Valley of Strength

Shulamit Lapid

VALLEY OF STRENGTH

TRANSLATED BY

Philip Simpson

The Toby Press

Valley of Strength

First English Edition 2009

The Toby Press LLC
POB 8531, New Milford, CT 06776-8531, USA
& POB 2455, London W1A 5WY, England
www.tobypress.com

First published in Hebrew as *Gai Oni*

ISBN 978 1 59264 230 4, *hardcover*

A CIP catalogue record for this title is available from the British Library

Typeset in Garamond by Koren Publishing Services

Printed and bound in the United States

Chapter one

It had all happened too quickly. The wedding in the Ajiman synagogue in Jaffa, the journey. Fania decided to not even try to understand. If she starts to think—she will go crazy! Better just to gaze at the landscape. The bare monotonous plain had given way to a range of hills with tall crags protruding as if uprooted from their flanks. Until they reached Haifa they were accompanied by other travellers: there were ten of them, crammed tightly into Haim Yankel's wagon. To Fania, with the baby in her lap, they offered the seat of honor, which in fact was nothing more than a pile of bundles. Most of the time she sat in the wagon alone. When the road climbed, Haim Yankel asked the passengers to step down "to make life easier for the beasts"; on downward slopes he asked them to step down "for fear of breaking bones"; while on level ground he suggested that they step down and stroll at their leisure. And every time he commanded Fania: "You, stay where you are!" The travellers were apparently familiar with the carter's "system" and didn't protest unduly. After travelling through the night and half of the following day they finally reached Haifa and parted from the other wayfarers. Yehiel hired mules, and because time was pressing, decided not to wait for a convoy to assemble but to take the risk of setting out at once for home, for Jaoni.

Fania peered at him furtively. Since leaving Jaffa they had exchanged no words between them. The swaying motion lulled Tamara to sleep, and sometimes she quite forgot the little bundle in the box tied to the mule's flanks. The time for feeding had passed a while ago, and Fania wondered what she would do when her daughter woke up and demanded her food. How could she bare a breast in the sight of this stranger, her husband of two days? She remembered the words her uncle, Shura, said to her when he parted from her in Jaffa: "Don't worry, Fania." As if words had the power to erase what had befallen them. And as if to belie her uncle's words, there was a sudden roar of artillery and the passengers gathered beside the wagon frozen in terror. A woman, the only other female traveller, cried: "Albert, mon Dieu!" But Haim Yankel counted the salvoes, and when the number reached twenty-one and the noise ceased, he explained solemnly to his charges that "this day the Lord has done great things for us," adding that "this is the anniversary of the Constitution."

"May it be good fortune and a blessing," murmured the men, and Fania said to herself, Amen, Amen, so be it, and wondered what kind of a life awaited her with her husband there in Galilee.

"When will you come to me in…in Jaoni?" she had asked her uncle.

"I shall come!" His voice was loud, confident, but she sensed the fear in his heart, the same as in hers.

"If one of our people comes to Jaffa, you can return with him in the cart," said Yehiel.

"When?" Fania insisted. Her uncle laughed, hearing in her voice a hint of the old obstinacy. "If anything happens will you let me know?"

"Nothing's going to happen, Fania!" A note of impatience crackled in his voice and he added hastily: "It's time for you to start worrying about yourself!"

As if this were possible, she thought now, remembering her uncle's words. The baby in the box, her brother Lulik tied to the back of the mule like a bundle of rags…she can't help them and doesn't want to think about herself.

"Do you want to rest?" asked Yehiel, and his voice startled her. The monotonous swaying had made her forget for a moment the man riding beside her.

"No. I'm all right. Where are we?"

"In about an hour we shall reach Tabor. We'll stop there. The mules need to rest."

The moist warmth was spreading in her breasts and the baby in the box stirred and wriggled, her rosy button-mouth demanding food. Fania felt her nipples swelling. Both she and the baby needed to suckle. Suddenly Tamara was crying loudly, her face contorted and covered with red blotches and her little thimble-nose turning white.

"She's hungry," said Yehiel. Fania remembered the man's two children, waiting for their father's return. What a surprise is in store for them! Daddy went to buy grain in Jaffa and here he is returning with a stepmother and a stepsister and a stepuncle. A big marten suddenly darted across the path, seeking refuge in a clump of cactus bushes.

"Do you want to get down?"

"Yes."

Yehiel led the mules to a little spring flowing among thickets of oleander. Fania hastily unbuttoned her blouse and bared a breast to Tamara. The little mouth clamped firmly on the full nipple and after the initial, searing pain she abandoned herself to the urgent sucking which gradually became steady and monotonous. Soon Tamara fell asleep, her little mouth still sucking. Her eyes closed as well as if of their own accord, and she could barely stay awake long enough to cover herself before Yehiel's return. True, in Jaffa she had seen Arab women baring breasts in the street, but in her home, in her parents' house, bodies were never exposed. Until that bitter and frantic day when they were laid out before her eyes, shattered bodies drenched with blood. Her screams mingled with their screams when that Gentile raped her on her parents' bed, and she couldn't understand why no one came to her rescue, until a silence descended on the house that was even more terrible than the screams.

"Have you finished?" Yehiel startled her from her sleep and Fania cried out.

His lips twisted sourly, and her heart was filled with depression and fear. Who is this man that she married the day before yesterday with the blessing of Rabbi Naphtali Hirsch, the rabbi of Jaffa? What does he know of the baby in her arms? He married her so she would care for his two orphans, but he could have married another woman, healthy in body and in mind, a woman without relatives hanging like millstones around her neck.

"I told him your husband was murdered in the pogrom together with your parents," said her uncle Shura. One of his eyes was watering and a wad of cotton wool protruded from his ear.

"What's the matter with your ear?" she asked, irrelevantly.

"Loud noises."

"And the cotton wool helps?"

"I think so. It reduces the noise."

The signs of old age were clearly evident in him, and she felt guilty for having dragged him with her to the ends of the earth.

Her uncle, Alexander Shura, was her father's brother, and like all the Mandelstams he had strong white teeth and a ruddy beard, a pleasant voice and an excitable nature. The brothers argued incessantly, but little Fania seldom listened to them. "They aren't quarrelling, Sofgania," her mother used to assure her when their shouting rose to the heavens, "they're discussing, that's all." Her father managed the sugar refinery that he inherited from his father and bore a grudge against his brother, who accepted a share of the proceeds but preferred not to share the burden of administration. "I too want to live," he used to say. "To live" in his dictionary meant to study a page of the Talmud, to read David Gordon's *Hamagid* and Tolstoy's letters, to correspond with Rabbi Shmuel Mohilever of Radom, who believed in the revival of the Jewish people in the Land of Israel… Secretly Fania sided with her uncle. "I am a Russian!" he insisted. "A solution for the Russian people will bring deliverance to the Jews as well." Words like "deliverance", "emancipation", "cosmopolitanism", echoed around the house. Then the uncle disappeared and Fania heard whispers that he had joined some revolutionary group. On her twelfth birthday, in the evening, he suddenly appeared in their house, bringing her Pushkin's *Eugene Onegin*, inscribed with the dedication: "To my Fanichka Tatiana, on her twelfth birthday, from her loving Uncle Shura, Elizavetgrad, 9 November 1878." Now the book was in her trunk. During the same visit, after the kisses and the good wishes, the uncle informed his brother that deliverance was close at hand. Tomorrow or the day after, two and a half million Jews would join the family of the great Russian people and become equal citizens in the eyes of the government. But these words were said after the blood libel in Kutais and this time the breach between her father and his brother was deep and final. Fania didn't see her uncle again for some three years, until two weeks after the pogrom in her town.

He arrived in the evening after travelling all day, and found Fania in a neighbor's house. A shutter in their house was open, hanging loose and banging against the lintel of the window, and it was this that warned him of the disaster. "My heart quivered with dread," he said later to the neighbor, "as if all this had happened before, as if this wasn't the first time. How I hated this feeling! The door was locked and I climbed in through the coal-cellar, as scared as I used to be when I was a little boy. By the light of the moon I saw the wreckage..."

Fania's father had only stayed in his home because he was waiting for the return of his beloved son Lulik from the army. If not this year—then next year. If not next year—then the year after. The grown-up daughters had immigrated to America and were urging their parents to take Fania and join them. "When Lulik returns from the army we shall all go to the Holy Land," her father said. Lulik was twelve years old when he was conscripted into the army. A few months after he was taken they received a letter from another conscripted youth, a certain Elyakim Zuntzer. He said he had met their son Lulik Mandelstam in Kazan, and he was well. About a year later the law of Jewish conscription was repealed, but still Lulik did not return. From time to time rumors reached them of a young Jewish conscript who had died in Kara, in torment, a martyr's death. Fania hardly knew her brother, but in her young heart there was resentment against this brother, who had cast such gloom upon their home. Her parents were too old and tired to bother about her education. It was Fania herself who decided to study in a secular school, and she who decided to learn to play the piano and to learn English rather than French, so she could correspond with her relatives in America. Her father promised that one day he would buy a tract of land in the Land of Israel, and meanwhile? Meanwhile he used to sing the song of Mandelkorn, "I am the lily of the Sharon, the rose of the valleys."

Fania hummed the song to herself. The sky was clear, cloudless. Among the rocks on the hillside black goats grazed, and on the slopes stretched a line of oleander bushes, masking the horizon. Yehiel's horse whinnied when they entered a grove of acacias. The heat was intense and summer flies buzzed around her, sometimes sticking to her sweating face. She was afraid to open her mouth lest she swallow one of them, but her breathing was heavy. Is this what spring is like in this country?

"Who is Tamara named after?" asked Yehiel.

"After herself."

"A pretty name. It's Russian and Hebrew as well."

Fania was pleased that he liked the name, and that he understood her intention. Her uncle Shura advised her to name the baby after her mother, Henya Deborah. But would this not be a kind of desecration of her mother's memory? One day she would sew Torah scrolls in memory of her parents, with their names embroidered in silver threads. When the Turkish midwife asked her the child's name, she replied "Tamara," sure in her heart that in a little while she would dispose of both the birth certificate and the baby, and erase this unhappy episode from her life. But the wily midwife laid the tiny, damp and yelling bundle of flesh in her lap and waited until it began to suck the aching nipples. For three months they lived in Constantinople, in the house of the midwife. All those weeks Fania saw no one. Her whole world was the baby, the midwife and her uncle. When at last the ship arrived to take them to Jaffa, it was no longer possible to sever the bond that tied her to her daughter.

A green field of crops appeared beyond the range of hills and behind it a few scattered oaks, each standing in isolation. How few were the trees they had seen on the way! The ride across the flank of the hill jolted the boxes tied to the mule's back, and Tamara wriggled and cried, relaxed and wailed again. Fania peered at the man walking beside them. Most of the journey he made on foot, his eyes fixed on the path and his expression blank. She too would have liked to walk, to stretch her limbs and breathe fresh air, but she was tied to the back of the mule along with the bundles and boxes. On the other mule her brother Lulik tossed like a sack filled with rags, his head slumped and his chin thumping rhythmically on his chest. The doctor in Jaffa gave him a sleeping potion, and when they reached Haifa Fania again mixed a little opium into his food, to keep him calm until they could bring him safely to their new refuge. Every now and then his eyes would open and the grey face came to life. A fine dowry I'm bringing with me, she thought, and glanced for the hundredth time at the man who was her husband. Her eyes met his and she asked: "Aren't you tired?"

"When we come to the downward slope, I'll ride," he replied. But when they came to the downward slope he was busy controlling the animals and keeping them from slipping. The big black stones looked like a stream of lava, its bubbles frozen on the belly of the hill. No track or footpath was visible, and she wondered how the man knew his way. The vestiges of winter were still evident in the bleak colors of the hills. There were a few isolated patches of anemones, cyclamens, peonies, but most of the time they picked their way among thorns and brambles and the going was hard for the animals. A thick haze covered the mountains to the east. Tamara continued crying and Fania wondered: Has he any regrets? Suddenly he pulled on the reins and stopped the mule.

"She's wet," he said.

Before she understood what he was saying he had taken Tamara from the box, and already she was laid across his knees, her dress pulled up and the wet diaper tossed into a corner of the box. Yehiel swaddled the baby expertly, and when she stopped crying, it seemed to Fania that a faint smile lit up his face and disappeared at once.

"When…?" she began, but the sound of the wheels drowned her question.

"What?" He glanced at her.

"When did your wife die?"

"A year and a half ago."

"What did she die of?"

"Fever."

A year and a half! And she had supposed in her innocence that his wife died a few months ago and he set out at once for Jaffa to seek a nurse for his children. Obviously until now he had failed to find a woman who would agree to live with him. No matter, the arrangement suited her well enough. The conditions between them had been clearly stated. Her uncle presumed that by means of this marriage he would solve her problems, not realizing that he himself was one of these problems. There was a kind of insanity in this journey to the Land of Israel: she, a sixteen-year-old girl, saddled with an elderly uncle, a lunatic brother and a baby. If she were to read of such a foursome in a novel, she would seriously doubt the good taste of the writer. How she used to love reading romantic fiction! To stretch out on the sofa with a bowl of sweets and shed tears over the fate of noble heroes. In the meantime she had discovered there is no nobility in suffering, nor consolation in tears.

Fania met Yehiel about two weeks after her arrival in Jaffa. He had come from Galilee to work in the orchard of Shimon Rokeah, his relative, and earn money to buy seeds. Fania was standing on the roof of the old house, which actually constituted the main living quarters of Haim Becker's hostel. She was stirring a steaming cauldron full of diapers with a wooden pole. The wet laundry was very heavy and the sleeves of her dress were soaked every time she raised the pole. Her face blazed in the hot vapors, and she was trying, by means of these mechanical actions, to subdue every thought that popped into her head. From the lower floor rose the repellent smell of sesame oil. The regular movement of the camel turning the machinery of the oil press seemed somehow to mirror her own movements.

Why did she imagine that here in the Land of Israel her grief would be erased? What made her think that here all her problems would be solved? What had she hoped for, really? The money was running out and she had come to realize with mounting despair that her uncle, to whom she had clung with all her strength, was powerless to help them. Every morning he went out to the offices of the central committee of the "Lovers of Zion" society. When she asked him what he was doing there, he told her he was organizing "the labor committee". Several times she went to Shlomo Grossman's store, the only Jewish shop in the town, hoping to hear of some vacancy that might suit her uncle. In Grossman's "club" they knew everything and everybody. She herself could not find work as long as she was nursing Tamara. As for Lulik—it was lucky that the owners of the hostel let him lie in the yard behind the oil press, by the sycamore tree. But what will happen when winter comes and the rain begins to fall? She, she alone inflicted these hardships on them, when out of the enveloping gloom there suddenly flashed before her wounded eyes the light of the Land of Israel.

When Shura Mandelstam discovered the relics of the pogrom in his brother's empty house, he went to a neighbor's house to find out what had become of his family. On the bed he found Fania, dumb and a mere shadow of herself, and in the yard he found Lulik, the lost son, dressed in his soldiers' coat, and the neighbor tossing food to him from a distance, since if anyone tried to approach him he would run away, howling. Only from Fania's hand would he accept food, but Fania herself was far from well.

The uncle hired a peasant woman and with her help began to clean up the house. But Fania said firmly that she would never again set foot in that house.

"What then?" the uncle asked her. "Shall we go to Kharkov?"

"Father was waiting for Lulik, to take him to the Land of Israel," she replied.

"Do *you* want to go to Israel?" he asked.

Fania shrugged as if to say: What has it to do with me? Since when have my wishes counted for anything?

Three camels appeared suddenly, approaching them, laden with heavy sacks. She felt anger at the man walking beside her and making no effort to explain to her the sights and sounds of the journey. After all, he knows she's a stranger here and doesn't even know the names of the places they are passing by. Or perhaps he thinks he's bringing a simpleton to his home?

"In another hour we'll reach a spring and there we'll rest. In the night we'll go on," said Yehiel.

"What are they carrying, those camels?"

"Charcoal."

"Idiot!" That was the first word he said to her. She was trying to put out the fire burning under the laundry-tub, and the flames leaping up from the wick suddenly caught her hair. Before she understood what was happening, something dark and woolly was thrown over her head and she was already choking with shock and fear under the suffocating pall of darkness. Someone slapped her head again and again, and only then was the heavy coat removed from her head and her startled eyes met an angry stare. She just had time to hear him say "Idiot!" before she fainted.

"There, there, my dear, it's all right my darling." She heard the tired, kindly voice of Mrs. Becker, the landlady, and felt a hand lightly slapping her cheek. "What more does this poor girl need to suffer, God in Heaven? Come on my chick, here, drink a little…" Drops of brandy scalded her throat, and she touched the landlady's hand to express her gratitude.

"The color of your cheeks, dear God! Stay where you are and don't move! I'll bring you some hot sweet tea. And you, Mr. Silas, keep an eye on her and don't let her budge until I return."

A shadow moved by the window and muttered something. The landlady left the room and Fania closed her eyes, afraid of meeting the angry stare of the stranger again.

He stood above her, his face grim, his eyes and his hair black as coal, and she wondered if he had some oriental blood. Most of the Jews of Jaffa were oriental Jews, no different from the Arabs in clothing and headdress, or in language and appearance. Her uncle told her that the majority of them came from Morocco, Tunisia and Algeria, and a minority from the Mediterranean ports of Turkey and

Greece. Why shouldn't there be Arab blood flowing in his veins? she thought. In my daughter's veins isn't there the blood of a Russian Gentile? And who knows whose blood is mingled with *that* blood? The blood of murderers, madmen, cripples—anything is possible and we'll never know... While she was working with the laundry on the balcony Tamara had been left in their room, alone. Fania was suddenly alert, listening for the sound of the baby crying.

"How long have you been here?"

"Two weeks."

"Where are you from?"

"From Russia."

"What were you trying to do?"

"To put out the fire!" She felt a sudden surge of anger at this man, berating her and not believing her. "How was I supposed to know how to put it out?"

"You could have asked."

Fania turned her face to the wall. She was still lying on the floor with the man's coat under her head. The landlady came back, bringing her a cup of sweet tea. Fania felt her strength returning to her and she tried to sit up. But the room whirled about her and she hurriedly closed her eyes. When she opened them, she again met the glowering looks of the stranger. Why is he still here, she thought angrily.

"Oy, Yehiel, blessings upon you!" cried Madame Becker. "And you, my chick, don't be in such a hurry to get up!"

"But the baby!"

"I'll bring her to you—"

"No! I won't allow it! You've enough work to do without bothering about me!" Fania protested.

"Where is she?"

Her objections were to no avail. The landlady explained to the stranger how to find the room where Fania and her uncle lodged. They were counted among the "privileged guests" who rated a room of their own, as they had stayed in the hostel longer than the two or three days usually spent here. Most of the guests used to sprawl on the roof with their bundles, waiting for the camels or wagons that would take them on the bone-breaking, forty- or fifty-hour journey to Jerusalem. The house was very old, having miraculously survived the earthquake that had wrecked Jaffa forty years earlier. The room allotted to the Mandelstams contained a long table, two chairs, mats that served for beds, divans and other odd items of furniture. Tamara slept on a feather-cushion laid on one of the mats.

Some time passed before Yehiel returned with Tamara in his arms.

"The nappy was wet," he said, explaining his delay, and before she had time to thank him, his lips curled into something resembling a smile and he said: "A pretty baby."

"Thank-you for everything!" replied Fania curtly.

Without a word he turned and left. The big room seemed to grow bigger still. Mrs. Becker will no doubt repeat to him her uncle's account of her past, namely, that her husband and her parents were murdered in a pogrom. Why should she care who knows her story?—she demanded of her uncle—it isn't her shame but the shame of humanity! "And the little girl?" the uncle protested, "How has the little girl sinned? Look, besides you and me, nobody knows your story, and why should this innocent baby endure the mark of Cain all the days of her life? For her sake—be silent!"

Because she wasn't speaking to anyone anyway, for better or worse, she promised him that her lips would be sealed. She sensed that her uncle's version was current among the guests at the hostel, judging by the furtive way they glanced at her.

"Is this Sharon?" she asked Yehiel.

"No. This is Lower Galilee."

He too was engrossed in his thoughts. Since they left Jaffa he had barely exchanged words with her. Even after they parted from the rest of the travellers in Haifa and were left alone, he had spoken little. Is he having regrets? Instead of bringing home a strong and healthy nurse, he's bringing an inexperienced and helpless girl saddled with a baby and a mad brother. Why did he agree, really, to the conditions she set before him? And how did she dare to set conditions at all, knowing the gravity of their predicament?

The morning after the incident with the fire she met him in

the dining room of the hostel. She wanted to flee the place at once, but her uncle was sitting with her, and so she concentrated all her attention on the plate in front of her. Her uncle was reading *Havatzelet*, which had arrived that day from Jerusalem.

"Next month we shall go to Jerusalem!" he informed Fania, who wondered where they would find the money for this journey. "A quarter of all the Jews in Jerusalem are already living outside the walls! I'd like to see the new developments."

"Are there many Jews in Jerusalem?" she asked.

"Twenty thousand. More than half the population of the city! Frumkin writes that they are divided—the Ashkenazis, that is—into twenty sects. Twenty!" The uncle's voice rose and Fania felt embarrassed before the other diners. "And every sect naturally has a leader and a deputy leader and an agent and a treasurer and a scribe and a burial company and a prayer-house and a beadle for the sect and a beadle for the prayer-house and a beadle for the cemetery...this fragmentation is a disaster! If there were one central office to supervise all the sects..."

Fania stopped listening to her uncle. Again and again her worries for tomorrow racked her brain. If only she had some skill! Sewing, cookery, midwifery...Instead of piano lessons and English classes she should have studied some useful occupation...

"May I take a look at *Havatzelet*?"

Mr. Silas stood beside their table and Fania stared intensely at the plate before her. "Good morning to you!" Again that scornful smile hovering on his lips. "And how are you this morning?"

"Very well, thank-you," she said in a peremptory tone, but her uncle hurriedly invited the stranger to join them at their table, and he accepted, although Fania's feelings towards him must have been obvious. The uncle lost no time lecturing the stranger on his proposed solution to the problem of the sects in Jerusalem.

"The answer lies in abolishing our dependence on charitable donations!" said the stranger, and a flush of anger lit up his face. "We have become a nation of parasites!"

"True! Absolutely true! Where are you from, sir?"

"I'm from Galilee."

"From Galilee!" the uncle exclaimed, impressed, and Fania knew he'd already decided to go not only to Jerusalem but to the Galilee as well.

"From Jaoni. Gai Oni."

"What's that? Where is it?"

"It's an Arab village near Safed. You've heard perhaps of Eleazar Rokeah's project? We're working the land."

"And what did you say your name is?"

"Yehiel Silas. I'm related to Rokeah. Also to Frumkin, the editor of *Havatzelet*." He pointed to the newspaper in the uncle's hand, but the uncle held on to it, apparently oblivious of the hint.

"And where were you born? And what are you growing there? Is your family with you?"

"I was born in Safed, like most of the pioneers in Jaoni. At the moment we are harvesting stones and weeds."

"And there's a synagogue? And a shop? And a doctor? And Bible classes?"

That tolerant-scornful smile twitched again at the corners of his mouth.

"We were seventeen families when we moved to Jaoni. Today there are three families left there. A shop? Bible classes? Everything will come in its time…"

Fania rose silently and left the dining room. Her uncle would now be engrossed in a long conversation with the stranger, and when they part he'll know everything there is to be known about his village. It's as if he's the child and I'm the old woman, she thought bitterly. Sitting there and prattling on and not pausing to wonder where his next crust of bread will come from. It was Fania who organized the shopping in Shlomo Grossman's store, and she knew that the bundle of money was growing lighter from day to day. Yes, she knew that in the sects, Jews were living without working for their keep, but the very idea of "charity" made her shudder. She will never hold out her hand! And perhaps she should offer her services to the landlady? She would do the Arab women's work in exchange for a roof over her head and meals for herself and her family. Yesterday Mrs.

Becker paid two *matlik*s to each of the women who sat on the roof and sifted flour with their big sieves. This work even she could do. If only her uncle were younger and if only her brother were healthy and if only and if only! This "if only" that haunts her night and day and gives her no rest! She must find a solution by her own resources, since it is pointless looking to her uncle for deliverance. He goes on behaving as if he's still working in the legal department of the Russian railway company.

Her uncle appeared in their room, a gleam in his eye, and announced that he and Yehiel Silas were going out to buy grain and barley. The hours passed, darkness fell, and her uncle didn't return. As the evening wore on, the streets were thronged with people raising a fearful din, beating on drums and cymbals. From far away echoed the booms of explosions. Fania went down to the yard to take food to Lulik, and on returning to the building went into Mrs. Becker's room and told her of her concern for her uncle.

"If he went out with Yehiel Silas, you've nothing to fear, my chick," said the good woman, setting a cup of tea before her.

"But it's like a riot out there!"

"The Muslims are celebrating the feast of Ramadan. Your uncle has probably been held up by the crowds. He'll be back soon, you'll see."

And sure enough, while they were still drinking tea the uncle appeared, his red beard awry and his face gleaming, and told them that after going to the produce market they called in at the "Lovers of Zion" office, and on their way back he accompanied Yehiel to his aunt's house, where he was lodging.

"Is Bella Rokeah's daughter still here?" asked the landlady.

"No, there was no daughter there. What daughter?" the uncle replied.

"She must have already gone back."

"A very pleasant lady, Mrs. Rokeah."

"She's related to Yehiel both on her own account and through his late wife. His wife Rachel belonged to the Adis family from Ein Zeitim, and they are related to the Silases from Safed and the

Rokeahs from Jerusalem. The families were united when they were barely more than children, Bella Rokeah told me this was 'a marriage made in Heaven.'"

"A delightful woman," remarked the uncle. Clearly his hostess had made a powerful impression on him.

"And her husband?" asked Fania.

"She's a widow. Her husband was an agent for Russian and French shipping companies and an agent of the Austrian postal service, and when he died he left her a fine inheritance. Both her sons are studying in Beirut, and of her three daughters one lives in Alexandria, one in Jerusalem and the youngest in Paris."

Bella Rokeah had apparently aroused the curiosity of her uncle, since he went on interrogating the landlady. Fania returned exhausted to her room, praying she would be able to sleep in spite of the din erupting from the street. Luckily, they were staying in a room and not on the roof, where sleep would have been quite impossible. Her uncle was still talking when he entered the room, and she smiled in the darkness. This Bella Rokeah had simply captured his heart, and Fania wondered suddenly why he had never married. She listened to the muffled sounds in the darkness, his shuffling feet, the rustles and soft thuds as her uncle undressed. And suddenly it was as if the world stopped spinning. Her uncle cleared his throat, paused and whispered hoarsely: "Fanichka?"

"Yes?"

"Yehiel asked about you."

"What?"

"He sees me as your father. And so I am, my dear."

Fania stared at the ceiling, at the moving reflection of the clouds.

"He asked for your hand! Please!" he cried at once as if fearing her response. "Please, don't be in a hurry to reply, my dear. You mustn't think I don't know what you're going through. My heart bleeds. After all I know who and what you are. I told him about your parents' home. I told him you were the child of their old age, their favorite. I told him of the love and the high ideals to which you were brought up, I told him what an outstanding pupil you were in school, and I told him about your love of reading and playing the piano, and all the things that were important to you once and may yet return to you and make your life full. I'm an old man, my dear, and Lulik is a poor creature lost in the dark...perhaps he will recover one day, who knows...but we can't go on being a burden on your frail shoulders. You're so young. You can't bear the responsibility of all our lives without collapsing under the weight. I drag my feet from one office to another, looking for work, but there is no work even for men younger than me. I'm an old man. I'm superfluous. And even if I did find something, I doubt it would be enough to support the four of us. And the baby is your daughter, and she too deserves a life with a future. And the boy strikes me as a decent sort, strong in body and in spirit. We spent a long time together today. We said morning and evening prayers at the synagogue of Rabbi Haim Schmerling and then I went with him to his aunt's house and she made a very favorable impression on me as well. He too has known sorrow and he'll understand you, my darling. I went on purpose to his relatives' house to see how he was received there—and everyone greeted him with love and respect. He is the son of an illustrious tribe. The ancestor of the tribe, Rabbi Israel Bak, came to the Land of Israel from Berdichev as long ago as the thirties."

"And I thought he was a Sephardi."

"The Silases come from Damascus, but his mother belonged to the Bak family...It's possible I'll go to Jerusalem and offer my service to *Havatzelet*...Frumkin and Bak are in dispute with the rabbis and I, as an outsider, could mediate between them."

"Father used to say that the Mandelstams don't ask favors of anyone."

Her uncle was suddenly silent. He was silent so long Fania thought he was already asleep. But at last he spoke again and his voice was weary: "The decision is a hard one, my dear, but it's yours alone. I must tell you that I like him, but I don't want to influence you, not at all. It's your life. And your daughter's life and the lives of the children that will be born to you in the future, God willing."

"He knows about Tamara?"

"He knows about all of us."

From his answer she understood that he hadn't told Yehiel the circumstances of Tamara's birth.

It shall not be! she told herself. But the more she thought it over, the clearer became her conviction that there was no way out of the morass. Her heart melted with grief for her uncle. So, in spite of everything she had thought, he knows their state is critical and he's dragging his old legs back and forth in search of work. On her account he descended to this level, submitting to her whim and coming with her to the Land of Israel. She seemed to see the tolerant smiles with which various employers turned him away. For thirty years he was a respected lawyer in government service and all at once he had become an old man, homeless and unemployed, with three helpless relatives hanging round his neck. She had considered all kinds of weird and wonderful solutions in recent days, but never marriage. No! She will never marry! Never will she allow a man to assault her body again… or does *this* man just want a nurse for his children? All night the thoughts reverberated in her mind. If she marries him—bad. If she doesn't marry him—bad. Which is the lesser evil? No one will help her to decide, it is for her to turn it over and over until she knows what she wants. She is only sixteen years old, but already she is used to decisions, since it was she who decided to come to the Land of Israel and she who decided to sell the sugar refinery and the smoke-blackened walls that were once her home. Of the hundreds of books that were in the house, books sacred and profane, about half a dozen had survived. There was *Eugene Onegin* and *The Demon* by Lermontov, which had been a present from Ossia P. on her fourteenth birthday ("To Fania M." he wrote, "as an everlasting reminder, that all your life should be poetry") and Smolenskin's *Revenge of the Covenant*, which her father had not had time to read, and a volume of short stories by Bendetson, from which she was trying to learn Hebrew with the aid of Mandelstam's Hebrew-Russian dictionary—no relation according to her uncle. This was the sum of her inheritance.

Fania entered the dining room nervously, fearing she might find *him* there. Her face was pale and swollen from the sleepless night and her big eyes had deepened and darkened. At the long table sat a few

Jews, their voices raised in animated conversation. Mrs. Becker set a cup of hot tea before her and sat beside her until she had drunk it. Then she smeared a slice of bread with olive oil and goat's cheese and urged her to "eat, young lady" in a voice that reminded her of her mother's. Her heart melted at the sight of the good woman, working from dawn till night and catering to the needs of the flustered immigrants, guiding and directing and consoling and encouraging. Not wanting to detain her or hurt her feelings, she ate the slice of bread, and felt her strength returning. She remembered her uncle saying that Yehiel was staying at his aunt's house and wondered why she had been so worried. Near the window sat a little man, his face red, angrily shaking his stick as he spoke of the latest edict issued by the Turkish government, an edict restricting the immigration of Jews, the purchase of land and establishment of settlements. In spite of his anger, she liked the sound of his voice because he was speaking Russian. All the time she had been in Jaffa, these last two weeks, she had heard little other than Spanish and Arabic.

"Do you hear, my dear?" Mrs. Becker smiled at her. "It's your lucky day!" As soon as Fania finished eating, the landlady hurried back to the kitchen.

"Jews will continue to immigrate!" the angry man's friend consoled him, "And land will continue to be sold, and the only difference is we shall need to grease the palms of a few more officials and agents."

"You should have seen Yosef Effendi Krieger, the Pasha's interpreter, and the look on his face when he gave us this terrible news. He was happy!"

"Thy destroyers and despoilers shall go forth from thee. So what is new?"

"And he is related by marriage to Haim Amzaleg!"

"What of it?"

"And he negotiated the sale of land to Levontin!"

"Really? But there's no need to worry: Our Jews will not bow to this edict. What are they to do? Where can they go?"

"The beggars of Jerusalem are afraid the rain of charity will stop falling upon them. You know, after Levontin published his article in

Halevanon, he was contacted by Jews from Kremenchug, Kharkov, Elizavetgrad—"

Fania looked up, startled, at hearing the name of her town. What did he say? She couldn't understand what she had heard; did he say that someone from her town was here? And suddenly she saw Yehiel, sitting alone by the window and watching her calmly. How long had he been sitting there, watching her? She felt an impulse to flee with all possible haste, but didn't want to show him she was afraid of him. She rose to her feet slowly, gathered up the utensils from the table and turned towards the kitchen.

"Are you coming back here?" he asked her as she passed him. For a moment she hesitated, and then nodded. When she returned to the dining room, he pointed to the chair facing him. In the meantime the other occupants had left the room, and the Arab woman who carried the jugs of water was shouting for someone to open the kitchen door for her.

"Has your uncle spoken to you?" Yehiel Silas asked Fania Mandelstam.

Fania nodded again without speaking. It seemed that a shadow of annoyance passed for a moment over his face and disappeared at once. Fania stared at the window and then looked again into his face. His black eyes were sunk beneath finely chiseled eyebrows. His face was tanned by the sun, and his hands, resting on the table, were clearly accustomed to hard work. His eyes wandered over her face and Fania asked, "Inspecting the merchandise?" and was shocked by the words that had slipped from her mouth. A dark flush washed over her face, and she feared his response. His lips slackened suddenly and the hint of a smile flickered on them for a moment. This smile, that she remembered from yesterday, irritated her and she decided to hold herself in check and not betray her feelings. He was the one who made the proposal, so let him do the hard work.

"I know, I should have engaged a marriage-broker, but I'm pressed for time. What is your opinion?"

"My opinion?" Fania shrugged as if saying: what does it matter, my opinion? "The children, how old are they?" she asked.

"Bella is four and Moshe five and a half."

"And who is caring for them?"

"I am. And my neighbor used to help, too. Their mother was sick for nearly two years. Now they are with my sister-in-law in Safed."

"Why me?"

"You don't like the idea?"

"I have a baby of my own, a little girl."

"I know."

"Did my uncle tell you?"

"I've seen her! Remember? Yesterday, when you tried to set the house on fire."

"I didn't try to set the house on fire!" God, how infuriating this man is! she thought, and felt her face blazing like a beacon. Of all the girls of the family it had to be she who inherited the ruddy complexion of the Mandelstams!

"Have you any other relatives besides your uncle and your brother?"

"Yes, two older sisters. In America."

"Do they know what's become of you? I mean, that you're here, in the Land of Israel?"

"I wrote to them as soon as we arrived in Jaffa. They say it takes months for letters to get there…But I don't expect anything from them. They have had problems as well. They have children of their own…"

"And why didn't you join them there?"

"Why did *you* decide to come to the Land of Israel?"

The note of irritation in her voice didn't perturb him. He laughed suddenly and his laugh startled her. His teeth were white and strong and there was a deep furrow etched along his cheek. Suddenly he looked young, boyish, and she wondered how old he was.

"I wasn't consulted. Just as you didn't consult your daughter. I was born in Safed. My father came to Safed from Damascus after the blood libel in 1840. There he met one of the daughters of the Bak family, and this was the first mixed marriage in Safed."

"But you don't live in Safed?"

"No. I live in Jaoni, which we call Gai Oni, Valley of Strength. Another grandson of Israel Bak, Eleazar Rokeah, was the one who conceived the idea of this settlement. We wanted to leave Safed, escape from 'charity' and work on the land. Today there are only three Jewish families left there. One of them, the Frumkin family, is also related to us. I've been working here in Jaffa with Shimon, Eleazar's brother."

"Why? Can't you make a living in Gai Oni?"

"There's been a drought there for two years. Eleazar is trying to get help for us."

"He isn't living with you there?"

"No, he had to flee for his life. The synagogue treasurers of Safed hired murderers to assassinate him, and he escaped by a miracle."

There was a note of agitation in his voice, and Fania sensed that he was reluctant to discuss the subjects most important to him. The cleaning-girl came in for a moment, and went out at once when she saw the two of them talking.

"Even if the rain falls, we won't have enough money for all our needs: seed, livestock, fodder. That's why I came to work in Jaffa. With the money I've earned I've already bought seed. If the rains come and Eleazar succeeds in getting help, there will be bread in Jaoni." For a moment he hesitated and then looked at Fania. "At the moment our life is hard. We live like Arab peasants and alongside Arab peasants, in stone cottages. I can offer you only this: the roof over my head will cover your head, too, and the food that we eat you shall eat, too."

Fania racked her brains. The most difficult question of all had not yet been asked.

"Ask!" he said as if reading her thoughts.

"You said 'you'. Does that include…all of us?"

"Your uncle says he wants to find work here in Jaffa, in the 'Labor Committee'. Or with *Havatzelet* in Jerusalem. My aunt, Bella Rokeah, has promised to help him as far as she can. Has he any money? Or are you supporting him as well?"

It seemed to Fania that she detected a note of scorn in his voice.

"My uncle didn't want to come to the Land of Israel. He came here because of me. He isn't as young as me. There he had a respectable profession, a guaranteed income and...a purpose."

"Why did you decide to come here?"

"My father swore that if my brother returned from the army, we would all go to the Land of Israel. My brother returned, and I'm keeping my father's oath."

Fania was silent for a moment, and as Yehiel said nothing she continued:

"After selling the house and paying for the journey I have just forty francs left. If my uncle stays in Jaffa, I'll leave the money with him."

"Will he agree to take it from you?"

"He must agree! He'll need the money, not I."

"So, you've decided to come?" A spark of interest was ignited in his eyes.

"But what will become of my brother? I can't abandon him..."

"Your uncle will look after him."

"No! Lulik is my responsibility. He doesn't know where he is, who he is...I think he recognizes me..."

"Mrs. Becker told me that he runs away if anyone tries to approach him."

"That's right. But perhaps he'll get his senses back in time. And then—I must be with him, to explain everything to him...When he's left alone with his food, he eats. If he isn't left alone—he doesn't eat. Who but me will remember to do this for him? Look!" She touched his hand and withdrew her hand hastily. "Perhaps you think I'm ungrateful: you're offering me a home and I'm coming to you with demands. But I can't abandon him. I can't."

"How did this happen to him?"

"Lulik was a conscript. One of the last. They press-ganged him in the very year that the law was repealed. But he didn't return. I don't know where he was taken and what became of him, but my father was waiting all those years. We were three sisters and he was the only son. When the pogroms broke out he ran away from his unit. They caught him, charged him with desertion, and in prison he went mad. The poet Elyakim Zuntzer met him—they were drafted together in '56—and he identified him and brought him home. Meanwhile the pogroms had reached us."

"Yes, your uncle told me."

Fania wondered what else her uncle had told him. He made her swear not to reveal her secret, but the oath didn't bind him... Perhaps it was better so. If he hadn't spoken this man wouldn't be offering her a place in his home.

"I'm not used to household chores."

"You'll learn."

"You haven't answered my question, about my brother."

"I'll talk to your uncle."

"I'm responsible for my brother. And my daughter. And I'm the one who decides."

"How old are you?"

"Sixteen and a half."

Fania's heart pounded. Throughout the conversation they had not touched on one subject. Now she felt it could no longer be avoided.

"Look!" she cried hastily, her face flushed and her big eyes blazing. She shook her head, tossing the dark bronze curls from her face. "I need an occupation and I'll come to your house to look after your children. There aren't many men who would take into their home an inexperienced woman saddled with a baby, an elderly uncle and a mad brother. I know that. But I shall not marry you!"

Now, when the words had been said, she sat erect in her chair as if preparing herself to face a firing squad. She fixed her gaze on the window. From outside came the sounds of Jaffa. The whole of this oriental city looked like the aftermath of some riot that had left its mark in broken stones, in crooked streets, in the sea lashing against the walls, in the hoarse cries of drovers and peddlers.

"Why?"

"Not because of you."

"I asked why."

"I can't."

"Because of him?"

"Because of who?" She turned to him in alarm.

"Your husband?"

Her husband! Fania almost laughed aloud. God, if she could only wipe from her memory the horror of that day. All her life would be divided, since then and forever, between what was "before" and what was "after". She felt that the consolation of madness had been denied her and she was doomed to carry this searing wound in her womb forever. And if she could forget for a moment, there would be Tamara there to remind her, the child that she wanted to hate but could not.

"You can't live with me under one roof without marrying me. You're too…"

"What?"

"People will gossip."

"People don't interest me. What about the children, do you expect them to rejoice when you bring a strange woman to your house and tell them this is their new mother? After all, what you want is a nanny and not a wife. And that suits me better, too."

Yehiel looked at her for a moment, a curious expression on his face. Then he roused himself from his reverie and said curtly: "We'll take your brother too."

And this was what tipped the scales. Fania knew the offer was too good to refuse. Although unacquainted with the ways of this country, she knew there were very few possibilities open before her. The money in her purse would be enough only for a few more weeks, and even if she found some work, her wages would not buy accommodation and food for the four of them. For a moment she was relieved that the man had taken on himself the responsibility for their fate. During the past year all the decisions had been hers and hers alone. For better or worse. Even as a child she had been independent and rebellious, but then her mother's arms had always been there, and she could bury her head in her lap and let the warm tears flow, feel the loving hands caressing her head and the noisy kisses planted on her wet cheek. "I won't be in a hurry to get married," she used to inform her mother. "I want to study to be a doctor first of all, and I'll only marry someone when I fall in love with all my heart!"

"And who do you think is going to fall in love with you?" her mother teased her. "Look what a gypsy face she has! Who needs such a fireball in his house?"

"There must have been some pogrom that we don't know about!" her father used to say, winking at her mother.

Yehiel interrupted her thoughts.

"I want to return to Jaoni in a day or two. If you agree, I'll talk to Rabbi Hirsch and fix the wedding for tomorrow."

"Tomorrow!" she was dumbfounded.

"I should have returned a few days ago. The harvest is nearly finished. My friend and neighbor Frumkin went back to Jaoni a week ago with the first batch of seed-corn, and he told my sister I was on my way too."

Fania stared at the man and tried to understand what he was saying. The conversation between them seemed more like a business negotiation than a betrothal. Who is this man, with whom she will perhaps be spending most of the years of her life? She knows nothing about him!

"Yes, well…" he rose to his feet, and when she rose with him he suddenly took her hand in his and said: "Congratulations, Fania."

The words stuck in her throat, and she was afraid to speak lest she burst into tears. He grimaced, and the familiar shadow of annoyance lingered on his face. She cleared her throat and whispered: "Congratulations, Yehiel."

"I'm going to talk with the rabbi and my aunt and reserve places for us in the carriage to Haifa tomorrow. And in the meantime you'd better pack your belongings and speak to your uncle." He was talking quickly, his movements brisk and his eyes shining.

"How old are you, Yehiel?"

"Twenty-six."

"How are we going to take my brother?"

"I'll find a way."

And already he was going. Fania watched him as he went. He

was taller than average and leaner than average, and the tarboosh on his head made him seem taller and leaner still. The woolen coat reached to his knees, and the yellow Damascus caftan peeped out from under it. His shoulders were erect, and she knew he was aware of her gaze, although he did not turn back.

Chapter two

Fania's back was hurting. From time to time she felt stabbing pains between her ribs and in her thighs. For the past hour she had been holding Tamara in her lap, rocking her until she relaxed. Now the blue eyes were fixed on the clouds drifting in the sky. The air became sharp and clear. Bedouin women passed them by, carrying huge piles of firewood on their heads, climbing the hill-path as sure-footed as goats. The mountain ranges were bare, without a tree, without a shrub. The white peak of the Hermon was their compass, and their faces were constantly turned towards it, heading northward. The snow-covered range was at odds with the summer heat of late May. Suddenly, a big lake appeared in the valley. A basin of blue tranquility tinged with gold. On the shore of the lake, a small township had been constructed.

"What is this place?" Fania asked.

"The Sea of Tiberias, and the town of Tiberias. Next to it is the valley of Ginossar."

"How far is it from the lake to Jaoni? Is it within walking distance?"

"We don't do much walking round here."

"Why not?"

"Galilee is swarming with bandits. Besides, the work tires us out."

"But it's such a lovely view!"

Yehiel glanced at Fania. The rays of the sun streamed over her heavy curls in jets of bronze and her skin was tanned by their golden light.

"At Succoth we'll go out walking and come down to the lake. We'll bring the children here."

A small settlement appeared on one of the ranges to the west, white houses nestling in the lap of the hill. Fania felt herself falling in love with this landscape ablaze with the light of sunset, as her heart was open and she was happy that this was to be her new homeland.

"Safed," said Yehiel, following the direction of her glance. "I was born there."

"How long will it take us to get there?"

"Not today."

"But the children!"

"Tomorrow I'll go and fetch them. Or the day after. I want to get home. Look!" His voice was hoarse with emotion. "That's Gai Oni over there!"

About a dozen single-story houses, built of blackened stone and daubed with a coating of clay, stood in a line, submerged among thorns and long grass. A few mud-built huts had fallen into the crevices bisecting the ridge. Yehiel halted the animals and they looked straight ahead. The tinkle of running water mingled with the sound of the breeze blowing over the tops of the olive trees. Is this it?? Fania didn't know whether to laugh or cry.

"There were seventeen of us when we settled here as youngsters in 1878, determined to turn ourselves into agricultural workers." Yehiel was suddenly speaking with enthusiasm, in a rush. "Our house is at the end of the line, next to the cypress tree. Out of the seventeen, four families were left, then three...You'll be meeting them soon. Schwartz, Keller, Friedman, Frumkin...Last year we were all forced to leave Gai Oni and buy grain from other farmers. But Frumkin has already come back, and now I'm here too. I hope the others will be returning soon."

"Is it safe to drink from the spring?"

"Yes. The water is fresh. We have three springs. This one is Ayn Abu Halil and it's the biggest of them. Water levels are low now, because of the drought."

An Arab girl suddenly appeared before them, crouching by the olive tree. It seemed she was hiding, but once discovered she smiled at them, peering curiously at Fania.

"This is our neighbor, Maryam Alhija. Her house is next to ours, between us and the Frumkins."

Fania greeted the girl, whose face was wet from the well-water. The girl looked about her own age.

"What's she doing?"

"Pruning the wild growth from the olive trees—the 'pigs'. Those branches are good for firewood."

"Why Jaoni?"

Yehiel looked at her, surprised.

"Why did you choose to settle here?"

His eyes scanned the landscape around them. The gleam of Hermon to the north, the Golan hills to the east, shrouded in silvery vapors, and the darkening mountain to the west, behind the setting sun. Now, on reaching their destination, he slowed the pace. Fania held the reins of the mule, getting caught from time to time on the dense and spiky raspberry bushes growing alongside the spring.

"My family came to the Jarmak fifty years ago, together with Rabbi Israel Bak. He was given the place by Ibrahim Pasha, after Arab rioters wrecked his printing press in Safed. He founded his farm on the Jarmak, and at Ein Zeitim, about an hour's ride from Jaoni, he rebuilt his printing press. You see those walnut trees on the hill? That's where Rabbi Israel wanted to set up a khan, midway between the farm on the Jarmak and the Sea of Tiberias. He studied Torah and practiced medicine, and his son, Rabbi Nisan, worked the land, planted and sowed and reaped. His son Shmuel was born here too. Rabbi Israel hoped that in his village on the Jarmak he'd find a refuge from the plunder and pillage that the Jews of Safed had to suffer, but Heaven decreed otherwise. The earthquake that hit the land in 1837 wrecked the village. Rabbi Israel moved to Jerusalem, and all that survived from his plans for the salvation of Galilee were the relics on the Jarmak and those four walnut trees. The Arabs call this place Hirbet el-Yahud—the ruin of the Jews. When my friend and companion Eleazar Rokeah started mentioning a return to the land, it was obvious to both of us that this would be the place. The place where our grandfather Rabbi Israel began, there we would continue! In our innocence, we reckoned all the five thousand Jews of Safed would follow in our tracks. But they are too devoted to the leeches who are sucking their blood..."

The sound of metallic jingling was heard. A peasant appeared on the path, leading a small donkey laden with massive panniers. He said something to Yehiel that made him smile. When he moved away from them, Fania asked: "What did he say?"

"He congratulated me on the wife I bought."

Fania thought to herself: the Arab is right, you bought me.

"Does he live in the village?"

"No, that's Isa, the oil-seller. I think he's taken a fancy to Maryam Alhaji..." he smiled.

"The Arabs stayed in the village?"

"A few stayed. It is an Arab village. We bought half the land from them, but we didn't have the money to build houses. There aren't any settlements in Galilee occupied exclusively by Jews. In all the villages Jews and Arabs live side by side—that's the way it is in Tarshiha and in Pekiin, where Jews have been living since the plague of 1825, also in Kfar Yasif and in Hazbia, in Baram, in Kfar Hittim and in Shafram, where the Ravanite from Shoklov is buried."

"Are they all agricultural workers?"

"Yes...and members of my family are living in Ein Zeitim. It used to be a major metropolis. Today it's a village..."

"Yehiel!!"

From around the curve of the mountain two men appeared and pounced on Yehiel, hugging him joyfully.

"I've brought seeds!" he told them, as if announcing that he had brought the Sultan's treasure. "Has rain fallen?"

"No, not yet. But the peasants say they sense it will fall soon."

"They've been sensing that for two years now!"

"The drought won't last forever."

"Where have you been working?"

"In Shimon Rokeah's plantations. Near Jaffa."

More people came and gathered round, women with heads covered, peasants, children. The men embraced Yehiel, prodded the sacks of seed. The women stared curiously at Fania. At her uncovered hair, at the baby in the box, at Lulik, tied to the mule. Fragments of conversation reached her ears, in a mixture of Arabic, Hebrew and Yiddish. Even the Hebrew sounded different here, more like the Arabic spoken by the peasants. Someone had bought a bull, someone else had sold a horse, building permits hadn't arrived yet…From the end of the village a figure approached riding a horse, and stopped right beside them.

"Yehiel! You're back!"

Fania was surprised to hear the voice. On the horse sat a girl of about eighteen, with two long black plaits of hair hanging down to her chest. A necklace made from coins of pure gold adorned her neck, and from under her broad dress peeped white cotton trousers, tight at the ankles. The girl flinched at the sight of Fania, and at last Yehiel remembered to introduce her.

"Friends and comrades, this is Fania, my wife. And you, Fania, please meet my fellow residents of Gai Oni—Mordecai Leib, Issar Frumkin, Riva Frumkin…and this is Rivka Adis from Ein Zeitim, the younger sister of my late wife, Rachel…"

The people shouted "Good luck!" and "Happy times!" and asked when and where, but the chorus of congratulations did nothing to obscure the shocked silence of Rivka, still sitting on the horse and fixing Fania with a hostile stare.

"And the children?" Yehiel asked Rivka, "Are they well?"

"They are well. They were at our house for the Sabbath, and on Sunday I took them back to Safed, to Leah's house."

"Tomorrow or the day after I'll go and fetch them. Will you give Fania a hand, Rivka? You'll need to show her…"

"Whatever you ask of me, I'll do!"

"They say that Klisker intends to sell his land!" someone interjected, in an effort to soften the impact of Rivka's words. The information was indeed enough to distract Yehiel's attention.

"Why?" he asked, astonished.

"When he went to Safed some time ago, our Jews pelted him with stones and shouted 'Jaoni Turk' at him. He came back from there bruised and distraught. His wife has come down with a fever, both of his children have contracted trachoma, and he says he's not going to wait for them to make an attempt on his life, the way they did with Eleazar Rokeah and Rabbi Moishe Yosef…"

"If it weren't for the drought, he'd have stayed."

Is she in love with him? But he's so much older than her! Ach! She expelled the thought from her mind with disgust. She had read too many romantic novels in her childhood. In love! And where are we? For love you need rose gardens and the scent of musk, you need silk and velvet and crystal and marble. What does she have here among the thorns and the scorpions…

"How long have you been travelling, Yehiel?"

"Four days since we left Jaffa."

"By yourselves?"

"No. As far as Haifa we travelled in convoy."

The people escorted them to the gate of the front yard of one of the houses. A rusty iron fence surrounded the yard. Near one of the windows grew a tall and dusty cypress. But this was the house's only decoration. Unruly weeds sprouted both beyond the fence and inside the yard. Wind and rain had eroded the walls of the house, and dust blown in from the denuded valleys swirled around the grey stonework. Inside the stone arch which formed the entrance to the house was a wooden door; its paint had long since peeled away and deep cracks gaped between the panels.

Fania was glad. The sight that greeted her meant work! This house had been waiting for her to come and rescue it from its desolation. All her time and all her strength she would devote to tending the house and cherishing the children, so she would be left with no leisure to think about herself and her fate. Flower beds and vegetable patches she would plant in the garden, she would paint the lintels and shutters and doors...Yehiel opened the gate of the yard for her, and she slipped past him quickly, scared of being touched by him. A shadow covered his face. She had learned to recognize these clouds of anger which deepened the dark hue of his skin. The other people went on their way, leaving the young couple alone for this first hour that they would spend in their home. Rivka hesitated for a moment and then she too turned away, digging her heels into her horse's flanks.

Yehiel brought the animals into the yard, and after setting out water and fodder for them, straightened up and stared at Fania, who all this time had been standing and watching him, expectantly, with Tamara in her arms.

"Welcome to our home, Fania."

"Delighted to be here, Yehiel."

She resisted the impulse to smile at the portentous tone of his voice. His polite welcome was at odds with the thorns in the yard, the rusty gate, the broken shutters.

"Will you bring the box inside?"

"There's a cradle in the house."

He stepped forward, opened the low door with a key that he took from the pocket of his coat, and kissed the *mezuzah*. The passage was narrow and she was obliged to turn sideways to avoid physical contact with him. It seemed to her his hand was held out to her, and without thinking she hurriedly slipped inside, into the room.

"Are you afraid?

"No, why should I be afraid?" she was quick to answer, but her voice was high, strident. A musty smell hung in the air and Fania pulled back the bolts and opened the shutters. A bluish light shrouded the mountains now, and a green smell breathed on them tenderly.

"There's the cradle. I'll go and untie Lulik."

"I'm coming with you."

"There's no need."

"I want him to see me."

Yehiel pulled away the blanket that covered Lulik and released the leather straps that restrained him. Lulik squinted up at the sky, its blue deepening, still lying on his bed of sacks. He resembled her father, and at the same time was so very different.

"Lulik? Come on, get down, we've arrived."

Lulik looked at Fania who was holding out her hand to him, climbed down from the back of the mule and immediately began walking.

"Lulik! Come back!"

Hearing her cry he quickened his pace, clutching the collar of his coat in his fists. When Fania's cry was repeated, then uttered a third time, he broke into a run. She watched him go, feeling helpless.

"He'll be back," said Yehiel.

"Back where? He doesn't know where he is. He only speaks Russian and he can't explain to people who he is and where he lives."

"He won't get lost. It's a small village and they've all seen him. I'll bring the baggage inside."

"No! Wait! I'd rather clean the house first and only then bring the stuff inside. How long till sunset?"

"About two hours."

"I need water. Lots of water. And soap."

Yehiel hesitated for a moment, looking at her, and then left the house. A fine dowry I've brought you, she thought. She opened all the windows and doors and began taking all the household items outside. The landscape open to her all around gave her a thrill of pleasure. Now and then her eyes rested on the four walnut trees on the top of the hill, and she decided she would go up there as soon as she had the time for it. She longed to explore the crevasses and the heaps of stones and what appeared to be tiny caverns, and the wasteland and the thin coppice and the stunted olive trees. I love this landscape! she discovered to her surprise, while spreading the cushion-covers on the fence and beating them with all her might.

How good it was to move the limbs, stretch the legs and puff out the chest. She dragged out every piece of furniture she was capable of dragging. In the cubby-hole next to the kitchen she found a broom and dusters and began cleaning the apartment. Above the sideboard hung a wedding portrait. Yehiel and Rachel. He looked so boyish, his cheeks smooth and his big eyes staring at the photographer with bashful innocence, his mouth like two leaves of clover. The bride's dress was sewn from several layers of white lace, and there were small gems set in her hair and crescent shapes gliding over her temples like drops of silver.

"She was the most beautiful girl in Galilee."

The voice startled her. In the doorway stood Rivka, carrying buckets of water.

"What is this? Where's Yehiel?"

"I met him by the spring, among the Bedouin women. Don't you know that this isn't man's work? What will the peasants say about him?"

"And how was I supposed to know? In my house the water came out of taps."

Fania felt uncomfortable. She had shamed Yehiel in the eyes of the peasantry. "Why didn't he tell me? He could have told me this isn't the way things are done."

The two women looked at each other. Then Fania said: "Where's the spring?"

Gathered around the shallow pool at that time were Bedouin children and young women who had brought their flocks of sheep to the waterside. The bleating of the sheep and the cries of the shepherds intimidated her. She stood beside them, wondering how to gain access to the water. Rivka pushed the children aside brusquely and called out to Fania: "What are you waiting for?" Her legs seemed to have turned to stone. The shouting, the bleating, the quarrelling, the laughter—all of these raised other voices in her ears. The language of the mob is the same everywhere—in Arabic or in Russian. Enough! her heart cried out. Enough! I have to wipe away that memory, wipe away the old fear and start afresh. This is my home now, this is my land, this is my village and this is my spring. I have to keep on repeating this until the words become as much a part of me as the air that I breathe, to be like Rivka, one of the native plants of this country.

"And what will *they* do?" she asked Rivka when she had succeeded in filling the buckets.

"They can go down to the Jordan! This pool belongs to Gai Oni!"

Twice more Fania went down to the spring to fetch water. In her childhood they had travelled one summer to the countryside. And there she saw peasants drawing water from the well in the middle of the village. And now I'm just like them, she said to herself. When evening came there was a clean smell in the house, the windows had been washed and the dark night sparkled in them, casting starlight on the gleaming floor.

The big bundles were still out in the yard, and Fania waited for Yehiel to come and help her bring them inside. Where has he disappeared to? He brings her to his house and goes off by himself! All her body ached. Hunger nagged at her and the darkness was beginning to make her feel uneasy. Tamara cried and stopped, and cried again. Sounds of the night were menacing in their unfamiliarity. Animals wailed in the distance, an owl hooted. From the ground came the rustling of living creatures and there was a distant murmur of voices. Fania curled up on the chair, rocking Tamara's new-old cradle. Despite her tiredness she was afraid to go to sleep. Her eyes followed the dancing shadows and tried to decipher the sources of the shapes. There was the sound of footsteps approaching the house and she froze in alarm. The door creaked on its hinges and a human shape appeared in the doorway.

"Mrs. Silas?" a woman's voice called out.

"Yes!" Her voice sounded to her like the whimper of a frightened child.

"Where are you? Why are you sitting in the dark?"

"I d-d-don't know how to light the l-l-lamp..." she stammered.

"And where's Yehiel?"

"He went to deliver some sacks of seed, somewhere or other."

"Men!" cried the woman in disgust.

"Who are you?"

"I'm your neighbor, Riva Frumkin. I heard the baby...Come on, my dear, let's go. Pick up the baby and come with me."

"Where to?"

"To our house. We live next door to you. I've known Yehiel since the day he was born and he deserves a good thrashing."

The woman took her hand and led her outside, stepping carefully in the dark. What a joy it was, coming into her neighbor's brightly lit house! After closing the door behind her, the woman let go of Fania's hand and turned to look at her.

"Oh, how beautiful you are! Issar, take a look and see what a jewel Yehiel has brought to Gai Oni. It would be a shame, covering that wonderful hair of yours! And the baby! Blond hair and blue eyes like those haven't been seen in Galilee for years. You'll have to hang a talisman round her neck. Look at him…" she pointed despairingly at her husband, who sat at the table studying by the light of the lamp. The good woman hurled insults, first at her husband and then at Yehiel and finally at the entire masculine race, while putting a plate of hot soup and a large hunk of bread in front of Fania. Issar Frumkin mumbled some pleasantry, moving slightly in his chair and responding with a smile to his wife's words, and for a moment she imagined it was her father studying at the table, at the end of the working day. How she wished she could kneel beside him on the floor, as she used to do as a little girl, to listen to the murmuring and to dream…

While she was eating, the woman told her she too was a native of Safed, and her husband was the uncle of Israel Dov Frumkin, editor of *Havatzelet* and son-in-law of Rabbi Israel Bak. So they were related to Yehiel, too.

Fania felt her strength returning to her. In the other room the woman set up a tub of hot water, and in it Fania bathed Tamara and then bathed herself. It was a real pleasure, taking a bath after the long journey and after all the housework. As she was wondering how she was going to put her dirty clothes back on her clean body, from behind the partition the neighbor's hand appeared, holding out to her a long cotton robe.

"Here, my dear, put this on. And these are for the baby, they're my granddaughter's. I've put hot bricks in your bed. And don't worry about the baby—generations of babies have wet this cradle."

Fania came out from behind the partition, shivering a little at contact with the cool gown, which was too broad and too short.

She had been the tallest in her class, taller than the boys and the girls alike, and they called her "clothes-post" when they were making fun of her. Every few months, her bemused mother had to adjust the hems of dresses that were suddenly too short. Riva Frumkin's gown reached only as far as her knees, and she hurriedly hid herself in the bed, under the big feather quilt, pushing the hot bricks to the end of the bed with her feet.

From the other room, Yehiel's voice was suddenly heard.

"Don't move!" Riva commanded her and left the room.

Fania laughed inwardly, hearing the abuse that Riva was inflicting on Yehiel. Suddenly his head appeared in the doorway.

"Fania?" he asked the recumbent form in the bed.

"Yes?"

"Out!" Riva berated Yehiel. "Tomorrow you're going to stay at home and show your young wife where everything is and how to use it. Tonight she's staying here. What are you waiting for? Food? What were you thinking of eating tonight? You weren't thinking? What were you thinking about? Men!"

Through the open door Fania heard the clatter of utensils as Riva put food in front of Yehiel.

"On the Sabbath you can invite your relatives from Safed and Ein Zeitim here so we'll have a *minyan*. And you can go up to the Torah and recite the 'Who has blessed' and then we'll all come back here for the Kiddush and we'll sing and be happy...No! I don't need any advice from you!" she silenced Yehiel, who was apparently trying to say something. "You've already shown what a clever man you are. I'm doing this for Fania's sake, not for yours. Poor woman. A lot of happiness she's going to know with you!"

"God has punished me, Yehiel," Issar was heard saying, laughing. "I've been getting this for thirty years, Heaven help us, and every year it just gets worse."

"What's this, Yehiel, not at home? Has she thrown you out already?" Someone else had come into the house. In the playful words Fania detected a tone of affection. Again she wondered about this man whom she had married in such haste. After all, he isn't an impulsive boy. He's twenty-six years old and has been married before...

Riva came into the room, covered Fania well and stroked her head. “Good night my dear, and welcome to Gai Oni.” Fania didn’t answer, afraid that her voice would betray her. For the first time in many months she missed her mother. That’s all I need! she thought to herself. Just don’t think about it! But the tears broke out of their own accord, and now, now of all times, when facing up to the kindness of her warm-hearted neighbor, suddenly the dams that had been sealed in her were breached. Riva brought her a cup of hot milk and sat beside her until she had drunk it to the end, wiping her eyes, whimpering, apologizing, panting for breath and bursting into tears again… “It doesn’t matter, it’s all right, don’t apologize, please! I’ll sit with you here until you go to sleep.”

From the next room murmuring voices were heard, and she feared that the sound of her weeping might reach them in there. Yehiel would wonder why she was crying, and she couldn’t explain.

“What are tears for if not to be wept? Weep, weep, you’ll feel better afterwards. I want to weep too when I look at my Issar. My mother used to say, ‘The dew and the rain He brings down and tears—are for us to shed’. You’re tired, my dear. You’ve travelled a long way, and now you’ve come home. It’s all right, it’s all right. Yehiel is a wonderful lad. All the families of Safed wanted him for a son-in-law. He was a prodigy, and as handsome as the Prince of Wales. He could have gone to the rabbinate, applied for grants from the charitable funds and lived like a king…”

Riva lowered the wick in the lamp, and the pale flame cast flickering shadows on the walls. The sounds of hushed conversation from the adjacent room blended with Riva’s gentle voice and the soft breathing of Tamara, lying beside her in the little cot. Her eyes closed finally, but her sleep was fitful. Several times in the course of the night she woke, struggling for breath and unable to stifle her whimpers. Sometimes it seemed Yehiel was sitting by her bed, watching over her sleep. At last she sank into deep and dreamless sleep.

In the morning she was awakened by the crying of Tamara. Points of light glittered on the thin curtain and the air was sharp and clear. Fania took a deep breath, filling her lungs. She felt she had strength and energy and…hunger! Sleep had done her good.

She changed Tamara's wet diaper for a clean one that had been left beside the cot, apparently belonging to one of the Frumkin grandchildren. Tamara sucked with gusto, easing the weight of the milk in her breasts. How long must she go on suckling? And how is it stopped? She must ask somebody. Tamara opened her big blue eyes and from her throat a kind of gurgle emerged, a satisfied sound that she used to utter when she was replete and dry. In two or three years from now this little blonde doll will be chattering away in Arabic like one of the peasants, she thought.

Beside the bed she now saw a basin and a jug of water and a towel. The neighbor must have left them here early in the morning, while she and Tamara were still fast asleep. I'd better hurry up and get used to hard work, she thought. These good people—I'm not the child of their old age. Suddenly she remembered Lulik. She laid Tamara down in the cot and hurried outside.

"Where are you going?!" Riva's voice stopped her.

"Good morning! I…my brother…he's outside…"

"Yes. I've seen him. The peasants say: 'Every madman has a language of his own'. Has he always been like that?"

"No. It happened about a year ago. He can't be approached."

"Is he dangerous?"

"Only to himself. If people come too close to him, he runs away. I want him to get used to the place."

"The people of Jaoni will love him! Come on, sit down and have something to eat. Sleep well?"

"Yes. Thank-you."

"Don't thank me, thank Yehiel. He watched over you."

So, that hadn't been a mirage or a dream.

"Where is he now?"

"He went to Safed to fetch the children. He borrowed a donkey from Samir Alhijja, our neighbor, so you can use it when you go to fetch water. The donkey's tethered to your cypress."

"When did he go out? I didn't hear anything."

"Just as well. You're going to need your strength. There's a lot of work to be done, and very hard work it is, too. Two years of drought we've had. Most of the time we're clearing stones from the ground in

Majuez. Now go and find your brother. In the meantime, I'll make you some breakfast."

"No! Please!"

"And what are you going to eat?" Suddenly Riva began to laugh. "Men! He brought a wife and a baby here and a sack of seeds, and never gave a thought to food! When he comes back from Safed, he'll be bringing flour and oil and sugar and grits and candles and charcoal…I gave him a long list."

"Oh, thank-you. I'd never have thought of all that."

From the hollow recesses of the stove fixed to the wall Riva took out a handful of wooden faggots and shoved them into the black cooking oven.

"The food will only last you a week or two. You'll have to stockpile stores for the winter. A few weeks from now the Bedouin will start arriving from Hermon with grain to sell. You saw the big wooden bowls in the kitchen?"

"Yes."

"You'll need to fill them. I'll come with you when you buy so they won't try to sell you black grain. Maryam Alhijja and her sister Latifa will help you with the winnowing. After Succoth, before the rains start, you should buy a few hundred rotels of charcoal and store them in the cellar to last the winter."

"Our house has a cellar?"

"Yes. Each of these houses has a cellar. I used to keep charcoal in mine along with eggs in slaked lime, also the wine we used to prepare before Rosh Hashanah. And oil, and olives…When you've fed your brother we'll go down to your cellar and see if anything's left there."

Fania noticed that Riva was speaking in the past tense. It must be two years since she filled up the cellar of her house.

How am I going to cope with all this? she wondered, and went in search of Lulik. She found him in the toolshed in the yard. On hearing her footsteps, he was out of there in a flash, staring at her with frightened eyes.

"Lulik! Please! It's me, your sister Fania. I'll bring you some food right away. This is our home now, Lulik…"

She took a step towards him and he fled, his trousers reaching to his ankles, as if he had shot up in height since losing his wits. "Every madman has a language of his own," Riva had said. In what language could she speak to him? The bronze hair of the Mandelstams was growing wild on his head and already reached the shoulders of his army coat. She stood and watched him go and then slowly returned to the neighbor's house.

"If I may, I'll take a slice of bread and a cup of tea for my brother too," she said to Riva.

"It'll be ready in a moment. What happened to him?"

"He was a soldier in the Russian army and his unit took part in a pogrom."

Riva took a hot loaf from the oven and brewed tea. Her back still turned to Fania, she said:

"On the fifteenth of June 1834, Arab rioters wiped out my entire family in Safed. I was spared by a miracle, one baby out of a whole family. And I thank God in Heaven that I was an infant and I didn't see with my eyes and didn't hear with my ears."

"Not everyone is so lucky…" Fania murmured.

"When the harvest comes we women work in the fields alongside the men."

"What happens if this year too there's no rain?"

"Heaven forbid! Why should it be so? Another year?!" Riva was shocked. "Impossible! We've poured our blood into this land! Most of us here are the offspring of Rabbi Israel Bak and we grew up on stories of the plenty that was his lot in Galilee. He himself wrote, and Issar read it to me, that on the Jermak he had built houses to settle in. He planted gardens, sowed fields, and from the very first year he ate his fill from the fruits of the land. By the second year he had sheep and goats, donkeys and horses. And what is more, our master the Sultan, His Imperial Majesty, took a personal interest in him and guaranteed his safety!"

"And was it all lies?"

"Heaven forbid!"

"What then?"

"I'm still searching for the relics of his gardens and orchards. I'm sure I'll find them…"

"Riva!" Fania burst into laughter.

Riva looked at her with a warm smile. "Nice to hear a girl laughing. Since my children moved away from here, I've had no one to talk to, just talk, a casual conversation…Fania?"

"Yes?"

"Be patient. The first year is the hardest. And you're so young, almost a child. Yehiel is a good boy. Wise, sensible, but stubborn. Who isn't stubborn in this place? There were seventeen of us and only the stubborn ones are left. My Issar and Mordecai Leib and Yehiel. Help him. He deserves a good wife."

"I'll try."

If she only knew! Fania reflected as she left the house. What would she say if she knew that our marriage was an arrangement, purely for the sake of appearances?

Fania spent the whole morning scrubbing every corner of the house. From the chest she took bedclothes and children's clothes and men's shirts and women's blouses, and her thoughts returned yet again to the woman who had sat and embroidered them. From time to time she glanced at the wedding photograph standing on the cabinet. It seemed to her that Rachel's eyes were following her and watching her every move. If she had dared she would have turned the picture to face the wall. Beside the spring, among the Bedouin and the peasant women, she washed the clothes and the linen, scrubbing them with soap and rinsing them in the meager, miserly stream. On returning home she hung the laundry to dry on the bushes and on the fence. From time to time she peered into the toolshed but didn't dare go inside for fear of scaring Lulik away again. Hours had passed since she had left the bread and the tea on the little box by the door. She pushed a mat and a woolen blanket, taken from the house, into the shed. Over the fence and the hill, the four big walnut trees, the remains of Rabbi Israel's khan, caught her eye. At the first opportunity she would go up there, she promised herself again. Once more she was assailed by hunger and she began searching for morsels of bread in her house. In the larder she found a few stray tea leaves and a little flour. A sense of unease accompanied her as she opened the various boxes. As if she was trespassing on the preserve of others. She knew she needed to wean herself from this feeling. If only she could move that photograph. She decided to clean out the larder as well before Yehiel came back with the children and the food.

For the fourth time that morning she filled the buckets with water and loaded them with effort onto the back of the donkey. Her arms ached and the muscles of her back seemed on the point of breaking. Suddenly, Rivka appeared on her horse and as she passed by, kicked her heels into the horse's flanks and broke into a gallop. The donkey took fright, picked up his hooves and fled, the buckets on his back spraying the precious water in all directions. Fania watched anxiously as the donkey disappeared down the slope, beyond the ridge.

"Why are you so worried?" Rivka smiled at her. "Donkeys come back."

"He isn't ours…" Fania stammered, a flush of anger swamping her face.

"I know he isn't yours. Why didn't you tie him up?"

"I only stopped to fill the buckets…"

Her anger seethed. Most of all she was furious with herself, for the stammering, for the excuses and for the look of childish petulance which she was sure must be visible on her face. She picked up the remaining bucket, and without another word turned towards her home. From time to time she put the bucket down on the ground to catch her breath.

"Do you need some help?"

"No, thank-you."

"You look as if you could collapse at any moment."

Fania didn't answer. Sweat poured into her eyes, and if it weren't for the girl watching her she'd have emptied the bucket there and then. The Bedouin women can do this and so can I! she repeated to herself stubbornly.

She dropped the bucket by the larder and went to wash her face. Her long hair was coiled on her head now like a burnished crown.

She looked at the black iron stove and wondered how to use it. In the yard stood a baking oven, and in the morning she had watched her neighbor taking hot pitas from her oven, but the neighbor's oven had been burning all night. She put the small quantity of flour she had found into a bowl, added a little water and some salt and began kneading the dough. The sound of approaching hooves was heard outside, stopping in the yard.

"I caught the donkey and took it back to Fatima," said Rivka.

"Is Fatima Samir's wife?"

"Yes…What are you doing?"

"Baking bread, I hope," Fania shrugged her shoulders in despair.

"Bread! How are you expecting to bring up a family? You don't know anything!"

"How do you light this oven?"

Rivka crammed some pieces of charcoal into the stove, also twigs that she found in the yard. She had the body of a boy and black plaited hair like Rachel's. Does she resemble her late sister?

"Don't you go to school?"

"What do I need to learn?"

Fania shrugged again. What could she possibly say about the delight, the intoxicating joy of studying history and literature and music and languages…

"Rachel embroidered these clothes for Bella."

Fania looked up from the dough. Rivka was standing by Tamara's cot.

"She doesn't look like you."

"No."

"Does she look like her father?"

"No! She's just herself…"

Fania knew that confusion was showing in her face. Rivka narrowed her eyes and peered at her suspiciously. In vain she tried to calm her turbulent heart.

"How old is she?"

"Four months."

Rivka said nothing. She's working out when I conceived, Fania thought. She's going to uncover my secret soon. I have to suppress this panic that I feel, so it doesn't give me away.

"Moshe and Bella had no idea that Yehiel had married. Even his sister Leah didn't know."

"Have you been in Safed?"

"Someone had to prepare them."

"Yehiel went there specially to tell them."

I need to take care when this girl's around, she reflected.

"This dough's no good for making bread. Pitas, perhaps." Rivka took the dough from her hands and started rolling it into little balls which she then flattened. While she worked, from outside the sound of approaching cart-wheels was heard. Rivka carried on with what she was doing and Fania went to wash her hands.

The cart drove into the yard and right up to the door of the house. On the front seat, beside Yehiel, sat the two children. They climbed down from the cart with Yehiel's help, then stopped and stood their ground, as if confronting a high wall. All at once Fania was inundated by waves of joy and fear. She had felt like this only once before, as a little girl sitting on a carousel, on a ride shaped like a swan, hanging on with all her strength to the wooden feathers, choking in her excitement. The first thing that caught her eye was the lank mass of dark reddish hair, coloring similar to her own. The two little heads were very tousled, grubby and sticky. The dark eyes were half closed and swollen. It seemed they too were victims of trachoma, the ailment she had seen in the majority of the children of Jaffa. They looked at her with serious expectation and she knew she was supposed to do something, but suddenly she was as shy as they were. She was afraid of doing something that would spoil any prospect of a good relationship developing between them. If only there were no other people there, just her and the children! Between them they could have found exactly the right words to say on an occasion such as this. Precise words, like musical notes, which cannot be faked. In her home, in her childhood, children were always *getting* something, kisses or tickles or presents. Mouths were always full of cherries or sweets or cake, pockets bulging and hands full and faces ablaze with anticipation beforehand and excitement afterwards...Trembling with the irresistible urge to give something to these children, who would henceforward be *her* children, Fania stood before them empty-handed, face blank and tongue silent.

From the cart another figure appeared, someone who had been hidden there up to now, and the whole group hurried to get inside the house. The door was closed behind them and Yehiel and the stranger burst into laughter and embraced.

"We crept in like mice!" said the stranger, who was about the same age as Yehiel. He was dressed in "European" style, without the oriental caftan which even emigrés from Europe tended to wear on arriving in the Holy Land. The lapels of his jacket were velvet and he wore a hat rather than a tarboosh.

"Fania, this is my kinsman and mentor Eleazar Rokeah, who has come from over the sea. Lizar, this is my wife Fania. Bella! Moshe! Have you said hello to Fania? I see you took the donkey back to Samir..."

"I took him back."

Surprised, Yehiel and Eleazar turned in the direction of the voice.

"Rivka! What are you doing here?"

"Baking pitas."

"Perfect timing!" Yehiel laughed. "We're hungry."

We're hungry! Fania fumed, and the blushing quotient that always reflected her moods swamped her face now with a dark flush. Here is the good and efficient Rivka baking pitas for hungry men while she, the lazy and clumsy one, doesn't have the intellectual capacity needed to provide for them herself. And what about her? Doesn't she get hungry too?

"There's no food in the house," she said to Yehiel, careful to keep the anger out of her voice.

"I've brought flour and oil and olives and sugar and charcoal and eggs. And Leah has sent us wine and raisins...I worked for Lizar's brother in Jaffa," he explained to Fania, "for Shimon Rokeah."

"You want me to light the baking oven?" said Eleazar.

"You sit down!" Rivka commanded him.

"Where's Tamara?" Bella asked, finally breaking her silence.

"Come with me and I'll show you." Fania was glad to escape to the other room.

The children stood on opposite sides of the cot. Bella put a grubby little finger in Tamara's hand, and the tiny hand closed on it at once. Tamara pulled Bella's finger into her mouth and began sucking it to the sound of the girl's giggles.

"My turn now," said Moshe. He was so serious! Bella's finger was pulled from Tamara's mouth and for a moment it seemed the baby had lost her balance, but immediately Moshe's finger was gripped in the little fist and was being sucked with relish.

"Mahmud's cow has calved," Moshe told Fania. She nodded without smiling. Her heart was full and her mouth empty of words.

From the other room the voices of Riva and Issar were heard and another voice, that of Mordecai Lieb perhaps. There was animation in Yehiel's voice.

"I'm going back in there so they won't be cross with me," Fania told the children.

The table was set and all those present took their seats around it, the glow of good fellowship in their faces. She was a stranger among them.

"You're not alike," Fania said to Eleazar Rokeah.

"We're both descended from Rabbi Israel Bak, but Yehiel takes after his grandmother from Damascus and I'm closer to the Berdichevs."

"Why did you leave Gai Oni?"

"His life was in danger!" Yehiel interjected in a passionate tone. "The burghers of Safed were scared by his ideas! We here, are the sole surviving relic of his revolution. According to the plan, more of the Jews of Safed were supposed to follow in our footsteps and finally begin earning a living by the sweat of their brow. And for this terrible idea they pelted him with stones! They were afraid the Jews of the Diaspora would stop sending them charitable donations, if they heard that Jews were producing food from the land. Every time I pass your house in Safed and see the broken windows, it makes my blood boil, such an insult!"

"Yehiel!" Eliezer broke into his friend's tirade, "In my house in Safed 'Elijah's Chair' is still there, the one on which Montefiore sat when Shmuel Ben Nisan Bak was initiated into the covenant of our father Abraham. Take the chair! A wedding present to you and Fania. And may you put it to good use."

"Moishele, Belluna!" Riva had found the children and was embracing them, planting noisy kisses on their cheeks. "What's this? Oh dear!" she exclaimed, seeing their swollen eyes. "In the morning come to your Auntie Riva and she'll put some ointment on your eyes."

"No," said Moshe.

"No," Bella echoed.

"You'll go blind! Like Pharaoh!"

"If you're brave, we'll go up in the afternoon to the hill with the walnut trees," Fania promised.

"The place is swarming with snakes and scorpions," Yehiel warned.

"I'm not afraid," said Moshe.

"I am," said Fania.

"I'll take sticks," said Moshe.

"Me too," said Bella.

"I was hoping to meet more of the comrades here," said Eleazar with feeling.

"They will be back, God willing, after the first rain," said Mordecai Lieb.

"They haven't sold the houses," said Issar apologetically.

"You can't blame them, Lizar my dear," said Riva. "The Friedmans and the Schwartzes and the Brochsteins sold their last bootlace to buy the land and register it with the authorities and pay the mukhtar his cut. And when they were completely broke, the drought set in. We weren't left with one dinar to buy seeds with. Not to mention an ox or a plough. People were hungry for bread. They couldn't breathe any more. And all of them parents with young children."

"You stayed," said Eleazar.

"Yes, because we've nowhere to go back to. Don't let the pitas on the table deceive you. For three years now we haven't sown or reaped."

"So where does the flour come from?"

Riva hesitated and then said: "We glean ears of corn after the peasants have reaped, like Ruth the Moabite."

Fania was dumbfounded. For the first time she realized the dire conditions in which these people lived. That evening, when she stood surveying the empty tins in the larder, was like a forewarning of the future. Yehiel had apparently set aside some of the money he earned in Jaffa to buy food for his family. But what would the future hold? They had to find some other source of income, in addition to the land. And who could guarantee that the drought would end? She had supposed in her innocence that he was saving her and her family from the scourge of hunger. Some salvation! Feeding three children and three adults was now her responsibility.

For a moment her eyes met Yehiel's and he seemed to be reading her thoughts. Fania made a point of sitting up straight in her chair as if saying: I have no regrets! She would plant vegetables in the little garden and write to her sisters in America, asking them to send her things she could sell at a profit. Some of the proceeds she would send back to them, some she would send to her uncle and the remainder would support her family. God! For one moment it had seemed to her that the man sitting opposite her had taken the burden off her shoulders.

"We read your articles in *Jezreel*," Issar said, as if Eleazar needed cheering up. "Israel Dov Frumkin sends me the paper from Jerusalem. Is there really any prospect of Romanian Jews coming to the Holy Land?"

"God willing, a hundred families will be arriving in Gai Oni immediately after Pesach!" was Eliezer's sensational announcement. "Some three hundred souls from two cities: Batushan and Moinesti. Two envoys have already been sent to the 'Sublime Porte' to apply for the settlement permit. They will claim they are seeking the opportunity to shelter again under the benign patronage of the Sultan. And two agents will be coming here soon to buy the land."

"And they're coming here? To Gai Oni?"

"We certainly hope so. In all my articles I sing the praises of the pioneers of Gai Oni."

"What are they going to eat?" Riva asked.

"They are affluent people. Many of them liquidated their businesses prior to emigrating and they'll be coming here with full pockets. And what's no less important: they are all God-fearers and keepers of commandments. The Jews of Safed will have no cause to complain about them. 'The vanguard'—that's what they call them in *Hamaggid*."

Riva sat up straight in her chair and said in a quaking voice: "*We* are the vanguard."

"And what about the tracts of land bought up by Oliphant, the Minister? Will he sell them to the Romanians?"

"If he hasn't sold them in the meantime to the Effendis."

"Oliphant? Never!" Eleazar exclaimed. "He believes in the 'Return to Zion' more than our Jews believe in it! If it weren't for him, they would never have woken up. After all, the Alliance Israelite Universelle is opposed to the concept of settlement of the land! Ten thousand Jews sitting in Brody since the pogroms began are waiting for the chance to leave Russia. And the A.I.U. is racking its brains and wondering what's preferable: Spain, perhaps? Or how about central Russia? Anything other than the Land of Israel. Why?!" he cried suddenly. "Because life is hard in this country? So it is! And in America it isn't hard? A significant proportion of the fifteen hundred Jewish refugees who went to America last year are facing starvation. The local committee is refusing to accept any more Jews. Who are these refugees? Orphans, widows, the elderly, tradesmen, peddlers… We're prepared to take them! All of them! They can irrigate the soil of the land with their tears! If I could, I'd harness my own body to the plough! Oliphant, too, is trying to inspire them to immigrate to the Land of Israel. With his own eyes he has seen the pogroms, and this has only reinforced his conviction that the safest haven for the Jews is Palestine. After all, it's only five years since Disraeli signed the Treaty of Berlin. We were all deliriously happy, you remember, Yehiel? The western powers committed themselves to defending the rights of the Jews in the Balkan countries. We might have known what the outcome would be—one hand signs and the other goes on hitting. I just hope that *he* doesn't despair. The 'Sublime Porte' suspects his motives. They're afraid that Britain is using Oliphant and the concept of return to Zion as a means of subverting the Ottoman Empire. Now he's sitting in Haifa with his wife, Lady Alice, and his secretary, Naphtali Herz Imber, and sending all around the world articles singing the praises of the land. He tells of its beauty, of the safety of its roads, of its fertility..." Eleazar grinned suddenly. "I can't blame him. I've been guilty of this 'sin' too. I baulk at no measures, may God forgive me...When the delegation arrives from Romania, I hope one of you will make a point of introducing them to Oliphant. Their immigration to this country is in no small measure to his credit."

"You won't be here?"

"I'm leaving tonight. Before anyone in Safed discovers that I've returned."

"And what language does he speak, Mr. Oliphant?"

"English."

All those present exchanged glances, shrugging their shoulders.

"I understand English," said Fania.

All turned to her in surprise. As if they had suddenly become aware of her existence.

"Your husband is a lucky man!" said Riva Frumkin. Now they remembered the other reason for the gathering. The bottle of wine was opened and all drank to their health. This is my marriage feast, Fania said to herself.

Before taking his leave of them, Eleazar again mentioned the 'Elijah's Chair', their wedding present.

The guests departed and Fania and Yehiel were left alone. The children had just gone to sleep on the mattress. When Yehiel laid his hand on Fania's shoulder, she flinched in alarm at his touch and her heart pounded.

"The house is spotlessly clean," he said, but on his face there was no sign of the radiance that had lit it just a moment before. From the pocket of his coat he took a small parcel wrapped in thick paper. "This is for you."

In the parcel she found a green headscarf decorated with colored tassels and inlaid with a tiny row of pearls.

"Thank-you."

"Your hair is wonderful. 'Like a flock of goats descending from Mount Gilead,'" he smiled. "But you will have to cover your head."

"Yes."

"Come on, let's go to bed."

"I…that is…I want to write some letters. To my sisters…to my uncle…"

"Now?!"

"Yes. Eleazar Rokeah can post them for me…Is he staying at Riva's?"

"Yes." He hesitated for a moment. She saw his knuckles whiten and was scared, but he turned away and left the room.

Fania wrote to her sisters telling them about her circumstances, but omitting any facts liable to distress them and embellishing where embellishment was required. The light of the lamp faded. Fania stood on the chair and glanced into the tin container hanging from a hook fixed in the ceiling. There was very little oil left in the container. She pushed the wick down hard into the oil, praying the light would last until she had finished writing her letters. She was still writing when she heard Yehiel stripping off his clothes, washing and getting into bed. She remembered the paraffin lamp she had seen in a shop in Jaffa. A glass bowl contained the smoke, stopped it from spreading. All right, then. Lamps like that one she would ask her sisters to send! A lot of people would jump at the chance of possessing one of these.

"Fania, come to bed."

A shudder passed through her body. Then another, and another. She couldn't sleep beside him! She had been brought here to serve as a nanny, not as a wife and bedmate. Hadn't these things been made clear from the start?

"I'll sleep with the children."

A sour smile hovered over Yehiel's face. He got out of the bed and lay down himself beside the children. Fania snuffed out the lamp and under cover of darkness, stripped off her clothes. How could they live like this side by side, undressing, washing, making all the noises that people make in privacy—and go on being strangers?

"I thought we married just to avoid scandal..." she whispered.

"When you change your mind, let me know," Yehiel's answer was heard in the dark. "I'm not asking for any favors except from the land." His voice was hoarse, out of anger perhaps, or out of fatigue, but there was a tone of finality in it. If he thought he was bringing a wife home, he hadn't gotten much of a bargain. Now he was trapped with her and inwardly he must be blaming her. His angry whisper continued to reverberate in the room a long time. "He deserves a good wife," the neighbor had said. And what am I?? Fania's heart melted. Don't I deserve a little kindness? But she rapidly shook off the self-pity and in her heart she resolved to compensate Yehiel for the "deception".

Chapter three

The sound of a shriek split the air. The stone-clearers stopped working abruptly, looking anxiously in the direction from which the cry had come. Imber sprang up, and with the staff that he carried he struck again and again at something on the ground at his feet. Moshe stood beside him, his lean face as pale as the rocks. In a flash they were joined by Yehiel, who smashed the snake's head with a stone. Then he held aloft the long, sinuous body of a black cobra. People stared, open-mouthed, or uttered panic-stricken gasps. Fania was afraid she was going to be sick. She ran to Moshe, hugging him tightly and kissing again and again the pale, sticky and dirt-stained face. Then she turned to Imber and clasped his hand, shaking it repeatedly and thanking him for his courage and his heroism. Imber suddenly started to laugh and Fania joined in his laughter, as relief and deliverance misted her eyes with a film of tears.

"I suddenly saw something black between the two rocks close to the boy," Imber explained. "The snake was dozing in the sun and Moshe woke it up. You shouldn't be giving women and children work like this," he added, turning to Yehiel. "I know! I know I have no right to interfere. I'm a guest, and a temporary one. And I'm deeply moved, seeing the work that's being done here. But it's hard work even for men."

"We're only clearing the small stones, and leaving the bigger ones to the men," Fania assured Imber with a charming smile, trying to cover the fact that Yehiel hadn't even thanked him for saving his son's life.

Eka Riva shouted to them, calling them back to work. Since the day she and her husband, the "honest and upright" Shalom Halpon, settled in Jaoni, she had been spurring her colleagues on without mercy. Not for nothing did the Arabs call her "Karima al-Wakila", meaning "Big Boss". Possibly, if it hadn't been for her egging them on through all the hours of the day, they wouldn't have kept up the effort, since there wasn't a single patch of ground on the hill without a rock.

Dig in the hills with all your might
Dig by day and dig by night
Dig and with a joyful sound
Find precious jewels in the ground...

Imber recited again the poem he was in the process of composing while Yehiel and Fania returned to their work.

"At least in public you could try to hide the friendship between you," Yehiel whispered angrily.

"Why should I hide anything?" she protested. "He's always nice to me and he's a wonderful man! And he saved your son's life and you couldn't even be bothered to thank him!"

She turned away from him in fury and walked to her "patch". Before dawn they had started working here and still it looked as if nothing had changed. As if the invisible hand of Satan had sown new stones in place of the ones removed. At the top of the hill rose the four walnut trees of Hirbet el-Yahud, and Fania reflected bitterly: That's what they'll say about us too when we're gone. A monument to a dream that used to be. Yehiel's face looked terrible. No one knew better than she that he was barely eating anything. The accursed land was sucking out their very marrow. All these people, they're a gang of lunatics. They have no food to give their children, and they're going to war against the stones. They could have stayed in Safed or in Jerusalem or in Hebron, studying the Torah and working at trades...If she were a washerwoman in Jaffa, she would be bringing more food into her house! Luckily, onions were sprouting in the vegetable plot, and the cucumbers had cropped, and there were still a few olives left in the can...Again she wondered why there had been no response from her sisters in the United States. Several months had passed since she wrote to them. She tried to match the rhythm of her movements to those of Riva Frumkin, stooping, picking up a stone, throwing it on the pile and repeating the process. Riva's old face was green, really green, as if it wasn't only hunger that was gnawing away at her but some mysterious disease. The frantic zeal with which these people tore the flesh from their hands alarmed her, the pain in her loins and her back was unbearable, but she carried on working in a kind of intoxication, saying to herself again and again: if Riva can do it, I can do it too. When the "Wakila" called a break, she was afraid to stop, afraid she'd be unable to start again.

"Sit down," said Riva.

Fania stretched her long legs and sat. Her head was purged of all thought and her eyes stared at the dust dancing in the sunlight. Her body was so tired she couldn't even raise her hand to wipe the sweat from her face. After a while she began to feel the cooling breeze and surrendered herself to its caresses, closing her eyes.

"Fania, drink!"

Riva handed her an earthenware jug containing cold water. It tasted sweeter in her mouth than any of the sweets which her mother had concocted for her in her childhood. She took a good swig of it and then took a deep breath and smiled at Riva, who responded to her with a wan smile. She's sick, Fania thought to herself again. A kind of greenish haze covered her tanned, desiccated skin. People began getting up to go back to work. They were dressed in a variety of costumes, a mix of peasant clothing and yeshiva-student attire: tarbooshes, turbans, caps, kaffias...Yehiel was working in his vest, in trousers hanging from his broad shoulders, held by the suspenders

Eleazar Rokeah gave him. This is our destiny, Fania reflected, to implement the visions of others. For Yehiel—Eleazar's dream, and for me—the ideals my uncle preached: equality of living, cooperation, work...Imber moved away to the edge of the field, as if wanting no disturbance in the performance of his sacred task. Something in his gait suggested a rhythmic beat, and his long hair rose and fell like a scythe in the standing corn. How easily the lyrics flowed from his lips! With what avid intoxication he observed these Hebrew farmers! He brought with him the vibrant spirit of the exiled Jewish scholar, like those "Lovers of Zion" who used to visit her father's house. His very appearance gladdened her heart, and she lavished unbounded affection and friendship on him, but this, apparently, was resented by Yehiel. Could it be that he's jealous?—she wondered.

On Sabbath morning, after the prayers, she went out with the children to the hill where the walnut trees stood. Ever since coming here she had been promising herself and the children that one day they would walk up to Hirbet el-Yahud. In her pocket was a pomegranate which had been left on one of the trees, and which she had hidden specifically with this trip in mind. They climbed along the channel of Ayn Abu Halil, drawn by threads of enchantment towards the summit. The sound of their footsteps as they trudged through the dust of the mountain was the only sound they heard. How she loved this wild landscape! The bare hills dotted here and there with an ancient olive or a lone terebinth, the chilly peak of faraway Hermon, the chalk cliffs crisscrossed by rivulets of lava. A pair of eagles circled in the sky, descending a short distance and then soaring up again. When at last they reached the summit, a rabbit fled from out of the thorny bushes and Moshe tried to chase it, much to the amusement of Fania and Bella. Tamara gurgled in her arms, smiling at the faces appearing above her and uttering little squeals of joy before turning serious and inquisitive again, looking round for the faces that had suddenly disappeared. Imber arrived, bringing with him a sense of all the fullness of the land, his tie awry and the fringes of his long "German" trousers rolled up to protect them from sand and dust. When he saw Fania he cried, his voice vibrant:

> *Flowers, meadows, arms that embrace*
> *And love! My eye's delight.*

Her heart overflowing with joy, Fania answered him, with a coquettish tilt of the head:

> *To which of the maidens, tell me,*
> *Is this song of yours dedicated?*

Again Imber followed her lead with quotations from *Eugene Onegin*, and they both stamped their feet to the rhythm of the words, their eyes laughing and weeping, while the children listened with bemusement to these adults, reciting rhythmically in a strange language.

"Where?" Imber demanded of Moshe, "Where in all the world will you find another farmer's wife who recites poetry? And what about you? What's that you have in your hand?"

"A tortoise. And there was a rabbit, too, and I chased it."

"A rabbit!" Imber exclaimed as if this was a sensational revelation. "What is the difference between a rabbit and a rabbi? And by the way, where are you from, Fania?"

Briefly, Fania told him the bare minimum about her past, and was relieved that he chose not to pursue the subject.

"What is this place?"

"Fifty years ago a Jewish printer from Berdichev settled up here on the hill, Rabbi Israel Bak, together with his wife and children and his entire household. He's the great grandfather of Moshe and Bella, here. Everything that he sowed and planted bore fruit, and the people built houses and lived in them, and they had livestock and chickens, too, and they were happy in their lot. Nisan Bak, the Rabbi's son, printed charity tickets and distributed them among the poorer peasants. The tickets were printed with six Hebrew letters to represent six days of the week, and the gleaners would show their tickets when they came into his fields, so that charity would be apportioned fairly."

"Boaz from Berdichev! King David was descended from you!"

A big red-legged partridge suddenly scuttled past Imber and startled him. Fania and the children stifled their laughter. And when

Imber had recovered his composure Moshe said to him: "The letter 'T'!"

To the surprise of Fania and Bella, Imber lifted the boy aloft and planted a resounding kiss on his cheek.

"Right! Right!

Take the 't' from the rabbit and then you will see,
Hiding behind it, you can take it from me,
Is the rabbi!

You're a clever lad, Moshe! Where are you going to school?"

"He isn't going to school at the moment, but two weeks from now he'll be starting Bible classes in Safed."

"No!" Moshe's face, which had lit up for a moment, darkened suddenly.

"But you have to! Didn't you hear? The famous poet Naphtali Hertz Imber, in person, says you're a clever lad."

"Go to the Talmud Torah school, my boy, and do as Imber the poet did when he was a kid and they called him Hertzli. I hid under the desk and from there I listened to what the teacher and the pupils were saying. It's a good place, believe me!"

"Imber!" Fania laughed.

"You're so pretty when you laugh!"

Sweet girl, how lovely you are!
But this nose! But this neck!
Who would believe it possible?

Fania replied to Imber with a proverb of Karilov, and he followed suit with a play on words that they both enjoyed:

And what a vista of feathers! What a flash of eyes!
And your voice too, surely—as the voice of an angel!

"Tell them!" Fania demanded of Imber. And he sat Moshe on one knee and Bella on the other and recited to them with relish the fable of the raven and the fox.

Their eyes were misted over with concentration, and Fania felt this was the most wonderful day she had spent so far in the Land of Israel. How good it was to exercise the brain again, to trawl up from memory the favorite rhymes of her childhood, to exchange witticisms, to be a member once more of the glorious family of poetry-lovers… The children demanded more, and Imber told them about the eagle and the cockerel and the lion and the gnat. Again and again they recited the rhyme:

And who was it? One tiny gnat
It was he who caused the whole of the spat!

Every time Imber cried, "And who?" he would point to one or the other of the children, who would then declaim the reply.

And this was how Yehiel found them, full of enthusiasm and hooting joyfully, clapping hands. All at once the group fell silent, as if caught red-handed in the commission of some crime. Yehiel, sensing the simple, good-natured friendship that had been woven here in his absence, struggled to conceal his jealousy and resentment.

"I asked you not to go up here without me," he said to Fania.

"I'm looking after her," Imber smiled at him, and she looked down, embarrassed.

"And I found a tortoise," added Moshe, who had become Imber's friend.

Fania remembered the pomegranate in her pocket and was glad to have something to do with her hands, peeling it and distributing it. Hands were blackened by the red pips, and teeth set on edge by their bitterness.

"Are you coming back?" Yehiel asked.

"Soon."

He turned away from them and started down the path, with his tall stature, lean body and broad shoulders. She watched him go as if he were a stranger, a wayfarer, a nomad whose path had crossed theirs. What's his problem? Why did he run away from us? Now, as he receded from them, their happiness evaporated like smoke.

"Fania!" Eka Riva, the "Wakila", roused Fania from her reverie. Riva Frumkin opened her eyes as well. She supported her head with her hand. Hunger inscribed its marks on the people's faces. How long will it be before their spirit succumbs to the weakness of their bodies? They will never succeed in clearing the mountain of its stones. Those stones will bury them and become the monuments marking their graves.

"Come on, Riva, let's go home." Fania helped her friend to her feet and led her away, supporting her with her arm. When they reached Riva's home, she helped her take off her shoes and stripped off her grimy clothes. She filled a tub with water and washed the old woman's face and legs. How old is she? Fifty? Fifty-five? She needs a doctor, medicines, decent food, rest. This is the fate that awaits all of us here. We shall all die before our time, of hunger, fever, grief and disappointment…

With a heart soured by wrath she left Riva Frumkin's house, determined to get some fresh milk at least for her sick friend. She knew there was no point approaching the homes of the Arab peasants, since they were just as hungry as their Jewish brethren. The spirit of the hunter setting out in search of prey was aroused in her, impelling her to walk, to run, to seek…Her legs carried her as if of their own accord to the place where in those days the Banu al-Zangariya were encamped. This was one of the smaller Bedouin tribes of the north, peering with covetous eyes at the lands of Jaoni. They tended to visit the place once or twice a year, bringing their herds of goats and sheep to the springs of the village, avoiding the need to go down to the Jordan to water them. There were periodic disputes and confrontations between the Bedouin and the villagers, over pasturing rights and the ownership of water. Fania knew she was breaking an unwritten law when she crossed the invisible boundary separating the *fellah* from the semi-nomad.

The familiar stench of burning camel dung greeted her as she approached the encampment. Grubby dogs assailed her with a chorus of enthusiastic barking, and a gang of inquisitive half-naked children came running in the wake of the dogs. In the tent in the center of the encampment a group of men sat around a heap of stones, with burning coals in its maw. On the altar of stones stood a jerry can full of water. Some distance away, two women were bending down, one of them young with flashing eyes and face covered with decorative incisions. A string of gold coins adorned the full length of her nose and reached as far as her throat. She was grinding coffee with a long wooden pestle, pounding the black mortar rhythmically. The other woman, older, was kneading dough for pitas, shaping them dexterously with the palms of her hands. The smell of baking dough made Fania's head spin for a moment. She approached the two women and told them she had come to ask for milk for a sick friend. More children came and gathered around her, as the news of her arrival spread through the camp. They were touching her dress, their inflamed eyes oozing pus. I won't be taking just milk away from here, she thought to herself, but trachoma too. She had barely managed to cure Moshe of this infernal eye affliction. Prolonged treatment with cobalt powder and tea leaves, bandages and compresses and constant rubbing, caused great distress to the children, as well as to her and to Riva, who had been helping her. It's too bad that I have to ask them for a favor, she reflected. Except that these homeless nomads were better off than she was, in that when the last blade of grass was consumed, they could strike camp and go in search of new pastures. Whereas for her—this would be the site of her grave. Yehiel and his comrades would rather die than leave Gai Oni.

The women looked quizzically at the men, and they explained to Fania that they had no milk, since their goats were scattered over the mountainside and had not yet come in from pasture.

"If I don't get milk right now, you won't be watering your flocks any more in the pool of Jaoni!" she threatened them. Women and children alike immediately uttered loud cries of protest, surrounding her with curses and oaths. She knew they wouldn't harm her since she was a guest, but in her heart she felt stirrings of that old fear of the faceless human morass, of the crowd. The faces blended before her eyes and the cries in her ears fused into rolling thunder. For a moment she hesitated. Should she flee? She knew she had nothing to offer in return, not a penny or anything worth a penny, and they saw water as a gift of God, to which every living and breathing creature was entitled. Luckily for her the tattooed beauty, who was apparently the youngest wife of the clan chieftain, took a fancy to her dress. Her husband proceeded to negotiate with her over the dress, and all the time she was talking to him, her brain was pierced by the thought that two years before, in her wildest dreams she could not have imagined this situation. A deal was struck, and the two women went into another tent to strip off their dresses. Fania hesitated. This was one of the few dresses which her neighbor in Elizavetgrad had sewed for her, that kind-hearted Jewish woman who took her into her house when it became clear that of her own house all that remained were a few smoldering embers. The seamstress had sewed the dresses "by sight" as Fania was still laid out on the bed, beaten and bruised and in too much pain even to lick her wounds…The stench in the tent was almost unbearable. Now it was going to cling to her too. So what! The sooner she becomes like one of the Bedouin women, so much the better. These are the clothes that suit this country. I'm not a Russian high school student any more, I'm a Jewish Bedouin. It's all in vain, trying to preserve the relics of my past. The more my previous life is erased, the better for me and for mine. The Bedouin dress will protect me on the roads, make my movements easier.

After stripping off the dresses they peered at one another the way young women peer at their friends, curiously, and with a shy smile. Then Fania remembered the pistol concealed in her underwear and hurriedly covered herself with the new dress. The Banu al-Zangariya were renowned for their love of weapons, and she hoped that in her excitement over the new dress the Bedouin woman had not noticed the pistol. The small tribe was notorious for its savagery and violence and its readiness to seize the property of others. In the past the Zangariya tribesmen used to collect the "Huwa" from the peasants of Jaoni, allegedly to defend them against attacks from other tribes. The Turkish governor issued a new edict forbidding the villagers to pay any more protection money, and his objective was twofold: he was determined to extend the power of the government over the

Bedouin, and at the same time he meant to levy taxes on the land himself, tax on the livestock and tax on the produce that was yet to be harvested. The Jews of Gai Oni had inherited from the Jaonians the cordial relations which had prevailed since then between the Bedouin of Galilee and the peasants. For the time being there was little serious conflict, since the drought had prevented the seeding of the fields, but on a number of occasions Fania overheard discussion of the precautions which should be taken to protect the crops against raids mounted by Zangariya bandits…

"I am Fania."

"I am Tenaha."

By the time they emerged from the tent the coffee was already brewing on the fire, and Fania was invited to sit with the women and drink some of it. The appearance of the two young women was greeted by laughter and cries of amazement. The children fingered Tenaha's new dress, and she didn't discourage them. Then it was time for the exchange to be made. The "bandits" clearly felt they had struck a good deal. Besides the milk, the older woman put into Fania's hand three slices of cheese and two hot pitas.

The warm dress smelled of goats and their excrement and chafed against her skin. Once she was out of sight of her hosts Fania broke off pieces of a pita and crammed them into her mouth. If it weren't for the bronze-colored hair spilling out from the green headscarf, I would look like a Bedouin, she reflected. She knew she was obliged to cut her hair short or hide it completely under the headscarf, but she didn't feel she was really married, and even Yehiel had not demanded this of her…

"Where's the milk from, Fania?" Riva asked.

"Drink!" Fania commanded her.

After drinking a little of the warm milk Riva lay down on her back and closed her eyes. The fever seemed to be abating a little, and within a few minutes her breathing stabilized and she sank into sleep. To all appearances, her condition was due to hunger, not just to disease. Fania racked her brains, wondering whether to leave the remainder of the milk for Riva or take it home, for her children. It was lucky for her that Tamara was still suckling, though she sometimes feared hunger might dry up this source of milk, too. Where would she find food for another mouth? Bella and Moshe wandered around hungry most of the time, their stomachs shrinking. Bella's eyes were inflamed and there was neither food nor medicines in the house. The day before yesterday she did as the peasant women did and burned sheaves of wheat on the fire, beating them to separate the grains from the straw. The taste of the charred grains was pleasant to the palate, rather like the taste of pumpkin seeds. And something like the smell of freshly baked bread wafted through the house, but this only intensified their hunger. She had her work cut out, persuading Yehiel to taste the grains. She knew he didn't want the children to go short, but how long could he carry on working without proper food? In the cottage garden there were a few onions and cucumbers left, and these staved off the worst of their hunger for the time being. In the end she decided to leave the milk for Riva, but to take the slices of cheese and the pitas home.

The stamping of a horse was heard from outside and a moment later Rivka's head appeared in the doorway.

"What's this?!" She burst into laughter when she caught sight of Fania.

"A Bedouin dress."

"I can see that!" she replied petulantly, waiting in vain for an explanation. Finally she said: "A parcel has arrived for you. From America."

"Oh! Thank God! Where is it? At long last!" Fania felt as if manna had descended from Heaven. If it weren't for the stench emanating from the dress she would have kissed Rivka there and then. She had already laundered the dress twice and still it was not entirely cleansed from the stink of excrement.

"My father was in Safed, visiting Leibel the postal clerk, and he heard him asking one of the community leaders if he knew a woman by the name of Fania Mandelstam. The parcel has been there for a week."

"Rivka! Please! I have to get to Safed! Can you stay here a few hours and keep an eye on Riva Frumkin and the children? I'll be back soon. Could I borrow your horse and harness it to Issar's cart? Please!"

Rivka finally yielded to her entreaties and agreed to hand over her horse. Fania remembered to take the key to Eleazar Rokeah's house with her too, and Rivka explained to her how to find both Leibel's house and Eleazar's. For a long time she'd wanted to bring home "Elijah's Chair". It was only once Eleazar bequeathed it to them that the thought occurred to her, this was the only wedding present they had received. Like a thief on the run she had married, without ceremony, without presents, appropriately perhaps for someone as "flawed" as she…

The horse climbed the hill at a cautious pace and Fania felt no inclination to use the whip. In her imagination she saw the dishes she would cook and the concoctions she would prepare to feed the children and Yehiel. Now she could finally wean Tamara from the breast. She would need to manage the household economy with great care and act with restraint. She would sell the lamps, and with the money she made from them buy wheat and oil and salt and eggs and vegetables, as well as ointment for Bella's eyes and tobacco for Yehiel, whitewash for the walls and paint for the *mezuzah*s. Unconsciously she began to hum some popular song she had heard in her childhood, about a sailor using his girlfriend's knickers to make sails for his ship. "Yo ho ho and a flag on the mast!" was the refrain, and she sang it repeatedly. The mare turned her head from time to time, flicking her tail to dispel troublesome flies and peering at Fania with a curious eye. It seemed to Fania she was smiling at her. She remembered arriving here on the first day, wondering how Yehiel was managing to find his way on mountain trails where there were no signposts. And now it was so simple! After two months, the mountain was like the face of an old and familiar friend.

When she finally arrived at the house of Leibel the postal clerk, she remembered she had no money on her to pay for the parcel. She left some of the lamps with him as a pledge, and with the rest she set out for the shop of Haim David. Negotiations took some time, with Fania sometimes counting on her fingers and sometimes jotting down her calculations on paper, trying to find her feet in the confusing world of the currencies circulating in Safed: each lamp costs two dollars, which equals ten francs, which equals half a Turkish pound, which is slightly less than two majedas—and what is this in roubles or guilders or the banknotes that are issued exclusively in Safed?..

Children gathered in the street, running after the cart and spreading the word throughout the town about "Americans" heading for Haim David's shop. Fania turned to a lanky youth who was standing nearby and asked him to help her with loading the lamps on the cart and transporting them from Leibel's house to Haim David's place.

"What's your name?" she asked the boy.

"Bezalel. Ben-Moreno Bezalel."

"Stick with me, Bezalel. I have more shopping to do. I'll pay you one matlik."

"I'm with you."

Haim David sensed that Fania needed the money. He pretended that just for her sake he was prepared to buy the lamps, although in fact he didn't need them at all, and she for her part pretended she didn't need *him*, either. "My husband will be in Haifa at the end of the week," she said, "and I can sell them there." Again and again she reminded herself that she had to have this money to feed her family and she was not cowed by his threats, even when it seemed to her there was no deal in sight. Eventually they worked their way toward a compromise and Fania went out again into the street. The money in her pocket made her giddy with excitement. She went into Pilpel's shop, which was nothing more than a dark cavern in a curved stone wall, a relic of the earthquake which had devastated the town fifty years before. It was a long time since Frumkin's little cart had been graced by such a cornucopia of good things! Charcoal and wheat and sugar and salt and tea, and plaster and paint for walls and candles, and she even bought medicines: quinine for malaria, silver nitrate for trachoma and castor oil for upset stomachs. In a small shop selling clocks and watches, she noticed a few books and paused to glance at them. In the town where she lived as a child, she used to love feasting her eyes on the display window of the big bookshop located between the school and her home. Every holiday, she received books as presents, and almost the entire “classical series”, with the bindings of gilded leather, already adorned her bookcase. Most of the books in the horologist’s shop were sacred tomes, and finally she bought a guide to land husbandry written in German. She would find someone to translate it for her…

Fania and the boy, Bezalel Ben-Moreno, maneuvered the cart along narrow, winding lanes, wheels clattering on the paving stones. She felt she had conducted her business with talent and skill. My father would be turning in his grave, she thought. “No longer a people of tradesmen and shopkeepers,” he used to declare, and “When we arrive in the Holy Land, we shall follow the plow!”

“And who’s preventing you from starting that here?” her mother used to ask, irritably. “Like that Tolstoy of yours!”

Tolstoy “belonged” to her father until he began to suspect his motives. He felt that a significant proportion of his ideas was derived from his Christian-religious background. When a letter arrived from Lulik, enclosing a translation of the article by Eliezer Ben-Yehuda, “Important Question,” her father knew what he must do. Tolstoy looked for “Russian” solutions and he found a “Hebrew” solution. As soon as Lulik was released from the army they would all travel to the Land of Israel, and there they could be a people like other peoples, plowing and sowing and reaping.

Of her father’s dreams only one echo remained—his cry of “Hear O Israel!”—and in her nightmares this still reverberated in her ears. A number of times Yehiel had woken her when she cried out in her dream—and there she was, engulfed in the fumes of brandy, her screams mingling with the screams of her parents and the body of the foreigner piercing her body. No more! This was the strongest of all the feelings that had accompanied her since then. No more! Nothing would ever scare her again and nothing divert her from her purpose. Not the east wind, not the snakes nor the hunger, nor the hard work. She was the monument to the slaughtered members of her family, and she had one objective in life: To survive. To go on living. In any way possible. She would trade like the most abject of merchants, the last of the pedlars, if only this meant she could support her new family.

"Are you from the commune?" the boy asked.

"Yes."

"Whose wife?"

"Yehiel Silas."

"He used to be a friend of my brother, Gedalia. They studied together in Bible class."

"Are you a Sephardi?"

"Yes."

"Are all the Jews of Safed Sephardis?"

"No! We're in the minority. There are about four thousand Ashkenazis here and only two thousand Sephardis…the rabbis in Safed are after your blood."

"God preserve us!.. Do you know where Eleazar Rokeah's house is?"

"Yes."

"Show me the way."

When they arrived at the house of Eleazar Rokeah, she promised him another matlik for watching over the cart and the provisions.

The gate opened to a small yard. Along the wall stood tin cans full of dust, which had formerly served as vases. Inside, the room was dark and damp, and under the east window, in the exact place described by Eleazar, stood the chair. Fania took one step toward it and suddenly a big stone hit the wall beside her. A moment later a barrage of stones was unleashed on the outer walls of the room. She bent down, searching around for a safer place. What's going on?! Beyond the din created by the hail of stones, it seemed to her she heard the sound of the horse's hooves. No! her heart shouted, No! From outside she heard the children shouting, "Jaoni Turk! Jaoni Turk! Shiksa! Heretic!" She huddled into an alcove in the wall, shouting at the top of her voice, "Jews! Stop! Jews!"…The stones went on falling around her, chipping plaster and pitch from the walls. What do they want, in God's name? What have I done to them? Why this hatred?…From time to time the fusillade of stones abated and then began again, resuming with added force. What will make them stop? What sign are they waiting for? What will become of the food on the cart? The vital need to feed her family filled her whole being. Besieged in this alien room, she feared only for the spoils she had acquired for her household, and she could not bear the thought that she had lost them. She stood her ground, motionless, not knowing if minutes had passed or hours, as a kind of mist of fear and anger enveloped and choked her.

The door of the room opened suddenly and was closed again at once. Fania couldn't believe what she was seeing. In the doorway stood Yehiel. Coming from the light into the dark, he was momentarily blinded.

"Fania?" he shouted.

"I'm here!" she called out from the stone alcove in which she was cowering.

Yehiel ran toward her, his head bowed, and before she knew what she was doing she leapt into his arms, hugging his body firmly, her head nuzzling his neck, part of her weeping and part of her laughing. "Fania, Fania," he was repeating her name and choking, as if speech was stuck in his throat. When she finally heard his voice through the emotion and the fear, he also felt his arms embracing her, his heart beating, his cheek caressing her hair, his lips exploring her face, his rapid, frantic breathing. She felt to her amazement that she never wanted to be parted from him. This was the best place for her to be—in his arms.

"Come on. Let's get out of here," he said, pulling away from her embrace.

"How did you know where I was?"

"Rivka told me you went to Safed to collect a parcel you got from America. You shouldn't have gone to Safed by yourself."

And suddenly the memory struck her: "Yehiel! I bought food and we lost it!"

"No, the cart's in Leah's yard."

"Thank God!"

"I went to Leah's house because I didn't know where to look for you, and there the boy told me they were throwing stones at you."

"Elijah's Chair!" Fania cried when they were already in the doorway.

Yehiel laughed and went back, stooping, to fetch the chair. They climbed through a window that opened on the roof of a neighboring house, and from that roof they moved to another, a lower one, and finally reached a small alleyway leading to Leah's house. In the yard stood the cart with the horse and the full load of provisions. Fania resisted the impulse to kiss the boy. Kissing the horse was an even harder one to resist.

"What kind of person goes to Safed alone?" There was real severity in Leah's tone. "Don't you know we only travel in convoys?"

"We have to get back," said Yehiel. He watched Fania as she paid the boy a matlik and an extra matlik. Then she opened her purse, emptied the contents into her hand and asked Yehiel: "Is there enough here to buy seeds?"

"There is." Suddenly he laughed, impressed. "What's this? How much money did they send you? No!" he interrupted her as she was about to answer him, "Tell me later, on the way home. In the meantime you should stay here. You come with me!" he said to the boy.

"Come back soon!" Leah called after him. "You can't go home after dark…and I don't want them to start throwing stones at my house, too," she said to Fania after the men had left.

"But why?" cried Fania with emotion. "What's this hatred for? What have we done? I was on my own, a lone woman! And outside there were at least twenty youths! We're not doing any harm to anyone, except ourselves. We're a people of haters. I don't blame Eleazar anymore for running away from here."

"What are you waiting for? Waiting for them to make your lives a misery, the way they treated him. If once they don't succeed, the next time they will."

Fania looked at the bony, anxious woman, who had paused for a moment from the preparation of coffee and was fixing bird-like eyes on her. Despite the unpleasant experience Fania had gone through, a kind of radiance flickered over her face, a radiance that irritated Leah more than anything, but she herself didn't know this, and even if she had known—she would never have admitted it.

"I heard that some Jews have even left Jerusalem and gone to live in some commune near Jaffa."

"Isn't that more respectable than living on charity?"

"We are not living on charity!" cried Leah, her thin, gibbous nose turning white with anger. "Jews are meant to study Torah! We're not Bedouin!"

There was an evil expression on Leah's face, but her words left Fania unperturbed, as if Yehiel's brief embrace had put armor on her skin. She knew Leah was referring to her Bedouin dress, and this pleased her immensely!

"Your future and Yehiel's future are your business, but it's the children I'm concerned about, my dead sister's children, growing up in hunger and squalor and ignorance."

"Moshe will be going to the Talmud Torah school after New Year."

"I thank God I wasn't married to him." Leah was like a bird pecking away with her sharp beak in every available crevice. "Poor Rachel…"

Is she hinting that *she* was supposed to be Yehiel's bride and he chose Rachel in preference to her? "The most beautiful girl in Galilee," Rivka had said.

Fania peered at her tattered dress, at the blackened soles of her feet, as if seeing herself for the first time. Rags, dirt…what have I to offer? She's right, this old witch! With all the hardship and hard work and hunger, I've sacrificed my femininity. When I get home—home!—I'm going to start shampooing my hair with the new soap…

"Are you pregnant?" Leah asked.

"No!"

"So what do you want with 'Elijah's Chair'?"

"Eleazar Rokeah gave it to us as a wedding present."

"Rivka says you're not living together as man and wife."

"Rivka talks too much," and to herself she added: So do you, witch!

From outside, Yehiel's voice was heard. He and the boy came back and loaded a sack of fodder on the cart. Leah laid the table for them, setting out coffee, dishes of jam and dry wafers. Fania watched Yehiel as he sipped coffee and munched wafers. Leah will never know how much we need this food, she thought. For a moment their eyes met over the coffee cups, and knowing he was thinking the same thing, she wrinkled her nose. A tiny smile flickered in his eyes and she thought to herself: I planted that smile in his eyes. She remembered their embrace in the alcove in Eleazar Rokeah's house, and lowered her eyes. Whenever there were troubled times for her family, her mother used to say: "God knows what good will grow from this." When she looked up again she realized Yehiel was still watching her, with a smile hovering over his face. He's grown so thin these last weeks! His black eyes blazed in their dark sockets. God! Let the rains fall soon! They can't stand another year of drought.

The hills shone with light, shone down on them as they boarded the little cart to return to Gai Oni. Suddenly everything made her glad, the dancing of the cart, the sunlight gleaming on stones, the green valleys. She couldn't help but utter little cries of fright and surprise. The joy finally infected Yehiel, too. His laugh was boyish, rolling. She had never heard him laugh like this.

"Leah says I look like a Bedouin."

"That's right!" Yehiel declared after glancing at her.

"Yehiel!" she protested, and he laughed.

"How did you like Safed?" he asked.

"They threw stones at me!"

"One day I'll show you the house where I was born. You don't regret coming to Gai Oni?"

"No! I love the place! I love the children! And Riva! And I love the idealism that brought us here! And I…" She had run out of breath and she put a hand to her throat, the place where the dress ended.

Yehiel waited for her to continue, but she didn't add anything. For some reason he seemed amused. She was reminded of their first journey together, when they came up from Jaffa to Galilee, two strangers. In fact, they had carried on being strangers to each other. She asked herself if she would ever succeed in taking the place of the late-lamented Rachel in his heart, and then she was shocked to realize what she was thinking. Was that what she wanted to do?

"What have you decided?" he asked.

"What…what?" she stammered.

"I don't know what. You're looking at me and sizing me up as if you'd like to sell me as well to Haim David."

A loud screech split the air and a big bird crossed their path. Yehiel reined in the horse and took Fania in his arms. His beard tickled her cheek and his lips clamped on hers. She submitted to him at once, as if she had been expecting this, absorbing the sweetness emanating from him, feeling the thrill of joy from her toes to the crown of her head, the head brimming over with waves of warmth. She wanted him and knew that she wanted him, his body, his soul, his love.

"What's this?" he asked in surprise, when his hand brushed her thigh.

"A gun." And it was as if a cloud blotted out the radiance.

"You bought this today?"

"No, I brought it from Russia."

Fania seemed to be losing her balance between one word and the next. The landscape was barren again, and flies swarmed around the hindquarters of the horse. The bird screeched again above them, and Yehiel picked up the reins again and his face seemed leaner and darker.

"That's the Boomer," he pointed to the bird. "That's what the Arabs call it because of the sound it makes. We should hurry. The Boomer only appears at nightfall."

"Is it dangerous?" she asked, her voice hoarse.

"Only if you're an insect."

"Where does it spend the day?"

"Among the rocks. Hollow trunks of trees…"

Some distance away a small column of revelers appeared, making its way up the hill. This was a Christian wedding party setting out for the church in Nazareth. The youths surrounded the groom singing and clapping hands. A veil covered the face of the bride, who was riding a mule, and a little boy sat behind her, supporting her and keeping her from falling. Her friends, elegantly dressed and with faces uncovered, responded in song to the chanting of the youths and matched their hand-clapping. The chorus was swelled by three drummers, bringing up the rear.

The revelers greeted Fania and Yehiel, and they responded with gracious smiles. Once they had left the procession behind, they continued their journey in silence. Was he remembering his wedding to Rachel? And what was Leah hinting at—that Yehiel had preferred Rachel to Leah? Could it be that she had misunderstood and Yehiel wanted to marry Leah, but she rejected him and that was why he married Rachel?

On the flank of the hill an impoverished village appeared, crumbling mud huts attached to caves carved into the rock, where destitute peasants lived with their emaciated cattle. A hedge of dusty cactus was the only patch of green in sight. Not a tree, not a bush. Grubby old crones were alarmed at the sight of the strangers and emerged from one of the caves to confront them, shouting abuse. Yehiel used the whip to speed the horse on, and when they were finally clear of the village, suddenly shouting was heard and the ground vibrated beneath them, when from around a bend on the hillside a gang of Bedouin emerged, yelling and waving big swords and long rifles. Yehiel pressed the horse on, lashing out with the whip in all directions.

"Fire in the air!" he shouted to Fania.

Fania took the pistol from its hiding place and aimed it above the heads of the Arabs. Now, as she struggled to steady her hand, she realized there were only three of them; because of all the noise they were making it had seemed to her before that scores of bandits had descended on them. The sound of the shot went on reverberating long after the assailants had disappeared from sight. Darkness began to fall, wrapping the mountain ranges in a grey veil. Fania was still scanning every rock and every tree apprehensively.

"They won't be back."

"You're injured!" she cried in surprise. "Yehiel! Stop the cart! You've been injured!"

"No, I want to carry on and get home before it's dark."

Fania pulled on the reins to stop the horse. Since they were on a downward gradient the horse was pushed forward by the weight of the load. Yehiel had to jump down and use brute strength to stop the cart and prevent it careening down the slope. Fania took off the green headscarf that Yehiel had given her after their marriage and bandaged his shoulder with it. The blood was absorbed by the scarf and the hot smell of his body vaporized between them. Now she knew her heart yearned for him and a frisson passed through her when he took her in his arms. His lips were hungry for her, caressing her eyes and her cheeks, lusting after her mouth. Was he trembling too or was it just the shaking of her body? Something terrible and wonderful was happening to them, and she didn't know herself, afraid of the new happiness that was flooding her senses. She felt she was being dazzled by a light that was too bright, exposing everything and shrouding everything, and even as she clung to Yehiel's body with all her strength, at that very moment she wished she could flee to the ends of the earth. The wail of a night creature split the silence, the horse shied in alarm and she was startled as well.

"That's a bird," said Yehiel, "an owl."

The darkness hid his face, but she knew he was smiling.

"What's so funny?" she asked.

"You weren't afraid of the bandits but the cry of a bird scared you stiff."

"I wasn't scared!"

"Let's get home before they have another go at us. Rumors about the merchandise on the cart will have spread by now to all the villages. You looked like a pretty good bandit yourself when you were shooting at them."

The cart jolted and their bodies touched fleetingly. How ascetic was his face! Only today, when she heard him laugh for the first time, did it occur to her that he was capable of being different. In other circumstances he might even sing or laugh or dance. In other circumstances...Sooner or later she will have to tell him about herself. But how will he relate to her when he knows the truth? And what if he feels cheated because she didn't reveal everything at the beginning?

On hearing the rattle of the cart's wheels the children came running out to meet them, their red hair blazing like torches on their little heads. A lamp was burning in the house, and just as Fania was wondering who had taken the trouble to light it, appearing in the doorway was the congenial figure of Imber, without a tie around his neck and without a hat on his head.

"Imber!" Fania cried. "Oh. Imber!" She hugged him warmly and planted a resounding kiss on his cheek.

"What's up, Fanichka? Why so excited?"

"What are you doing here?" she replied, ignoring his question.

"Keeping an eye on the children. You abandoned them, bad parents! What is that thing you're wearing, dear young lady?"

"A dress!"

"Oy, Fania!"

They both burst into laughter, and then the poet suddenly struck his forehead and exclaimed: "Oh! Oh! Tolstoy! Do you want to resemble the *mujik*s? Fania! Fania! Let them copy us! I wrote a poem about this: *When your fathers like savages/ Lived in trees/ Or under stones or rocks/ And walking naked.../ Our fathers already were plowing the land/ Wearing clothes of silk/ Studying Torah and wisdom...* Two thousand years of Torah separate you from them."

"It's just a dress, Imber!" Fania laughed. "And why shouldn't I be a Bedouin? Those are the people I have to live with!"

"They ought to resemble you."

"Why? Are Russian clothes more comfortable in this climate? I'm sure that even you in—where were you born?"

"In Zelochov."

"In Zelochov they didn't wear long trousers! Even you had to conform to your surroundings in—where was it?"

"In Lvov. Oy, my poor mother! When she heard I had trimmed my curls and exchanged my silk coat for a short one, she left all the children behind in Zelochov and came to rescue me...All right! I give in!" Imber laughed and winked at Yehiel, who all this time had been unloading packages from the cart. Fania also turned with a smile towards Yehiel and saw that his face was blank. Hoisting a sack of food on his shoulder, he headed for the storeroom.

"Just a moment, Yehiel! Your shoulder!" she cried.

"It doesn't hurt, it's only a scratch," he replied without looking at her, and went on walking. Why was his tone suddenly so cold? As if a door had slammed in his face. She watched him go and felt utterly desolate. All at once the happiness that had fermented in her since their encounter in Safed drained away.

"Rivka went back to Ein Zeitim in the afternoon, and Riva Frumkin asked me to keep an eye on the children till you came back. Riva didn't want to get too close to them, didn't want them catching her disease."

"Thanks, Imber. And were they good, the children?"

"They were good. Tamara was the only one who cried. My stories didn't appeal to her and I've never learned how to breast-feed."

"Oy, Imber!" Fania laughed. Yehiel passed by them again, the other sack on his back.

"Where is Lulik?" she asked him.

"He isn't in the hut."

"Did he run away from you?"

"No. He isn't afraid of me. You can be sure he'll be back as soon as Imber goes."

"We've been teaching Imber to count in Arabic," said Moshe. His eyes had swollen up again. Fania remembered the boys who threw stones at her and wondered how they could possibly send Moshe to Bible classes in Safed, among the fanatics.

"Will you stay and eat with us?" she invited Imber. "We brought food from Safed."

"No, thank-you. Another time. Riva will be offended."

"Imber says you're a queen," said Bella, "and you've got a crown."

Yehiel returned from the hut and now stood beside them, his arm round Moshe's shoulder and a furious expression on his face.

"She doesn't want people to know about it," Imber said to Bella as if sharing a secret. "Don't tell anyone."

The children nodded their heads solemnly, and even on Yehiel's lips there was the faint flicker of a smile. She was so angry with him now: Imber's a good man and he looked after their children, and he isn't giving him the time of day! If Yehiel had said one word Imber would be staying and eating supper with them.

After Imber had taken his leave the children helped Yehiel to bring the packages into the house. Fania went to feed Tamara, and from the place where she was sitting she watched the children. The rhythmic sucking made her head spin, her eyelids heavy. So many things had happened that day! This was the first day in two weeks that she hadn't spent at work, clearing stones, and the sense of freedom reminded her of the way she used to feel as a child, when the summer vacation began.

The satisfying meal made the children sleepy, and Yehiel carried them to the mattress.

"They're pale and weak from hunger," said Fania.

"The peasants live like this too."

"And *they* are setting us an example?"

"That's what you said to Imber!"

"I was talking about myself! Not about the children! I'm an adult..."

Yehiel grunted sarcastically, but Fania continued, undeterred:

"I chose this life! I know that the hunger and the stone-clearing on the mountain and the snake among the rocks and the drought and the horseflies under the shirt—every night I'm scratching like some flea-ridden peasant!—I know all this is leading to something! I'm also doing this for the sake of my father and my crazy brother and my mother...but the children! Why should they suffer?"

"They are ours."

"They're young, innocent. They don't *understand*."

"They're a part of us. They are us."

"No! No!" She was impassioned now, eyes flashing as she tossed the bronze curls from her face. "We *know* what we want. But we're responsible for them, too. I'm saying this now of all times, when there's food in the house. I haven't yet heard a child singing here! I used to sing! I sang all through my childhood! I knew hundreds of songs!"

"Teach them then!"

"I'm doing that! But I'm also responsible for their nourishment, for their health!"

"We do the best we can."

"But the best we can do doesn't amount to much."

"No, it's *everything*. It's all that we can do and that we need to do. We don't know what the future has in store for us. This is all we can do: the best we can!"

His face was grey with fatigue, his eyes lurid.

"Come to bed."

"Soon. I'll wash the dishes first."

"Leave the dishes, Fania."

"No. I'll be along soon."

A look of bitterness passed over his face again. She was afraid of being too close to him, afraid of his body, of his breath on her face, of the warmth generated by their bodies. She knew that if he touched her, she would be consumed like paper burning in the fire. First of all she must tell him about her past. *That man* must not be allowed to come between them! And she feared so much the prospect of scorn and disgust taking the place of anger. Anger she could live with…

Yehiel left the room. For some time she listened to the noises he was making, and when they were completely silenced—she too went to her bed. I'm not strong enough yet to take any more blows, her heart pleaded.

Chapter four

An idea occurred to Fania: she would hire herself out as a laundress for the women of the village. Anyone who had a few coppers to pay—would pay, and anyone who didn't—could give a little flour or a few olives in exchange for her work…But the Jews averted their eyes, embarrassed on her behalf, while the peasants laughed. Whoever heard of a Jewish woman washing clothes for peasants?

The larder was empty, and there was enough flour left for just one more day. Tamara had been weaned from the breast during the happy days that followed Fania's return from Safed with a cartload of good things, but since then she hadn't succeeded in earning a single cent. Frumkin said that Eleazar Rokeah had been distributing charity boxes in Romania and England and collecting contributions from the Jews of the Diaspora towards the settlement project in Gai Oni. There was fierce competition between the redoubtable Rabbi Meir with his "Halukkah" fund, and those raising money for the pioneers, and Eleazar Rokeah continued going from city to city, preaching to Jewish congregations and urging them to help the redeemers of the Holy Land. And meanwhile…and meanwhile…

Fania had one objective in coming to this land: she came to

settle in it. This had been her father's lifelong aspiration. She was too agitated, too scared and too hurt to think of ways in which this aspiration could be fulfilled. She was choking in the dark, like someone drowning striking out towards the light above the surface of the water, so she clung to Yehiel. On arriving in Gai Oni she realized she had chosen an extraordinary path, but at heart she felt easy with this. Almost all of the two thousand Jews in Safed lived on the "Halukkah" and their way of life repelled her. Every beggar or bogus fundraiser had been charitably received in her father's house, but as soon as they had left her mother used to exclaim scornfully: "scroungers!" The people living on the "Halukkah" seemed to her like the blood relatives of these "scroungers". Old women in snoods, knitting in their courtyards; Jews running to the seminaries or the ritual baths; and even the cobblers and the tailors, the metal-workers and smiths and market traders—all thinking only of the next handout. To her mind, the rigors of working on the land were infinitely preferable. But what would her father say if he saw his daughter turning his dreams into reality? How did he imagine it would be, in the chosen land? Words! Words! He used to sit in his spacious and comfortable home, contented and at ease, discussing social justice and national salvation… would her hands, torn by the clearing of stones, bring salvation to the people of Israel? Would the hunger they were suffering turn them into "new Jews"? They were carrying on with the work of clearing stones simply because they were afraid to stop! The oxen had been sold last summer, and then the plows.

Fania climbed up "her hill". She loved sitting in Hirbet el Yahud, among the walnut trees, and looking down at the valley. Sometimes she could see as far as Kinneret. She no longer believed the communal legends about Rabbi Israel Bak. It was all a delusion, a lie! She no longer believed in the miracles of the field and the vineyard, the ground and the trees yielding their fruits in abundance, the song of the land. Stories about the Bak family and their khan sounded like the tales told by the Bedouin and the peasants. A few days before a certain Arab had brought oyster eggs to her house and tried to sell them as goose eggs. When she told him that geese don't lay their eggs in water, he snorted scornfully. Why does *she* think geese dive into water, if not to lay their eggs there? Yesterday one of the peasants from Jaoni reported that the al-Zangariya Bedouin were planning to attack the village. Sentries were posted at strategic points, and every few minutes one of the peasants let out a yell which sent shivers down her spine. In the morning, Samir Alhija told Yehiel that the Zangariya hadn't shown up, but that he and his fellow sentries had repelled a tiger!

Slabs of basalt patched the low-lying plains, and the tall thistles spreading between the fenced areas magnified the feeling of neglect. The stones burned under her feet and Fania quickened her pace. A warm wind blew, bearing swarms of little flies that penetrated through her clothing, even though she was wearing trousers under the dress, drawn tight at the ankles, and her hair was bound up in a head-scarf. She knew Yehiel would prefer her to cover her head in the manner of Jewish wives, but she didn't see herself as a married woman. Her eccentricities appealed to the peasants. They respected "mad people" and credited Fania with supernatural powers. They were particularly impressed when she treated the eyes of Maryam Alhija, her neighbor, with some of the silver nitrate that she brought back with her from Safed. Within two or three days the infection had cleared up and an army of mothers turned up on her doorstep, accompanied by children with inflamed eyes. The mothers brought milk and cheese and eggs to offer in exchange for treatment, and for about a fortnight their table was laden with good things, with the fat of the land. Fania made the mothers promise to wash their children with soap and water, and now they were more certain than ever that she was a sorceress. Washing the body? Wasting precious water? And what for? Once in every few weeks the peasants used to give their clothes a good shake, expelling any unwanted wildlife, and that was quite enough!

The line of whimpering children seemed to upset Lulik, and one day he broke out from the shed and fled to the hills. Rumors about the lunatic spread rapidly and added considerably to Fania's prestige. In the evening, Lulik returned without his tunic. His white body gleamed for a moment in the yard before he disappeared again into the shed. Fania wondered who was now wearing the Russian army uniform with its shiny brass buttons.

She sat down under one of the walnut trees. It soon became clear to her that the shadow it cast was only an illusion. The air blazed even in the gloom, as if a steam boiler was seething in the bowels of the earth. Her lips were parched with thirst and involuntarily she recalled the “good times”. If only she could get her hands on another bottle of medicine! In her childhood she had loved playing “doctors,” and she even dreamed of going to medical school one day. Of course, she knew that very few women made it into higher education, and even fewer Jewish women, but she had already studied in high school, and when her time came she would prove she wasn’t inferior to men! Well then, now, in her adulthood she was proving her gender equality with a broken back, with unbearable fatigue, and with work that promised no reward.

A thin figure was climbing the hill, walking fast on long legs, with confident tread; shoulders hunched and eyes fixed on the path. Any moment he’ll look up and see me! she thought, wondering what the meaning of this sudden visit was. Yehiel knew this was her spot, this was where she escaped to when she was in low spirits or when her heart was longing for something. He was panting from the rapid ascent, and when he reached her he seized the lapels of her dress and yanked at them roughly, hauling her to her feet. His eyes were livid with rage.

“Have you offered your services as a washerwoman?” he demanded.

“Yes.” She was afraid he might hit her. In her panic she could feel her legs buckling under her.

“To the peasants?”

“To them as well.”

All at once he released his hold and she fell backwards onto the hard ground. He was as pale as the crags of the mountain and his lips clenched now, as before, that time when he was injured by the bandits. He sat down on the ground, his head in his hands. For a long time he was silent and finally he said:

“We’re getting out of here.”

“Leaving Gai Oni?!”

“Yes. We’ll find another place. This is only land after all.”

"Safed?" she asked in a quavering voice.

"No!" he exclaimed. "God forbid! Why Safed?"

"You said it! This is only land."

"Around Lake Huleh there's good land…and bumper crops…"

"Izber?" she asked querulously.

She had heard of Jews settling in that area. There were two brothers, scions of a Mograbi family, protégés of some emir from Damascus. Everyone knew that spending even one night beside that lake exacted a very heavy price, and everyone waited to hear news of their deaths.

"Why not? There are Jews living there."

"You know what the people of Safed call the place: Ugly Valley! If the land there is really that good why haven't more settlers gone there? Even the Bedouin avoid the place. It's prolific all right—with diseases! Malaria, jaundice, death!"

"The Banu Abbu and the Banu Mizrahi have been living there for eleven years now! And they have two thousand dunams and wells, too."

"Yehiel! Gai Oni is your whole life!"

What right had she to urge him to stay in Gai Oni? He had grown so thin his cheekbones were piercing his skin. The light shone on his forehead. If only she could have met her Black Prince in other circumstances, she thought for the thousandth time. Sometimes, in a moment of goodwill, he showed flashes of charm and gaiety, but most of the time something wild and hostile was burgeoning in him. She had no doubt it was for her sake he wanted to leave Gai Oni, for her sake and for the sake of the children. If it was up to him, he would never leave this place.

"The children won't settle down there, near Lake Huleh."

"I'll go by myself."

"No!" she cried out. "Are you going away to die a heroic death and leave us stranded?"

A rabbit ran out from between the rocks. "*Tabsun*. The peasants would give something for that," said Yehiel, watching sorrowfully as the rabbit escaped.

"Sell your land to Oliphant."

"No!"

"Why not? You said yourself, it's only land. And you told me yourself, he paid more than a hundred napoleons for two plots! And what good is this land doing you?"

"When the rains come…"

"What then? What will you do? You have no ox and no plow and no seed. You don't need to worry, Oliphant's not going to sell the land. You can carry on working it the same way as you have up to now."

"If anything happens to me, this is what will be left for you and for the children."

And what meaning would there be to this land and to this place, without him? Fania longed to bury that ascetic face in her bosom and caress and caress until he felt relaxed. She would have liked to tell him that if anything happened to him, she would not need this land at all. When she finally began to speak, her voice was soft, sighing like the warm breeze.

"A year and ten months ago the pogrom began in my city…I came to Gai Oni to lick my wounds, and the place gave me back my dignity. I'm not sorry and I have no regrets, Yehiel. I'm proud of my bruised hands. I'm even proud of the hunger…my torn clothes… The rain will come, Yehiel. It has to come."

Before dawn Yehiel set out to fetch the horse from Ein Zeitim. Fania wanted to accompany him so she would finally get to see with her own eyes this Jewish-Arab village in which several members of Yehiel's family and two of his friends from Safed had put down roots. He promised her that one day he would show her the ancient tombs of Rabbi Shimon Bar Yochai, Rabbi Yosef of Saragossa and Yehuda Bar Eylai, the sacred caves and the wells. But today they were preparing themselves for a journey to Haifa, to visit Oliphant, and Yehiel feared that going to Ein Zeitim as a twosome would cause them unnecessary delay.

Fania took out from the storeroom the chest she had brought with her from Russia. She was opening it now for the first time since arriving here. Moshe and Bella stood beside her, staring goggle-eyed at the bright fabrics, the silk ribbons, the leather bindings with their yellowish, secretive aroma, the big woolen shawl, the embroidered handkerchiefs…She herself didn't know what her neighbor had put into the chest. It was her uncle who sold the house in Elizavetgrad and he who gave the neighbor the money to buy for Fania all that she needed for the journey. One by one she took the objects out of the chest, no less goggle-eyed than the children, breathing hard and with feeling, pressing the pink silk pillowcase to her cheek, burying her face in the soft woolen shawl…as the faint scent of an ancient perfume wafted from the chest.

Wrapped in thin and rustling paper was a sensational secret and Fania lifted it carefully, her hands spread under it, as if she was presenting a gift. Very cautiously she peeled off the wrapping to reveal a green dress with a dense frieze of tiny buttons adorning the front, from the high collar to the waist. She shook the dress with light movements, letting air and light into the dark spaces. For a moment nothing existed in the whole world other than this dress. Then, having recovered her wits, she hurriedly stripped off the Bedouin clothing, stepped into the skirt and inserted her arms gingerly into the sleeves, which were voluminous above and tight below. She seemed to grow taller, as the tight-fitting bodice lengthened the space between her bust and her waist. Since she had stopped nursing, her breasts had shrunk to their former dimensions. Her handsome neck rose from the round collar with its trimming of velvet ribbon. She saw her reflection in the mirror, and she lifted the hair from her nape and turned this way and that, inspecting first her right profile and then her left.

"Behold thou art fair, my love, behold thou art fair…"

Yehiel's melodious voice startled her. Now, hearing him, she knew that all this obsessive behavior was for him, the frantic scrabbling in the chest, the gyrations in front of the mirror. When she lowered her arms, rings of dark bronze glided over the green fabric. Little beads of sweat sparkled on her brow. In Russia they believed that woolen garments warded off malaria, and all dresses were tailored from woolen fabrics. She wiped her brow and her chin, then laughed briefly, awkwardly, and cleared her throat hoarsely.

"You can't travel in that dress."

"Why?" she protested, "Yehiel!"

"The local bandits will attack us."

"But we're on our way to the city! To see the minister!"

"To ask for money."

"To sell! We're not asking for anything, we're selling! When my mother was going to sell something she always used to dress in style, so the buyer would know she didn't need his money. If she was going to buy something—then she wore her old clothes."

"Oliphant will buy the land to help us. If he buys. He doesn't want it."

"It's a business! You're selling him land and he's paying for it. You're not doing him a favor and he's not doing you one."

"The horse is outside. I've hitched it to Frumkin's wagon."

"Yehiel!" she pleaded.

"If he agrees to buy the land we'll stay over in Haifa until tomorrow. We can buy food. Rivka will be here soon and she'll stay with the children."

"Yehiel!"

For a moment she hesitated, then, without another look in the mirror she stripped off the green dress and put on the grimy and tattered Bedouin garments instead. Bella suddenly ran to her and hugged her thighs with her little hands, then looked up at her.

"I haven't told anyone you used to be a queen," she said to Fania.

"That's good, duckling, that's good…" She kissed the cool little face and hurriedly put all the objects back in the box, without bothering to wrap them again. The light in the room dimmed, as if lightning had flashed and then turned the sky dark with thunder clouds.

Imber opened the door of Oliphant's house, and his delight at seeing Fania was so obvious she almost forgot her disappointment over the green dress.

"Fanichka!" he cried. "Sir Laurence, this is the young lady I told you about, the one who picks up stones on the mountain while reciting Pushkin! *Sabakh alkhir*, Yehiel, *kif hallak*?"

"*Alhamdu li Lah*!" Yehiel replied with a smile.

"I'm learning Arabic. How was my pronunciation?"

"Fine, just fine…"

"Lady Alice, if you please…"

The room was large, its whitewashed walls hung with embroidered tapestries, and small carpets covering the floor. In the corner stood a black piano and on it a silk cloth embroidered with roses, long tassels draped over the lid. There was a key in the lock of the piano, and Fania remembered the story her mother told her in her childhood about the goblins who stole the white keys and replaced them with new, black ones. The lace curtains were tied with big ribbons, and through the windows she saw a strange-looking carriage travelling along the broad road running between the houses of the German Settlement.

Lady Alice laid the napkin she was holding on the table and rose to meet them. The other two men in the room, Sir Laurence and someone introduced as the engineer Gottlieb Schumacker, also stood up.

"Mister Silas is the third generation in Jaoni," the minister explained to his wife and his guest.

"I was born in Safed," said Yehiel.

"But your grandmother came to Jaoni after the Damascus blood libel in 1840, is that right?"

"Yes, that's right." Yehiel was obviously surprised to find that the minister knew so much about him.

"They lived with the peasants?" asked Mister Schumacker.

"Yes. They bought a few padans of land and built a dairy."

"I've heard about the cheese that Jews used to sell in the villages around Safed. Is the family still running the dairy?"

"No." The minister's perspicacity brought a smile to Yehiel's face. "The Bedouin rustled the sheep, and in the conflict with them the sheikh's son was killed. My grandmother's family fled to Sidon, and only a few family members stayed around here. There's one branch still living in Hazbiya, and the other, the Adis clan, is in Ein Zeitim."

"I wanted to buy land in Ein Zeitim," said the minister. "They're offering it to me at less than a dollar a dunam. There's no problem raising the money, but the land is divided into small plots and each one belongs to a different family. I'm sure that if we have land the Jews will come."

Less than a dollar! In other words, for Yehiel's hundred and fifty dunams, the minister will pay him about fifty napoleons. Too little! Too little! Fania peered at Yehiel. His face was gloomy. Similar considerations would surely be running through his mind too. The thing more precious to him than all else, he was about to give away in exchange for fifty napoleons, and this would barely last them three or four months. Less than that, if they wanted to buy a mule or a plow…

"Will you take tea?" the hostess asked. She was a very pleasant lady, around thirty-five years of age and evidently some twenty years younger than her husband.

"Thank-you."

"You had a good journey here?"

"Yes. Thank-you."

"A year ago you couldn't have travelled that route without being attacked. You have to thank the Germans for this. They protest loudly over every incident, and it seems to work," the minister smiled at Schumacker. "Did you know, a year ago, when we arrived here, we were attacked by local bandits and Keller beat them off with his whip and saved us."

"All he was short of was a sword…" Lady Alice laughed softly. The men turned to look at her and she fell silent, a mysterious smile on her face. For a moment Imber's black eyes seemed to cloud over and Fania wondered about the relationships between members of the household. Is he in love with the lady? And she?

"That German arrived here with one sausage in his hand and one mark in his pocket!" said the minister.

"Who is he?"

"The German vice-consul in Haifa and Acre, Fritz Keller. Excellent man! He initiated all the development work that you see in the city."

"How long have you been living in this country?" Lady Alice asked Fania. The French accent gave her words a charming lilt.

"About a year and a half."

"From Russia?"

"Yes."

"I was in Russia during the Russian-Turkish war, four years ago," said the minister, "and I was back there again last year. I went to help the refugees who fled to Galicia after the pogroms. Tell me, why aren't they coming to Palestine? Why?!"

"You shouldn't be having a go at her, Laurence," his wife came to Fania's rescue. "She came here, after all…Mahmud?"

An Arab who had been sitting on a small stool by the door approached the lady to heed her instructions. Fania didn't hear what Lady Alice was saying, spoken as it was in a whisper, but she couldn't help but see the thin white hand stroking the servant's head. Fania looked away in embarrassment and Imber shifted in his chair and stared out of the window.

"In Romania they told me they were deterred by the desolation," the minister went on to complain. "But if they come here, then it won't be a desolation anymore! It's so simple! And they're afraid of the Bedouin, too. I explained to them that the Bedouin in the streets of Jerusalem are no more numerous than the Bedouin in the streets of Constantinople."

"Now they're going to start conscripting the rabble into the Turkish army," said Schumacker the engineer, "and the roads will be even safer! And when we start work on the railway…"

"A railway? Where?" asked Yehiel.

"I wondered how long it would be before Herr Schumacker mentioned the railway!" said Imber.

Lady Alice was looking at Imber with a sad smile. He was about ten years younger than her, an eccentric and a stranger in their house, his flashing black eyes suffused with pain and indignation. To all appearances the lady preferred the servant to the poet, while as for the minister—it seemed that of all the company present only he was unaware of the ugly undercurrents of jealousy—did he not care? Or perhaps he didn't know? Of course he must know…

"My friend Herr Schumacker is planning to build a railway that will connect Haifa and Acre with Damascus."

"It was your idea, Sir Laurence."

"Do you have a license?" Yehiel asked.

"A pertinent question! We have indeed—a broker in Beirut obtained the license on our behalf, and Mister Schumacker is already drawing up the plans, with all the diligence and energy that we have come to expect of Germans. If I ever succeed in obtaining the Moab concession, this railway can link up with the industrial plants that we'll be developing around the Dead Sea."

"You don't need a railway!" his wife objected. "Laurence has already travelled the world by steamship and by camel, by carriage and on foot, from Cape Town to China and from Japan to Ceylon, and as far afield as America and Canada and Russia. He hunted elephants in Nepal and sailed a raft the full length of the Volga on the eve of the Crimean War…you really need a railway?"

"I'm talking about the Jews, Alice, not about me," he rebuked her, in the tone of one who won't allow any hint of levity in the discussion of such a serious topic, but his eyes sparkled with nostalgia, with the zeal of the young adventurer that he used to be.

"Have you had time to tour the township?" he asked Yehiel.

"Township!" exclaimed Schumacker, sounding aggrieved, "Jews alone—there's already more than a thousand there! And Germans—four hundred!"

"I know Haifa."

"Where will you be lodging tonight? I hear that some Muscovite immigrant has opened a new hostel."

"No, I have relatives in Harat el-Yahud."

"Yehiel Silas! Sell your last shirt before you lodge there!" cried Imber. "The garbage is knee-high in the streets and the place is full of feral dogs and flea-ridden children with eye infections…And I've seen the souk in Constantinople, so I know what garbage is!"

"Oh, Herzli!" the lady laughed.

"Please, O Mama Mia!" Imber insisted. "It isn't funny…look, I'll lend you my bed! The place is cramped, but it's clean!"

"No!"

Yehiel's face was livid with rage. True, Imber had spoken out of turn, insulting Yehiel's relatives with the implication that they lived in squalor, but all the same, how had these good people here offended? And how would they get to talk to the minister about the sale of land with so many people present?

"Do you play the piano?" Fania asked the lady, who was flexing her fingers nervously while peering at her husband like a trapped butterfly.

"I used to play, but since coming here I haven't felt able to. How can I play when there's so much desolation all around? We are trying to bring harmony into the world in our own way, Madame Silas…"

"You play, don't you, Fania?" Imber broke into the conversation.

"I haven't played for a long time."

"Play now!"

Fania glanced down at her coarse, calloused hands, also taking in the peasant trousers peeping out from under the tattered dress and her bare feet.

"Why not?" she said, suddenly smiling and rising from her seat. "If it's really terrible, you can throw shoes at me!"

"The Jewish immigrants have set up a musical society in Haifa," said Herr Schumacker.

Behind her back they went on discussing the Jewish musical society and the women's choir of the German Templars, but now their conversation sounded far away. Carefully she moved the embroidered cloth, lifted the lid and touched the keys, letting her fingers become acquainted with the unique acoustic register of the instrument. The light in the room changed, with the silence seeming to alter the angle of the shadow. Very slowly and cautiously, she started playing Tchaikovsky's Barcarolle…

The sounds filled the bright void of the room, gliding smoothly from between her fingers, and in all the world nothing else existed anymore. The cool touch of the pedal on her foot sent a thrill of delight through her body, as if nothing had happened, as if she were still a student, getting to grips with the new, romantic sounds of Tchaikovsky. "Slow down! Slow down!" her teacher used to cry, "Pyotr Ilyich doesn't need any help from you!" Despite her opposition to Tchaikovsky's "Europeanism", apparently at odds with the

"Russian spirit"—her teacher worshipped him like a god. Some said she was the sister of Nadezhda von Meck, Tchaikovsky's enigmatic patron. Others said she herself was that enigmatic patron. Not everyone earned the privilege of being numbered among her pupils, and Fania, accepted at the tender age of eight, was considered a prodigy. The "Black Witch"—as they used to call her—took her pupils to the Opera House to experience *Eugene Onegin*, and to the Ballet for performances of "Sleeping Beauty" and "Swan Lake," and she even contrived to send one of her most talented pupils to the Conservatoire, to study with *him*! In those far-off days Fania used to imagine herself sitting at the piano and playing the "Seasons" suite, the composer himself sitting behind her and listening with rapture…

When she finished playing the *Barcarolle* she paused for a moment, lost among the sounds. Then Imber swooped on her, like a young dog lovingly greeting his mistress on her return home. His eyes were moist and he wetted her face with his kisses as he cried: "Fanichka! Fanichka! That was wonderful! Marvelous! Where else in all the world will you find peasants such as these? Where?!"

"When the Romanian Jews come to join you, you too can set up a musical society," said Herr Schumacker.

"What was that?" asked Lady Alice.

"Thirty families have already registered to immigrate to this country, and they will be arriving in Gai Oni."

"When?" asked Yehiel.

"I've heard people talking"—Schumacker's voice was firm, but confronted by Yehiel's astonishment, it seemed he was no longer sure of just what he had heard—"Sir Laurence has heard these discussions too, is that not so, Sir Laurence?"

"Even I have heard," said Imber, "they'll be arriving after Passover. Eleazar Rokeah drew their attention to Gai Oni in his articles. And they have already managed to raise a hundred thousand francs to fund the new colony."

"A hundred thousand francs!" cried Fania, moved by this exciting news, "And thirty families! Yehiel, this is the 'first caravan' that Rokeah told us about."

"Jews are quick to feel enthusiasm," warned Herr Schumacker.

"Afterwards they sink into despair. Things have to be done in moderation."

"Moderation?" objected Sir Laurence. "This is salvation we're talking about! This really appeals to me! A true believer has to put deeds before words. When all the Jews have come to this land, salvation will come to the world."

"But look at what happened in Jaoni and what happened in Umm Labas! Even faith demands caution. Look at those Americans who settled near Jaffa fifteen years ago. Weren't they believers? They came to this country to wait for the Messiah! And what happened? They went back to America and gave up on the Messiah!"

"The Messiah of the Americans is Mammon. While we were working like black slaves in the settlement of Reverend Harris, he stole all our property from us! My poor mother…"

"Laurence! Herr Schumacker's father is American!"

"No, no, he's of German extraction. But the lady is right: one scoundrel can't teach you about a whole nation…I beg your pardon! That isn't what I meant to say! Of the Reverend Harris I know nothing, but I know something about the Americans who settled in this land! They didn't check what kind of a man their leader was, and it turned out he was a drunk. They didn't know what could be grown in this country, and they didn't have a clue about tenancy laws, taxes, local customs, climate…All these things have to be learned. Then they go back to their homeland and malign this country. The land is good! In precisely the same place where the Americans used to be, these days our Templars are living, tending vineyards and orchards, and they've built a school and a hospital as well. Why have we succeeded where the others have failed? I know! They say of us that fellow members of our sect in Wirtenburg are helping us financially. Nonsense! We proceed with caution! We don't go in for delegations of thirty families with a hundred thousand francs to spend! Learn from us! At first our Doctor Hoffman sent a party of five here, to spy out the land just as Joshua's spies did. No one knew of their coming and no one heard them go. Before they left they entrusted a reliable and discreet agent with the task of buying a tract of land on their behalf. And once the land had been bought, a small group of people arrived and they took on all the obstacles that stood in their way and learned by heart the ways of the land. When they were reasonably settled, more comrades joined them, all according to the needs of the community: doctor, architect, brewer, carpenter and metal-worker, priest, merchant. I'm not claiming that all problems were solved. For all our astuteness we failed to take into account, for example, the obstinacy of the Carmelite monks. But I'm a religious man and I believe that in the end the French will hand over to us the land on the hill that belongs to us…and in the meantime we already have enclaves in Jaffa, in Sharon and in the Valley of Ghosts outside Jerusalem, and here on Carmel. All settlement is a difficult business, and I want to say no more than this, that the land is kind to its settlers so long as things are done with moderation and with diligence and with love of order…"

"Moderation! Diligence! Love of order!" Imber chortled. "Are you talking about us? The Jews?!" He turned to Yehiel and said: "In *Hamelitz* I read an article by Rabbi Pines which went something like, 'The pampered and the frivolous and the lazy and the arrogant won't be going!' So now we know who won't be coming to this country and all we need is to find out who will be."

The Arab servant returned to the room carrying a tea-tray. He put the tray down on the round table beside the lady, and as he leaned over her she raised her pale face to him. She's making no attempt at all to hide her desires!—shocked, Fania cast her eyes down and stared at her fingers.

"Not for me, thank-you!" cried Herr Schumacker, hurriedly taking his leave.

"One cup?"

"No, no, I'm already late for dinner. No doubt my wife is already sharpening the carving-knife!"

"That's the way our husbands talk about us, too, when we're not listening," Lady Alice smiled at Fania, clapping her hands lightly. Fania smiled and then looked up, to see how Yehiel was faring. It was obvious he was agitated and embarrassed. She didn't know if he had noticed what she noticed, but she sensed that these parlor games were not to his taste. Given the choice, he would conclude the deal and get out of here as quickly as possible. But why is he so agitated?

Is he afraid that Sir Laurence might turn out to be a missionary? No! If he believed that, he wouldn't have come here in the first place. So what's his problem? She was still basking in the delight that playing the music had instilled in her. Her fingers were stiff and clumsy and at first had refused to obey her. She felt ashamed at the pleasure she was deriving from the company of these people, from the manicured house, the elegant clothes, the agreeable conversation. The lady's bedroom antics were not her concern! She was a guest, enjoying the unfamiliar sensation of drinking tea from a fine china cup! And why not?—she protested to herself—is there any virtue in poverty and penury? Why shouldn't she enjoy all this?

"How come you speak English?" Lady Alice asked Fania. "Laurence told me that intellectuals in Russia speak French."

"My older sisters immigrated to America. I wanted to learn English so I could correspond with them and with their children."

"I had a very hard time of it in Russia. They all spoke German or French…" said Sir Laurence. "How old are you?"

"It isn't polite to ask a lady her age, Laurence!"

"Seventeen, Sir Laurence."

"So, let me see, how old were you—"

"Lady Alice wrote my mother a letter in German," Imber interrupted the minister, "and because my mother only knows Yiddish, our tailor in Zelochov translated the letter for her. The words spoken by the tailor sounded very similar to the Yiddish spoken in Zelochov, and my mother decided I was in safe hands!"

"The mass immigration to America is a disaster!" cried Sir Laurence. "I don't understand your leaders! If only they planned to send at least *some* of the Jews to Palestine. I know that the leaders of 'Lovers of Zion' are pleading with the 'Alliance Israelite Universelle' in Paris and with the 'Society of Brothers' in London to steer in this direction at least a few of the Jews looking for refuge from the pogroms, but they support immigration to America of all places. Why?"

"We want to sell the land," said Yehiel suddenly in a high and resolute tone. Fania burst into laughter and then hurriedly apologized to Lady Alice: "Forgive us for discussing business at teatime, but it's already getting dark outside."

Yehiel handed Oliphant the bills of purchase.

"These are our holdings in Jaoni, Sir Laurence. In total, about a hundred and fifty dunams."

"But why? Where are you going?"

"Herzli!" Oliphant rebuked Imber affectionately. "Would they be coming to me if they wanted to leave the place? Everyone knows that settlement in Gilead is the dream of my life. They want to sell so they can stay there. Is that right?"

"Yes."

"I've heard," said Sir Laurence, "that Jews are even leaving Jerusalem to settle in Umm Labas, after the former residents abandoned it four years ago. We can hope that the second time round, in both places, will be more successful than the first."

"Rabbi Pines is helping them," said Imber.

"They have influential friends. We asked for help from Rabbi Pines and didn't get anywhere."

"Look here, young man," Sir Laurence said to Yehiel, "I can give you seventy-five napoleons for your land. I'll give you fifty now, and the other twenty-five on signature of the deeds of sale. Who signed the purchase document?"

"I did."

For a moment Fania heard no more of what was said, as if she had gone deaf. Something fluttered in her breast—a joy too great to be contained, frightening! There will be food in the house again! She can sleep at night again!

"You will stay on the land," said the minister, "you will plow, sow and reap. It will be my privilege to lend a hand to the realization of the dream of Return to Zion. You may well feel isolated and abandoned just now. But you will be remembered for generations to come as the first Hebrew farmers to work this land after two thousand years of neglect!"

"Please, Laurence, don't preach!" Lady Alice implored, putting her hands together in a prayerful gesture.

Fania resisted the impulse to laugh. Yehiel's eyes were glinting with a dangerous spark. For an instant she caught sight of the look that Imber was fixing on the lady: confused and tormented and… loving?

"You have livestock?"

"No."

"No?" The minister was surprised. "How will you manure the land?"

"When the rains come we'll buy manure."

The minister looked at Yehiel dubiously. Was he regretting the deal?

"By law you will be required, as the tenant, to set aside the 'kisam' for me, as your landlord—my share of the produce, in other words. I won't be insisting on this, but there is one condition that I stipulate: if the immigrants come and want to settle in Gai Oni and there isn't enough land for them, you should allocate them some space on your territory. It's possible there'll be no need for this at all; perhaps Romanian Jews really will be arriving with bundles of cash. All the same, I'm a bit alarmed by the propaganda that your friend Eleazar Rokeah is putting out. He seems determined to convince the Jews that this is a land flowing with milk and honey."

"It's easy for him to talk—sitting there in Romania," said Fania.

"He can't come back!" cried Yehiel indignantly.

"Even from there he's doing some good," said Imber in conciliatory mode. "It's true he exaggerates a bit when he describes the fertility and the safety of the country, but Jews will be coming from Romania and from Bulgaria and from Turkey, and Jewish immigrants to the Holy Land won't be here for the fleshpots. Do you know what they're calling their ship— 'Titus'! Come on Fania, play us some more!" Imber urged, sensing that the cheerful mood was fading.

Yehiel's anger seemed to dim the light in the room. He had so much admired Rokeah! And she? Was she jealous of him? Why be jealous? But Yehiel was more precious in her eyes than a thousand Rokeahs—preaching and not practicing.

"Oh no, I can't."

"Lady Alice loves Chopin."

"Would you like to play, ma'am?" Fania asked. "Just this once."

"No! No! I swore..." The lady stopped abruptly, breathing hard, as if she had said more than she intended to say.

"Come on, Fania," cried Imber, "God gave the birds wings to fly high in the sky, and to us he gave ears to hear you play...Chopin!"

Fania lifted the lid of the piano again. Wood came in contact with wood and uttered a reedy sound. Her stiff fingers moved clumsily from note to note, segueing gradually into a Chopin impromptu. Steadily the stiffness eased and the soft, heart-rending sounds hovered in the void of the room, her eyes cast down on the keys, the dense lashes shading her eyelids. She was sitting firmly on the wooden chair, her back straight, and the space between her shoulders and her waist resembling the shape of a perfect inverted triangle. When she finished the room was plunged into silence. Then the sound of hand-clapping was heard and the final reverberations were dispelled.

"You could be queen of the salons in Saint Petersburg! Vienna! Paris!" cried Imber, wiping his eyes. "What talent and good taste you have, Fania, allow me to kiss the hem of your garment, my little queen, queen of the land of Naphtali!"

By the time she had grasped what was happening he was already kneeling at her feet and pressing the hem of her shabby dress to his lips. For a moment the Bedouin trousers peeped out above the dirt-blackened feet.

"Imber! Imber!" Fania protested with a laugh and leapt up from her seat. Yehiel also stood up at once, incensed by Imber's behavior.

"You're not old enough to prostrate yourself like that!" the lady rebuked Imber with a smile.

Yehiel approached Sir Laurence Oliphant and held out his hand with a solemn expression.

"Thank-you very much, Sir Laurence."

"Don't thank me! Without Jewish settlers all my dreams would go up in smoke! On land that was sold to me by Kolisker and Gorochovsky I intend to settle four families, two from Russia and two from Safed. Jews will settle in the land of Naphtali and the land of Moab and the land of Gilead. Those are wilderness territories, and I hope that when the Turks see the Jews succeeding in making their deserts bloom, they will agree to give them autonomy under the protection of the Sultan. We would all benefit from that."

"Laurence! You're preaching again! Mrs. Silas, you're welcome to play the piano in my home whenever you find yourself in Haifa," said the lady, turning to Fania. "In fact, we shall be moving soon to Dalyat el-Carmel, but I hope you will visit us there too."

"Thank-you! That would be wonderful! Really wonderful!"

"Come on, Sofgania, give a kiss to your foolish old admirer!" said Imber, offering Fania his cheek.

As they were leaving, Fania looked curiously at her surroundings. The district differed from the residential quarters which she had visited previously in this country. She made mental notes of the way the picket fences were constructed, the shape of the double wooden shutters, and where precisely the ornamental trees were planted. The houses of the German colony rose to two stories and were large and spacious and stone-built, with beds of flowers and vegetables adorning their extensive gardens. Good roads ran between the houses, and on the flank of the hill, the Templars had planted orchards, set in straight lines and standing out against the untamed desolation of the rest of the hill, a wasteland strewn with boulders and bushes growing wild.

"Those are strange carriages over there," said Fania.

"They have their own workshop and they adapt them there."

"They look convenient. You could load them with a stack of merchandise and not worry about it falling out."

"The Germans use them to transport tourists from Haifa to Jaffa. Now you have a choice: you can do the journey by sea or in one of the Templars' carriages."

"How do they get through the gates of the city?"

"They widened the gates."

"Specially for carriages?"

"The wall was falling down anyway."

"Could we travel in a carriage like that to Gai Oni?"

"What's got into you today?" he cried in a sudden surge of anger, stopping and turning to confront her. For a moment she was afraid he was going to slap her.

"What are you talking about?"

"We arrived here in Adis's cart! Is that not good enough for you?"

"Yes, of course, it's fine. I was just expressing an aspiration. I know we came here in a cart…"

"You should be ashamed of yourself!"

"Why? What have I done?"

"Your behavior with…all those kisses! That drunken reprobate… Imber!"

Yehiel pronounced this as if spitting something out.

Fania was so enraged at this she could not trust herself to speak. For some time she walked beside him with veiled eyes that saw nothing. They were walking now in narrow streets, between low flat-roofed houses, built of mud and stone. She was trudging through garbage and the slimy contact with her bare feet disgusted her. Her throat was constricted, as if unseen fingers had her in a stranglehold. Hordes of people were crammed in the stinking alleyway; there were children with inflamed eyes and scavenging dogs everywhere. Safed with its grimy streets was like a royal court compared to this neighborhood. In one of the alcoves men were sitting on low wicker benches. They raised heavy eyelids from their nargilehs and looked lazily at Fania and at Yehiel, sizing them up.

"What is this place?" she asked.

"Harat el Yahud."

"We're spending the night here?"

"Yes."

Yehiel suddenly stopped and turned to her: "Oliphant has many enemies: Abd el Hamid, the Sultan, suspects he was sent here by the British to appropriate Turkish land; the Carmelite monks, who control most of the real estate in Haifa, hate him because of his support of the Templars; the Jews are afraid he might be a missionary…I don't hate him, I don't suspect him and I'm not afraid of him. He's an eccentric, there's no denying that, but he's one of the righteous Gentiles. All the same, better not to tell anyone we've visited him."

Both of them felt uncomfortable and they exchanged no more words, walking on in silence until they stopped in front of one of the alcoves. Yehiel spoke to a middle-aged man, heavily-built and red-haired, who was sitting in the entrance to the alcove, wearing a striped cloak and a sash with a tarboosh on his head. On recognizing Yehiel, the man rose to greet him. In the interior of the alcove stood two sacks of pulses, giving off a musty smell. Yehiel and the man embraced once, twice, and it was only then that Yehiel remembered Fania who was standing behind him.

"Fania, this is Musa Adis, a cousin on the Grandma Silas side. Musa, this is my wife, Fania."

"Congratulations, congratulations! Even if they are belated. Come on, let's go to our house."

"No, you stay in the shop! We'll make our own way," Yehiel protested.

Musa Adis clapped his hands and a boy appeared from the yard and took over the supervision of the little shop.

Three steep stone steps led to an iron gate with a meshed window set in it. A knocker in the shape of a clenched fist was hung on the door. Inside, a small square courtyard was revealed. The sounds of the street were muffled now behind the walls. Musa opened one of the doors and called out: "Allegra! Guests!"

Cool dimness reigned in the room. Woolen rugs covered the stone couches. Clumps of onions and garlic were hung over the windows and hand-shaped talismans over the lintels of the doors. The lady of the house, a plumpish, shabby woman, sat beside the window and sewed. In her hands was a Turkish military tunic, and laid out on the bench were Turkish army-issue trousers and a white *abbayeh* trimmed with gold ribbons of the damascene silk favored by the sheikhs. Hey, I could do that, thought Fania happily, only to be struck down by despair a moment later, when she remembered she couldn't sew. And while she was learning, what would they eat? And how was she going to learn?...No, she must think of some other solution. But what??

Could she sell pulses, like Musa Adis? No, only men went into trade. But why should that be? The business that Adis was engaged in looked a lot easier than the work Allegra, his wife, was doing.

Allegra set the table for them and served them black lentil soup, thick as porridge and smelling strongly of garlic. While they ate she talked about her children and her children's children, her big eyes instilling in her audience a sense of guilt. She told Fania of the good times they had known in Safed, in the house of Yehiel's parents, when they were very young. On Lag Ba'Omer the family used to gather in Meron, and at Succoth they used to travel in convoy to Tiberias, to bathe in the lake. Yehiel was devoted to his father and could only bear to be parted from him when he was sparring with her son Amram. The brothers and cousins of these two used to divide into teams, each team egging on its champion to attack his rival with redoubled ferocity. One time, when they were about ten years old, they returned from a family gathering, Yehiel with a severely scratched cheek and Amram with a broken ankle.

Now Fania knew the origin of the deep grove on Yehiel's cheek, and she tried to see him in the form of a little boy clutching his father's hand. Allegra described a different Yehiel, a Yehiel belonging to a world in which she had no part. Ostensibly she was being told these things to bring her closer to the family circle, but the tone in which they were spoken meant: what have you, an outsider, to do with us? But the proximity of Yehiel inspired her with confidence, and soon she began to feel drowsy. The unremitting drone of the nasal voice, the hot soup, the trials of the day—all of these weighed heavy on her limbs and eased her into slumber...When she opened her eyes again, bobbing in front of her were the affronted features of Allegra.

"You fell asleep," said Yehiel.

"Come on!" Allegra Adis rose to her feet. "We don't have a lot of space, but Amram's room happens to be vacant at the moment. Yesterday he went to Acre to pick up goods sent from Izmir. Sometimes when we're lucky and the port of Acre is full, the boats dock in Haifa instead. These journeys! I won't be able to rest until I see Amram again. Here it is," she added, turning to Fania, "and in the morning you can tell me about yourself."

Amram's room was nothing more than a stone cubicle with a narrow skylight set close to the ceiling. Fania watched the fleshy, short-statured woman as she removed the counterpane from the stone bed, covered the mattress with a white sheet, plumped the pillows and spread the blanket. Yehiel came in with a pan of water, closely followed by Musa Adis who was brandishing a bar of soap. "From the German factory," he said. "They make excellent soap there, oil of myrrh, and it's exported to America. Afterwards just throw the water into the street."

Fania stood petrified, staring goggle-eyed at these two people who had unwittingly taken on the role of their bedroom attendants. What was going to happen now? The one and only bed wasn't big enough. What were they going to do?

"Come to bed, Fania," Yehiel said when their hosts had left them. He blew out the lamp and blackness filled the room, as colored specks flashed in her closed eyes. Water poured noisily into the iron bucket. Suddenly she sensed that Yehiel was coming closer, and she opened her eyes again. He removed the kerchief from her head, and locks of her dense bronze hair tumbled down onto her shoulders. She sat in silence while he unfastened the buttons of her bodice, the touch of his fingers leaving scald-marks on her body. In her single bed in Gai Oni she longed for him at night, and now she was petrified with fear. "When you change your mind, let me know," he had said to her then, when she pushed him away. Scores of times since then her heart had yearned to draw him close to her. If only she could explain that it wasn't him she was recoiling from. She wanted so much to tell him about her past before he approached her. That way, he wouldn't say afterwards she had behaved deceitfully. But the words stuck in her mouth and refused to be said.

She felt on her skin the flutter of his fingers unbuttoning her blouse. His touch was apparently unintentional, tender and flimsy as the wings of a butterfly, and yet her body was on fire, burning up, and involuntarily she recalled that ancient, devastating fear, "those" hands, forcing and beating and crushing without mercy. I'm so tired, she thought, and so afraid. God forgive me, I love him!

A sigh emerged from her lips and she clutched at his arms and stood up, shaking convulsively and unsteady on her feet, her eyes scouring the dark.

"Please, Yehiel, no!"

"It's Imber you want, I know that! But I'm your husband! I!"

His mouth bore down on hers, bitter and demanding, and his strong arms clasped her to his body, his fingers digging deep into the flesh of her shoulders.

"No!" the cry escaped her while her heart was still calling out: Not like this, not with anger, please, I've been trampled on enough…

His grip on her eased, but he went on holding her. Fania was unable to move, feeling her legs buckling beneath her. She lusted for him and feared him, burning with an unfamiliar fire. Yehiel moved a lock of hair that had fallen over her face and planted hungry kisses in the recesses of her neck. "Fania, Fania!" he whispered as he caressed the body with its overflowing youth and vitality. There was a tenderness in him such as she hadn't known until now. This was how he would be, she told herself, if he were a young and carefree man. He would have aroused the hearts of all the maidens of St. Petersburg, my Black Prince. A shudder passed through her body.

"Are you crying?" he was alarmed when her tears splashed his hands.

"I…" She wanted to say to him: I'm weeping for joy, my love, but the words running around in her were too many, too garbled to be spoken. This wasn't the way Yehiel interpreted her tears. Suddenly he pushed her away, and before she realized what was happening, he had left the room and closed the door quietly behind him, slipping out into the night.

She wanted to shout after him, but the thought of the other residents asleep in the next room deterred her. The little room was suddenly empty and cold, with the night air blowing through the yellow skylight. A short while before this she had been falling asleep out of sheer fatigue, but now all her senses were thoroughly awakened. A donkey brayed mournfully, and in the distance somebody cursed. Her nostrils were assailed by the all-pervading smell of the street, that blend of sewage and oriental spices. Where is Yehiel? Why hasn't he come back? Has he gone out for a stroll in the alleyways of the quarter at this hour of the night? Admittedly she had heard of the good relations prevailing between Muslims and Jews in Haifa, but thirty Jewish families were a negligible minority amid the six hundred Muslim families populating the quarter. And a minority never feels entirely safe. Perhaps she should wake Adis and ask him to look for Yehiel? She rejected this idea, seeing before her eyes the angry expression on Yehiel's face. What was to become of them? She immersed herself in the memory of those moments when his lips touched her body. He sensed the old fear in her, the fear over which she has no control, and he didn't know, didn't understand: she's in love with Imber, he thought. How could he even entertain such an idea? Doesn't her love for Yehiel show in her eyes? In all her movements? Don't her hands speak of it when she folds his shirts? Or when she puts a plate of food in front of him? She loves her husband and she's so afraid! For a moment it seemed they were about to share a bed, but the moment passed as if it never was. Grief filled her heart, and from grief over herself and over Yehiel it spread and enfolded all the creatures precious to her. She pitied the three barefoot children, growing up wild and knowing only poverty; she pitied her old uncle, who accompanied her on her madcap journey to the Holy Land and was left behind without family and without acquaintance in a strange, oriental city; she pitied her brother, hiding in the darkness of the shed, his bones quaking in fear; she pitied Riva Frumkin, her good neighbor, lying sick in a mud hut, her face yellow and her eyes longing to believe all the promises...How she wanted to help them all! To feed and clothe and cure, to take in her arms and console. I'm the unhappiest woman in all the world, she thought. And what if there's another year of drought? And what happens when the money they received from Oliphant runs out? In the morning she'll write to her sisters again and again ask them for...She'll have to rack her brains and think of something offering a secure income. If she could just find some form of business that would benefit both her and people in general, if she could trade in something that people need and can't do without. But what can she sell to this backward population, dirty, ignorant and riddled with boils? Suddenly she remembered the medicine that she had used to treat trachoma. That's it! Medicines! Medicines for trachoma, fever, typhus, psoriasis…the range of medicines stocked by pharmacists was limited and meager: quinine for malaria, castor oil for all stomach complaints and cold compresses for typhus. Other ailments and diseases simply didn't figure in their lexicon…That's it, then! She'll ask her sisters to send medicines and later she'll share the proceeds with them. Medicines don't take up a lot of space, they're easy to transport and the market for them is stable. She'll have to think about proper postal services, that won't jeopardize her plans. Under no circumstances will she use the Turkish mail system. Passing today by the precinct of the mosque, she saw how the postal clerk was dumping all the letters on the pavement and the passersby were rummaging in the heaps looking for letters addressed to them or to their neighbors. When she asked Yehiel why the clerk was letting people handle mail not belonging to them, his answer was the clerk couldn't read or write. "Most services are provided by the residents for themselves," he explained to her then. "The best schools are run by Jews or Christians; medical services in the city are organized by the British, the Germans and the Jews; and anyone who wants his letter to reach its destination uses the Austrian, the French or the Russian postal service. That is standard practice not only for the seven hundred foreign nationals living in the city but for the six thousand indigenous residents as well."

When she opened her eyes, Yehiel was once more standing by the water-bucket and washing his face. The room was lit by the blue-yellow light of morning, and sounds of crowing and bleating came in through the walls. Where did he sleep? If only she could find the strength to explain to him that he'd misunderstood her tears. How she wished he would turn to look at her and see her eyes talking to him.

"I want to buy medicines."

"Are you sick?"

Fania laughed. And with the sound of her laughter a kind of spasm passed through his body and he turned to peer at her, then immediately looked away.

"I want to buy medicines to trade. For trachoma, malaria, fever, intestinal diseases."

"The money is yours, too."

"No! No!" She rose quickly from the bed. Her bronze-colored hair, which he uncovered last night, was cascading over her shoulders, disheveled. "If you want, we can buy something else…I just wanted to guarantee…because of the drought…"

"As you wish."

"But first we'll buy flour and seeds…Yehiel?"

Yehiel didn't look at her and didn't answer. He hates me, she thought, and with good reason. What kind of a wife am I?

Chapter five

Fania sat on "her" hill, under the big walnut trees, and plaited a rope from rags. No wind blew. The heat settled on the ruin, heavy and stifling. Bella held the end of the rope in her little hand. Moshe and Yekotiel, grandson of Issar and Riva Frumkin, competed with the younger brothers of Maryam Alhija in throwing stones. Maryam herself was rocking Tamara in her lap and watching Fania at work. Yesterday she tore a surplus sheet into strips and now she was weaving them into a long plait. When the "rope" was ready, she put one end of it in Moshe's hand and then moved away from him holding the other end and began tugging it, cautiously at first and then with force. The children understood at once what the game was about and they shouted encouragement to Moshe. Then she organized them into two teams of more or less equal weight, with each child clutching at the waist of the one in front. There were howls of laughter when one of the teams fell to the ground. Fania returned to the walnut trees and watched the children playing through the spiraling dust. Two weeks had passed since she decided the time had come to keep the children occupied with games and with study. An air of decline and dejection had hung over Gai Oni since Mordecai Leib and his family left the place. Out of the seventeen pioneering families that settled in Gai Oni five years before, only the Frumkins, the Silases, the Kalirs and the Schwartzes had held on, and now there were just two Jewish families left. Most of the peasants had abandoned the place as well and gone to join their relatives in Horan. Besides the Alhija family, only three other peasant families remained. The incredible had happened: a third year of drought. The ground was hard and barren, and even if they had oxen they would have been unable to plow it. The faces of the residents were dark with hunger and with worry. Oliphant's money had run out, and the days when they ate their fill had turned into a dim memory. Every day, Fania woke up with the thought: today, today Yehiel is going to decide to leave. But Yehiel said nothing. It was as if he had made up his mind: I shall die with this land! Every morning, at dawn, she went out with Maryam Alhija to glean ears of corn. I'm like Ruth the Moabite, she thought to herself, although I shall never have a Boaz. She moved as if in a daze, her eyes scouring the clods of earth and the dry thorns, the sweat drenching her body as she stooped and stood up again, reminding herself constantly: this is I, Fania Mandelstam...Her heart rebelled only when she looked into the faces of the children, the big eyes and the blank, listless features. Perhaps this was why she decided one day to start a kind of school, to keep their spirits up at least. In one of the drawers in the house she found cards with Hebrew letters printed on them. They made words with the letters and added up their numerical value. The children of the peasants also learned the Hebrew letters—it could do no harm...Now the boys were pulling on one end of the rope and the girls on the other, and the girls were being dragged forward; they were determined to resist, but the boys were older and too strong for them.

Yesterday Yehiel went to Safed to pawn "Language of Truth" by Rabbi Israel Bak. He had been given the book by Eleazar Rokeah and it was his most precious possession, as it was the first book printed by Israel Bak in Palestine. He personally molded the letters and personally cast them. The book had been published in the first year following Rabbi Israel's arrival in the country in 1832, and its frontispiece bore the inscription: "Upper Galilee is the gateway to the Holy City, may it be restored and prosper, under the governance of our master, the Chief Minister Muhammad Ali Pasha." Books produced by the printer of Safed enjoyed wide circulation in the Diaspora, and the printing press even attracted large numbers of tourists, who came to see the Galilean miracle with their own eyes. The good times lasted eight years. When Muhammad Ali was overthrown, Rabbi Israel Bak's home was wrecked and his printworks smashed. Looted *tefillin* were transformed into reins for horses, and of the precious books, the Galilean books, all that remained were fragments scattered to the winds. Miraculously, a few copies were preserved in the hands of the Frumkins and the Rokeahs. When Fania saw how reverently Yehiel was handling the book, she tried to persuade him not to sell it. "The lives of the children are more important," he answered her stubbornly. In the end he promised he would make an effort not to sell the book but rather to mortgage it to Leah, so it would at least stay in the family's possession. She hoped that when the medicines finally arrived from America, she could redeem the book. But the weeks passed and not a word was heard from her sisters, as if the people living here had been wiped from the memory of the whole world. We shall all die here and no one will even know, she thought. At night she listened to the wailing of the jackals and the rustle of insects, heard the wood of the furniture cracking in the heat, thinking: if only I could curl up in Yehiel's arms. How close he is and how far away! Days went by without her exchanging a word with anyone. Not a word of inspiration, not a word of real meaning. Sometimes she would pick some book out of her chest, but her stomach complained and the letters gyrated before her eyes, in a dizzy dance of hunger and loneliness. Sometimes she would stand in the yard and watch the door of the shed. If she could at least talk to her brother. But Lulik was living his mysterious and secluded life in the mute serenity of the insane. Had hunger sapped his strength? Or had time brought him healing? At times she remembered her childhood, the school, her large and tempestuous family, the aspen trees in the little street, music lessons, the soaring hills outside the kitchen door. All of this now seemed like a distant dream. Did it exist? Or did none of it exist?

From time to time Fania glanced toward the path, expecting to see Yehiel there. Of Ayn Abu Halil all that remained was a channel of dark earth. The mulberry bushes had dried and turned into a layer of thorns, interwoven with dusty spiders' webs, which hampered access to the spring. At last she noticed some movement on the slope, but it wasn't Yehiel. Rivka was sauntering up the hill in leisurely style, in the wake of her tired horse. A sense of foreboding set Fania's heart racing. This girl always aroused a fear of impending doom in her. When she was still some distance from them, she tossed the long plait of hair over her shoulder and called out: "Moshe! Bella! Come and say hello to your Auntie!"

In Rivka's hand was a purple sugar-stick, and she took a knife from her pocket, cut off two pieces and handed them to the children. But the little ones didn't start sucking the sticks; they were embarrassed by the looks of their friends. Fania was so proud of them! Her stomach too contracted suddenly, as if a fist had struck her, and saliva filled her mouth.

"Cut shares of the candy for all the children," she said.

"I brought this for Moshe and Bella," she said. The look in her eyes asked indignantly: What are you saying? Am I supposed to be looking after all these kids?

"What's this?" she cried suddenly, snatching from the hand of one of the children a card with the letter B written on it.

"I'm teaching them the alphabet."

"With Rabbi Israel's cards?! Are you out of your mind?"

"What? What?" Fania stammered, "I didn't know…"

"You didn't know!" Rivka mocked angrily. "What *do* you know?"

She snatched the cards from the children, who were frightened and only too eager to hand them over.

"Rabbi Israel printed these cards, here in Jaoni, so the gleaners in the field could take turns. The Baks had a bumper crop that year." She shot Fania an accusing glance, as if it were her fault that the rains refused to fall. "Where did you find them?"

"At home, in a drawer." There was a hint of apology in her

voice and she was angry at herself. She hates me and she's in love with Yehiel, she thought.

"Yehiel brought flour and oil. He's at home. Moshe! Bella! Would you like to ride on the horse? Did you notice there were only six cards?" she asked, turning again to Fania.

"I thought the others were lost."

"No. A card for every day of the week."

"Divide up the candy for all the children!" Fania commanded Rivka, but her voice was shaking. Rivka didn't reply. She lifted Moshe and Bella in turn and sat them on the back of the horse. Fania felt she didn't have the strength to cope with Rivka now. You wait!—she threatened her in her mind—I'll settle things with you yet! Had Rivka met Yehiel at her sister's house in Safed, or had she accompanied him from Ein Zeitim? And was she perhaps the one who mediated between him and her sister Leah? Rivka's family, living in Ein Zeitim, had also been hit by the drought, and they were being helped by their daughter Leah, who was one of the recipients of the Halukkah. In the eyes of the Jews of Safed, the drought was a sign from Heaven, telling them they were in the right. It wasn't by chance that Yehiel set out on his way toward evening. Like a thief he crept into Safed, not wanting to advertise his plight publicly lest his enemies rejoice.

Yehiel was waiting for her by the door, his face dark and blank.

"I brought food."

"Yes. Rivka told me. Did she travel with you to Safed?"

"Her horse...Why did you give her the gleaning cards? I don't want to dispose of *all* the family's assets."

"I didn't give them to her."

"Took them by force, did she? And why didn't you let the children eat the sugar sticks I sent them?"

Fania didn't answer. Fuming, she passed by Yehiel and went into the house. On the floor stood a sack of wheat and a can of oil, and there were onions and olives too—a treasure trove! She hurried first of all to light the fire in the oven and then stowed the food in the larder, took what she required and started kneading the dough.

Her strength seemed to return to her all at once. Yehiel came and stood facing her, watching her at work.

"You've turned into a peasant woman!" Was she imagining it, or did a smile really flit across his face? "Are you angry?"

"There were other hungry children there besides ours!" she burst out. "But she didn't say the candy was from you and she wouldn't let me distribute it!"

"Don't worry, Moshe and Bella will give some of it to their friends. You're very quick to lose your temper"—and this time he definitely smiled. "I heard good news today in Safed. The thirty families from Romania—already on their way! They've bought up almost all the land in Jaoni: two thousand five hundred dunams for plowing, plus pasture for cattle and sheep!"

"Plowing!"

"The drought won't last forever."

"I've been hearing that remark since the day I came here."

"Any regrets?"

"No…Why are they coming here specifically?"

"You know. Eleazar Rokeah influenced them."

"When are they arriving?"

"Before New Year. Who knows, maybe Rabbi Israel's dream will be realized at last, and two hundred Jewish villages will spring up in Galilee!" Yehiel laughed with feeling.

The excitement infected Fania too. The signs were good: there was food in the house and soon more Jews would be coming here, partners who would share the burden with them, fresher than them. No more hunger! No more loneliness! She would draw a big "Welcome" sign in their honor, and teach the children a song with which to greet the new arrivals—maybe that song that Imber composed, "Hatikva"? That song has a tune already attached to it.

"I'll set aside some of the flour, and when they arrive we'll greet them with bread and salt. Let them see that working the land is the way to eat well!" she laughed.

"What is it that keeps you here?" he asked suddenly.

Fania was taken aback. She hesitated and then answered: "Stubbornness."

Fate stepped in, and when the Jews of Moineshti arrived in Gai Oni they weren't greeted with salt or with bread. Fania returned from the gleaning, the cloth bag tied at her waist and Tamara in her arms. From the distance came the sound of a Psalm, and her legs almost buckled with the impact of the emotion. The "Song of Degrees" was her father's favorite, and he used to chant it every Sabbath after the midday meal, fingering the crumbs of bread left on the tablecloth. Now the song was soaring aloft from far away, a high-pitched and harmonious sound, and Fania broke into a run in the direction of the village, the heavy child bouncing on her shoulder.

From a distance she saw them: Jews! A great many Jews! Perhaps a hundred, perhaps more! Not Jews of the Holy Land, natives of Tangier, Izmir or Safed, but Jews from her father's home. The sudden surge of joy alarmed her; it was as if her father and mother had descended unexpectedly from Heaven, to assume from her young back the heavy burden laid upon it. She scoured them with her eyes: the dark suits, the woolen dresses...they too had heard the rumor about woolen clothes warding off malaria...

The newcomers wandered among the houses, peering into the yards, and then gathered on the hillside, looking stunned. Fania saw the place through their eyes, the dilapidated mud huts and the black tents of the shepherds. She felt on her skin the hot blast of wind that was searing their skin, and her lungs were filled with the same dust that was choking them. They examined everything with the attitude of landowners, and Fania was reminded that the land did indeed belong to them. Her heart fluttered with the fear that they might yet decide to abandon the place.

At the entrance to her house she met two women in kerchiefs, coming out of the yard. Evidently they hadn't opened the door of the shed, Fania reflected, smiling at them; if they had done so, Lulik would almost certainly have scared them away like a pair of frightened chickens.

"What does she look like, God help us!" one said to her companion in Yiddish, in response to Fania's smile.

"Menahem Mandel says the Arabs will be joining their families in Syria now."

They think I'm an Arab! she realized, and lowered her head to hide her face, slipping into the house without saying a word. If they find out she's one of the Jewish settlers, they'll flee for their lives... Despite the stories she had heard about the hardships suffered by the Jews of Romania, they appeared to her like "landlords". Perhaps she could hire herself out to them as a washerwoman or a nanny.

Flushed with shame, she decided to take off the dirty clothes. Again and again the words reverberated in her ears—*What does she look like, God help us!* She peered at herself in the mirror—the first time she had done so in weeks—and decided they had a point! Isn't she just skin and bone? Grubby and sick with hunger and worry? But now, since they are here, everything will change. They will be one family, all helping one another, protecting one another and standing by comrades in times of strife. It's a shame I'm having to depend for my renewal on the wealth of others, she thought, I who grew up in a household where they were always giving...I just hope the rains come and they don't have to suffer everything that's been inflicted on us. Jews have come to the village and henceforward, henceforward the situation cannot go on being the same as it has been!

Fania brought a basin of water into the room, and having closed the windows and the doors, hurriedly took off the tattered Bedouin trousers and the shabby Bedouin dress. The Bedouin clothes were a symbol of the change that had come about in her life. How happy she was when she began wearing these garments—how proud she was! And now, for the first time, she hesitated. Along with this sharing of fate, she had also decreed upon herself the standard of living of the peasants, the submissive acceptance of hardship. There was no real bond between the peasants of Jaoni and the pioneers, but still they lived in one village, on one patch of land, looked up at the same sky. But there was one big difference between them: the pioneers—or those of them who were left—settled in the place in obedience to an ideal, and they were prepared to pay the price. And so, while the vast majority of the peasants were leaving for Horan in search of seasonal work, she and Yehiel and Issar and Riva lowered their heads and dug their heels in the ground like the meanest of the Bedouin, praying for the grace of Heaven. Just like the serf who will not abandon his village in frost or in drought, so is she! Fania remembered the arguments that used to rage between her uncle and her father. Her father was right. What kind of percipience could be credited to Tolstoy the cobbler, when in the background his ancestral estate always awaited him...Much of what was shared between her and Yehiel came down to the stubbornness with which they held on to this barren land, the unremitting self-laceration...the mud daubed on the walls of their house was baking in the heat, and only yesterday Yehiel killed a scorpion that had crawled under Tamara's cot, but until now he had never asked her what was keeping her here. It was Rivka who put this thought into his mind. She's wondering why I'm staying, but she doesn't have to wonder about herself because she belongs to the place and the place belongs to her. That's how Tamara will feel when the time comes. Belonging. Without thinking about things. The way the river belongs to its bed.

For the second time in a year Fania lifted the lid of her chest. She took out a long brown skirt made of a soft woolen fabric, a belt with a brass buckle and a white blouse with voluminous sleeves. In the depths of the chest she also found a pair of sandals with pointed toes, more suited to the dance hall of the high school in Elizavetgrad than to the dust paths of Jaoni.

Again, like the first time, the children stood and watched her, enchanted by the miracle taking place before their eyes. She remembered what Imber had told them, that she was really a queen in disguise. She was combing her long hair and twining it into a plait when suddenly the door opened and the room was filled with light.

"Fania!" Yehiel cried, "They've arrived!"

She almost expected him, this time too, to tell her to strip off her glad rags, but he smiled.

"Yehiel, put on something else. We don't want to scare the Romanians away."

"Are we really that scary? Away with you, children. Daddy's getting dressed."

"There's clean water in the basin, Yehiel."

"Washing as well?" he smiled, and then suddenly embraced her and kissed her lips. Her arms rose as if of their own accord and clasped his body hard, while in her head lightning flashed and thunder rolled.

"Issar says there's a meeting outside the synagogue," the voice of Moshe was heard, before he fell silent, taken aback by the sight of Fania and Yehiel embracing. Yehiel extricated himself from the clinch.

"Yes, we're coming."

Fania went on twining the plait, looking at Yehiel as he leaned over the basin. She watched the play of the muscles moving in his back, watched the way he put his arms into the sleeves of the shirt, how he moved his chin up and down to adjust to the stiff collar… After he had shaved off the stubble, the cleft in his cheek became visible, and on his temple, beside the ear, three brown freckles appeared, arranged like a little triangle.

"Are you happy?"

"Yes, Mr. Silas. And you?"

"Yes, Miss Mandelstam."

From outside the racket of the people thronging the village could be heard. New voices speaking Yiddish and Romanian, the cries of mothers calling to their children, men arguing and babies wailing. The sounds of Jewish life.

"What's happening in the village?"

"A riot!"

Fania wound the thick plait around her head like a crown. Yehiel looked at her with delight and planted noisy kisses on her cheeks and her forehead, as if she were a little girl. Suddenly he burst out laughing.

"What is it?" she pressed him, "What's so funny?"

"Issar told me that at the close of Sabbath the Romanians held a meeting in Safed, and every one of them was asked to declare how much money he had brought with him…" the words stuck in Yehiel's mouth, held up by the laughter. "It turned out most of them are penniless and some are even relying on public assistance to feed themselves!"

"No! But surely they were told every family needs two thousand gold francs—on top of the land!"

Fania looked at Yehiel in alarm. He was talking as if he were drunk, halfway between laughter and tears.

"Ah! But our Jews are a clever bunch! They sat down and debated it logically, a bit of pedantry and some analogy and inference, and decided that if most of the Jews were going to bring two thousand gold francs, it wouldn't be such a disaster if a few poor men came along for the ride. Will the compassionate Jews let the paupers starve to death? Of course not!"

"What's going to happen, Yehiel?"

"Their leader, Rabbi Moshe David, is so worried he's tearing his hair and his beard out. In the meantime the meeting decided to set up a communal fund for all. Poor and rich alike will put their money in. They've also elected a committee that will distribute the money in installments for the building of houses, and share out the land and the agricultural labor."

"And the rich agreed to this?"

"A good question. Six families have already decided to return to Romania."

"Why go back? They could settle in Safed or in Jaffa or Jerusalem. Gai Oni isn't the only place in the Land of Israel!"

"On the subject of Gai Oni—they want to give the place a new name, call it 'Rosh Pinnah'!"

Fania stared at Yehiel in blank incomprehension.

"*The stone the builders rejected has become the cornerstone, Rosh Pinnah.*"

"What's wrong with 'Gai Oni'?"

"What's wrong with 'Rosh Pinnah'?"

"Gai Oni has a nicer sound to it! And why change it, when there's a Hebrew name ready-made?"

"Come on, Fania, you've made yourself beautiful enough."

Fania stared straight ahead without seeing anything. The four walnut trees had been silent witnesses to all her experiences in Gai Oni, to the many hours of hardship and the few moments of joy that had fallen to her lot. Even now, having made up her mind to abandon the place, she came here. At this of all times, when "reinforcements" had arrived—she was running away. The decision had been made suddenly, but once it was made, time was suddenly pressing. She had to leave this place at once! Before Yehiel returned from Damascus. She didn't want to see him. Not for fear that he might prevent her—he was too proud for that. It was herself she was afraid of. Perhaps she would not have the strength of mind to leave after setting eyes on him. She knew that jealousy was guiding her actions now, but there was no consolation in this knowledge, or any incentive to change her decision. How ugly was jealousy, petty and destructive, sister to slander and hatred.

When the Romanians arrived they thought that here, at last, a new day was dawning for them. But the newcomers were shocked by what they saw and, having no regard for the feelings of the two families still residing in Gai Oni, they didn't hesitate to express their disappointment. Immediately upon their arrival the Moineshti contingent declared that *they* weren't going to live in mud huts alongside peasants, and *their* children wouldn't be contracting trachoma and fever. Anyway, do you call this land? It's a barren desert! Sold under false pretenses! The cattle in the villages of Romania enjoy better conditions than the villagers of Gai Oni.

The leaders of the committee, Rabbi Moshe David Shub and Motil Katz, enlisted the aid of the honorary presidents of the council of Rosh Pinnah, the Sage Yakov Abu Hai, French consul in Safed, and his brother Yitzhak Mordecai, and exerting their joint authority they addressed the committee and persuaded the settlers not to return to the flesh-pots of Moineshti. In her heart Fania couldn't blame these Jews for their bitterness. She knew that the state of shock she had been in at the time of her arrival in the country had dulled her senses and made it easier for her to conform. She wasn't expecting a land flowing with milk and honey. She wasn't expecting anything, and she saw little of what was going on around her. With the meager willpower that remained in her, she wanted only one thing: to fulfill her father's dream. She didn't mind wearing her body out with all kinds of hard work, its punishment for betraying her in accepting the seed of a drunken *mujik*. She went on living because Tamara and Lulik depended on her and because she never gave a thought to her future. She wasn't brave, nor was she faint-hearted. When they had bread to eat—they ate bread, and when there was no bread—she gleaned ears of corn in the fields of strangers, and when there were no ears of corn—she picked mallows. But this wasn't the lifestyle that the Jews of Moineshti had been expecting: inspired by flimsy dreams they had financed their journeys, only to be confronted by the stark reality of Jaoni.

Riva Frumkin's arm was entwined with Fania's, and the two of them stood apart from the other women when the meeting was convened to settle the question: whether to stay or return to Moineshti. From the fingers digging hard into her arm, Fania could sense the tension in her older friend. One of the Jews opened the Holy Ark and cried: "Jews! Let every man who is timorous and faint-hearted confess in public that he is leaving this land and returning…"

"How do they have the gall to look them in the face?" Riva whispered in Fania's ear and pointed to two women, one old and the other young, who were likewise standing arm-in-arm. "Who are they?"

"The mother of Rabbi Moshe David Shub and his wife. Their baby daughter died at sea before the father even laid eyes on her. He left his family and came here to find a place where his fellow citizens could settle, and they…!"

Fania studied the faces of the people, going from one to the next: is he staying or not staying? Her gaze rested now on a young girl who had drawn her attention before. She was as pale as the children of Safed, her breathing labored and her cheeks flushed. The skies lowered, enfolding them in ominous silence.

The wife of Rabbi Tzevi, known to the people of Moineshti as the "Cossack", suddenly stepped forward. "Jews!" she cried in a voice that cast confusion into their agitated hearts. "Here we shall live and here we shall die! We shall not abandon the land!"

"She used to be a leading advocate of 'defection'," Riva

whispered, in a voice somewhere between laughter and a sigh of relief. Sure enough, following this statement of faith on the part of Madame Bendel, the bundle unraveled. Suddenly they were all talking at once, interrupting one another, splitting into groups and arguing passionately. In Rabbi Tzevi's eyes there were tears and he cried in a loud voice: "In the place where the penitents stand…"

In the end there were only six families left that had not reversed the decision to return to Moineshti. Fania peered at them and didn't know which party she should feel sorrier for: those who had decided to stay or those who had decided to leave.

Suddenly there was a kind of festivity in the air. There and then the foundation of "Rosh Pinnah" was proclaimed, and Rabbi Motel Katz, brother-in-law of Rabbi Moshe David, pronounced the blessing "of the One who has given us life". Riva whispered, "Amen," and abruptly held her breath. Her eyes shone with hope, but experience had taught her not to be carried away by such hope. She is the real heroine at this feast, Fania thought to herself, and on a sudden impulse kissed her friend's cheek. As if to add the finishing touches to the ceremony, Lulik appeared from somewhere shouting, "Jews! Fire!"—his coattails flapping and exposing his white legs. For a moment Fania was alarmed, but the general mood was by now so ebullient that even Lulik's appearance was seen as a good omen.

"Who is he?" asked the young woman, approaching the place where Fania and Riva were standing.

"My brother," Fania replied.

The young woman was about her own age. Her eyes black and effulgent, her skin clear and her forehead bright, as if lit from inside. There was a mixture of coyness and mischief in her, and Fania felt that *this* was someone she could talk to. Even the Yiddish-Romanian that she spoke sounded melodious. For the first time in months she suddenly longed for a sense of companionship. Days and weeks passed during which she exchanged words only with the children or with some itinerant shepherd encountered by the spring. Admittedly, Riva was a good friend, but she was forty years older. Fania wanted to chat with someone of her own age, to stroll and laugh, to sit amid the olive trees overlooking the spring, the way the peasant women do, and talk about babies and clothes and sewing and cooking, and perhaps even share more intimate thoughts sometimes…

"Are you staying?" she asked the first question that occurred to her.

"Yes! Were you born here?"

"No!" Fania burst into laughter, her laughter of long ago—loud and resonant—and she noticed Yehiel looking up and staring at her, curious and smiling. "I'm from Russia."

"And the children?"

"The youngest is mine, and the other two belong to my husband. Are you married?"

"Yes." The black eyes flickered. "I married a month before we set out on the journey. My parents are here too. And my sister and her husband."

"Who are you lodging with in Safed?"

"With Michel the baths-attendant. You know him?

"Yes."

"He may keep the baths clean but his house is filthy!" she twisted her face into a sardonic smile.

"It's hard to find accommodation in Safed. Thirty families arriving at once!"

"They assigned me and my husband a separate room, being a young couple." A flush colored the pale face. "Since we married we've had hardly any privacy. And it will be months before houses are built here."

"You can live with us, if you like."

"Thank-you…but no, we'll wait…there's no *minyan* here and no *mikveh*…my husband is very devout."

"My husband says our father Abraham didn't have a *minyan*, or a *mikveh* either. But all those things will be coming here soon. A *minyan*, and a *mikveh* too. Everything!."

"Who is your husband?"

Fania pointed with her chin toward Yehiel, who was standing and talking with Issar Frumkin and two of the Romanians. The stiff collar was bothering him and from time to time he stretched his neck as if trying to escape from the constraints imposed on him. He was taller than most of the men around him, and his jacket hung loosely on his shoulders, hinting at the muscular frame beneath. On his swarthy face, planed like basalt rocks, was an expression of serious attentiveness. Fania glanced with pride at her new friend.

"The little one doesn't look like him," she tilted her head and smiled at Tamara, who stared unblinking at the newcomer. Her tiny shell-earrings sparkled with drops of light.

"No."

"And is this your mother?" She pointed to Riva Frumkin.

"No." And after a moment or two Fania asked: "And who is your sister?"

"My sister is in Haifa. Her husband's from the town of Galatzi. Twenty families from Galatzi travelled with us on the ship, and at the last moment they decided to settle in a place called Zamarin. Their agent in Beirut, Mr. Frank, promised to buy the village for them. Until the money arrives from Galatzi, they have to sit in Haifa and wait. My mother is very worried. She misses her grandchildren, misses her daughter, even misses her son-in-law. How long will it be, do you think, before the money arrives?"

"I don't know. Sometimes the post is delayed for months. It takes at least three days for the messenger to reach Beirut. Then you have to wait for a ship that will take the post to Romania, and from there the post comes back to Beirut and from there to Zamarin... and if there's a storm at sea... But why don't they settle here, in Gai Oni? The land here is cheap. Five francs a dunam. And the family is here, too."

"My brother-in-law wants to be with his fellow townsmen... by the way, my name is Helen Leah Joseph. And my parents"—she pointed to a middle-aged couple—"are called Moses."

"And I'm Fania Silas."

"I thought there would be more local inhabitants. Was your husband one of the seventeen original pioneers?"

"Yes."

"I admire them. Rabbi Eleazar told us about them."

"My husband is Eleazar's cousin."

The two young women smiled. Fania didn't even know why. She hadn't said anything funny, but all the same, she felt an urge to laugh!

"The peasants will be happy to help with the building!" she overheard Yehiel saying. There was a note of anger and concern in his voice, and she was tempted to listen.

"No! We shall build our own houses!" one young man insisted.

"Because of the drought they are hungry for bread," said Yehiel. "And you're going to need help. You can't do it all by yourselves. Why not use them?"

"They're going to have to leave the place. This land belongs to us now, and the village is ours too. They've already proved what they're capable of. We're going to turn this place into a fertile garden."

It's lucky we're living on Oliphant's land, Fania thought. Suddenly an alarming idea occurred to her: What if the Romanians approach Oliphant and offer to buy back the land he bought in Gai Oni? No! Oliphant will never evict them from his land!

Heaps of stones and earth were piled up in front of the house of Yehiel and Fania. Rabbi Moshe David Shub had prepared everything needed for building, and the planks to be used for construction his fellow townsmen had brought with them from Romania. Deep pits had been dug for the foundations of the houses, and dust filled the home of the Silases. All day the din of building was heard, and only at four P.M. did the Romanians return to Safed and sweet silence descend on the village. As it was the day before yesterday.

"Why here of all places?" Fania asked Yehiel. "Why the overcrowding? Are they short of space?"

"It's better this way," Yehiel replied. "They wanted to build a 'European'-style settlement. Big houses with extensive grounds and pretty gardens, with a lot of space in between. But Issar and I explained to them it's better for the time being to build their houses in the village itself. Under Turkish law it's hard to get permission to build on 'Miri' land. Better to exploit the licenses that have already been issued. Besides that, there's water here, and the further they go from the springs the more problems they're going to have with supply. The burghers of Safed had some influence on them too, and advised them to build close to the houses of the village to guarantee their safety, in case of attack."

"At long last the good folk of Safed are in agreement with us! This must be the Messianic Age!"

"They've bought livestock for plowing and milking, and until they come to live here we shall be tending the animals."

"Me too?"

"The children as well. There's a lot that needs doing—milking, pasturing, feeding and watering."

"And they'll be paying us for this?

"Of course."

"Oh, Yehiel!" Fania's eyes were moist from happiness.

"They bought seeds as well."

"And the rain? Have they bought that too?"

"From now on everything's going to be different, you'll see!"

But their hopes were dashed even sooner than they expected. The very next morning soldiers appeared in the settlement. They had been sent on the orders of the governor of Safed, and they brought with them an edict on behalf of the Wali, the governor of Syria and Palestine, demanding that all building work be halted. The building-ban carried over from another edict, authorized by the "Sublime Porte" in Constantinople, ordering that no more immigration permits be issued. It seemed the Turks were alarmed by the number of migrants arriving in the country that year. Most of the Moineshti contingent were now forced to sit in Safed doing nothing and using up the remainder of their savings. Many homes had not been started at all, while others stood half-built with roofs open to the sky. Even those whose homes were completed looked anxiously to the future. What if the permits were never to be issued? Would they be marooned in this God-forsaken place, abandoned and cut off from their loved ones? And if the rains came, who would help them with the cultivation of the fields? And why had Rabbi Moshe David promised them the permits in the first place? On the head of the unfortunate Rabbi Moshe David all the blame was laid; he and only he was responsible for everything...

It was actually Fania who remembered Yakov Adis; she had heard him talked about in the home of Musa and Allegra Adis.

"Isn't the Wali's secretary a relative of yours?" she asked Yehiel.

"Yes."

"Could he get the order rescinded? After all, these migrants are living on land that belongs to them, land they paid good money for! And all they want to do is work and grow crops! And everybody stands to benefit from this, the peasants too, and even the government!"

"You've convinced me!"

"Yehiel! It's so logical!"

"For that very reason we'll need to find some additional arguments."

Fania's suggestion appealed to Rabbi Moshe David Shub, and the very next day he went to Safed and obtained letters of recommendation from the Sage Yakov Abu Hai, French consul in Safed, and from his brother, the Sage Yitzhak. The letters were addressed to the Bashi Sage of Damascus, the Rabbi and Gaon Mercado Alkalai and to other luminaries of the Damascus community. Now, with the letters of recommendation in his hand, Rabbi Moshe David asked Yehiel to accompany him on the journey to Damascus, to serve as interpreter and advocate in his consultations with the Wali. Yehiel went to Ein Zeitim, to see his in-laws and collect letters for delivery to Yakov Adis, their relative, and ask once again for the loan of their horse.

At dawn the next day Rivka appeared in Rosh Pinnah, a bonnet on her head and a bag in her hand. Fania stared at her in astonishment.

"Where are you heading for?" Yehiel asked.

"Damascus!" she replied and took her seat in the buggy.

For a moment he hesitated and then asked: "Are they expecting you there?"

"Father says I should help you persuade Uncle Yakov."

Father says! He has a lot to say for himself, the old idiot! Rivka and Leah and their mother ruled over the patriarch with a high hand. Fania wondered what Rivka's mother was thinking, letting her daughter make such a dangerous journey in the company of two men. She peered at Yehiel. It seemed he too was embarrassed. The horse and the buggy belonged to Rivka, and how could he change his mind about travelling without making a fool of himself? And she, what could she say to him? Don't go with her because I'm jealous? Oh yes, she was jealous all right. Her heart was seared by jealousy! And all the same, he could have said something, invented some excuse. *You can't come with us into the house of the Sheikh in Banyas*, or *I'm worried about your good name, Rivka*, or something like that…

Fania turned her back on them and went into the house. She couldn't bear the sight of them sitting together on the small seat, side by side. And the triumphant look that Rivka flashed at her! And how is it that Yehiel doesn't see what's obvious to everyone else? Or perhaps he does see it and takes it as a compliment, having two hens pecking at each other over him. And who knows? Perhaps they planned this joint journey from the start.

Yehiel came into the house to pick up his bag. Fania had prepared a change of clean clothes for him, and food for the journey. Now they could pull up by the headwaters of the Jordan or at the foot of Hermon, spread a cloth on the ground in the shade of the trees and eat their fill to the sound of birdsong…Well, he won't be finding her when he comes home! she thought wildly. When he leaned towards her for a moment as if meaning to kiss her, she recoiled from him, and the old look returned to his eyes, black and brooding.

Fania watched as the dust receded on the road and then turned and climbed the hill. She sat amid the walnut trees, looking out over the valley. Flies filled the air in grey clouds and she huffed again and again to repel them from her face. The air was hot and sticky, sweat ran down her back and her dress exuded vapor. Her mind was made up, to leave the place and find somewhere else to live, far, far away from Yehiel. The sight of his face would be unbearable to her, after that journey with her. Sitting there like a regular couple for all the community to see! Oh, please! She won't get in their way. She'll be out of here before Yehiel is back from Damascus. So where to? Where can she go? And who, besides Yehiel, is going to take into his home a girl saddled with a baby and a lunatic brother? And she herself, isn't she contemplating an act of lunacy? If she were to appear like this, as she is, before the eyes of her relations and her former acquaintances, they would declare without hesitation that poor Fania has gone out of her mind. Her father's dream of revival had turned into a holy mania for which she was burning out her youth, her life. She was determined to carry on the way she had started, but not here. She tried to remember things she had heard about Jewish settlements in other places. She was adamantly opposed to the idea of living in a town; better to die of hunger than tag along with the "charity Jews"! If she had succeeded in surviving in Gai Oni, she could survive anywhere. She knew that five families had revived the settlement in Umm Labas, and in Yahud eighteen families were already living. And according to Issar, Jews from Novopavlovska were negotiating over the purchase of land near the Arab village of Akir. She could talk to them at least...In Mikveh Israel, too, a group of fifteen young Russians had settled, mostly students, from the Bilu movement. Although she already spoke Hebrew and Arabic, Russian was still her mother tongue. But no, Hirsch the supervisor was a pedant, and he wouldn't allow a woman who had left her husband to join them...She wasn't asking for much! Just a mat to sleep on, and a vegetable patch so she could grow food for Tamara and Lulik. How about Rishon le-Zion? Since July, ten affluent families had been located there and a further six impoverished families, living, rumor had it, on the generosity of Baron Rothschild in Paris. No! No! She will never hold out her hand for charity from anyone! Shame on her for even thinking such thoughts...No! She will go to her uncle's house, in Jaffa, and there she can stay until she finds a solution.

A slim figure was climbing the hill: Helen Leah, her hands holding up the hemline of her skirt and her olive complexion pale from the effort. She sat herself down on a stone beside Fania, panting and wheezing.

"What's new, Fania?" she asked when her breathing had steadied.

"Look around you," said Fania. "This is what our dreams look like."

"I love these trees, they remind me of the countryside in Romania."

"This was the first agricultural settlement in Jaoni. Did you know? You didn't know! Well, no one wants to discourage you. The Arabs call this place Khan el-Yahud. It belonged to Yehiel's family. Fifty years ago his great-uncle received it as a gift from the Egyptian general Ibrahim Pasha."

"I saw you running away suddenly. As if someone was chasing you!"

"He was a Jewish printer from Berdichev, a farmer and a physician too...He founded some flourishing villages here. There are testimonials! The minister Montefiore visited him and was so impressed by his success, he decided that over a period of years he was going to establish a hundred to two hundred Jewish villages here. A hundred to two hundred! He reckoned, all that the land here needed was a little dose of manure and bumper crops would follow!"

Fania was aware of the sarcasm in her voice, but couldn't suppress her feelings. She shouldn't be weakening the resolve of this young woman, who had left behind the fleshpots of Romania and came here to redeem the soil of the Holy Land.

For some time the two of them were silent. Fania was thinking: what a pity! She had just now found a friend and already she was having to part from her.

"I'm leaving this place."

"What? When?" Helen Leah was astonished.

"I'm going to stay with my uncle, in Jaffa."

"When will you be back?"

"I don't know."

"Is it...because of her? Does he know?"

Fania rose to her feet, unable to look Helen Leah in the eye. Am I really so transparent? she wondered and started walking down towards the village.

"That's a shame." Helen Leah's black eyes flashed with affection and sorrow. Then she said shyly: "There are no girls here of my age."

"What's the problem? The Frumkins' girls are here, and the daughters of the Katzes and the Bergmans and the Fishels and..."

"Yes, yes, but you're different. You're...special..."

"I don't know what's different about me, and I never wanted to be 'special'...I saw the list of regulations drawn up by the committee of the settlers of Rosh Pinnah. All the signatories to it are men. Anyone reading this rule-book a hundred years from now would think there were no women here at all. And they are the true heroines of Rosh Pinnah. Rosenfeld's wife who set out to travel here in the eighth month of her pregnancy...old Mima Yankowitz...Riva Frumkin... When I arrived here she was the only Jewish woman among all the Arab peasants. I *really* had no friend. Riva is kind-hearted and as tender as a mother, but she's so many years older than me and besides that she's related to Yehiel. Both the Frumkins and Yehiel have been so persecuted by the 'charity' Jews that she'll never do anything likely to hurt Yehiel. She worships the ground he walks on! If I went to her with any complaint she'd try to convince me I was in the wrong..."

"She sent me to you."

"Riva??"

"Yes." Helen Leah hesitated. "She said that she's old and you need me...and I need you!" She raised her voice suddenly and then smiled awkwardly. "My fellow citizens from Moineshti talk of nothing but salvation of the land and national revival. Of course, that's the most important thing and it's why we're here, but..." Helen Leah waved her hands in mock despair, then asked in a serious tone: "Isn't he worth fighting for? I wouldn't give up so easily. I wouldn't give up at all! No, I wouldn't give up. And anyway..."

"I don't want to see him," Fania declared as an established fact, walking fast and with head bowed.

Helen Leah was shocked into silence and then, perhaps in an effort at conciliation she asked: "Will you be in Haifa?"

"I'll be stopping there on the way to Jaffa."

"My sister is in Haifa, with the people from Galatzi. I'll give you her address and if you need anything—turn to her. Will you promise me that?"

"I promise."

The two of them had arrived in the meantime at Fania's house. Fania went round the building and approached Lulik's shed. She would have to take him with her somehow. Helen Leah stopped by the gate, watching the proceedings in the yard nervously and from a safe distance. The interior of the shed was dark. "Lulik!" Fania cried. But before she could even take one step forward, her brother rushed outside. She grabbed at his shirt with both hands and cried, pleading: "It's me! Fania!" But he managed to free himself from her grip and ran, long-legged and barefoot, shouting his usual refrain of "Jews! Fire!" Fania watched him recede in despair.

"I'll bring him food," said Helen Leah.

"Thank-you! Thank-you very much! He barely eats anything! A mug of water and a slice of bread will be enough for him. And I'll leave you my uncle's address in Jaffa. If anything happens here—let me know."

"Why, Fania? Why?"

Fania didn't answer. Could she describe in words the confusion churning around inside her? The anger and the jealousy and the pain? For a moment she felt an urge to take to her heels, like Lulik, run into the hills and shout and shout.

Chapter six

Fania recognized the house of Musa and Allegra by the "hand" on the door and the bundles of garlic on the windows. The "Ishmaelite" carried her trunk into the apartment while Allegra watched what he was doing with her big, accusatory eyes. She wasn't happy having guests turn up suddenly in her house. Yehiel was a relative, and the trunk was evidence that the girl had left him.

Fania was very tired from the tribulations of the road. All day she had been riding, lashed to the back of the mule like one of the saddlebags. Although she knew Yehiel had travelled to the north, heading for Damascus, the impulse for flight was irresistible, and were it not for the darkness and the dangers of bandits and wild animals, she would have carried on. She was tossed about on the back of the mule like a little boat on a stormy sea, as her mount stumbled on the shifting stones. Sometimes she collided with a dense bush and thorny branches scratched her cheeks, and at other times she came close to dropping Tamara. She envied the escorts on their horses, their bodies unrestrained and free to move as they pleased. If she could afford it she'd do the stage of the journey from Haifa to Jaffa in the German carriage. The thought of a further twenty hours of jolting on the back of the mule horrified her. They stopped just once to rest on the way, near a Druze village, and sat down to rest in the shade of a tree. One of the escorts fetched eggs and honey and water from the village, but she refused the food offered her because she didn't have the money to pay for it. Her fellow travelers ate sociably, passing the pitas and the water-skins from hand to hand and sharing out the tobacco, and then pronouncing the blessing for food in chorus.

In the house of Allegra and Musa a letter awaited her, from her sister. It turned out it had been in their house for two weeks. Musa recognized her name in the pile of letters dumped in the square by the mosque.

> *My dear little Fania…*—her sister Sonia wrote—*Today I mailed you a parcel containing medicines. I don't know exactly what you need over there in Palestine, so I've sent salts of silver and bronze nitrates for trachoma, aspirin for fever, ether and chloroform for anesthesia (mostly used by dentists for extractions, but surgeons and midwives use it too; in America it has become very fashionable since Queen Victoria gave birth to Prince Leopold under anesthesia), quinine for malaria, syringes and listening-tubes. Write to us and tell us what else you need. I tried to get you the agency for 'Park Davis' of Detroit, one of the biggest pharmaceutical manufacturers, but they said the market in your part of the world is too small and there could be problems with transport and distribution. After a lot of correspondence back and forth we've been appointed the company's representatives in Woodbine, and we can supply you with whatever you order from us. So you see, thanks to you we've started a business that has a future. When you start trading at a profit—you can pay us back, but don't worry about it too much. Incidentally, you'll also find five kerosene lamps in the parcel. Here, more and more people are using electric light and the price of lamps has fallen. We bought everything in partnership, Lili and I.*
>
> *A month ago Lili left us, along with Kalman Leib and their children, and they moved to Boston, in the east on the Atlantic coast. You know Lili, she's already found "friends of heart*

and spirit" there, some Lithuanian family, name of Wolworinsky, whose son is the same age as their Yankele. Incidentally, they're calling him Jack now. I've had two letters from them already, full of big plans but not a word about anything practical. I'm worried about her. She's turned against the pioneering principle— "Life is the objective!" she says—as if our life isn't life, perish the thought! True, we're not bathing in milk, but we're not hungry for bread either. We were given the land free of charge and we have the support of the J.A.S. *and the* A.I.U. *They distributed sewing machines to the women, and now we too are helping to finance the family. It's true some settlements have already disintegrated, like Sicily Island in the state of Louisiana and settlements in Kansas and New Jersey. But we are holding on. My dear Fanichka! I'm writing these things to avoid writing about what's really distressing me. A few days ago we had a visit from Lipa Yudlevich, the butcher, Sila's brother, our neighbor in Elizavetgrad. He told us what happened to you and what happened to Lulik. For days I've been unable to stop myself crying. I don't sleep at night, and during the day I'm choked by my tears. Your sweet face is before my eyes all the time. I so, so want to kiss your soft, fragrant cheeks, to comfort you and compensate you for all that you have suffered, my sweet. You're just a child after all—my daughter Mina is only three years younger than you! Would your husband agree to immigrate to America? There are Jewish agricultural settlements here too, and we can send you the necessary documents. How happy I would be if we could live together again! There's no denying the work is hard here, but everyone who works—eats. And I understand that in Palestine, too, life is far from easy. Please think about this, my dear.*

With us, all is well, thank God. Haimka will be Bar Mitzvah in six weeks from now and he's learning his Haphtarah. He has the voice of a nightingale. Evidently he has inherited the musical talent of the Mandelstams, because my Yosef has the musical ear of a block of wood. Our unlucky father was destined not to see it. All our joys are mingled with heartache: that's the kind of people we are. I've had a few back problems and the kids had to

> *run the household for a few days, but I'm better now, thank God, and the old mule is pulling the cart again. How is Uncle Shura? What's he doing? In his last letter he told us he was going to get work on a Hebrew newspaper. He also told us your husband's a widower from the Sephardi community and he has two children of his own. Have you gotten used to their ways? How are you coping with this burden? Are you getting any regular help with the housework? You shouldn't have any qualms about dismissing unsatisfactory staff while you're waiting for someone really good to come along. That's the way I do things. I'm enclosing the recipe for Mother's strudel and Lili has promised to send you the recipe for raisin cake. Wishing you every success! Write me a long letter and don't hide anything, from me, from your loving sister,*
>
> *Sonia*

By the time she finished reading the letter her face was already awash with tears. In vain she tried to stop them, but they were positively streaming from her eyes. Clearly, one word of compassion and love was enough to break her heart. She wept in isolation, choked by self-pity, croaking, her nose streaming and her eyes swelling, unable to stop. Allegra brewed her a cup of tea with banana, and she tried to take sips from it between one sob and the next. She was so engrossed in her weeping, so crushed by sorrow, she was no longer abashed in front of this strange woman. She knew Allegra had no sympathy for her, and was almost glad that the floodgates had opened here, here specifically. She could not have endured a gesture of solidarity.

Amram, son of Allegra and Musa, came home and was surprised to see a stranger weeping at their table.

"This is Fania," Allegra explained, "Yehiel's wife".

"What's the matter with her?"

"She's had a letter. From America."

Allegra's explanation brought a sudden smile to Fania's lips, and she wiped the tears from her eyes and hair and throat and apologized profusely. Allegra set the table, and after eating more of the black lentil soup, thick as porridge, which she remembered from her previous visit, Fania felt her strength returning to her. If only she could put aside some of this soup for Moshe and for Bella, the foolish thought occurred to her. She refused to touch any of the other foodstuffs that Allegra offered her, and not wanting to embarrass the other diners she went to the next-door room, Amram's room. She lay on the couch listening to the clatter of cutlery on plates and thinking of the little children in Rosh Pinnah, weak with hunger… Mother's strudel! God!

Fania hugged Tamara, pressed the little body to her heart. Tamara opened her mouth wide, like a chick. Poor baby! Sonia hadn't mentioned her name, hadn't said a single word about her, as if she had never come into this world. As if the very mention of her name was enough to contaminate. Even without the stain of her conception, a hard life was in store for her. This land wasn't going to coddle her. Yehiel gave her the most precious gift he could give: a surname. Now this too had been taken from her. He never asked about Tamara's father, never demanded of Fania anything that she didn't give voluntarily. He could have insisted on her sharing his bed and could have thrown her out for failing to comply. How, really, was he interpreting her actions to himself? Again and again she tried to dismiss Yehiel from her thoughts, and without success. His image hovered all the time before her eyes, popping up and disappearing and popping up again. She thought about him constantly, trying to understand him, his thoughts, his heart. Because he spoke very little, his actions spoke for him. Now, having torn herself away from him, she gave some consideration to the fact that he had allowed her, from the first moment of their marriage, to lead her life as he chose. He never said "Do this!" or "I told you to do that!" and was she not, all of her, just a young and battered sprig, struggling to be accepted in new soil…

Next day she went out with Amram to see if the package had arrived from America. How happy she was, finding her name on the wooden crate! If she dared she'd have retraced her steps immediately and gone back to Rosh Pinnah to give food to the little children. She had to remind herself she was heading south, toward Jaffa, and not north, toward Rosh Pinnah. Yehiel was there, and she wasn't going back to him! She was like the rope of rags that she made for the children. One end was being pulled toward Yehiel and the children, and the other end stretched in the opposite direction. And she was in the middle, being torn to pieces…Amid the melee of voices in the square by the mosque, suddenly a familiar voice was heard, hoarse and full of vitality, and utterly unmistakable.

"Imber!"

For a moment he stared in astonishment at the tall red-haired peasant woman, and then he recognized her and embraced her warmly, kissing both her cheeks.

"Fania Silas!" he introduced her proudly to an elegant man whose pale face revealed he was a newcomer to the country. His immaculate attire set him apart from the throng—all gowns and sashes—and even his shoes had miraculously retained their shine, despite the dust and dirt.

"She's one of the colonists from Jaoni, near Safed. Did you ever meet a peasant woman who plays mazurkas by Chopin?" he asked the foreigner, his eyes sparkling.

"I played the Impromptu! I remember it better than you do!… This is the poet Naphtali Hertz Imber, secretary to Sir Laurence Oliphant," she explained to Amram, who was standing beside her, in a state of shock. She knew he had never before seen a man and a woman kissing in public. "And this is Amram Adis."

"Where have you come from, Fania, and which way are you heading?"

"What about you, Imber? Which way are you heading? And how is Sir Laurence? And his good lady? New settlers have come to join us in Jaoni, did you know? Thirty families from Romania! And the place has changed its name to 'Rosh Pinnah', did you know?"

"Yes, yes, some of them are here in Haifa," Imber laughed on hearing the fusillade of questions. "Sir Laurence intends to visit Rosh Pinnah next week, and he told me he's looking forward to meeting the Queen of the Land of Naphtali there. That's my pet-name for Fania," he explained to the foreigner. "Is it hot where you are?"

"Very. Do you know where the people from Galatzi are staying? I have a message for one of the families."

Fania spoke quickly, afraid of bursting into tears again. How can she hide from him the fact that she's left Rosh Pinnah? And he's so proud of her!

"Yes, certainly. They're staying in the 'Odessa' hostel, in Ard el-Yahud, near the Alliance school. Come with us, we're going that way. This is Signor Veneziani, representing Baron Hirsch and the A.I.U., and envoy of Baron Rothschild in Paris. He brings them good news. The Baron has agreed to support Zamarin."

"Have they settled in the place yet?"

"No. The men work there all week, and for the Sabbath they join their families in Haifa."

"Have you visited Zamarin yet, Sir?" she asked Veneziani.

"I've just come from Jerusalem."

"We met the Bilu people there!" Imber enthused.

"Who are these Bilu people? Where are they living?" Amram asked.

"Thirteen of them live in Rishon le-Zion and work land they leased from Levontin," explained Signor Veneziani, "seven work in Mikveh Israel. They earn a franc and a half per day and live in a rented hut in one of the orchards. Three are in Jerusalem learning trades, and they are the ones I met just now; three are still based in Constantinople, although I hear that two of them are planning to come to the country soon. One of the Biluists went on a mission to Europe and another is convalescing after illness in Tiberias. That is all the Biluists."

There was a disdainful note in the words of Signor Veneziani, and Fania wondered how anyone could open his heart to this man, with the cool aloofness encasing him like armor. He was polite and detached, and she felt ashamed of the peasant clothing she was wearing, and fear gnawed at her heart for Yehiel and the children and all her brothers in Rosh Pinnah. As if trying to shake him off she asked Imber:

"Schumacker the engineer, how is he?"

"Not well! He hasn't succeeded in raising the money for his railway." Imber stood up from the heap of letters and cried: "The miracle has happened and I've found my mail! And now we're going to visit the Romanians. Would you like to join us?"

"I'm coming too," Amram was quick to say, and Fania laughed awkwardly. His stiffness was such a contrast to Imber's overflowing emotional warmth.

"Are you related to Yehiel Silas?" Imber asked him with the hint of a smile in his eyes.

"Yes. Second cousin."

"So I thought."

The "Odessa" hostel stood in the center of the city in a new enclave built by "The Muscovite Émigrés". The latter set themselves the objective of working for the advancement of their brethren from the eastern communities. The construction of the new enclave and the opening of the "Alliance Israelite Universelle" school in 1881 did indeed improve their living conditions, but the more affluent of the Jews—Sephardis and Ashkenazis alike—continued to live in the German Colony or in the western quarter, and ignored the plight of their impoverished brethren.

In three big rooms in the hostel some fifty women and children were crammed, most of them sprawled on mats spread on the floor, feverish and hungry. Veneziani's news stirred up a wave of worrying elation among the wretched woman—as if salvation was just around the corner! If their hopes are dashed, Fania reflected, the disappointment will be more than they can bear. She asked where she could find Helen Leah's sister. In the corner a woman of about twenty-two years old was stretched out, trembling with fever, her face yellow and her teeth chattering. Fania knelt beside her and told her about her relatives in Rosh Pinnah. The woman moved her head rhythmically from side to side, opening and closing her eyes, racked by violent convulsions, sinking and drifting.

"What does the doctor say?" Fania asked a woman who was sitting nearby.

"He prescribed quinine. He prescribes quinine for all the invalids."

"And did it help?"

"We have no quinine."

Fania opened her box, and with trembling hands took out a

cardboard box full of quinine tablets. With the help of the neighbor she fed tablets to the invalid, and then gave the woman a small stash of tablets to distribute among the other sufferers. She felt giddy for want of fresh air and at the sight of the sister's face, yellow as curdled milk. Every way she turned groaning women were stretched out on the floor, drenched in sweat, helpless. Someone was praying in the next room. Fania remembered the "Song of Degrees" and the tears of joy of the settlers in Rosh Pinnah. Her heart melted with compassion for the suffering children, who were the victims of a dream and its frustration. How much hope did it take, wandering like this to the ends of the earth, to open up new channnels for a new people… Just now it all seemed crazy! Crazy! Crazy!

"Let's get out of here," said Amram. He closed the box and tied it with string, as if afraid Fania was going to distribute everything in it to the residents of the hostel.

"And they still say we're a wise people!"—Imber's animated voice was heard from the next room.

"We're a people that want to live!" she heard Veneziani's reply. "And this is the basic right of all human beings, isn't it?"

"Yes, of course. But you know as well as I do how inefficiently we're managing our resources. Look at these women! Multiply this picture and you'll get the twelve thousand refugees in Brody. Twelve thousand! After the second thousand they should have taken refuge somewhere else. But no! They all had to go to Brody!—I was there too!"

"Three thousand we've already sent back to Russia."

"And what about the rest?"

"Eight thousand we distributed among the communities of Europe, and the remaining thousand are waiting until their relatives in America have put down roots in their new homeland and then they'll go and join them. Anyway, by January this year there'll be none of them left in Brody."

We sent back…We distributed…spoken like a true Chlestakov! In her father's house the name of Gogol's character was applied to any pompous bureaucrat. She signaled to Amram and together they slipped out into the street. Once outside she took a deep breath, but the hot and humid air brought her no relief. Oh, for the clear and cold air of her homeland! The avenue of tall birches in her street, the grove of beeches visible through the kitchen window, the squirrels in the conifers on the hill…in vain her eyes searched for a patch of green, in vain her heart longed for the fragrant darkness between the pines…If she were a poet she would surely have found a way of evoking the humiliation inherent in her new homeland, describing the blight that makes a mockery of the dreams of salvation. Well, for a moment fate was kind to her, when the case of medicines from her sister arrived, and then a moment later she had to hand over a sizable batch of quinine free of charge—the quinine that meant food for her children!—to these strangers. She was angry that she had been forced into this position, and at the same time she knew she couldn't have done any different. If she had insisted on her rights, they wouldn't have been able to pay for the medicines. As for Veneziani, she'd rather die of starvation than ask him for a subsidy. She consoled herself with the thought that Yehiel would have done the same. Ouch! Yehiel again!

"Where to?" asked Amram.

He had a big, pudgy face and red hair, the hair of the Adis family which also adorned the heads of Moshe and Bella. His legs were thin and it was as if they hadn't been designed for his stout body, the body inherited from his mother.

"I want to check when the German coach leaves for Jaffa."

"I'll make sure of reserving you a place on one of them. They're completely reliable, the German coaches."

"Thank-you, Amram."

"Whereabouts in Jaffa are you going?"

"I'll be staying with my uncle, Shura Alexander Mandelstam."

"A newcomer?"

"We arrived together about a year ago."

She was afraid he would go on to ask about the others: about her daughter, about her brother, about Yehiel. But Amram didn't ask any more questions. She couldn't help but be aware that since the morning he had been by her side, carrying her burden and putting himself out for her, simply and without affectation, as if he was just doing his job. He's a good boy, she thought. True, he doesn't smile and he isn't one for friendly conversation, but his actions speak to his credit. Yehiel is like that too: he gives his life for an idea that he believes in, but says very little about it. There we go, Yehiel again! She will have to wean herself off him if she really wants to erase him from her life.

Chapter seven

In a booming voice the town crier announced that a child had gone missing. Fania's heart skipped a beat. Only two months had passed since she arrived in Jaffa, but the Arabic spoken by the residents was no longer alien to her ears.

She stepped carefully between the puddles, trying hard to avoid the mud. The rain that fell in Jaffa ten days before had left behind it channels of black, stagnant water, which turned to a repellent sludge. The people here were accustomed to throwing everything into the street, from bodily fluids and laundry water to scraps of food. The *kawwas* threatened them in vain with punishments and fines. For a few days they would practice hygiene and then revert to their former ways.

Fania wondered if in Rosh Pinnah, too, there were puddles now, and soggy ground and slippery mud, or perhaps the water had drained into the springs, to be discharged on the hillsides…Had the plowing started, and was there enough livestock, and when would sowing begin… She remembered the excitement that enveloped her when she heard the sound of the first raindrops falling on the roof of the house. In the middle of the night she woke to the sound of a tap, and then another, and these grew in volume and intensity and finally became a glorious orchestra of torrential rain, which didn't stop until morning and continued most of the following day. For a moment she was in Rosh Pinnah again, laughing, rejoicing, bathing in the water as it streamed from the buckets of the Heavens.

She held up the hem of her skirt and quickened her pace. Since coming to Jaffa she had taken off the Bedouin attire and reverted to her "European" dress. The vast majority of the Jews of Jaffa, some two hundred families in all, came from the Mediterranean basin, a minority from North Africa, plus a handful of Europeans, but they all dressed like Arabs and even the language they spoke was Arabic. But Fania felt the time of the Bedouin clothes was over. Wearing them, it was as if the bourgeois girl from Russia was announcing her acceptance of an oriental code; now she no longer needed this "flag". She laundered them and stowed them away in the trunk. She doubted she would ever wear them again.

Bella Rokeah tried once or twice to encourage her to talk, to understand the nature of the change that had come over her, but Fania avoided giving answers. Yehiel's aunt treated her as a true relative and even suggested she should move in with her, she and Tamara too, but Fania was afraid of getting too close to anything involving Yehiel. In the early days she walked around with dulled senses, and all the time the image of Yehiel was before her eyes. Her heart was soured by grief and envy every time she remembered the spectacle of the man setting out for Damascus with Rivka at his side, the bonnet on her head and the locks of her hair entwining on her back like two black snakes.

Through the good offices of Bella Rokeah she succeeded in selling two of the lamps at a good price to the merchant Señor Azriel Levi. He wanted to buy the medicines too, but she decided to hold on to them for the moment. The money she earned enabled her to live in her uncle's house without being a burden to him. Since their ways parted, the uncle had managed to settle down among the Jews of Jaffa. Bella Rokeah had taken a shine to him and Fania sensed a friendship developing between them. Tamara had put on weight since they returned to Jaffa and her cheeks were rosy. Fania often remembered Moshe and Bella, with a sudden pang of sorrow. She once thought of suggesting that Bella Rokeah invite the children to Jaffa, but she was afraid Yehiel would realize whose idea it was. She never stopped thinking about him. The profile of a tall man passing by at the corner of the street reminded her of him, the color of his jacket, the sound of his voice at prayer.

Even the nights brought her no relief, because then he came to her unrestrained and the pain of waking was almost too much to bear. I'm in love with him! she realized to her amazement. To put thoughts of him out of her mind, she kept herself busy from morning till night. Her uncle's room, in a house near the fish market, she cleaned and polished until not a speck of dust was left. Then she started doing the rounds of the chemists and the tradesmen, looking for ways of making a living. One day, in Bella Rokeah's house, she met Aharon Schloss the money changer, who advised her to delay selling the rest of the lamps until the end of Elul, when the Bedouin would be coming up from the Negev with their pockets full of the money they had earned from the sale of their produce. Fania used to love standing in Aharon Schloss's shop. At first sight this was nothing more than an empty room where nothing happened, but over time it became clear to her that the leisurely, almost sleepy conversations concealed in typical oriental style a lively trading enterprise. Even though she was a woman and dressed in European style, Mr. Schloss gave her all the help she needed. From him she learned the value of the coins, when was the best time to buy, and which ones were worth more melted down. She used to go down to the port to meet the tourists and change their European currency for Ottoman currency, or visit the produce market and change the Bedouin's thalers and pounds for Turkish gold sultans or silver rials. Her business activities were anathema to her uncle. "They smell of exile," he complained, wrinkling his nose.

"We have to eat," she replied.

And to herself she thought: as if his involvement in public affairs doesn't smell of exile! She avoided arguing with him. She had spoken little since she returned to Jaffa, and now, with tight-lipped obstinacy, she worked to support her little family. The Mograbis and the Aleppans were already used to the sight of the "Muscovite" girl coming and going among the money-changing booths or negotiating with the Bedouin at the gates of the city. The only place where she could relax a little was Bella Rokeah's house. In the afternoons the ladies of the small community used to come visiting, and Fania felt comfortable among the dignified, pale-faced Jewish matrons. They would sit on embroidered cushions while the maid came in slowly, bearing a big silver tray with little coffee cups, sweets and fruit. The fully-fleshed women, sensitive and sedate, were very pleasant toward her, as she sat quietly in her corner and listened to their conversation. Here she met the wife of Reuben Robert Blattner, the Danish consul, Esther Amzaleg, wife of Haim Amzaleg, British consul in Jaffa, the daughters of Yosef Bey Moyal, the Persian consul. The ladies of the community peered at her as though she were a strange bird, wondering at this young girl, living in a weird kind of triangle with her baby daughter and her uncle, who, as everyone knew, had caught the fancy of Bella Rokeah. At this time Ashkenazi immigrants from European countries were already arriving in Jaffa, but these were young bachelors for whom the Land of Israel was a kind of crossroads between riots and salvation. Usually they only passed through Jaffa and carried on to Jerusalem or to the recently established agricultural settlements. If fortune smiled on one of these young men, he would summon from his distant homeland his mother or his sister or his betrothed. And here's this Fania, all in all a girl barely in the first bloom of youth, and she has done everything that these youngsters have done, the ones that Imber calls "pioneers", but unlike them she's not looking for salvation through working on the land. Sometimes the women would try to help her: Hannah Luria for example, daughter of Avraham Schloss, who held her in special affection. "We have something in common," she smiled at Fania. "We're both married to natives of Safed, and in both families there's a mixture of Sephardis and Ashkenazis, even though your Yehiel isn't pure Sephardi." One day Hannah Luria escorted her to the little shop belonging to her husband, who was known by the nickname of "the French silversmith". Fania handed over to him the small change given her by the Bedouin, and Alter Luria made it into a nice necklace which she sold at a profit to her neighbor Faida. In the wake of Faida, a bride appeared and after her a pregnant wife, and even a negroid prostitute. And Fania was running back and forth hunting for little coins that could be beaten into jewelry, and at the gate of the city there was sometimes someone clutching her sleeve or calling after her "Saida Fania!", then opening before her eyes a fistful of shiny coins for sale or exchange.

On several occasions, when the ladies had gone away to their homes, Fania would take her seat at the piano and play, while Bella relaxed in her armchair and listened. The sun blazed through the stained glass of the windows and their shapes were projected onto the pink marble floor. When the sun began to set, the aunt moved in her armchair and reminded her she must go home before darkness fell.

"How nice it would be if you came to live with me," Bella said to Fania one day. "The house is big and empty. Five children we raised here, my late husband and I..."

"Thank-you, thank-you but no. My uncle needs me."

"Your uncle doesn't need anyone," Bella laughed, a laugh tinged with a hint of bitterness. "The destiny and future of the Jewish people rests on his shoulders, God preserve us!"

"And what's wrong with that?" Fania laughed.

"I'm afraid of saints. They're fanatics."

"Uncle Shura isn't a fanatic! He isn't a saint either."

"Ah, that's because he's an armchair general. He sends others out to the battlefield. Where is he these days? Where's he disappeared to?"

"He's sitting up day and night with Berliavsky. They're writing the manifesto of the Bilu movement."

"You see? I was right! Anyway, I'm glad he isn't perfect."

That's true! Fania reflected. He was so proud when I went away to Jaoni, but he preferred to stay behind in Jaffa, putting the revivalist dreams of others down on paper, in words of fire.

"He's too old."

"Your uncle?" Bella Rokeah laughed. "He isn't old! And you don't need to defend him to me; I'm very fond of him. And as for you!"—she suddenly went on the offensive: "How long are you going to torment yourself over Yehiel? No! You're not wriggling out of this one!" she cried, when Fania stood up to leave. "You're in love with him! Every movement of yours, every look, speaks of the travails of love. Don't try to deny it! There's not a lot of love around, whatever the poets say. Not everyone gets to enjoy it, and there's nothing easier than being hurt by it. There aren't many boys like Yehiel, Fania. He broke the hearts of all the maidens of Jaffa when he was staying with me last year. He's as handsome as a prince and as wise as King Solomon, decent…and stubborn! One of you is going to have to bend, Fania."

"I don't want him."

"Why? You know you're in love with him!"

"What makes you think I'm in love with him?"

"There's no escaping it. Love is reflected in every move you make, and in those big sparkling eyes of yours! If I were a man you'd break my heart. You have no idea how beautiful you are, Fania. Don't you like living in Jaoni? Is that the problem?"

"No, I want to work. Even clearing stones was a job I loved. I thought every scar on my hands hastened the coming of the Messiah." She laughed suddenly, surprised at herself. "I wish he'd send the children here. They're going hungry there. Some days there's no food in the house, nothing at all!"

"I wrote to him and suggested he send the children to me. This was before the rains came. And his answer was, 'wherever I am, my family is too' or something like that, full of masculine pride. I don't understand you people!" she went on, suddenly angry. "All the girls in Jaffa would follow him to the ends of the earth, and he didn't want any of them until he found you and decided you were for him. He married you in a hurry and whisked you away from here so no one else would discover his treasure. What happened?"

"There's…another…woman."

"Yehiel has another woman?! I don't believe it! No! I don't believe it!"

Bella Rokeah was so shocked, Fania regretted the words she had spoken. But what was done couldn't be undone.

"Please, let's leave it. It's late, and the sun's going down." Fania bent down and kissed Bella on the cheek, hurrying to take her leave.

She went down the steep steps, her shoes resounding on the gilded stones. On the high, cool ceiling, was the reflection of the waves of the sea, shot with golden rays.

The conversation with Bella Rokeah unsettled her. Bella's feelings were apparently conditioned to no small extent by the absences of Uncle Shura. If he had returned her affection, she wouldn't have been bothering Fania with loud proclamations about love. Fania already knew that her love for Yehiel would remain an incurable wound, but she hoped that over time the wound would heal and she could learn to live with the scars. Now she was glad she had a little girl, a living creature needing her attention. Sometimes it seemed it was Tamara looking after her mother. On her account she got out of bed in the morning, on her account she cooked meals, and on her account she set about earning a living as a currency broker.

Sometimes rumors about Jaoni filtered through to her. In the Haim Schmerling synagogue her uncle heard that an Arab had been killed there, when the first Jewish wedding was celebrated in the place. All the local residents had participated in the festivities, and when "joy-shots" were fired in the air, an Arab laborer was killed by a stray bullet from the pistol of one of the Jewish settlers. The Arabs pelted the revelers with stones and the festivities gave way to lamentation. All the money remaining in the hands of the settlers was squandered in the judicial process. They were obliged to pay the wages of the Turkish soldiers guarding the settlement, in addition to compensating the family of the deceased, and were finally left penniless. Someone said he had read in *Hamaggid* that an international fund had been launched with the aim of rescuing Rosh Pinnah from its plight. "Has the rain fallen there too?" Fania asked her uncle, but he didn't have an answer to this.

From the harbor, down below, came the voices of the porters. Two barefooted youths were urging on an emaciated horse with loud cries, and they almost collided with Fania as she passed under the sturdy stone arch. For some reason she had felt no fear since coming to Jaffa. The commotion was endless and the noise deafening, but this was the vibrant voice of ignorance and not the cold voice of malice. All the same, she never left her home without the revolver tucked into the folds of her clothing. As a Jewess taught by experience, she had concluded a permanent contract with doubt.

She went into the little courtyard and arrived at Faida's apartment, to collect Tamara from her. The baby greeted her happily and Fania held both her little hands and led her along step after step, counting "one-two, one-two…"

Her small apartment was cloaked in darkness. A faint light from outside turned the window into a milky screen. Fania picked Tamara up and stopped suddenly. On a chair, near the window, sat Yehiel.

"Hello Fania."

"Hello."

The panic clearly reflected in her voice raised the ghost of a bitter smile to his lips. Fania felt uncomfortable, as if she had been caught invading his space.

"How long have you been here?"

"About an hour. I came by boat."

"From Haifa?"

"Yes. Twenty-five hours we were at sea."

Yehiel bent down and picked Tamara up and sat her on his knees.

"Hello sweetheart!" he smiled at the baby.

"*We* were at sea?" Fania whispered. Has he dared to come here with *her*?"You and…the children?"

"No, I and the other passengers."

"How are the children?"

"Bella has been ill."

"Oh! What was the problem?"

"Stomach infection."

"My poor darling! And how is she now? Is she better?"

"Yes."

"And who…where is she?"

"In Safed, with Leah. Moshe's there too."

In the turmoil of her mind, Fania was glad of the semi-darkness in the room, hiding her face. If only she could hide the emotion in her voice as well. Feelings of guilt overpowered her. Perhaps, if she had stayed in Rosh Pinnah, she could have prevented Bella's illness. In her imagination she saw Leah's face, lips set grimly and a censorious look in her eyes, and her heart ached for the little children.

"Did you succeed in your mission?"

It seemed to Fania that for a moment a spasm of pain passed over Yehiel's face, but when she took a closer look at him, again that dismissive smile was on his lips.

"In Damascus? Yes, we succeeded." Yehiel suddenly began to laugh quietly. "Moshe David Shub explained to the Wali that all the settlers in Rosh Pinnah are émigrés from Romania, which used to be ruled by the Ottomans, and now it is their fervent wish to take refuge once again under the benign protection of the government of His Majesty the Sultan…The Wali was persuaded by Yakov Adis to forward the request to the 'Sublime Porte' in Constantinople. For six weeks we were stuck in Damascus waiting for the permit to come through."

Six weeks! Fania's heart missed a beat when she heard they had spent six weeks together in Damascus.

"Was Adis friendly?"

"Friendly? He was reliable as an intermediary…Outwardly he resembles Musa Adis, has the same ruddy complexion. He and Moshe David Shub have found a common language. Rabbi Moshe David speaks Jewish Hebrew and Rabbi Yakov speaks Damascus Hebrew, but they managed to understand each other. Adis convinced the Wali that the "Musawi" peasants of Jaoni near Safed are industrious farmers, and thanks to them Galilee will bloom and the Sultan's revenues will be swelled. For the time being we can levy labor tax for the stones we've cleared. After our return to Rosh Pinnah, the governor of Safed turned up there and informed the residents that the concession had indeed been issued. He suggested to them—bearing in mind their love of all things Turkish—that they become Ottomans. All the inhabitants of Rosh Pinnah became Turkish subjects overnight. This document and the goodwill of the governor cost us a load of money."

"Have you stopped building?"

"No. We are building, but not the way we planned it at first. Two small rooms and a cowshed. That's all."

"And you? Are you building too?"

"No, I already have a roof over my head. Just now there are five young lads billeted with me."

"Five!"

"Men with families go back to Safed in the evening. But these are bachelors."

"And Moshe and Bella?"

"They're enjoying having guests. These men miss their families and in the meantime they're spoiling Moshe and Bella."

"And Lulik?"

"We hardly see him. Riva insists that we're all mad and he's just a little bit more so. She's feeding him, don't worry."

"Helen Leah promised to look after him."

"She sends her regards."

"Yes? And how is she? I visited her sister in Haifa. Have the women and children moved into Zamarin yet?"

Yehiel hesitated. He put Tamara down from his lap, and rose to his feet as if to move towards her.

"There's been a tragedy in her family."

"What?!!"

"Her sister."

"Dead?!"

Rage blinded Fania. She remembered the feverish woman, sprawled like a rag doll on the mat in the Odessa hostel in Haifa. It seemed to her the most hurtful thing was the lack of dignity in the death. A dream and its dissolution! And it was to safeguard their lives that they came here! And what is it, this Zamarin, the altar on which she was sacrificed? A word! Just a name! Letters flying in the air! What an ugly life this is!

"The rain has been falling in Galilee," said Yehiel, in an effort to console her.

"Here in Jaffa too! All night. It fell and fell and fell! And have you plowed?" So the miracle had happened, and she hadn't been there to see it.

"The rain began to fall at the end of Kislev. On the second of Tevet we started plowing."

"How? Tell me how!"

"We all gathered in the field: men, women and children. And we upheld the injunction 'In tears you shall reap', since we were all weeping for joy. All day we sang and wept and preached and exchanged blessings. Rabbi Moshe David preached a sermon taking as his text the Song of Degrees, *When the Lord turned again the captivity of Zion*. And when we returned from the field we put up tables in the middle of the settlement and all sat down together to eat, and there was more singing and more benedictions. It was decided that henceforward the second of Tevet will always be celebrated as the foundation day of the settlement."

"But it was founded long before then! When was Gai Oni established?"

"In Tammuz 5646, 1878, but we're talking about Rosh Pinnah… The same day a wedding was celebrated…" Yehiel broke off suddenly and his face turned grey.

"Yes, I know. What became of the boy who fired the shot?"

"Still in limbo. We wanted to plant vines and limes and apples and lemons and five hundred olive trees…After we paid compensation to the family of the deceased, the settlement was fourteen thousand francs in debt!"

"*We* paid! You too?"

Yehiel shrugged and said:

"The word is that in Paris, Baron Rothschild is planning to take Rosh Pinnah under his wing."

"Yes, I met Chlestakov…" mumbled Fania.

"Who?"

"Signor Veneziani, the Baron's representative. Are you happy about it?"

"No, I'm not happy about it. I'd rather not take refuge in the shadow of any philanthropist." Fania smiled in the darkness. She guessed this would be his response.

"Do you know who led the defenders of the village? Samir Alhija, our neighbor. And our friends among the local peasantry ran and appealed for help to the Zangariya Bedouin, and they protected us bodily from the attackers until the police arrived. There were at least two hundred rioters, armed with sticks and stones and accompanied by women and children, wailing and yelling at the tops of their voices."

"God!"

Her spirit was so troubled she was quite unaware of him approaching her, and she caught her breath when she suddenly felt his strong, sinewy hands on her body. He turned her to face him, parting her hair and leaning toward her, pressing her gently against his body. His face was close to hers, and she heard his rapid breathing before his lips sought out hers. He didn't relax his hold until she submitted to him, and then, after the first shock, she hugged his body and began to shake, as waves of shame and longing coursed through her unchecked. Their bodies spoke a language of their own, saying the things that their mouths refused to say. His fingers traced a furrow along the nape of her neck, through the heavy locks of bronze-colored hair, while his mouth was drawn insistently to her throat, before kissing her eyes and caressing her silky, blazing skin, transmitting to her body spasmodic shudders that she could not control. Her head was empty of all thought and the whole of her being was condensed into one desire: to sweep away all the barriers, all the masks, and be as one with him.

Voices were heard from outside. The door opened and there on the threshold were Uncle Shura and Yakov Berliavsky. They were so engrossed in their conversation they didn't notice the two young people in the room. Suddenly the uncle broke off, looked around him and cried: "Yehiel! What's this, Fania, why are you in the dark?"

Fania was glad of the excuse to keep herself busy, lighting the lamp. She felt her legs buckling beneath her and feared she might fall off the chair when she climbed on it to reach the lamp.

"See here!" cried the uncle as if he had found something really special. "Open your eyes and take a look at this man: He got there before you! He's a Hebrew farmer, from Galilee! He and his friends are all yeshiva boys from Safed and they settled in the Arab village of Jaoni. They're cultivating the land alongside the local peasantry and living a communal life. They've never heard of Tolstoy or Robert Owen, or even Peretz Smolenskin. Isn't that right, Yehiel?"

Yehiel smiled a non-committal smile and didn't answer.

"You could join them, Uncle Shura."

"At my age! Oh, if I was forty years younger I'd definitely be joining them...This is Fania's husband," he added.

"Where is this Jaoni?" the guest asked.

"Near Safed. And the settlement has a new name: Rosh Pinnah, the cornerstone."

"I protest!" said the uncle.

"The Gai Oni that the Romanians rejected has become Rosh Pinnah," Yehiel quipped. He smiled and the light of the lamp flickered on his gleaming teeth.

"Jews! First of all they worry about a name!" the uncle puffed out his cheeks. "Even the Bilu group was called Dabru at first—*Speak to the People of Israel and they will be moved.* Then they decided to drop the 'Speak' and put the emphasis on the movement, and they came up with Bilu—*House of Jacob come let us go*. We should act first and talk afterwards. Don't you agree?"

"Yes," the guest confirmed.

"Well, has it rained?" the uncle asked. "Fania was very worried."

"It has rained."

There was something strange about the tone of Yehiel's reply, and the uncle peered at him suspiciously.

"Have you plowed?"

"Yes."

"Sown?"

"No."

"Why not?"

"No money...Where are you from?" Yehiel turned to Berliavsky.

"From Kharkov," the uncle was quick to answer on his behalf. "That's the cradle of the movement, in Kharkov. He used to be a veterinarian..."

"A student."

"Uncle Shura is helping Berliavsky compose the manifesto of the Bilu movement," Fania explained to Yehiel with a smile.

"Do I detect a note of scorn in your voice, young lady?" the uncle asked. "Well, even before you were born I already had a lot of experience of composing manifestos. I helped to draft the manifesto of the 'Society for the Propagation of Enlightenment' back in 1863, and to my everlasting shame I also participated in producing the manifesto of Narodnaya Volia in 1879, after I had come to the gloomy conclusion that Enlightenment was not going to blur the distinctions between Russians and Jews. I'm an experienced jurist and I can still be useful, even if you think I'm over the hill."

Yehiel listened patiently, as if he were the older man and her uncle the impetuous youth. From time to time he shot curious glances toward Berliavsky. Fania felt that deep down he related to her uncle with tolerant scorn, and she remembered Bella Rokeah's comment: her uncle was nothing more than an armchair general…Yehiel obviously hadn't eaten properly for many hours and she remembered the "perpetual" hunger that she used to feel there. She spread a cloth on the table and served up cups of tea and fresh pitas, along with a slab of cheese and some dates.

"Are you from Rishon le-Zion?" Yehiel asked.

"Yes."

"How many of you are there?"

"On paper?—sixteen. In fact—thirteen."

"We started out with seventeen families…Out of the original group of pioneers from Safed, just two families are left, finally."

"Seven of our number are still working in Mikveh Israel. We're trying to transfer them to Rishon le-Zion as well."

"The boys want to move to Rishon le-Zion?"

"That's what some of them want. But the farmers of Rishon le-Zion won't be welcoming them with open arms. They claim we're apostates and we don't keep the commandments."

"That's what the people of Safed claimed when we settled in Jaoni. They were afraid the Jews of the Diaspora would realize it's possible to live in the Land of Israel without depending on charity."

"Money! Money! Money!" the uncle exclaimed vehemently.

"That's what bothers the people of Rishon le-Zion! Nothing to do with keeping the commandments! They're afraid of losing out when the Baron's support funds are shared between them and the Biluists."

"You have to succeed, just as we in Rosh Pinnah must succeed."

"Maybe I'll move to Jerusalem."

"You see Jerusalem as preferable to Rishon le-Zion?"

"I don't know. Rishon le-Zion is a temporary solution. It isn't what we planned. We feel we're the vanguard of a big army and I'm not sure Rishon le-Zion is the right flag to be flying…"

"You need to hold on to the land. In Jerusalem the fanatics will eat you alive."

"That's what Eliezer Rokeah says too. All the same, at Pesach I shall go up to Jerusalem. Let's hope that by then the comrades from Constantinople have arrived."

"What are you doing in Rishon le-Zion?" Fania asked,

"Working! We've built roads…dug a well…planted an orchard…"

"And what salary are you receiving?"

"A franc a day."

"Is anyone supporting you?"

Berliavsky's face fell. He hesitated and then said: "We hoped that Signor Veneziani, the Baron's envoy, would offer us help, but Hirsch dashed our hopes…"

"What a people we are! God, what a people!" cried the uncle. "Strife and quarrels and cliques and hatred and jealousy!"

"You have to hold on to the land," Yehiel repeated his mantra stubbornly. "How long have you been in the country?"

"On the nineteenth of Tammuz, a full year."

"We had a nice celebration here in Jaffa," Fania told Yehiel. "Uncle Shura preached."

"You were there too?"

"I was there!" she smiled.

"Would you like to live there, with the Muscovites?" he asked.

"Don't you go asking Fania what she wants!" the uncle

interjected. "She'll ask you for the sky! The moon and the stars! Have you told Yehiel about your business activities? She's a business-woman! And we, the Mandelstams, were so proud that money never sullied our hands!"

"You had food to eat, Uncle Shura."

"Our father, may he rest in peace, owned a sugar factory. He employed sixty workers! We weren't short of money, but in our house money was never discussed. My brother, Fania's father, continued to run the factory after the patriarch died, introducing social conditions such as had never been known in Russia before! From my childhood days I remember a house buzzing with intellectuals, yeshiva students, emissaries. They sent us to general schools so we could enjoy the liberalization inaugurated by Alexander the Second, and we were happy to resemble Russians. Russification was our ideal! I studied after that in the Academy of Law, a privilege that Jews had not enjoyed in previous generations. And I thought there was no difference between me and other citizens of my class. Fania's mother, who was a devout Jewess, knew hundreds of Russian songs by heart. Real Messianic times! We didn't see and didn't want to see the discrimination, the injustice, the incitement. Until nine years ago, in 1873, when *Diary of a Writer* appeared, written by the author I admired most of all: Dostoyevsky! And in this book I read the sentence: 'The Jew-boys will drink the blood of the people, and draw nourishment from the destruction and humiliation of the people.' Dostoyevsky!"

The uncle's voice suddenly rose in a bellow of pain, as if a sword had been plunged into his heart. "This wasn't new. Before that there had been talk of emancipating the Russians from the Jews. But Dostoyevsky?! I wanted to kill myself! Really! I wanted to kill myself! Everything seemed so hopeless! Then, when I calmed down, I decided that we, the Jews, need to prove to the world that we're better than the others. You ask me why we have to be better than the others? Today I say it's the world that has to change and not the Jews. But that's what I thought then. The salary I earned as legal advisor to the railway company I handed over almost intact to the 'Society for the Propagation of Enlightenment among the Jews of Russia'. Have you heard of this society, Yehiel? It was founded twenty years ago by wealthy Jews from St. Petersburg who believed that enlightenment would erode the distinctions between two-and-a-half million Jews and the great family of the great Russian people, and henceforward only fellowship and brotherhood would prevail between them. Ha! Even the revolutionaries of the Narodnaya Volia—which had a dozen Jewish members—soon adopted anti-Semitic viewpoints. This was legal tender! This the people would swallow and this was the way they decided to buy the people's heart. With anti-Semitism!"

His hands shaking with emotion, the uncle started fumbling in a big envelope. He took out a letter and ran a finger over the lines while muttering and reading aloud, until he found the passage he was looking for. "Here it is! My friend and colleague Leib Meirovitz, who was secretary of the 'Society for the Propagation of Enlightenment' sent me a copy of the proclamation issued by the Narodnaya Volia in the Ukraine in September 1881, *five years after* the pogroms erupted! We were already on our way to this country. Have you seen this proclamation?" he asked Berliavsky, who nodded. "Well, the rest of you listen to this! Listen!

> *Who has taken possession of the land, the woods and the taverns? The Jids*—Jids indeed! *Before whom does the serf plead, sometimes in tears, to be allowed access to his plot of land, the inheritance of his fathers? Before the Jids! Everywhere you turn—the Jids are there! The Jid curses and reviles his fellow man, cheats him and drinks his blood*—drinks his blood, you hear that? *It's no longer possible to live in the villages, on account of the Jids…*
> and so on and so on…And finally:
> *Arise then, you upright workers! The landlords have ruled us for long enough and the Jids have oppressed us for long enough, while the police force assaults us and harasses us at every opportunity.*

You understand? The landlords, the police and the Jids. They are the enemies of upright workers? And this was five months *after* the pogroms. It isn't the murderers that they castigate but the murdered. And in all of great Russia not one reasonable man came forward and demanded the blood of these helpless wretches, the pure and innocent ones! It's lucky I'm not in Russia, because I would shoot the man who wrote this article. Shedding the blood of Jews is endorsed both by the authorities and the revolutionaries. A true blood-covenant! It's a fact that among the conspirators of Narodnaya Volia there was also a Jewess, Hessia Helfmann, and for this reason Alexander the Third saw persecution of the Jews as an act of historical justice! My perverse brain, the brain of a Jid, is prepared to understand even this! But Jews provoking pogroms? Jews?! Which Jews?! Cosmopolitans, rectifiers of the world!"

"Anti-Semitism for them is just a means, to bring the revolution forward," said Berliavsky.

"Exactly! They murdered! They raped! They pillaged! From that utter turmoil they expected the horn of salvation to emerge!"

"Enough! Enough! Enough!" cried Fania in a terrible voice, and blocked her ears. The uncle seemed to wake up suddenly and looked at her in bemusement, as if not knowing where she sprang from. Yehiel leapt to his feet and embraced her, and she buried her face in his shoulder.

"Sorry…" the uncle mumbled. "How did I get onto that?" His face reddened and he looked confused and embarrassed. Berliavsky smiled suddenly and said:

"You were talking about Fania's business interests, and from there you somehow moved on to anti-Semitism in Russia."

"Ah! There is a connection! I'm not completely stupid as you seem to think. And you Fanichka, you've nothing to be ashamed of. This young lady is the greatest heroine I've ever had the privilege of meeting in all my life! Why are you crying?"

"I'm not crying."

"Well, let's leave it there, sweetheart. All I meant to say was that we, the Mandelstams, like many others and despite our reputation as Jews, never dealt with money for its own sake."

"He got a medal for that, my father!"

"What are you doing?" Yehiel asked curiously.

"Buying and selling currency. I'm also the deputy agent for an

American drug company, Park Davis, and as well as that...my sisters have sent me another consignment, more lamps."

Yehiel sensed that Fania wasn't keen to talk about her business.

"Where are you staying?" he asked Berliavsky.

"At Anton Iyyub's house. Yes, it's getting late." Berliavsky rose to his feet. "And you?"

"At my aunt's house, near Jaffa Gate."

"You can't go to Anton Iyyub's house in the middle of the night!" the uncle protested. "The house is surrounded by plantations and it's at least two hours from here!. Stay here. We'll put mats out, and there'll be room for all of us.

Berliavsky laughed. "I'm afraid I may be infested with fleas. In Rishon le-Zion we share our accommodation with the two horses, and every night we're battling the bugs."

"Ah, such are the throes of redemption. Go on, stay!" the uncle appealed to him in a conciliatory tone. "You too, Yehiel."

"My aunt will be offended if she hears I visited Jaffa and didn't stay at her house."

"Your aunt will be even more offended if she hears you endangered your life getting to her house. Who wanders around Jaffa in the middle of the night? And where your aunt lives they close the gates immediately after sunset. Fania! Unroll the mats!"

"At once."

Fania removed the eating utensils from the table and went out to fetch water from the well in the yard. What was going to happen now? Obviously Yehiel wanted to leave, and he was staying only because he couldn't resist her uncle's persuasion. It was hard for her to curb her feelings. Her uncle knew, of course, that her relations with Yehiel were strained, and in spite of this he forced him to stay here and sleep in one room with her. What would become of them? Sooner or later they must discuss their future. Is that why he came to Jaffa now? Rivka wants to marry him and he's asking for a divorce? Or perhaps he's decided to live with her here?. No, he'll never leave Rosh Pinnah. From a distance of two months, Rosh Pinnah—Jaoni, as she continued to call it to herself—seemed so remote, all arid rocky cliffs, where life was unbearably hard! Will he ask her to return with him?

"What have you decided?"

Fania woke from her reverie and a flush swamped her cheeks. Yehiel looked at her with that playful half-smile which always made her feel he was mocking her. She had been engrossed in her thoughts, standing and watching him without being aware of it.

"Does she still cry out at night?" he asked her uncle.

"Sometimes. Don't be alarmed," he added, turning to Berliavsky. "Fania has bad dreams and she cries out in the night."

"Where were you at the time of the pogrom?"

"In Elizavetgrad...When did you arrive in the country?" she asked hastily.

"A year ago."

"From Kharkov?"

"No, from Constantinople." It was evident that Berliavsky was still taken aback by Fania's response. She knew he couldn't help but wonder about the coincidence of events between her arrival in the country and the pogroms in her hometown in the spring of 1881. Everyone knew it was there, in her town, that the storm erupted. Nearly two years had passed since that bitter and hectic day, and with all her being she wanted to seal "that" episode in her life. But the wounds refused to heal: from time to time rumors were heard of new troubles affecting scores of thousands of Jews, in Warsaw...in Yalta...

Fania spread the mats on the floor and went into "her" room, which was nothing more than a corner of the communal room, separated from it by a curtain. She lay down beside Tamara who sighed in her sleep, protesting at the disturbance. From behind the curtain the murmured prayers of the three men could be heard. Berliavsky and his big mouth! Her heart pounded like the heart of someone saved by a miracle. In the end the truth would come to light. Someone from her town would arrive and tell the story—the way the truth became known to her sisters. How long could she hide what had happened to her? Better perhaps to reveal all and be freed from this terrible secret. She listened to the whispering of the men. How she longed to remove the buffer-stones between her and Yehiel. How embarrassing is this situation! He is lying beside her and she could stretch out her hand and touch him, and they are like strangers to each other. She needs to conquer her fears and her pride before it's too late to sew up the breach between them. Deep down she felt his heart was still hers. It wasn't for Rivka he came here. Would he have left Rosh Pinnah at seeding time if he didn't want her? After all, though she had left him, he had swallowed his pride and come to her here. Could there be a more convincing sign of his intentions? Her heart spoke in two languages. The memory of "that" rapist made her whole body shake convulsively, but in the meantime her love for Yehiel had compensated her and she dreamed of the consummation of this love. If only she had the courage to open her mouth and explain to him the reasons for her behavior. But what would become of her if the revelation of her secret repelled him?

In the night, knocking was heard at the gate of the yard. The uncle, accustomed to these nocturnal disturbances, didn't get up to open the gate. Fania hurriedly covered herself with a dress and lit the lamp. When her eyes adjusted to the gloom, she made out the shape of a man in Turkish uniform, evidently one of the governor's minions. Tugging nervously at his black moustache, he explained that his daughter was sick with a fever. Fania quoted the price of quinine tablets. The man turned out his empty pockets, and in spite of his indignation she wouldn't agree to hand over the medicine without payment.

"I'll be back!" he said and left in a hurry.

"His child is sick," said Yehiel, popping up suddenly behind her.

"I don't sell on credit."

"Not even to save a life?"

"He'll be back."

"He'll pay when he has the money."

"I'm not a charitable institution!" Her eyes flashed with anger. "And I don't want to chase after my money." Fania's eyes blazed in the moonlight and her young body, which had attained full maturity only this past year, stiffened in protest at Yehiel.

"Arguments won't help," said the uncle, and laid a conciliatory hand on Yehiel's shoulder. "Go back to bed."

The sound of running feet echoed from the street. The Turk returned, short of breath, and handed her the money. He thanked her emotionally when she gave him the medicine, and after closing the door behind him she turned and looked for a moment at Yehiel as if making up her mind about something, then walked quickly behind her curtain. She put the coins in the base of the candlestick which served her as a cashbox; she enjoyed watching the coins pile up in the glass vessel. She earned them herself, with her acumen and agility and diligence! She's not hanging around the neck of any man and she doesn't need people to pity her. Not in the least! She's providing for her uncle and her little girl. But she regretted having no one with whom she could share the satisfaction she derived from her business. She was waiting now for the month of Elul, having agreed to buy produce from the Bedouin. Instead of them coming to her with their coins, she would go to them. She was so different from them, they accepted her without undue surprise. Only the matrons of Jaffa looked at her with suspicion. Of course, they had seen women working before: the peasant women cultivating the fields, and the poor Bedouin women in domestic service, in their own homes…Walking into Bella Rokeah's house one day, she heard Nina Amzaleg saying: "But she meets men on her own!"

"They're different, the Russians," Bella Rokeah was quick to defend her. Then she saw her suddenly and hurried toward her, greeting her with extravagant tokens of affection. Fania entered the room, flushed with resentment. The vengeful impulse took hold of her. Who are they and what are they, daring to malign her? Sitting secluded in their homes, free from any concern over livelihood, protected by their menfolk, they had never known hunger, persecution, humiliation. If they knew what had befallen her in the past, they would certainly spurn her. Her uncle gave her good advice when he told her to hold her tongue. In her innocence she believed that here, in the Holy Land, the only residents were the pure and the upright among mankind, and she had since learned that people are people everywhere...It irked her that Yehiel had seen her conducting one of her transactions. The days in Jaoni had certainly strengthened her resolve: the memory of the hungry children, Riva on her sickbed, the fields that had been cleared, but they lacked the means to plow. And he must think she's hard-hearted...

Tamara started crying and then stopped. Fania woke from her sleep and listened to the silence. She sensed that the house was empty. Moving the curtain aside, she saw by the moonlight her uncle coming into the room, barefooted. The mats had been rolled up and there was no sign of Berliavsky or of Yehiel. For a moment it seemed she had dreamt his visit. What's going on, in the middle of the night? Her uncle put water to heat on the stove, and his words aroused her fears: it turned out someone had kidnapped Yosef Elyahu, son of Aharon Schloss. The boy had been missing since midday and all the men of Jaffa, Jewish and non-Jewish, were looking for him. In the night they had been roused by the shouting of the town crier, out on the street on the orders of the *kiamkam*, to report the disappearance. Yehiel and Berliavksy had joined the search party.

"I didn't hear anything!" Fania cried, thoroughly alarmed. She took Tamara out of the bed and hugged her to her breast. "How do they know he was kidnapped? Perhaps the child just fell asleep in some corner."

"Someone said that the child had been seen in the company of a Mograbi Arab, and Aharon Schloss confirms that a Mograbi visited his shop that day."

"But what does he want with the boy? What will he do to him?"

"He'll be found, Fania, don't worry. The *kiamkam*'s soldiers are out searching for him in the outskirts of Jaffa. I went with Yehiel and Berliavsky as far as the Seraya house. Yehiel got a horse there and went off with the soldiers. He asked me to come back home to you."

"And Berliavsky?"

"He can't ride, so he joined the searchers inside the city."

Fania forced herself to listen. It seemed to her she heard wailing. A tremor passed through her body and with her cheek she caressed

Tamara's little head, smoothing with her lips the soft downy hair, savoring the closeness and the sweetness of the child, humming, "I am the rose of Sharon, the lily of the valleys..."

"Who's with the family?"

"They've all gathered in the synagogue. You can hear the wailing. Rabbi Elyahu Mani is reciting the verses for Yom Kippur..."

Fania walked back and forth in the room, Tamara in her arms. The wailing grated on her nerves. In her imagination she saw Yehiel riding at the head of the troop of horsemen, into the desert...Oh—if only she were a man! And what if there are bandits out there? If they have firearms Yehiel could be in danger! Why didn't he ask her for her revolver? He must have known she had it. Fania sat down abruptly, her body convulsed by spasms as she stared ahead of her. The room was cold and silent...she remembered the nights in Rosh Pinnah, so cold. Had Yehiel sealed the cracks above the main entrance? If he were to say the word, even drop the faintest of hints, she would return with him without any hesitation! But from the very first moment, everything had made it abundantly clear to her that she was an uninvited intruder into the realm of Rachel. She had been impetuous when she decided to marry him. But he? He was no sixteen-year-old girl!...Just let him come back safe! She'll follow him to the ends of the earth if he says he wants her. Unconditionally and uninhibitedly.

"Drink, Fania." Her uncle handed her a cup of hot tea. The simple gesture touched her heart. She warmed her fingers and took small sips of the sweet tea, trying to control the shaking of her body.

"You love him."

Fania nodded. Her uncle looked so old! All the time running to and fro between all kinds of groups and factions, preaching, enthusing, and then coming home to grow old. She stopped believing all his stories about the revolutionary clubs that he belonged to, supposedly. He may well have believed in them—yes, but action—that wasn't for him! Her uncle Shura wasn't a natural activist. Two years he had been in the country and he hadn't yet found a job. If it were not for her, he would starve. But were it not for her, he wouldn't be here at all. Because of her he left Russia, left his home and livelihood and came here.

"I don't know how I can help you, Fania. You need a woman. Girls of your age learn everything from mothers, from aunts, from neighbors...Perhaps you should talk to Bella Rokeah. She's a reasonable woman."

"No...don't worry, Uncle Shura."

"I feel I'm to blame. I was so glad, knowing you had a roof over your head. A man to take care of you. A home..."

"He's a decent man, Uncle Shura. I'm the problem. I need time."

"Time for what?"

"Please!"

"All right, all right..." he tapped her hand lightly and then sat down beside her, at a loss. For some time they sat in silence, listening to the wailing that tore apart the hollowness of the night. In the end she couldn't stand the inactivity anymore and jumped up from her place.

"Where are you going?" her uncle asked.

"The washerwoman will be here soon. I'll go and prepare the cauldron."

"Perhaps I'll go to the synagogue. You're not afraid of being left on your own, Fania?"

"Why should I be afraid? Go, don't worry!"

She was glad of the work awaiting her. She drew water from the well in the yard and lit the fire, and by the time the water boiled, the washerwoman had arrived and the two women sat on the step and started scrubbing the laundry. Time in the yard passed slowly. Fania kept her hands busy, while her ears were attuned to the sounds of the street and her eyes hung on the gate. Sometimes the sound of a cry would split the air, and she stopped working and listened anxiously. At intervals she went inside and checked the clock, to find that only a few minutes had passed since she last looked. The washerwoman watched her and didn't say a word. If anything happens to him—I'll die! she thought, and was shocked by the intensity of her feelings.

Midday passed and still no news of Yehiel. Her uncle had promised to come back and tell her what was happening, and he didn't come. Esther Bushkila, her neighbor, was playing with Tamara now.

She would have to keep a close eye on the baby. In her childhood she had heard stories about gypsies who kidnapped Jewish children and for years her family lived with the nightmare of Lulik's kidnapping. Her father thought that when he came to the Land of Israel he would live a full Jewish life without any fear. Who would have imagined that even in the Chosen Land, Jews would live under the threat of kidnap and violence? Is there anywhere in the world where Jews can live without hatred and without persecution and without fear? Her father was lucky, in that he never came face to face with his dream.

Fania helped the washerwoman to drag out the laundered clothes. The fabrics were soaked in boiling water and the two of them struggled to lift the load out of the tub. Her arms were close to their breaking point and sweat dripped into her eyes, when suddenly the gate opened and into the yard came Yehiel and her uncle. All at once she threw the laundry back into the tub, jumped up from the step and ran towards him.

"Have you found him?" she asked.

"Yes." Yehiel's face was grey with fatigue and his black eyes seemed to have sunk into their sockets.

"Alive?"

"Yes."

"Thank God!"

Yehiel went into the house and Fania followed, as her uncle completed the story of the kidnap. That Mograbi was indeed the man who kidnapped the boy. Israel Simhon, the overseer of Montefiore's vineyard, came across them on the beach and rescued the boy from the clutches of the abductor. A double miracle for Aharon Schloss: the miracle that Israel Simhon's donkey strayed and the miracle that he recognized the boy.

"Esther Bushkila says the boy has a green vein between his eyes and this is a lucky sign. He was kidnapped in the hope that he would bring luck."

"The green vein didn't bring *him* much luck," was the uncle's comment on this.

"Perhaps it did!" Yehiel pointed out.

Does he really believe that the green vein between the eyes brings luck, and that's how the boy was rescued? And then she noticed he was biting his lips and realized he was mocking her.

"In the synagogue I heard Karl Marx has died," announced the uncle.

"Who? Was that what all the wailing was about?

"Not in Jaffa!" the uncle grimaced. "In London!"

"A relative of ours?"

"Fania! This is the man who showed us that all of history is nothing but war between the oppressors and the oppressed. His maxim was: *The proletarians have nothing to lose but their chains.* Remember that, Yehiel!"

"Yes…yes…" Yehiel nodded, but it seemed he wasn't really paying much attention to the speech. The uncle had apparently decided to find himself a more appreciative audience, because he said: "I promised Bella I'd go and see her this afternoon. And you, Yehiel, better get some rest. You've gone twenty-four hours without closing your eyes."

"Does he often visit my aunt?" asked Yehiel when the uncle had left.

"Yes. Nearly every day."

"And what do the gossips say? Are they going to marry?"

"I don't know."

"What kind of woman are you, Fania?"

"She's free and so is he."

Fania made up the uncle's bed for Yehiel, making an effort not to touch him. When she straightened up she realized he was standing close beside her, and when she turned to him he embraced her tenderly, and leaned forward and kissed her lips. Her arms went out as if of their own accord and wound around his body. And from her mouth a sigh emerged. He was so lean, her heart lurched. She lifted her eyes to him and submitted again to his warm and gentle lips, as they sought for hers.

"What's this? Where have the nails disappeared to?" he asked, pushing her hair behind her ears. Her ears burned and she knew they were reddening. She smiled when she noticed he was looking at them.

"Why did you run away? No, wait! I know it wasn't the hardships that drove you away. You're not a coward."

Now she knew for certain that she wanted Yehiel. No longer a confused aspiration, without a shape or a name, but tangible and conclusive knowledge. She hesitated, unsure how to talk to him. What to tell and what to conceal. And what will she do if it turns out he wants to marry Rivka after all? Where has her pride gone?

"Be brave, Fania!" Yehiel smiled and sat her down on the sofa, beside him. "Well?"

She detached herself from him and stood facing him, panting with emotion.

"I didn't run away. I left you because you went to Damascus with Rivka!"

His eyes opened wide in astonishment for a moment, and then he stood up and gave her a long and hard look.

"You were jealous?" he asked finally.

"Yes, I was jealous!"

So many times she had seen before her eyes the little carriage setting out from Rosh Pinnah, with Yehiel and Rivka riding on it. So many times she had been visited by the sensations of helplessness and humiliation and anger that she had felt at that moment. Yehiel took her by the shoulders and held her firmly, his face close to hers.

"It was really so important to you? That means I must be important to you."

"Of course you're important to me, you're my husband!"

"Oh!" Yehiel released his hold and she stumbled and leaned against the wall. His response confused her. Finally, she asked hesitantly:

"Did Rivka travel with you to Damascus?"

"No! Rivka did not travel with me to Damascus! Whatever gave you the idea I was travelling with her?"

"But…she had a suitcase with her…the bonnet…what was I supposed to think?"

"And that's why you ran away? Because you thought I was eloping with Rivka?"

"How far did you travel together?"

"Ein Zeitim! I took her to Ein Zeitim and carried on to Damascus with Rabbi Moshe David Shub. Oh, Fania!"

Yehiel began to laugh and held out his arms to her.

"At last you're a wife, Fania! You're jealous!"

Fania sat beside him, chastened, and nestled in his arms.

"Rivka came every day and looked after the children?" she probed.

"Yes."

"And…?"

"And nothing. Three weeks ago she was betrothed to Ishmael Nisan Amzaleg."

"Son of the British consul."

"No, an olive-oil merchant from Beirut. You can dance at her wedding."

"They're going to live in Jaoni?"

"No, in Beirut."

"She made my life a misery from the day I arrived in Jaoni."

"Why didn't you tell me?"

Fania shrugged her shoulders and Yehiel planted a kiss on the back of her neck.

"If it makes you feel any better, you might as well know, I thought you ran away from me because of Imber."

"Imber! He's ten years older than me!"

"And I'm not?

"But you're the one I—"

She broke off suddenly. But Yehiel wasn't letting up. He shook her hard and demanded to know.

"You what? Say it!"

"Love."

"Fania!"

There was a kind of sob in the voice that called her name, relief and heartbreak. She screwed up her eyes, as if sunlight had broken into a dark thicket. Yehiel took her to him and she, in turmoil, felt how her desire for him was blinding her senses. "Fania, Fania," he sighed, stroking her blazing skin, his kisses igniting new fires in her.

"Are you crying?"

"For joy, you fool."

"I feared you would never be mine. I was so afraid."

Fania seemed to wake up. The charm faded suddenly.

"I have to tell you something."

"Tell me," Yehiel pressed her to his body. Her face was buried between his jaw and his shoulder and she inhaled the warm darkness of his body. How to tell him what has to be said? Where to begin?

"Last night you heard from my uncle about the pogrom in our town," she whispered, her voice so faint it was barely audible. She closed her eyes, not wanting to see anything.

"Yes."

"My parents…were murdered…and…and…" she couldn't help bursting into tears. In vain she tried to say the words that were impossible to say. A rough hand again choked her throat, pressing her down on the big bed, her parents' bed…that stinking body and her cries, mingling with the cries of her parents.

"My love…sweetheart…my dear…"

Through the sobs she heard Yehiel's voice and felt his hands wiping the tears from her face, and through the turbulence of her heart she knew she *had* to tell him, and at this moment, or she would never be able to talk about it. Finally, in a halting voice, broken by tears, she said: "…Tamara…she's the daughter of a Russian goy who…who…I don't even know his name…I've never been married to anyone but you…"

Again there was silence in the room. And cold. Yehiel's arm was still around her body, pressing her to him.

"If you don't want me, I'll understand," she said after a pause.

"I love you, Fania! I love you the way I've never loved anyone before. I knew something terrible had happened to you. I waited. My life was destroyed when you left me."

She didn't dare move, scared by the intensity of her joy. Then she smiled suddenly, wiped her eyes, rested her head on her hand and looked at him. Now that they had bridged the dark gulf of her past, they could begin again in the place where a man and a woman begin.

Yehiel looked at her, his black eyes sparkling.

"Are you angry?" she asked.

"Angry?!"

"My uncle made me swear not to tell anyone about my past."

"Am I anyone?"

"I was afraid you wouldn't want me."

"That's a fine opinion you have of me!" The old sardonic flash returned to his eyes. "Why did you marry me?"

"I thought you needed a nanny…"

"Oh, Fania! How stupid you are!"

"That it would be a marriage on paper only."

"Has no one told you how beautiful you are?"

"No! Tell me!"

"From the moment I saw you there, in Mima Becker's hostel, I decided you were going to be mine. A wife, not a nanny…nanny indeed!" He started to laugh suddenly, holding her young and vibrant body to his.

Happiness coursed through her. From the feet that were brushing against his feet to the eyes that were devouring his face, in new and close proximity.

"You have three freckles on your temple."

"Inherited from my grandfather. 'The luck of the Silases'."

Fania ran her finger along the groove in his cheek.

"Tell me."

"What?"

"About yourself."

"There's nothing to tell."

"What kind of a girl were you?"

"A girl! With gangly legs. "

"What did you do? What did you like?"

"I don't remember…as if it's all been wiped away."

"A pity."

"Better that way."

"You shouldn't wipe things out."

"Better so. The present is more important. And the future."

"Who do you take after? Your father or your mother?"

"Grandma Devoshe!" she laughed. "But my love of music I inherited from my father…"

As if they had agreed from the start to approach their joy cautiously, they now let the desire flow between them, guiding them tentatively towards the rapids.

The room was in darkness when Esther Bushkila opened the door and brought Tamara inside. Fania's heart was filled with compassion for this daughter of hers who had come into the world unwanted by anyone. She sat her down on the bed beside Yehiel and went to light the lamp. Tongues of light licked the walls. Tamara drummed with her little hands on Yehiel's face. Every time he turned his head away, to avoid the onslaught, she squealed with laughter. Fania knew she would remember this scene for the rest of her life.

"The day after tomorrow there's a ship sailing to Constantinople and it will be anchoring for a few hours in Acre," she told Yehiel.

"Yes? How do you know?" He was surprised.

"I saw it in the harbor. They were repairing it on the Yarkon and now they're loading up with fruit. We can sail on it."

"I'm not boarding any ship."

"Coward!"

"For twenty-five hours we were being tossed around on the voyage to Jaffa, and all this time the passengers were crying out to the Heavens, and when we finally arrived in the bay and it seemed the boat was going to run aground on the rocks, the sailors told us that if we didn't pay a supplement they wouldn't take us to the shore! My last coppers I handed over to those carrion-eaters!"

"In that case, we'll have to walk."

"Why?"

"Because I swore I'd never ride in a carriage again!"

Chapter eight

Fania sat on "her" hill, in the shade of the walnut tree and read. Her uncle had sent her *Anna Karenina* from Jaffa and the novel entranced her, transporting her away to another world. The perfumed lotion of Stepan Arkadyich, the Venetian lace on Anna's black velvet dress…

It was good to read here, outside, in a place where there was no one to witness her. In recent days Yehiel had been sending her some awkward smiles. The women he knew didn't read books. Not like this. The distinguished minority, those capable of reading and writing, used to "skim" through the Holy Scriptures in the synagogue, and in a loud voice to be sure, so that the other women, gathered around them, could repeat the words they succeeded in catching. If anyone should ever be tempted, perish the thought, to read a "secular" book, all of Safed would hear about it. There was the case of a watchmaker, found to have in his possession a copy of Mapu's *Love of Zion*, and forced to leave the town. Even without the reading, there were some who denounced her as an "apostate", for not cutting her hair or making a point of covering it. She knew that if Yehiel didn't love her, he would have objected to her reading habits; because he loved her he said nothing, but he would peer at her sometimes with an air of utter bemusement.

From time to time she looked up from the book, and glanced at the path. When she arrived here two years ago, there were still no paths marked out on the surface of the hill. Nocturnal creatures used to carve out improvised paths, which disappeared as suddenly as they had appeared, leaving behind tantalizing speculations about hidden lairs and life underground. Now, as the inhabitants of the place had increased in number and were going up and down to the springs, a clearly marked and graveled path had been excavated out of the dark soil of the hillside. Down there, behind the bend and over the tops of the trees were the roofs of the village, reposing drowsily on what looked like a herbaceous bed, but in fact was little more than olive trees and bushes of raspberry and mulberry. First to be seen were the black roofs of the Arab village, and then the dazzling white rectangles of the new houses. The line disappeared from view in the place where the path dipped abruptly over the escarpment. Looking down, she felt as if she were falling giddily with the incline of the path, and she longed to see the plumes of dust which would herald Yehiel's return. At dawn he had set out for Safed as part of the delegation representing Rosh Pinnah in a legal dispute over water rights.

"We'll end up paying whether we win or lose," sighed Riva Frumkin.

"Why?" Fania protested. "The Bedouin attacked us and we're going to pay? We dug that pool! The water is ours!"

"Don't look for logic or justice. Even if we win the case, the 'Sulhah' will steal our last coppers. What's going to happen, Fania? It doesn't matter to me so much, I'm old, but our children…our grandchildren…"

Anna Karenina couldn't have come at a better time than this. In recent weeks Fania had suffered intense hunger and fatigue. Sometimes she feared for the baby in her womb. Since the incident with the Bedouin beside the reservoir, the settlers had stood guard over the access-points to the village day and night. Fania insisted on taking her turn. "A woman! And pregnant too!" Yehiel tried to dissuade her, but she announced she wasn't handing her revolver over to anyone unless she was allowed to do her share of guard duty.

Every morning, at dawn, Yehiel set out for work and Fania accompanied him as far as the flank of the hill. Until just two weeks ago, they had walked together to the actual worksite, but then, two weeks ago she thought that fatigue would never again leave her limbs, that the wounds on her hands would never heal, that pain had bought itself a long lease between her muscles. Even the consolation she found in Yehiel's arms was erased with the dawn. Yehiel tried to dissuade her from going to the worksite, but she insisted: "If the children are going there, I'm going too!" When the work was too hard for her because of her swelling womb, she began turning her full attention to the children. Moshe and Bella always stood some distance from her, using the other children as a partition to hide behind, the space between them speaking eloquently of their resentment at the way she had deserted them. When she returned from Jaffa she couldn't, simply couldn't, apologize to the little children, alienated as they were and painfully so, for abandoning them—not when her own skin was radiant with happiness. She tried to appease them, transmitting appeals for forgiveness in the form of an offer to mend their clothes, or a Russian lullaby with words they didn't understand. When her pregnancy became public knowledge, Moshe and Bella eventually heard about it too, and then embarrassment took the place of resentment.

Fania was pulling the small, powdery stones out of the ground, sweating profusely and humming the 'Rose of Sharon', a favorite of her father's, while Moshe, as tight-lipped as his father, was moving the stones she cleared to the edge of the plot, where a broad and compact heap was rising. When a break was called, Bella came and sat beside her, scrabbling in the sand with her little fingers and blowing from time to time on the thin snakes of dust. Dust covered her eyelashes and turned her hair grey. This is the childhood that awaits the baby in my womb, Fania thought. Do we have the right to rob our children of their childhood in the name of some vision? When she looked up to see what the other children were doing, she heard a sudden cry.

"Fania! Move!" someone shouted. Turning her head, she saw out of the corner of her eye a gigantic boulder rolling towards her. She just had time to leap aside, pulling after her Yekotiel Frumkin, Riva's grandson, who was working beside her. Her ears rang from all the shouting around her and for a moment she seemed to freeze where she stood. Her eyes darkened, and when she tried to focus them she noticed a human hand stretching out from under the boulder and she fainted.

There was still shouting after she regained consciousness. Eka Riva sat on the ground with Fania's head in her lap. A sour smell of sweat rose from her dark woolen dress. Eka Riva slapped her cheek and scolded her: "That's enough! That's enough!" Hearing the note of anger in her voice, Fania wondered why she was so upset. The pounding of running feet was heard, agitated speech. Someone shouted: "Pesach Lieb! Where's Pesach Lieb?"

"I'm here!" the answer came. "Where's Moishe?"

"He's coming!"

Eka Riva laid Fania's head on the sand and walked towards the group of people. Between the legs hurrying around her Fania caught sight of Rabbi David Buksheshter, lying flat under the rock. His face had turned blue and his breath was rapid with strange whistling sounds. The man was hovering between life and death. She rose to her feet and suddenly Yehiel was beside her. He tried to dissuade her from going any closer, but she was drawn to the place by a force stronger than herself.

"You should go on preparing the ground that has had the nerve to make our job so difficult," said Rabbi David to his sons who had gathered around him. His wife lay down on the ground beside him and began to wail. He took a deep breath, cried out with the last of his strength: "My country!" and was silent. For some reason Fania wanted to laugh. She had to work hard to restrain her lips from curling into a smile. And then she fainted again. When she opened her eyes, Eka Riva's lap was once again her pillow. Yehiel was helping the men to shift the boulder away from the corpse of Rabbi David.

"There's nothing for you to do here!" Eka Riva scolded her.

"You're in the way! What are you trying to do? Kill your unborn child? Don't come here anymore!"

Work on the "defiant ground"—so they called it from now on—was resumed the next day. But from now on Fania wasn't among the stone-clearers.

Before dawn Rabbi Zalman would go round from house to house and rouse the sleepers. While Yehiel was praying the dawn prayer, Fania was preparing a meal and packing a small bag of food for him. Then she would accompany him as far as the hill. The sight of the group of men gathering together at dawn, the silhouettes moving around in the bluish vapors of morning, the east turning gold with the first light of day—all of this held a real emotional charge for her. Ah! If only she were a painter! When she arrived at the worksite she would stop, as if encountering an invisible barrier, and turn her back on the stone-clearers.

This morning she was gripped by fear. There was barely any flour left in the sack and for weeks they hadn't earned a cent. What's going to happen? Where will the children's food come from? Her uncle still had some of the coffee she had bought in Jaffa, and weeks ago she wrote to him, asking him to sell the coffee and send her the proceeds. Instead of money, *Anna Karenina* arrived. She knew that her uncle detested "trade", but he could have deduced from her letter how desperately they needed the money. Another day or two and there would be no food left in the house. She remembered the foggy days she spent with her uncle in Constantinople, waiting for Tamara to be born. Her uncle made sure she ate fresh fruit and vegetables and drank plenty of milk...how was her baby being nourished now? Would he or she be born whole and healthy, despite the mother's hunger? She didn't share her fears with Yehiel. But from time to time he caught the look of concern in her eyes. His silences became longer and more stubborn. In fact, he was not so different from the rest of the men in the settlement, except in one respect: he had been enduring these hardships for five years. Since the death of Buksheshter, day after day they had been tackling the big rocks, which had come to symbolize the stumbling blocks that must be cleared.

"What will happen when you finish clearing stones?" Fania asked Yehiel.

"I don't know."

"How will you sow when there are no seeds? We'll have to acquire a loan."

"Who from? Come on then! You're the capitalist of the family! Tell me, who's going to give us a loan?"

"Captain Goldsmid? I've heard he's a regular visitor to Sage Yakov Abu Hai in Safed."

"We already owe him a hundred pounds sterling."

"What for?"

"He paid the legal fees when the Arab was killed at Rubinstein's wedding."

"Maybe someone in Safed?"

"Anyone who can afford to give—has already given. You're forgetting that most of the people of Safed hate us."

"No. I'm not forgetting." Suddenly she started laughing. "Yehiel! We must be crazy! Everyone here is crazy! Lulik is the only sane person in all Rosh Pinnah! We're frantically clearing the ground for sowing and the only thing we haven't got…seeds!"

"Well then, Mrs. Fire and Brimstone, prove your mettle! Find a solution!"

"I shall! I'll find something, you'll see…Maybe we should make the Bedouin pay us for the use of the water."

"They were here again today?"

"Yes. We tried to drive them away from the reservoir, but they weren't scared of us. Who would be intimidated by a pregnant woman and a few children? What did they do before we built the reservoir?"

"They went down to the Jordan."

"There's barely enough water for the cattle and sheep of Rosh Pinnah."

The blessing of Rosh Pinnah became its curse. It was the abundance of water in that place that drew the attention of Rabbi Moshe David Shub when he was scouting for a site where the Jews of his city could settle, and it was this very water that turned their lives sour. The water was drawn from three springs, discharging into a pool, and flowing on via an open channel to fill a reservoir. When the days of heat wave arrived, the peasants from the nearby villages, along with the Bedouin of the Al-Zangariya tribe, came to water their flocks in the reservoir of Rosh Pinnah. After she finished with the stone-clearing, Fania took to helping the children with the pasturing. But by the time they arrived at the reservoir there was barely any water left for the cattle and sheep of the settlement. Fania tried to drive the trespassers away, but there were so many of them, she abandoned the attempt. Yehiel, Rabbi Moshe David and Issar Frumkin went to the sheikh and explained to him the problems his tribesmen were causing for the settlement. The sheikh received them politely and promised he would take action against the "lazy shepherds". The style of speech was lofty and the promises reassuring, but the shepherds carried on stealing the water. When Fania announced she wasn't prepared to take personal responsibility for the survival of the livestock, the farmers posted sentries to guard the water. The next day the sheikh arrived on his warhorse, his sword at his side, and with him a whole contingent of horsemen and foot soldiers, spoiling for a fight. While the residents of Rosh Pinnah were negotiating with the sheikh and his armed escort, his shepherds made for the reservoir. A barrage of stones rained down on the defenders of the settlement and battle was initiated. Pesach Lieb Buksheshter, Menachem Greboski and Shmuel Katz blocked the path of the attackers and put up a spirited fight, staff against staff and stone against stone, while others attacked them from behind. Most of the assailants were young, strong and brave—which is more than could be said of the Jewish defenders, known to the Arabs of the country by the nickname *walad al-mawt*. One of the stones hit the sheikh on the head and he fell to the ground. When the Bedouin saw what had happened to the leader of the tribe—they turned and fled for their lives. News of the victory spread rapidly from one Jewish community to another, and the praises of the three warriors, Pesach, Menachem and Shmuel, were sung throughout Galilee. But the joy of triumph was tempered by fear of revenge attacks. For weeks on end the residents of Rosh Pinnah were compelled to guard the settlement day and night to ward off the vengeful tribesmen of the Al-Zangariya. Yehiel's face was black with fatigue. At dawn he went to the worksite to clear stones, and by night he was standing guard, Fania's revolver strapped to his waist. In the end, Fania announced she wouldn't give him the gun again, unless she was allowed to take her turn at guarding the settlement.

"I'll guard by day," she said. "Not at night."

"Women don't guard. Least of all, pregnant women!"

"If I'm fated to be injured, I can be injured just as easily at home," she insisted, and in the end he bowed to her wishes. The residents of Rosh Pinnah were shocked at first, but they were used to seeing her as a strange sort of creature, and this was just another of her eccentricities.

Helen Leah, coming from Zamarin to pay her a visit, tried to change her mind.

"I'm younger and healthier and stronger than your old father," Fania protested. "Why is it acceptable for him and not acceptable for me? Is my life worth more than his?"

"You're a woman, Fania!"

"True enough. And you must have heard that prayer, *God be praised for not making me a woman!* My life has to be worth less than theirs!"

"When's the baby due?"

"Two more months."

"Which do you want? Boy or girl?"

"I don't know…After the birth, when I'm feeling stronger I'll come and see you in Zamarin. What's it like there? Mountains? Same as here?"

Within minutes, the two young women were engrossed in a discussion of trivialities. Fania enjoyed looking at her friend and admiring her beauty, with her smoldering black eyes and smooth olive skin, her laughter and her yawns. Around them the vision of salvation burned like fire in the bones of the people, while they reveled in their banal conversation! In Helen Leah, Fania found a friend after her own heart, and she knew that her protests arose from concern for her welfare and were nothing to do with "principles".

A cloud of dust rose from the path. Fania inserted a leaf between the pages of *Anna Karenina* to mark the place and stood up. Her legs had "gone to sleep" from the prolonged sitting and her big belly impeded her progress as she descended the path. By the time she reached the settlement, the five members of the delegation were already standing by the entrance to the synagogue. Fania stopped where she stood and feasted her eyes on Yehiel. Every day that had passed since they returned from Jaffa had brought them closer and closer together. Whenever she felt that her heart was overflowing with love for her husband and mentor, a chance look or movement of the head would be enough to boost her love for him still further.

Yehiel inspected his surroundings, and she smiled, waiting for him to locate her as she walked toward him. From the jaunty tilt of his head, she could tell that the court had decided in Rosh Pinnah's favor.

From the fringes of the settlement the women and the children converged, and the men came running from the fields. Rabbi Moshe David, still on horseback, informed the settlers that the court in Safed had absolved the Jews of Rosh Pinnah of all blame. The Sultan's judges had decided that they were innocent of any offence since they were defending themselves against aggressors. "They have learned that the Jews are capable of standing up for themselves, and they have determined that this time the Law is on their side," said Rabbi Moshe David.

They all smiled on hearing the words of Rabbi Moshe David. For a moment the heart of the settlement was one heart, beating with pride. Justice had been done and the thieves had been taught a lesson. All would know that the Jews were not to be scorned, and that they lived under legal protection.

"As we were leaving the court," Rabbi Moshe David went on to say, "it was agreed between the two parties that a 'Sulhah' should be held, renewing the covenant that was supposed to last 'in perpetuity' between Jews and Arabs. The Kubra and the Awad, representing the peasants and the Bedouin, will be coming to the settlement next Tuesday and we hope for a successful outcome…Yehiel Silas will advise us on the conventions of the 'Sulhah'…"

Rabbi Moshe's polyglot language brought a smile to Fania's lips. The Romanians spoke Yiddish with a Romanian garnish, while the native-born inhabitants of Jaoni spoke a medley of Arabic, Hebrew and Spanish, with the result that Tamara was already fluent in a language of her own in which all these elements were combined, and even Bella and Moshe had to struggle sometimes to understand the weird expressions she came up with.

Meanwhile Yehiel had dismounted and was coming to meet her, closely followed by a gigantic fair-haired youth, dressed in the Russian style and casting curious looks around him.

"Fania, this is Alexander Zusmann. He'll be staying with us for a while."

"Welcome, Sasha!" Fania greeted the boy in Russian and laughed at his look of astonishment.

He was about twenty-three or twenty-four, and his face showed no sign of the expression of asceticism which typified the new migrants. His cheeks were ruddy from exposure to the sun and his blue eyes twinkled. The curls on his head mingled with the curls of his beard and together they framed his face in a gilded halo. He wore a Russian peasant shirt, embroidered with little blue crosses. They stood taking stock of each other, and Fania knew she must be a strange sight to him. Since she started her guarding duties the revolver had been slung from the belt around her waist, a waist that was steadily filling out from month to month. Her face had shriveled, as if the baby had consumed all her sap for want of any other source of nourishment. The skin of her face was taut and her eyes seemed to have grown bigger than ever.

When the men went to wash, Fania wondered about the boy. He looked like a wrestler. Tall, broad-shouldered, with a wide mouth and the solid jaw of a circus strongman, capable of breaking chains with his teeth. How did he get to be here? Did he come alone, or with his family? And where did Yehiel find him? What a joy it was, meeting a "Russian"! She had erased the land of her birth from her heart, but the memories came flooding back despite her efforts to repel them: the olive tree suddenly became a poplar encrusted with frost, the boulders covered with morning dew turned in her daydream into drifts of snow.

When Yehiel and the stranger returned to the table, his eyes fell on her book.

"Yours?" He shot a curious look at her. The men Yehiel knew weren't in the habit of looking women full in the face and Fania felt uncomfortable.

"Yes."

"Have you read his *Childhood*? *Youth*?"

"No, I haven't read those. But this is wonderful! Wonderful!"

It seemed to Fania the boy was smiling behind his sealed lips. She wanted to press him, ask what was amusing him, but didn't dare. Perhaps this is his normal expression and he isn't smiling at all. She'll make a fool of herself. And at once she regretted her caution, because in the meantime he had turned serious and it was obvious to her he had indeed been smiling before. Now she would never know what he was smiling about!

"Where did you get this book from?" he asked.

"My uncle sent it to me from Jaffa."

"Your uncle's Russian?"

"Of course he's Russian! What else?" she laughed.

"*He* doesn't like Jews!"—he pointed again at the book.

"Who does like them? Do we?"

"Yes! We do!"

"Aya! And all the quarrelling? And the rifts and the jealousies and the divisions? God preserve us!"

"Families are like that! Tolstoy doesn't even like the Old Testament because it belongs to us. And as for our national aspirations, he has already passed judgment. All peoples have the right to self-determination, with the exception of the Jews. He said that explicitly! In his opinion, our national revival is nothing but a symbol of degeneracy. Our leaders are intent on deceiving the people, satisfying their lust for power and their yen for military conquest! He didn't believe I was Jewish! He seems to think all Jews are hunchbacks with horns!"

"What?! You met him? How?"

"I was on his estate, in Yasnaya Polyana, along with a friend of mine who wanted to illustrate his stories."

"Are you an artist?"

"I used to be."

"Well? What happened?"

Sasha shrugged. "We met in the courtyard. Leonid Pasternak, my friend, waited until the old man came out for a breath of air. And I was with him. The courtyard was full of children—and thirteen of them were his! And when he finally came out, he asked me who my father was, and my mother and grandparents, to the third generation. He didn't believe I was Jewish. And then he spoke to us in Hebrew!"

"Tolstoy? Hebrew? I don't believe it!"

"We couldn't understand what he was saying. We thought he was making fun of us, and that annoyed him. He was learning Hebrew at that time, courtesy of a scholar from Yanur. Leonid had to placate him, but I didn't go inside the house. All that suspicion and anger… he was in a strange kind of mood…people bothered him…"

"Your uncle said similar things about another writer…" Yehiel interjected.

"Dostoyevsky."

"The Russian people apparently draw inspiration from on high."

"He doesn't need any inspiration!" said Sasha bitterly.

Fania cleared the plates from the table. For a whole month now they had been living on a diet of thin lentil soup. After the meal the boy's eyes lit up and his lips reddened. These "signs" were already familiar to her, and they barely aroused any emotion in her. She was glad that at her impoverished table it was possible to slake the hunger of barefoot and homeless refugees even more famished than they were themselves. Coming back into the room she asked:

"Where are you from, Sasha?"

"From Kharkov."

"And how long have you been in the country?"

"I arrived eighteen months ago."

"By yourself?"

"Yes."

"And where have you been until now?"

"In Jerusalem. And before that I spent three months with Tristram, the English cleric. His artist was sick and I filled in for him until he recovered. I'm sure you've heard of him."

"No, we haven't. Who is he?"

"An eccentric Englishman who's studying the natural history of the Holy Land. I'm surprised he hasn't been here yet. He arrived in the country twenty years ago and he's scoured the place from top to bottom and side to side. He knows every plant and every animal. I was with him by the Dead Sea when he discovered some bird hitherto unknown to science. He was so excited, you'd think he'd created it himself! I don't believe these scholars really love nature at all."

"No? Why?" Fania smiled.

"They kill animals. And stuff them. And they put flowers in the oven to dry them out. I don't like them. I was glad when his artist recovered, even though it was a good wage."

"He heard about us from Eleazar Rokeah," Yehiel explained to Fania.

"Where did you meet?"

"We didn't. Eleazar Rokeah was corresponding with some friends of mine who live in Constantinople. They sent us copies of his letters."

"Who is 'us'?"

"A group of friends in Jerusalem—"

"What did you do in Jerusalem?"

"Fania!" Yehiel cried suddenly, "Leave the boy alone!"

"Oy! Sorry, Sasha, sorry. You can ask me some questions for a change! Ask me anything you like!"

"Where's the water?"

Fania burst into laughter. She stood up to show Sasha where the well was located, but Yehiel put his hand on her arm to restrain her.

"The children will show him."

Bella and Moshe were entranced by Sasha and his larger-than-life personality, and they competed between themselves for the privilege of serving as his guide. "Heart-stealer," Fania called him to herself with a smile, and wondered what had brought *him* to this country.

When she woke in the morning, Sasha wasn't in the house. On the table there was a sheet of paper, a note from the children. According to Moshe, Sasha had prayed with Yehiel, then he had asked the way to Safed, picked up his bag and left. The house was suddenly empty. Fania was surprised to find how disappointed she was. For a moment her hunger and her worries for the future had been forgotten. Sasha filled the air with his vitality, with his outsized body, with his blue, laughing eyes. It seemed that nothing bothered him very much, and it was only when he spoke about art that a kind of reverence came over him.

From his account they had learned that he used to be a member of a Jerusalem society called "Return of the Craftsman and the Smith", which included some Bilu partisans among its membership. At first there were just three of them: Yakov Chertok, Shimon Belkind and Darya Sirot, but over time another five joined them. Their object was to learn trades: metalwork, engraving, the art of the blacksmith and the cutler. Pines and Ben Yehuda and Nessim Bakar, superintendent of the Alliance school, took them under their wing. "The Biluists of Jerusalem are different from the Biluists in Rishon le Zion or in Constantinople," explained Sasha.

"How are they different? Aren't they the same people?"

"In Jerusalem there's a special atmosphere. The city itself changes people. We were friends, soul mates. Without the pettiness and the machinations you find in other places. The personality of Ben Yehuda was influential, too. Day after day we ate our one and only daily meal in his house. Darya Sirot lodged in the Ben Yehuda family home, and she prepared our meals in his kitchen. Sometimes we shared the family's meager bread-ration."

"How does he make a living, Ben Yehuda?"

"He teaches in the Alliance Israelite Universelle school. On the quiet! The Alliance is opposed to the teaching of Hebrew in its schools. But the superintendent, Nessim Bakar, believes in the future of Hebrew and he smuggled Ben Yehuda in among the rest of the teaching staff. This discretion has helped us too."

"I have relatives in Jerusalem," said Yehiel. "The Bak family."

"The printer?" asked Sasha, his eyes sparkling with mischief. "I was his guest, a lodger in his house."

"Really! And how is he?"

"I don't know. He didn't know I was his guest. I'd been living for some time in Ben Yehuda's house, but in the summer his wife found some lodgers who were prepared to pay rent and I was forced to leave. I didn't have the money to pay for a hotel. One day, when I was praying in Bak's synagogue, which was the central room in his house, my prayers were answered from Heaven: I saw through the window a stairway leading to a cellar, a cellar formerly used as a grain store."

Tears of mirth filled Sasha's eyes. "A whole week I stayed there. But what then? Another relative of yours, Frumkin, was lodging on the upper floor of the same house. One morning he saw me coming out of the cellar, and ejected me. So you see, your family is fated to accommodate me!"

"And where did you go?"

"I went back to Ben Yehuda's house. He lives near the third gate, a neighbor of Fishel Nagid. Do you know Jerusalem?"

"No, Safed is my hometown."

"You were born in Safed?"

"Yes."

"And where's your family from?"

"We're a mixed bunch. From Morocco, Damascus, Russia, Israel…"

"In Jerusalem I met a lot of Jews from North Africa…Ben Yehuda has taken to wearing a Sephardi caftan and a tarboosh," Sasha grimaced. "And Pines smokes a nargileh!"

Fania and Yehiel burst into laughter. Sasha succeeded in amusing them again and again. Some spirit of frivolity entered them, and before long they were laughing without feeling they needed a reason.

In the meantime, Fania reflected inwardly that she had never laughed like this with Yehiel. How good is this friendship, she thought, and what a likable man is he.

"We too shall speak only Hebrew with our son, like Ben Yehuda!" Yehiel suddenly announced.

"And if it's a daughter?"

"It will be a son."

"God help the poor child!" sighed Fania.

"Eleazar Rokeah is related to Frumkin, is that right?"

"Yes. And his cousin Issar Frumkin lives next door to us here."

"Was he one of the founder-members?"

"Yes."

"I thought none of the original settlers were left. From one of Eleazar Rokeah's letters I got the impression Gai Oni had been abandoned..."

"It wasn't abandoned! Far from it! When the Romanians joined us, it came back to life, rising from the ashes like the phoenix."

"The phoenix..."

Fania and Yehiel stared at Sasha, perplexed. He was suddenly agitated. Something black and menacing wiped the laughter from his face. Then he perked up and spoke rapidly, trying to mask the change that had come over him.

"Eleazar Rokeah believed that we, the immigrants from Russia, should carry on the mission that you started. In a letter he sent to comrades in Constantinople, he said he'd come to the conclusion that natives of this country would never succeed in cultivating the land, and hoped that Bilu would carry on where the natives had started."

"Natives of this country don't want to work?" cried Fania angrily. "He doesn't want to work! He ran away from here. We're hanging on to the land with our fingernails! How dare he?!"

"Fania, please!" Yehiel tried to reassure her. "His objective is the same as ours. Settling the country, working the land..."

"Yes, Yehiel is right," Sasha agreed. "He even objected to the way we were living in Jerusalem for exactly that reason. He insisted we had come to this country to build agricultural settlements and not to sit in Jerusalem, among the fanatics, waiting for charity from abroad. That's one of the reasons I came here. I wanted to see the place with my own eyes."

"So that means you'll be running away from here pretty soon! Just like Eleazar Rokeah!" Fania taunted him, hoping to provoke him into agreeing to stay for a while.

At the turn of the day, Fania was leaving Lulik's shed when she noticed a large figure walking toward the house.

"Sasha!" she cried happily.

Sasha opened his bag and took out three oranges, a slab of cheese, a loaf of bread and a handful of olives, and put them on the table.

It turned out that he had visited every house and every tent in every village in the vicinity. In a certain dairy in the outskirts of Safed he repaired milk-churns, for a certain farmer he put shoes on his horse's hooves, while a certain sheikh had him paint a portrait of his favorite steed...

The bread was fresh, and the salt in the cheese made the fragrant oranges taste all the sweeter. Tamara sat in Fania's lap chewing a slice of bread that she held firmly in her little hands.

"We've decided that when the *kubra* and the *awad* come to the 'Sulhah' on Tuesday, we should entertain them with a meal of mutton and rice and coffee," said Yehiel.

"That's a scene I'm going to have to paint!" declared Sasha.

"You mean *you've* decided!" Fania's face flushed with anger. "Whose decision was it exactly?"

"It was down to all of us."

"When did you meet?"

"This morning, in the synagogue."

"Where's the money coming from?"

"Everyone will be asked to contribute to the best of his ability."

"Is that a joke?"

"No."

"*The best of his ability*, did you say? People here have had nothing to eat for two weeks! Men!"

Sasha roared with laughter, hearing how contemptuously she spat out the last word.

"They stole our water and we have to appease them! Where's the logic in that?"

"We beat them in the courts. That's the point."

"Because we were right. We didn't even need to bribe the judges! And now they're punishing us for being right? I want no part of this farce!"

"So all the others will contribute and we won't?" asked Yehiel angrily.

"We can't sow because we have no money to buy seeds, but stuffing the bellies of those bandits with mutton…Oh yes, we can afford that!"

Enraged, Fania left the room and stormed outside, slamming the door behind her with all the strength she could muster.

After spending some time in the yard, she finally came back inside, opened one of the drawers and rummaged in it until she found what she was looking for. She took out a small bottle and flung it down on the table.

"There it is! Our contribution!"

"What is it?"

"Quinine. I was keeping it for the birth."

"What am I supposed to do with it?"

"Sell it!"

"To whom?"

"To anyone! To the Mizrahi brothers living by Lake Huleh! The Izber tribe! Rabbi Fishel Salomon! Are there not enough lunatics sitting in swamps? Not enough malaria-sufferers? You'll find a customer!"

Yehiel rolled the phial between his fingers, staring at it awkwardly.

"Just as well my uncle didn't manage to send me the money for the coffee. I'd be hopping mad."

"You mean, you're not hopping mad now?" asked Sasha, and the three of them dissolved into relieved laughter.

"I suggested he should go out after you," Sasha told Fania, "but he was afraid you'd throw a bucket of water over him. Give it to me!" he took the phial from Yehiel's hand. "I'll sell it."

On the day of the "Sulhah" it became known to Fania that the women wouldn't be sitting with the men.

"So you men are going to sit, while we stand outside like Bedouin women and wait for you to eat your fill and throw us the scraps?"

"Yes."

"Why don't they conform to our customs? After all, they are our guests!"

"That's the way it is."

In the morning Fania went up the hill, taking *Anna Karenina*. She had sent the children with the men so they would receive portions from the banqueting table. The smell of smoke was wafted up to the heights. Fania swallowed her spittle. Her stomach was constricted by hunger, and she found it hard to concentrate on Princess Tverskaya's croquet game and gossip about the lords and ladies of St. Petersburg. In the days that had passed since she started reading this book, she had been in tears constantly. As if some dam had been breached within her. Fru-Fru the horse, wriggling like a fish, the diligence of Alexei Alexandrovich, the short legs of Madame Stahl—everything, everything reminded her of her parents' house, her lost childhood, the poetry, the warm aroma of plum purée, the dough of the *piroshkis*, melting in the mouth, the house filling up with all kinds of fabrics and ribbons and threads when the seamstress comes calling...And now, it was as if a magician waved his wand, and everything was an empty illusion! No Vronsky, no Kitty, no Levin with his diaries. Only the barren land exists, cracked by the heat. Only the baby exists that is soon to be born, and all else suddenly seems tasteless and absurd.

A big and radiant figure was striding up the path at a vigorous pace. Sasha, the hair of his head and his beard gleaming in the sunshine. He came closer, and Fania feasted her eyes on him happily. He was so big, and at the same time, seemingly helpless, as if he had not yet learned to live with his broad shoulders, as if he were afraid of his strength and his dimensions.

"It was a tough job, grabbing this helping out of the mouth of the bastard Sheikh…Oh, Fania, I'm sorry! Excuse my language!"

Fania's laugh, that fearless, rolling laugh, burst from her mouth. She tucked with gusto into the slice of mutton and the pita bread it was wrapped in.

"Is this your hiding place?" he asked, glancing around him.

"How did you know where to look for me?"

"How do you know I was looking?" he replied teasingly and then, as if taken aback by his own effrontery, he hastened to add: "The children told me. It's a pity I didn't bring my painting materials with me."

"Have the children eaten?"

"Ah! The children and the women stood by the table and looked with accusing eyes into the very mouths of the diners. It's a wonder none of them choked!"

"Bella? Moshe? Tamara?"

"They've all eaten."

"You're sure?"

"I'm sure."

On her return to the house she saw, from the street, Moshe going into the shed in the yard. The door was open and Fania was already imagining she heard Lulik storming out of there, shouting. But nothing happened. The cypress shed warm dust, living its inner life, while its gnarled, sticky trunk scored thin grooves on her wet hands. After a moment Moshe came out of the hut and Fania emerged from her hiding place.

"Is Lulik in the hut?" she asked.

"Yes."

"He doesn't run away from you?"

"No."

"What were you doing with him?"

"I brought him a pita…"

"From the feast?"

Moshe nodded his head, biting his lip awkwardly, and Fania planted a resounding kiss on his cheek before he could escape.

If it seemed hard times had come to Rosh Pinnah, there were still harder times on the way, and then the former days seemed almost heavenly. Not a cent was left in any of the houses of the settlement. The residents had sold their wedding rings and the tassels from their pillows to pay their share of the costs of the "Sulhah". There wasn't even enough left to guarantee the loans that they needed.

The time of the birth was approaching, and penury seemed to paralyze Fania. Even Yehiel barely spoke. At night she would lay her head on his shoulder and surrender to the caress of his fingers. They were driven to despair by hunger, by the lack of prospects, by fears that they didn't express.

Rabbi Moshe David Shub wrote to the Jews of Moineshti, asking for their help. He also called on the other residents to address urgent appeals to benefactors. A deputation of farmers met the representative of Baron Hirsch, but the best he could offer was a donation of two thousand francs. This money wasn't enough to hire mules or to sow crops, but it was enough to embarrass the farmers of Rosh Pinnah; they had founded their settlement precisely to avoid being dependent on the system of charitable donations prevalent in the old communities.

Rabbi Moshe David decided to go abroad to enlist the support of the "Lovers of Zion" in the effort to save the settlement from oblivion. When he came to their house to take his leave of them, Fania handed him letters to her sisters. She hadn't yet sent them the proceeds from the medicines and now she was asking them for a new consignment…

"Oliphant has transferred a thousand gold francs to the settlement committee," Rabbi Moshe David told Fania, "and I've instructed the committee to make provision for you and the baby. Much to my regret, I won't be here for the birth…"

"Oliphant!" Fania slapped her forehead, "Why didn't I think of him! He can buy one of the plots in Rosh Pinnah!"

"Sell to him? Who are you planning to evict from here?"

"No one will be evicted! We're already living on land registered in Oliphant's name," she enthused. "This is 'Miri' land and it can't be bequeathed. The question of ownership isn't important. What matters is working the land and producing crops. If it gets known to the authorities that for three years there's been no cultivation, the land will revert to state ownership. What's so disastrous about becoming Oliphant's tenants? He's not like the Efendis or the tax-grabbers. He's never asked us for a cent. All he wants to do is help farmers! This will be a sale on paper only. The farmers will still be living on the land and with Oliphant's money they can buy seeds and food for their families!"

"On condition that he really wants to buy, Fania," Yehiel whispered.

"I'm sure that's what he'll want!"

"Oliphant is a bit of a...fantasist..."

"And we're not?! His dream is the same as ours! I'm prepared to go and talk to him."

"You're not going anywhere!"

For a moment she opened her mouth to protest at Yehiel's vehement tone, but then she glanced at her swollen belly.

"No, I guess I'm not."

"Oliphant calls Fania 'the Queen of the Land of Naftali'," said Yehiel, a rare smile hovering for a moment on his lips. Fania was surprised that he remembered the nickname. "I'll go and see him tomorrow."

The next day, when Fania was walking to the reservoir with the children and the sheep, sharp pangs gripped her. Unlike the first time, when the process of birth began with delicate and barely perceptible warnings, now she was assailed all at once by the most ferocious of pains. Alarmed, she sat down beside the reservoir and sent one of the children to call Riva from the field. It seemed a long time had passed before the elongated figure of Sasha popped up beside her.

"Has it started?"

"Yes."

"Come on, let's get you home."

Fania rose to her feet, but after taking a few steps she felt warm liquid pouring down her legs.

"What's happened?"

"My waters have broken."

"Come on, honey." Before she realized what was happening, he had picked her up in his arms and was carrying her along the track leading to her home. Fania, her senses dulled by fear and pain, peered at the pink ear protruding from under the peaked cap, aware of the smell of the man whose curls were tickling her cheek. She was confused, things seemed out of place, his closeness, the strange feelings he aroused in her, the words he said…when the pain kicked in again she gripped his shoulders hard and then relaxed her grip.

"The pains are coming regularly, and we'll be home soon," he said tenderly. "I lit the fire and put the water on to heat. Moshe is running around looking for Yehiel and maybe he's already on his way. And Bella's gone to call a neighbor…"

"Put me down!"

Fania didn't want to be seen by Yehiel in Sasha's arms. Sasha did as she asked and they waited until the pangs eased and then they walked on.

"Where's Riva?"

"She'll be here any moment, don't worry."

Sasha stoked up the fire and then opened the chest and found the old sheet. The pains intensified and Fania tried hard not to cry out. Her head was covered in sweat and Sasha wiped her face and spoke to her in a soothing voice as if addressing a sick little girl, calling her Honey and Chick and Gosling and Sponge cake…

The children appeared in the doorway, their little faces frightened. Sasha went out to them and sent them away on long errands. She half-heard his words, her senses dulled by pain, and she groaned.

"Shout, Fania, it will make you feel better. Is that it? Has it passed? Well, he will be with us soon…"

"*She* will."

"She!" Sasha exclaimed with a kind of a laugh. "She'll have curly hair the color of bronze, like yours…Push! Breathe! Relax! Push!"

Through the pain and the swirling fog surrounding it, her fuddled consciousness was penetrated by the awareness that he *knew* what had to be done. In a moment of respite she opened her eyes, fixed him with a bemused stare and asked:

"Are you a doctor, Sasha?"

"No. But…I delivered a child once…my…my daughter…"

Fania closed her eyes. She knew he was exposing a little of his torment to her because she was so utterly exposed before him. Torment in exchange for torment. God! What kind of a world is she bringing her daughter into?!

Her thoughts were entangled. The pain pierced her body with increasing regularity and she called out: "Yehiel!" And as she panted between one stab of pain and the next, she heard Riva Frumkin's voice: "Why are you calling for Yehiel? You think he can help you? Call for Riva! I'm here!"

"Where's Sasha?"

"He's outside, painting on the door. The children are with him."

Her strength was exhausted and she stopped resisting. She was at one with the cows and the ewes. Crying out when the pains assailed her, sprawled out like a rag when they stopped. Someone wiped her brow, and when she opened her eyes she saw Yehiel standing beside her, pale and confused.

"What does he look like, your knight in shining armor!" said Riva with good-natured scorn and sent him out of the room. I wouldn't have gone out, the thought occurred to her between one pain and the next. As if reading her mind, Riva said: "We don't need him just now."

Then she felt her flesh tearing and from her crotch the baby appeared in a hot and sticky stream, and all at once the pains subsided and only weariness was left. From outside, her ears picked out the murmur of praying voices, and suddenly Yehiel stood over her, still pale, still confused, and for a moment she feared he was going to burst into tears.

"Congratulations, Fania, we have a son."

"Congratulations, Yehiel."

The next day, Yehiel told her that their mission had been successful. Oliphant did indeed agree to buy two of the allotments of Rosh Pinnah. It was all signed and sealed. He had paid one hundred and five Napoleons for the territory allotted to Nahum Klisker and Yakov Gorokovski, a total area of three hundred and sixty-nine dunams. He apparently intended to settle four families on their land.

"Oliphant has decided to prove to the world that Jews are capable of being farmers if they're just given the opportunity. He believes in us more than we believe in ourselves…Do you want to name our son after your father, of blessed memory?"

"No!" Fania had no intention of perpetuating in her son any echo of the pogrom which had brought death to her father. This son was a new beginning, a new world, a new man. She would not even tell him about the fate of her parents; that way the memory of their murders would not be inscribed in him.

"Moshe is named after my grandfather. This son of mine I'd like to name after my friend Eleazar."

"That absentee ass-licker?"

"Fania!"

"We'll find another name, from the Bible."

"Naphtali, perhaps? After all, Imber calls you 'the Queen of the Land of Naphtali'."

"Naphtali…" Fania rolled out the name as if tasting it, turning it over in her mouth. "Naphtali Silas…"

"At last we'll get to use 'Elijah's Chair'!"

They both smiled, remembering how the Jews of Safed threw stones at her when she tried to salvage the chair from Eleazar Rokeah's house.

"On this chair, Shmuel the son of Nisan Bak was admitted

to the covenant of our father Abraham. Not far from that favorite place of yours, up there. Montefiore was the sandak and he sat on the chair, and all the gentry of Safed were there, as well as the burghers of Pekiin and Baram and Ein Zeitim…"

"It was the noble lord's money that attracted them…"

"Don't be so cynical, Fania! These were simple Jews, workers of the land, keepers of the commandments. They made a big impression on the minister. Rabbi Israel exploited this impression and laid out his plan before him. According to this plan, all that the Jewish people needs is a little land—and Galilee will rise again! Everybody knows, it's excellent land: a little dollop of manure and hey, presto—bumper harvests!" Yehiel began to laugh. When he laughed, which didn't happen that often, it lit up his face all at once, as if a window had been opened, letting the sunshine into a darkened room.

"The only legacy of that convocation is our 'Elijah's Chair'…"

"That's where we'll hold the ceremony."

"In the Hirbet?"

"No. In the khan. We'll take 'Elijah's Chair' and the baby up there…"

"Fania!"

"Why not?" she persisted. "You see, you don't know!"

"Crazy Russian!"

"Where's Sasha?"

"He's gone."

"When?"

"Yesterday. Immediately after the birth."

"Strange."

"Are you sorry, Fania?"

"Yes, of course! He cheered us all up."

Fania knew this wasn't what Yehiel's question was about. Why did Sasha run away? What was he afraid of? Of himself? Of the woman who was revealed to him after the birth? And she? She needed time to understand her feelings. When she got out of bed for the first time, she found—painted on the front door—a red phoenix, wreathed in a cloud of flames.

Chapter nine

Fania was riding along the route from Safed to Rosh Pinnah. Rabbi Motel's mare proceeded slowly, planting thin, cautious legs between the steep cliff faces. From time to time she pricked up her sensitive ears, hearing the sound of falling rocks. She was heavily laden with packages, and Fania let her move at the pace that suited her. Soon, she had decided, she would buy a horse of her own. True, Rabbi Motel was happy to lend her his mare, but she knew that he, along with the other inhabitants of the settlement, viewed her activities with suspicion, and she didn't want to be beholden to any of them. Yehiel said nothing about her business, but she sensed it wasn't to his liking. Since her sister obtained the marketing rights for "Park Davis" pharmaceuticals, she had managed three times to send her consignments of medicine. Soon people would get used to seeing her as the supplier of medicine for Galilee and would flock to her door. And then she would no longer be forced to wander the roads. Every time she returned home, she felt as if she had been rescued from some disaster. The hill was rocky, without proper paths, and avalanches of stones blocked tracks that just yesterday seemed secure and permanent. On a number of occasions she had heard stories of bandits and beasts of prey. She had learned to recognize the tracks of the jackal and the wild boar, and on looking up from the ground, she saw before her the desolate valley, dotted with gleaming patches of marshland. In spring the hill was carpeted with flowers, in winter it became a morass of treacherous mud, and in summer it turned into an arid wilderness. Fania paused now on a ridge of rock. The hill fell away from its base as a sheer slope, and she looked out over the broad expanses spread out beneath her. She knew that this high vantage point gave the valley a glamour it didn't really possess, but this knowledge did not detract from her appreciation of the view. In her imagination she was Deborah the prophetess, standing on the summit and watching the forces of Sisera swarming toward treacherous Kishon. Or perhaps Gideon's three hundred warriors were down there in the valley, advancing on the Midianites…

The cry of an owl alarmed the mare, and she suddenly lost her footing. Fania dismounted and was adjusting the load to make movement easier, when suddenly blood-curdling shrieks were heard and horsemen appeared from the other side of the crevice. For a moment she froze where she stood, bristling with fear, but at once she drew the revolver from the recesses of her clothing and aimed it in the direction of the riders. She fired instinctively, without thinking, her only intention being to forestall the threat of attack. The horse of the first rider whinnied suddenly and reared on his hind legs, unseating his rider. Now she noticed there were three of them. The second horse collided with the injured horse and fell beside him. Fania fired one more shot in the air, while pulling on the reins of her mare with all her strength, to get her back on her feet. It was only after the bandits had fled that she began shaking all over, clinging to the mare for support. These were apparently opportunist thieves. The cry of the owl that she heard…someone had definitely passed on the word, telling them she was on her way back from Safed with money in her purse. Did she injure the horse or his rider? The horse was still running, so any injury could hardly be serious. And supposing, Heaven forbid, she killed the thief? His blood would be on her head. She already knew the ways of the East. They were allowed to ambush and rob—the "profession" of thieving supported whole villages—but woe betide anyone who dared to stand and defend himself! She must tell no one she had shot somebody. If they asked her, she would deny it. Even to Yehiel she wouldn't reveal her secret, not wanting him to be an accessory to her crime. With great difficulty she picked up the packages and loaded them again on the back of the horse. She was so glad to receive the books from the English doctor, so glad she hadn't stopped to consider the difficulty of transporting them to Rosh Pinnah. She couldn't leave them with Leah, because no Jew in Safed would dare bring "secular" books into his house, particularly books that were formerly the property of the missionary-doctor.

In the morning, when she set out for Safed, she had no idea these would be her proceeds. The idea of entering the house of the missionary-doctor only occurred to her when she happened to pass by his house and saw through the open windows the lines of books in glass-fronted cases. Months had passed since she last had picked up a book. *Anna Karenina* was a misty memory blended somehow with awareness of the fetus in her womb. A long time passed after Naphtali's birth before she felt strong enough to go back to work. Devorah, Rabbi Motel's daughter, called in every day to look after the baby and the other children, and Maryam Alhijah used to come down from Jaoni to do the heavy housework. Since her marriage to Isa the olive-oil merchant, she was spending a lot of time in the Silas house. The arrival of the Romanians in Rosh Pinnah brought to an end the mixed settlement system as instituted by the first pioneers. The Romanians wanted an exclusively Jewish settlement, and believed in their ability to keep marauders at bay without any help from the local peasantry. Yehiel didn't approve of this separation and he tried in all conceivable ways to maintain contact with his former neighbors. When Naphtali was born, it was his idea to invite Maryam into their house. She drew water from the spring, lit the stove and did the laundry. She returned to her home only after dark. Weariness descended on Fania. Her family now numbered six souls and suddenly the burden seemed too much. She was after all only nineteen years old, and most girls in Russia would be just beginning to think about marriage at that age...For several weeks she moved mechanically, getting up to feed Naphtali and going back to bed, wanting only to sleep and sleep and not wake up…

But the force of nature reasserted itself in her all the same. One day she got up, cut herself a slice of bread, spread it with olive oil, went outside and picked a radish from the vegetable patch for extra seasoning. And the taste of that bread, fresh and savory, seemed suddenly to open her eyes. She was impressed by the standard of the beds in the garden and she congratulated Bella and Moshe, the young gardeners. Their eyes shone with joy and pride and she hugged them warmly. It didn't take much to make them happy, although Moshe, already nine years old, avoided her embrace, blushing with embarrassment. He was very like his father, although his hair was red. He had the same long and shapely limbs, the same dark eyes and the same dignified restraint. Bella was more rounded and softer both in physique and personality. She repaid Fania with a firm embrace of her own, wrapping her arms around her waist. Fania suddenly saw the blue sky and far away, the lofty eminence of Hermon, its summit patched with white. In the land of her birth, Hermon would have been an unremarkable hill, but here, all were impressed by it.

A little bell rang when she opened the iron gate of the English doctor's house. With a pounding heart she climbed the house steps. The Jews of Safed not only boycotted the man, they spat in all directions when passing his house, and whispered a verse or two to be absolutely sure that the contagion he was spreading would not infect them. Doctor Bartlett knew she needed a lot of courage to enter his house. He greeted her with an ironic smile and was surprised to hear she came as the representative of an American drug company. Women in trade were not such a rare sight in Safed—so long as they stood in dark little booths, reached only by leaping over stinking channels of sewage, if they were lucky enough not to slip and fall in. Women were also seen in the marketplace, sitting next to their husbands like birds on a branch. They didn't go anywhere on their own, and under no circumstances were they allowed to socialize with men.

"Are you new in Safed?" asked the doctor.

"I'm from Rosh Pinnah. I see you have a fine library. May I take a look?"

"By all means! But the books are in English."

"Jane Austen is my favorite!" cried Fania in an emotional voice, clasping her hands over her heart, to the utter amazement of the doctor. "Dickens, I love too," she added hastily, her eyes flashing. "I've read *David Copperfield* three times. But Jane Austen is the best of them all. I love *The Scarlet Letter* too…"

"That's a scary story."

"Of course! But I like scary stories…*Ivanhoe!*" she ran her finger over the leather bindings. "And Ruskin…no, him I'm not so keen on…what a collection! Oh, I'm sorry! Excuse me!" she was suddenly embarrassed. "It wasn't for books that I came in here…"

"Oh, there's no need to apologize!" he smiled at her. "It's a long time since I've had the chance to speak English, and about books too!"

"No, no, I shouldn't be trespassing on your time."

And already she was taking bottles and phials and pillboxes from the bundle and arranging them on the counter. It was soon made plain to her that the doctor didn't need medicines at all, because in just a few weeks from now he was planning to leave Safed anyway.

"Oh? Yes? Why?"

"If I worked among the Muslims, the authorities would throw me in jail. And the Jews don't come to me. Three years I've lived in Safed and in all that time I've had three Jewish patients out of a population of five thousand! And you want to know the truth? I don't want them to come to me. I'll never forget one poor wretch who came to me: his wife and children disowned him, he lost his job, and in the end he hanged himself."

"And where will you go?"

"To Jerusalem. To the English Hospital. I'm not fooling myself"—again that sour smile appeared on his lips—"your rabbis have put armed guards around the place. Imagine it—any Jew who dies in the English Hospital will be denied burial! But at least there I'll have somebody to talk to…Have you been to Jerusalem?"

"No."

"They say the city's developing. They're building new quarters outside the walls of the Old City."

"I have a friend in Jerusalem."

"Russian?"

"Yes," Fania smiled, "a painter. He's learning metalwork there."

"Oh, one of the newcomers. I promise you, he'll be the only painter among the twenty-five thousand Jews of Jerusalem."

"Yes, I'm sure of that," Fania laughed. And then she asked the question that interested her most of all: what was going to happen to the books? Would he be willing to sell a few of them to her?

An hour later she left his house escorted by the *kavass*, carrying two sacks containing the finest specimens of English literature. She left the doctor with a hearing-tube and a tiny set of scales, and if he'd let her she would have given him medicines too, but he refused vehemently to take them from her. He had been wondering just how he was going to transport the books from Safed to Jerusalem. He accompanied her as far as the courtyard gate, but no further. Outside, she was greeted by the familiar tirades in the corn market and the vegetable market. One old woman who was sitting in her doorway knitting swooped on her suddenly and scratched her arm with the knitting needles. Fania urged the mare to pick up speed, stroking her flanks with her hands, blind with fury. Oh, how she hated Safed! She hated the streets with their running sewage, hated the residents since the day they pelted her with stones. If she could only share her feelings—but with whom? Helen Leah was in Zamara, while Yehiel found her activities repugnant and feared for her safety on her regular jaunts to Safed and Haifa and Tiberias…

Fania sat and winnowed wheat. Beside her sat three little girls reading from one book—Esther, youngest granddaughter of Riva Frumkin, Malcah, child of Rabbi Motel's old age, and Bella. Tamara leaned against Fania and put her head in her lap. Bella was reading aloud from *Message to the Children of Israel*, a book of short stories by Bendetson:

The raven saw the eagle sitting on its eggs for thirty days and said: Now I know why its chicks can see so well and why they are more powerful than any other bird in the sky. I shall try to do likewise.

In vain Fania tried to concentrate. She was too agitated. The bundle of books on the bed was the silent witness to the attack of the bandits and what had happened after it. The joy she had felt in these books had dissipated with the smoke from her revolver. She wanted to hide her perturbation of spirit, behave as if nothing had happened, but the words in Bella's mouth sounded meaningless. She glanced at the Russian translation appearing alongside the Hebrew text and then checked the word in Mandelstam's dictionary, but still it was as if her mind had been swallowed up. Some of the stories she remembered from her distant childhood days, from the fables of Karilov or Lessing. But the words didn't seem to hang together. Even the children seemed strange to her suddenly…and the whole of this session…

When Moshe started going to elementary school, Fania was concerned over the fate of Bella and the rest of the girls. Were they doomed to a life of illiteracy, as the ladies of Safed apparently were? This must not be allowed to happen! She informed her neighbors that in the afternoons she would be putting on classes for girls, and fished Bendetson's book out of her chest. The book was published in Warsaw, in 1872, turned up in Elizavetgrad, and made its way from there to Rosh Pinnah. She thought all the girls would take advantage of her class, but in the end the only takers were Esther Frumkin and Malcah Bernstein. The three-year-old Tamara wandered among them, listening, picking up the odd word and repeating it, tugging at her mother's dress or sticking a finger in the book. Her beauty embarrassed Fania. Involuntarily, she wondered about the man who was her father. She never saw him, as throughout that horrific episode she had been floundering in a dark whirlpool, but somehow she sensed he was young and strong. Does she resemble him? she wondered as a cold shudder passed through her. If anything happens to me she'll be all alone in the world, without a father, without a mother…

"Sit beside Maryam," said Fania to Tamara. Maryam loved sitting in the "madrasa". Now she was sitting to the side, nursing Tuli in her lap. Soon the young women would be coming here, the older sisters of the children, their mothers. After finishing the housework and before the time came for the stroll in the "Boulevard" as they called the main street, they came here with their knitting or sewing and read *Havatzelet* together. Israel Dov Frumkin, editor of *Havatzelet*, used to send a copy of the paper from Jerusalem to Issar Frumkin. And when Issar had finished reading it he passed it on to Yehiel. Sometimes long weeks passed before the paper reached Yehiel and Fania's house, but this didn't detract from the enjoyment of the women. It was like a compensation for the educational ban imposed on them. Men studied the Pentateuch and Rashi and portions of the Mishnah; the scholars among them sat down in the evening after a hard day at work and studied the Six Orders and the rabbinical injunctions; the minimalists contented themselves with the recitation of Psalms. But there wasn't a single one of them who didn't study something. Only women didn't study anything. Education, which was a kind of inexorable obligation imposed on boys of three years old and over, didn't apply to girls at all. Fania drew deep satisfaction from the progress the girls were making. They learned the letters of the alphabet without any real difficulty and took to reading avidly and with enjoyment. It was impossible not to compare Bella's diligence with Moshe's reluctance.

It was only today that time crept by slowly. Not only did Fania not dare to cancel the "class", she clung to it in the hope of distracting her mind. But her ears were attentive to noises coming from outside. From time to time she thought she heard the hooves of horses, the shouts of police officers, the yells of vengeance-seekers. Perhaps she should get the children away. Since the pogrom she had firmly resolved that if ever she was attacked again she would stand her ground; it seemed she was almost expecting riots to erupt around her. But now that the thing had really happened, she was quaking with fear. It wasn't just her life that was at stake, but the lives of the little children too.

She was picking grains of sand out of ears of corn, tossing

them behind her back with a rhythmic motion. Her hand movements matched those of her knitting and sewing companions. Someone read aloud:

> *Havatzelet, 7 Heshvan 5645, 1885. Although we derive no pleasure from depressing our readers with frightening rumors, we must at this time warn them that it will not be long before the world reverts to a state of primeval chaos, and perhaps when the anti-Semites hear that the end of all fleshly life is at hand, they will no longer concentrate their efforts on maligning the Children of Israel on the grounds that mankind as a whole has a very short time-span on this earth, and may this be our consolation.*

Silence descended on the room, as the young women tried to digest this ominous prediction. Suddenly Fania burst out laughing: "In my father's house they used to say: 'It's a good thing if the house catches fire—the bugs will be incinerated!' This is the same kind of logic!"

Abruptly, she stopped laughing. Yehiel was standing in the doorway. The young women hurried to get up and take their leave. Because he was home early they sensed something had happened. Although she was alarmed at the sight of him, she couldn't help feeling there was something pleasurable in seeing him through the eyes of her neighbors.

"Give me the revolver," he said, the moment the other women had left the house.

"What? Why?"

"Give it to me!"

"What's happened?"

"Fania!"

When she handed him the revolver, he peered into the barrel, paused for a moment, then sniffed it and went out of the room. Through the window she saw him approaching Lulik's hut. Lulik wasn't afraid of Yehiel just as he wasn't afraid of the children. Through the fog of his insanity he understood that they were his family. When Yehiel returned a moment later he asked her:

"Were you in Safed today?"

"Yes."

"Who saw you there?"

"Who didn't? Everyone saw me! Why do you ask?"

"An Arab from Tivaon was taken to the hospital in Safed. His friend said that a woman shot him on the road between Safed and Rosh Pinnah."

"Oy!"

"Oy indeed!"

"They attacked me! What are they saying? What's his condition?"

"We'll find that out tomorrow. Tonight I'm getting you away to Beirut, to Rivka's house."

"No!"

"When we know the extent of the man's injuries—we can decide what to do."

"I'm not running away," she said obstinately. "This is my permanent home, Yehiel."

For a moment he looked at her, questions flashing in his eyes. Then he said, whispering hoarsely in a tone of entreaty:

"They'll be coming here, Fania. There aren't many women riding alone between Safed and Rosh Pinnah."

"They'll have to prove it was me."

"That won't be too difficult."

"There were three of them and I was alone. A lone woman attacking three armed men—who's going to believe that?"

"What do you expect, Fania? Justice? Where do you think this is?"

"You're not running away, why should I?"

"It's getting late. If your own life isn't precious to you, at least think of Tamara and Tuli."

Fania felt choked. He didn't count himself among the ones precious to her. Not Bella and Moshe, either. Did he still think this was purely a marriage of convenience? How long? All at once she gave in to him.

"I'm not going to Rivka's."

"They'll be looking for you at Leah's. That's the first place they'll try."

"I'll go to Yesod Hamaaleh."

"No!"

"They won't follow me there."

"The toxic air of Yesod Hamaaleh is notorious. Anyone who has the nerve to spend one night beside Lake Huleh will get a whole year's worth of fever out of it."

"The Mizrahi brothers, your friends, they'll look after me."

"They can't protect you from malaria."

"I won't go without the revolver."

"Oh please, Fania, no need for that! I'll come with you."

"I'm not going to stand there empty-handed next time I'm attacked!"

Yehiel was about to say something but seemed to think better of it. He went to the hut and came back with the revolver in his hand. Meanwhile Fania opened the chest and took out the peasant outfit that she hadn't worn in more than a year. The trousers were a little tight in the region of the belly and the thighs. Several months had passed since the birth and her body had still not yet returned to its former dimensions.

At nightfall they set out in the direction of Yesod Hamaaleh. Or as Yehiel continued to call it, Izber, after the Bedouin tribe that used to visit the place. Yehiel wore a woolen shawl over his shoulders and Fania carried a bundle containing bread, onions and cheese.

"Have you taken quinine?"

Fania smiled into the night.

"Do you love me, Yehiel?"

Yehiel stopped suddenly and she collided with him. He hugged her and she laughed, panting from the effort of the rapid walking.

"You're my wife!"

"A lot of men don't love their wives!"

"Why are you asking now?"

"It's the fourth time you've asked me if I've taken quinine."

"I don't want you to get ill."

From the tone of his voice she could tell he was smiling. Stars lit the sky and they made an effort to keep to the dark side of the road, hidden from the eyes of ambushers.

"All this has happened before…" Yehiel whispered.

"What?"

"After the Damascus blood libel of 1840, a gang of marauders tried to break into the Jewish quarter. My grandfather, Musa Silas, killed one of the rioters, had to flee for fear of vengeance and didn't stop until he reached Jaoni. More refugees from Damascus followed him there. The wealthier ones among them bought land, the poorer ones rented land and paid 'Kisam'. A few of the families opened dairies and made cheese that was renowned throughout Galilee. The Bedouin started raiding Jaoni to rustle sheep and cattle, and in one of the raids the Sheikh's son was killed. Musa Silas was forced to flee again, and he moved to Sidon along with most of the residents. It seems we're repeating the same ritual…"

"What's going to happen, Yehiel? What's going to happen?!"

"When I moved from Safed to Jaoni, I made up my mind I would never move from there, not ever. What's going to happen? I don't know."

"But we're responsible for our children, Yehiel! We can gamble with our lives, but not with theirs!"

"I can only do the best I can. That's all. More than that I can't do…"

"I hope the robber wasn't killed. As far as I could see it was the horse that was hit, not the man. But it all happened so quickly!"

The trousers protected her legs from the thorny bushes. From time to time she tripped over a stone or slipped into a hollow, imagining she saw snakes startled from their repose. Suddenly there was a musty smell in the air and their way was blocked by a fence of cactus, entwined with prickly shrubs. When they started looking for an opening in the fence, they were greeted by a chorus of barking dogs. They stopped where they were, glancing anxiously toward the dark shapes of the tents. Silver plates gleamed in the moonlight.

"Those are the swamps," Yehiel whispered. "Keep clear of them! And don't drink the water."

"What about the Izber tribe? How do they survive here?"

"They pasture their sheep and camels here just for a few days, and then even they are forced to leave. Fania, we can still go back. You'd be safer in Jaffa. Or in Beirut."

"I'm not afraid, Yehiel."

The silhouette of a man appeared suddenly in an opening that they hadn't noticed before.

"Who's there?"

"Yehiel Silàs, from Rosh Pinnah."

"Yehiel! It's me, Shlomo Mizrahi."

The two men embraced in the darkness.

"Fania, this is Sage Shlomo Mizrahi. He and his brother Shaul are working the land of the Abu family here. Shlomo, this is my wife Fania. She needs to hide here."

"The responsibility is on me and on my head. Come on, Fania, I'll take you to meet the women and the children."

"Children!" Yehiel was shocked. "Since when?"

"New settlers have arrived. From Mezhirich. And I have brought my wife here too, and my children. He who dwells on high will be my helper. If they ask about her," he pointed to Fania, "we'll say she's from Mezhirich too."

The man spoke in an accent typical of the Sephardis of Safed. Perceptible in his voice was that stubborn and desperate devotion so familiar to her. She shuddered convulsively. Crazy! They're crazy, and I'm crazy too. Mother in Heaven! Do you see your little Fania? The pampered daughter who sewed herself a dress of blue velvet, who played the piano and was late for school every morning...what am I doing in this desolate land? Running away from Bedouin who are after my blood and taking refuge in this marshy death trap...

"What did you say?" asked Yehiel.

"Who will look after the children?"

"Don't worry," he squeezed her arm.

"What will you say, how will you explain my disappearance?"

"You've gone to Haifa, to sell medicines."

"Moshe can give Lulik his food. He isn't scared of him."

"I know."

The women and children slept in the only stone building. This was a big, windowless barn, and because the people of Yesod Hamaaleh hadn't obtained a building permit from the authorities, they were forced to accommodate the animals in the barn, too. The stench hanging in the air was unbearable. Fania told Sage Shlomo she preferred to sleep in one of the tents, and he put her in the tent where his own family was quartered. She lay down in a space she found between the children. The night was cold and she wrapped herself in the big woolen shawl. The chorus of coughing intensified the sense of chill and neglect. Through the canvas of the tent she heard the whispered conversation between Yehiel and Shlomo Mizrahi.

"Where do you sleep, Sage Shlomo?"

"Over there. There were more tents but some burned down."

"When will you start building?"

"Soon."

"No money?"

"No money. At the end of last year one of the laborers here killed himself, and the Turks decided we had murdered him. Almost all the villagers were arrested, and if it weren't for Yakov Hai Abu we'd still be in jail now. Our freedom cost a lot of money. We scraped together our last coppers, Yakov Hai 'fed' the bureaucrats sixty-five dinars, Oliphant sent fifty napoleons…"

"How many are you here?"

"Today? Eight farmers. A total of thirty-seven souls. Men, women and children."

"How many came from Mezhirich?"

"Twenty-two…most of them in Safed. Conditions here are hard, as you see, and they have no confidence in the future."

"And you?"

"I was here when there was just me and my brother in the place. I'm going to leave now? Anyway, a new worker has just arrived here,

Rabbi Israel Ashkenazi, and now he's learning the art of tent-making from the Bedouin. And Rabbi Fishel Salomon is here…"

"And the planting?"

"The planting…" Sage Shlomo sighed. "The Mezhirich contingent bought two thousand four hundred dunams from the Abu brothers and paid five hundred and fifty napoleons for them, and started out with such enthusiasm! If it weren't for the Abu brothers it would all have gone up in smoke. They provided the oxen and the plow and even the seeds…But you can't force the ground to bear crops…And you, Yehiel, how are things with you?"

"I have a newborn son."

"Congratulations! How many children do you have?"

"Four."

"Go forth and multiply indeed!"

"Look after my wife, Sage Shlomo."

"Are you going?"

"Yes."

"In the middle of the night?! Wait until morning!"

"No, I must go back."

"God be with you, Yehiel."

"God willing, I shall return tomorrow night. If not before."

Fania strained her ears, but couldn't hear the sound of Yehiel's footsteps receding. She lay on the hard ground staring into the darkness, listening to the coughing and the breathing of the children. She covered her whole body with the shawl, her head as well, to protect herself from the mosquitoes that swarmed in a warm cloud above the tents. She was tired and agitated and feared she'd be unable to sleep. She didn't know how much time had passed when she woke to the sound of weeping and wailing. Lanterns had been lit, and by their dim light she made out running figures appearing and disappearing, silhouetted against the canvas of the tent. The darkness was less viscous now, flecked with shades of metallic grey, but the cold froze her body.

"What's going on?" she asked a woman passing by the tent.

"Shavtai Likermann's wife."

"Is she in childbirth?"

The woman stopped at once and stared at Fania, looking bemused: "Who are you?"

"I'm a guest of Sage Shlomo."

"Russian?"

"What's the problem with Rabbi Shavtai's wife?"

"Black urine fever. She's dying."

"I have some quinine. Where is she?"

A reddish gleam shone through the silver vapors of the rising dawn. In the barn lay a young woman, her limbs distorted and gurgling sounds emerging from her throat. From time to time a spasm passed through her body, which flailed like a stranded fish dying in the sand. Beside the invalid sat women and men with helpless fear in their eyes. It was obvious nothing could be done for her. Fania turned on her heel and went back to the tent. Suddenly a shriek split the silence, like a period, a sign of the end. The children in the tent woke up and looked fearfully at the strange woman who lay beside them. Her gaze was fixed on the roof of the tent. The effort seemed to her so great and the price so exorbitant! Yehiel saw the sacrifice as a price worth paying for salvation. "In grief you shall bear children"—elevated to the status of a national motto. Well, she's had enough of grief! She wants to live! Her trade in medicines enables her to exist without hunger, and this is only the beginning. She's managed to pay for the first consignments and soon she'll be sending the third installment, and this too is salvation of a kind for the Land of Israel.

The sun rose in the east, beyond the Jordan. From the green swamps fetid vapors were rising. Sweat was now pouring from Fania's body. The heat and humidity made breathing difficult, and she feared the effects of taking the noxious air into her lungs. Through the flap of the tent she watched what was going on. The body of the deceased, wrapped in a blanket, had been loaded onto the back of a camel. A small cortege of sobbing men and women accompanied her as far as the gate.

"We don't have to go on living here among these infernal swamps!" one of the women exclaimed.

"It's a commandment! A stone crying out from the wall!"

Fania recognized the voice of Sage Shlomo.

"What stone?" she asked him.

"We found a stone with Hebrew letters on it, inscribed by a Hebrew farmer who lived here two thousand years ago...Who are you?"

"Yehiel Silas's wife. We met last night, don't you remember?"

Sage Shlomo looked in astonishment at the tall young woman in the Bedouin garb, as if he'd never seen her before. Fania was used to the impression her appearance made on people.

"Where have they taken the deceased?"

"To Safed."

"On a camel?!"

"We haven't got a cemetery."

"What do you call all this?" demanded the woman who had spoken before, waving her arms around. "Isn't it a cemetery?"

"We shall have proper housing here soon, and good orchards. A cemetery, too."

"At what price?"

"When we came here, my brother and I, thirteen years ago, we wanted only one thing: to plow a furrow for King David. And from Heaven we have been given the word that our offering is accepted: The stone that we found is a message from one generation to another."

"My brother-in-law ran away from here to Australia and he's pleading with us to go and join him," the woman said to Fania, her face pale and anxious. "And we're going! I'm not staying here and waiting for black urine fever to kill me too! That's my message to the next generation!"

"The inscription on the stone is in Aramaic, and it translates as: *All those who settle here will be well remembered.*"

Fania wondered if he was trying to fortify the woman's spirits or his own. Rosh Pinnah seemed a lively and bustling metropolis compared with Yesod Hamaaleh. In the light of day it turned out there was another case of malaria: one of the young girls in the tent had gone down with a fever and her mother sat beside her, swaying back and forth in silent prayer and massaging the little body under the blanket. The humid air hung heavy over the valley and the heat was stifling. But the mother tried in vain to keep her daughter warm, and the little girl's teeth chattered in the cold.

Fania started walking. She passed through the gap in the cactus fence, scratched by the thorns and stumbling against the rocks. Her steps lengthened and soon turned to a running pace. Her only idea was to get away from this place, go home! To her husband and her children, far from the plague fumes! She climbed the hill, taking the direction which, her instinct told her, would lead her back to Rosh Pinnah. Some force was pulling her to put some distance between herself and this place and not look back at those demented wretches sacrificing their lives among the swamps. The infernal malaria will kill them off one by one, the desperate women and the innocent children and the stubborn men and the geriatric zealots, but she won't be among them. She didn't slow the pace of her walking, dominated by a single impulse: homeward! After two hours of walking and running in a southerly direction, she could make out in the west the little houses of Rosh Pinnah strewn across one of the ridges. From time to time she missed her footing and her breathing was heavy, until at last she sank down and sprawled on the ground with limbs spread-eagled. When she opened her eyes a bright sky floated above her, feathery clouds drifting on a sea of blue. A feeling of serenity suddenly descended on her and it was if she couldn't understand what it was that had scared her just a short while before. Where was she running to in this headlong style? And why? What was the source of its strength, this inexorable impulse that was driving her home? Yes, she had heard of storks returning to their nesting-sites in Europe after migrating to Africa, of dogs walking hundreds of miles to be reunited with their masters, of people sent to penal colonies who endured all the torments of hell in the hope of returning to the four dilapidated walls that represented their home. And what of her home? Is it just four dilapidated walls? Four walls and a man. How strange it is, the bond of love that binds her to Yehiel! She married him because he offered her a roof over her head, and it ended up with her loving him more than any other human being in the world. If she had married any other man, could she have loved him as much? After all, even if given the opportunity to choose, she would be choosing her loved one from a circumscribed field, and with how many men could she have become acquainted between the ages of sixteen and twenty? Pupils studying at her school, neighbors, sons of friends…It's only an imaginary choice! Meaning, do the need for love and the aptitude for love count for more than the qualities of the loved one? And building the family nest is apparently a part of that misty amalgam of impulses motivating the woman to find a mate. How strange the thoughts running around in her head! She remembered a long letter she wrote to her friend, the last Passover in Elizavetgrad. "One thought worries me," she wrote, "who am I? Everything around me seems so superfluous, marginal and pointless…Are we doomed to copying the example set by our parents, with no opportunity to change it or stamp our own personality on life…" How precious to her now was the memory of that "marginal and pointless" life! And how hard had she fought for it! What a tenuous thread now links the young woman sprawled on the ground in the hills of Galilee with the spoiled girl, child of her parents' old age, tormenting herself with existential speculations.

She was lucky Yehiel was so different from the other people around them. Even though he had "bought" her for a loaf of bread and a roof, he saw her as a free person. She knew they were reckoned "strange birds", and indeed since arriving in the country she had not known a single family in which the relations prevailing between the spouses were even remotely similar to the relations between them. Since Yehiel was a man driven by the force of principle, she assumed his treatment of her was not accidental either.

It seemed to her she heard the sound of falling stones. It was good for her, sinking into thoughts like this, and she felt no inclination to move a muscle. In spite of this she leaned her head on the palm of her hand and looked in the direction from which she imagined she had heard the sounds. How desolate was the vista before her! A little cluster of black tents was visible now in a gully between the hills. The sheep of the Bedouin had consumed the meager pasture and the land was bare. The Sea of Tiberias and Lake Huleh reflected back the light of the sun and their surfaces gleamed like sheets of white-hot metal in which the dark hills of Gilead were reflected in their turn. Life began to stir around her: grasshoppers sprang from the sand, a tortoise poked its head out from the safe haven of its shell, a flock of jays flew past her, and a big wild cat suddenly broke cover and stopped to stare at her, as bemused by the sight of Fania as Fania was bemused by the sight of the creature. She remembered Moshe's tortoise which had lived in their house for the past two years, and suddenly she remembered the reason she had left Rosh Pinnah. What if she injured the Arab and he died from his wounds, perish the thought? If she returns to Rosh Pinnah she'll be endangering all the residents. No, she can't go home by daylight! For some time she sat, wondering what to do, and then suddenly, crossing over the crest of the hill, who should appear but Leibel the postman. He was clutching his sack of mail to his stomach as the donkey paced slowly and cautiously down the slope. When he was passing her she called out to him: "Hello, Reb Leibel!" He was so startled he nearly fell off his donkey.

"Silas! What are you doing here? I thought I was being robbed!"

"What have you got that's worth stealing, Reb Leibel?" asked Fania. She was so glad to be meeting Leibel. If she wasn't so bashful she'd have invited him to dismount from the donkey and sit down with her for a while and chat. "Where have you come from?"

"From Safed. And I'm on my way to deliver to those lunatics down there. Just now in Safed they're burying the wife of Rabbi Shavtai Likermann, bless her. Such a young woman!"

"You could have given them their post back there."

"Yes? And what about the maniac in Shoshanat Hayarden?"

"He's still living there?"

"And not alone! His son has come from America, and Abuhav from Safed has joined them. They say he was very rich, this Lubovsky, and he had a big estate in Russia, with gardens and woods. I met him last year, when he came to this country for the first time. Man of mystery! Then he went to America to bring both his sons back from there, but only one of them joined him. Do you know them?"

"No."

"They're so happy when I come to them! If only the favorite son in America could see how his father is watering the ground with his blood…"

"Why do they stay there, Reb Leibel? "

"Why indeed! Why do you stay in Rosh Pinnah, eh? Why did Yehiel Silas settle in Jaoni? People believe what's written in the Book of Books and don't believe what their eyes are seeing. They see thorns and brambles and imagine they're feasting their eyes on luxuriant orchards in the Bether hills! Rabbi Shmuel Abu presented the Jordan plain to Rabbi Mordecai Lobovsky as if he was handing over the crown jewels! If you could see them today! Lonely! Hungry! Where they draw their energy from, I don't know! I'm exhausted after a few hours riding on a donkey…So, where have you come from and where are you going?"

"I was in Yesod Hamaaleh. Did you hear any news in Safed?"

"News? What news? Ah! The chemist is going to reopen the pharmacy, and with whose money, you may ask—since the community has stopped allocating funds to the pharmacy—with the money of the apostate Utchert. This criminal will now be responsible for the health of the Jews of Safed! Where are the sticks? I ask, where are the fists and the stones? The Volhynians and the Lithuanians and the Romanians have been fighting one another like cats and dogs over any trivial thing—I don't need to tell you—and suddenly they're as meek as lambs. Money has sealed their lips! What will you do now with all your medicines?"

"I'm not worried."

"I delivered a letter for you."

"Yes?" Fania leaped to her feet. "Who from?"

"Your uncle in Jaffa."

"And what does he say?"

Now it was Leibel's turn to laugh. Among the residents of Safed the story was well-known: One day Awkil and his marauders attacked Leibel the postman and stole his sack of mail. The unfortunate Leibel was taken to the hospital, unconscious. When he came round he opened his eyes and said: "Tell Rabbi Ayreh Babis that his brother will be arriving from Damascus next week."

Since he had said nothing at all about a wounded Arab, Fania assumed that the man hadn't been badly hurt.

"So, I'll be on my way, Mrs. Silas."

"Goodbye, Reb Leibel. Take care of yourself!"

At the turn of the day Fania returned to her house and found Riva Frumkin, standing and folding laundry at the table. Tuli lay beside her, clutching his favorite cow-bone and chewing it with his little teeth.

"What are you doing here?" Riva was suspicious.

"I've come home. Where's Yehiel?"

"He's gone with the children to the flour-mill."

Riva—the best of neighbors! Her face so gaunt, with a hint of green about it.

"Are you well, Riva?"

"Yes."

"You don't look well."

"If you can open your eyes and see what's going on around you, you'd do better worrying about your own household!" She had never known Riva looking as angry as this before.

"I do worry about my household!"

"You're running around too much!"

"Yehiel forced me to leave!"

"You're not a child, you're a woman. A mother. Yehiel is grey with fatigue, he's lonely and miserable. You've turned into a gypsy!"

"He isn't miserable!"

"What kind of a home is this? Doesn't he deserve a home?"

"And what about me? Don't I deserve a home?"

"Improve it!"

"How? What are you talking about? Surely I don't need to tell you! What am I supposed to use to improve the house? We hardly have enough food to keep us alive! And even that's down to my 'running around' as you call it. Don't you know that?"

"You should be here waiting for him when he comes home from work. You're his wife."

"He goes out before dawn and comes back after dark tired to death, and goes to bed so tomorrow he can start all over again. Who am I waiting for? I'm trying as hard as I can to find extra sources of income, to make life easier for Yehiel. We're not short of men, Riva. The redemption of the land burns like fire in their bones. Everything else—means nothing!"

"Are you angry with him?"

"No."

"Talk to him."

"When? I told you, he comes home exhausted and goes to sleep at once."

"If you had the choice, would you leave him?"

"No!"

Riva took a deep breath and slapped the back of Fania's hand. Her bony hand was slightly damp.

"You're a good girl, Fania. And he—he's a big oak tree! Wise, upright, modest. He deserves a little happiness."

Fania wanted to shout: What about me? What do I deserve?—but she said nothing. Riva's anger eased a little.

"If he wasn't working so hard, what would the two of you be doing?"

"Oh…" Fania hesitated. The rancor was erased from her eyes and she spoke dreamily: "I'm not afraid of work, Riva! But if it was up to me we'd be working less, both of us. Just so we'd have time and energy for other things, things that to me are no less important than food. We'd read books, invite friends to our house and visit them in their houses and enjoy cultivated conversation. I'd play the piano…and one day, who knows, we'll put on our best clothes and go out for short excursions in the buggy, Mr. and Mrs. Silas…" Fania smiled. How banal these things sounded when spoken aloud! When she turned, she found that Yehiel was standing in the doorway and listening to her words. She wondered how much of their conversation he had heard.

"I'm not complaining!" she apologized hurriedly. "You didn't choose hardship out of love of hardship, either."

"Of course not…what are you doing here?"

"I'm going!" announced Riva Frumkin, blowing a kiss at Tuli. "Reb Leibel brought you a letter," she remembered and handed Fania an envelope.

The moment Riva was out of the house Yehiel turned to Fania: "Is this a new custom?" he asked angrily, "Complaining about your husband in front of the neighbors?"

"I wasn't complaining! Riva asked me how we would live *if* we had the choice."

"You wouldn't live with me."

Fania opened her mouth to reply and closed it immediately. A wave of anger and resentment swept over her and she couldn't trust her voice. Now Yehiel was confirming what she had suspected from the very first moment! For a moment she thought she could be a substitute for the lost love, but now she knew she would never succeed in taking the place of the dead Rachel in his heart. Rivka had told her this in no uncertain terms. Impossible to wipe out the past. Whether we like it or not, it accompanies us wherever we go. Yehiel, too, was apparently shocked by what he had said, since he hastened to add, as if to soften the impact of his statement:

"I was in Safed. I asked Doctor Blidin to go to the hospital and check on the condition of the Arab. By the time the doctor got there, the man had discharged himself. A grazed heel, that was all it was. They bandaged him and kept him in overnight, but in the morning his family came and took him home. He told the doctor treating him he had been injured when he was attacked by a dozen armed marauders…"

Fania didn't smile. His former words still rankled. One thought only was reverberating in her head: if he had the choice, *he* wouldn't live with *her*. He'd said as much himself. He could never deny this. And she, the fool, believed him when he said he loved her…

For some time her eyes wandered over the lines her uncle had written, and she saw nothing but the black smudges of ink. Then she managed to focus her gaze on the text of the letter.

"Yehiel!" she cried, forgetting her angry preoccupations for a moment. "My uncle is going to marry your aunt!"

"Good luck to them!"

"He's inviting us to the wedding."

"When is it?"

"About three weeks from now."

"Right in the middle of the plowing season!"

"What plowing?"

"I'm an agricultural worker, Fania."

"You haven't even got any seeds!"

"I have seeds! And oxen, too, and a plow. No, I haven't gone out of my mind! A miracle has happened to us, Fania! The envoy of Baron Rothschild was here—Mr. Elijah Shaid—and he's decided to help us."

"Elijah the Prophet!"

"Over the next nine months, he will pay every single one of us a monthly subsidy of ten francs. He will help us finish building the houses and the barns and the kitchen gardens and he's even promised to repair the water conduits. We're going to build a synagogue and a school…"

"Yehiel! I'm afraid! It sounds too good to be true."

"I know…Every settler will receive one ox and one cow, and a horse and a donkey and barley for fodder, and plows. For the husbandry of the livestock we'll be getting a subsidy of four thousand francs to tide us over until the first harvest, and one thousand two hundred francs for planting fruit trees—and on top of this, all the settlement's debts are being paid off. Who knows, Mrs. Silas, perhaps we'll be taking trips in that buggy yet!"

Instead of happiness, she felt only trepidation. The future looked altogether too rosy, and she feared they couldn't cope with another disappointment.

"We must go to the wedding."

"You go."

"They're inviting both of us! Just imagine it, a kind of double blood-tie…Are you happy, Yehiel?"

"About what?"

"About the wedding, of course!"

"I don't know. Mixed marriages don't always work out. Muscovites and Mograbis…"

Was he talking about *them*? She peered at him suspiciously. His face was blank, but she noticed a mischievous spark in his eye.

"Are you making fun of me?"

"Perish the thought, my dear!"—and he burst into laughter, hugged her round the waist and lifted her high in the air as if she was one of the children.

Chapter ten

Fania was taken aback by the mass of people. She took deep, urgent breaths, conscious of her lofty stature, of the festive plait wound around her scrubbed face. When did she last go to a party? At thirteen years old? Just like this, with the same kind of plait, feeling freshly laundered and confused. But then she was among friends, part of a little flock of chickens, poised and ready to erupt at any moment into a chorus of frantic giggling. And here she was in Jaffa, sitting with the women on a bench padded with cushions. The last light of the sun gleamed on the thin headscarves, on the dusty gold strands of their hair. It seemed she's the only one who arrived here alone; all the others came in groups, talking in restrained voices. If only she had stuck to her original intention and returned to Rosh Pinnah immediately after the wedding! But both her uncle and his new wife urged her to stay for the festivities. "You're my only surviving blood-relative," her uncle pointed out, and she gave in. As if there weren't enough people here without her.

"Elijah the Prophet…Elijah the Tishbite…Elijah of Gilead…"

The men sat at the table and sang, their eyes half-closed. Their bodies swayed and with their fingers they rolled the crumbs of bread that had fallen on the white cloth. White light was reflected from the sea and struck the high windows with dazzling force. The ladies sitting beside her accompanied the singing of the men with a soft murmur. Most of them she knew. There were ladies here belonging to the Blattner, Amzaleg and Luria dynasties, and maidens of the houses of Moyal and Schloss. She met them in the house of Bella Rokeah-Mandelstam, and on Sabbath mornings in the garden of Baron Ustinov. Some of the songs she remembered from her father's house, evidently appropriated by Shimon Rokeah from his father-in-law's house in Brisk. Unbidden, scraps of memory passed before her eyes, like black birds flying past. On the table were a big loaf and wine and dishes of salted wet fish. Perhaps it was these that reminded her of her father's house. She was seeing salted fish for the first time since arriving in the country. She wondered if her sisters were still singing the family songs, one of them in Woodbine and the other in Boston. Here she goes again, fleeing from longings for what is lost and will never return. How flimsy are the defenses that she wraps around herself. Sleeping at night, visions of the silvered poplars would return to her, a raft on the broad river, cherries in the basket, the tastes and smells...In Rosh Pinnah the memories were crushed beneath the stifling weight of fatigue and hunger and arduous labor, but here in Jaffa they had the space to rejuvenate. Two weeks had already passed since she arrived in Jaffa, and at least another week would elapse before her return to Rosh Pinnah, because that morning, in a light-headed moment, she had promised Imber she would accompany him on a visit to the settlement of Gedera. In fact, not so much light-headedness, more a palliative, a lump of sugar that she was offering him to sweeten his bitter and seething resentment. Oh, never, never, will she be "calm and free" like Varenka in *Anna Karenina*. Heart constantly fluttering and breathing tangled, and so quick to make decisions that are irreversible. She can't tell Imber now that she's changed her mind, that she's *not* going to Gedera with him tomorrow!

They met in Baron Ustinov's garden, when she was out walking with her uncle and her new aunt. All that week, the heat in Jaffa had hung heavy, and Fania was bustling from place to place, buying medicines and coins and farm-produce and selling them wherever she could, not sparing her dignity and her strength, and every evening stuffing extra coins into the ever-expanding "purse". She loved—yes, she really loved!—the pennies and the shillings and the rials and the pharos! And when she sensed the suspicious looks that virtuous Jewish men and women were casting in her direction, she would secretly weigh the warm and heavy bundle of cash that had chosen to nest in her hands. She enjoyed haggling with the Bedouin and the money changers, knowing instinctively what to buy and what to sell, and already she had amassed enough money to buy seeds and fertilizer and clothes for the children and even shoes for Yehiel…Perhaps that was the reason she wasn't too sorry when her uncle asked her to stay another week and join in the celebrations being held in honor of his wedding in the house of Shimon Rokeah.

In the morning they strolled in the Baron's garden like a real family, with Bella and Shura playing the role of grandparents to her children. Tamara and Tuli loved peering into the parrot cages and throwing tidbits to the monkeys. At this time Fania was straining her ears to hear the Baron playing, and considering all kinds of ploys and excuses—how to gain access to the house and how to get her hands on his piano…

"Fania Silas!"

Turning her head, she found standing right beside her, looking as foppish as the parrot in the cage, her dearest friend, Naphtali Hertz Imber, himself and no other! A black silk bowtie was strangling him, and a rolled-up newspaper stuffed into his pocket like a tube gave his body a distorted appearance.

"What are you doing in Jaffa?"

"The same as you!"

"Setting up a library, are you?" he laughed. "Eleazar Rokeah invited me to help get the new library started. And what about you? Still in the quinine business?"

"Yes!" she laughed.

"I visited Doctor Stein's new hospital yesterday."

"Eleazar Rokeah founded that one too," Bella Rokeah-Mandelstam interjected.

Once the introductions had been made, Imber asked Fania,

"Will you be coming to the 'Melaveh Malkah'?"

"She refuses!" the uncle complained.

"Cheapskate!"

"Why?" she smiled, intrigued.

"They're raising money there for charity!" the uncle insisted. "What did you think? There's a heavenly reason behind their meetings? Oh, Jews! Jews! Even the blessing over food they're selling for cash!"

"Anyway, I'm not entitled to pray with the community."

"You're entitled to contribute."

"All right then, I'll come."

"Oh, here in all his glory is Monsieur Nessim Bakar Alhadif, the poet of the flowers. This young lady is from Galilee, from Rosh Pinnah."

"They've invited me to Mai Merom," Baron Ustinov's gardener told them.

"Yesod Hamaaleh, they call it these days. I was there."

Nessim Bakar Alhadif peered at her furtively. He was wearing his Sabbath clothes: a green silk tunic with a broad sash around the waist and a red fez on his head.

"And how is the Jordan plain? Blooming? I wanted to go…but the flowers…"

"Monsieur Alhadif is a graduate of Mikveh Israel!" Imber boasted.

"And is Hirsch still in charge?" the uncle joined in the conversation.

"Absolutely!"

"My friend Berliavsky told me that Hirsch forced him and his Bilu comrades to leave the country."

"Forced him indeed!" Imber snorted derisively.

"They were hungry and he exploited that."

"And what about her?" Imber pointed to Fania. "She isn't hungry? Tell your uncle!" Fania shrugged her shoulders, embarrassed, and he turned away from her, crying angrily: "They gave an undertaking in writing to go to America and never return to the Land of Israel! In writing!"

"Hirsch got this undertaking from them by cunning," the uncle insisted. "They want to come back, they're pleading to come back!"

"Cunning! Try getting an undertaking like that from Fania! Phew! This is displaying the worldwide 'Lovers of Zion' movement in a really good light! High-sounding words, that's all. High-sounding words!"

"From high-sounding words, sir, new societies have been created! Continents have been conquered! And why do you, as a poet, object to high-sounding words?"

"Are you acquainted with them, sir, the Bilu people?" Aunt Bella asked Imber.

"Am I supposed to be acquainted with them?"

"Shura helped Berliavsky compose the Bilu manifesto!" said Bella in a reverential tone. "And my close relative Eleazar Rokeah is getting the building permits for them."

"Building permits! Castles in Spain!"

"I can't bear this kind of talk!" cried Fania's uncle, covering his ears with his hands. "They went away, those saints, Zevi Horowitz and...and...and Zuckermann and...they lived in a cave..." He was so agitated he could hardly string his words together in a coherent sentence. Bella tugged at his sleeve in vain. He roughly shook off her grip.

"I read the manifesto you wrote," said Imber, pressing ahead with his attack. "What is left of all those lofty ideals? Nothing! They're chasing donations! Exactly like the Halukkah people."

"Nothing is left?" cried the uncle hoarsely. "Is the Land of Israel nothing? Is working the land nothing? Is the communal life nothing? Are these three things not honorable enough in the eyes of the songster from Zelochov?"

Livid purple patches fringed with white coronas had sprung up on the uncle's forehead, and Bella pulled her husband away with real force, fearing the confrontation might turn violent. For her part, Fania dragged Imber in the opposite direction and said the first thing that came into her head: "I'll go to Gedera with you. We'll see for ourselves! Well?"

Imber took the rolled newspaper from his pocket and started slapping his thigh with it until his turbulent spirit had calmed a little. He turned his back on the Mandelstams, stared at Fania for some time as if seeing nothing, and then smiled suddenly and said, "You're a gypsy, Fania!"

"Why are you insulting me now?"

"I'm sure you despise me."

"No! Absolutely not! Who am I to despise you?" protested Fania, shocked. "It's just a shame…all this emotion…"

"They wanted to found a settlement and that's what they've done," said Alhadif, standing up for them.

"Nine people!"

"It's a start. A bird in the hand…" The two men stared at each other, and a mischievous smile suddenly danced in their eyes.

"I did a good job of upsetting your aunt!"

"She's a good woman."

"A businesswoman! Like most wives, watching over the merchandise."

"And what's wrong with that?"

"And you, my lovely gazelle, if there's nothing wrong with it, why don't you follow her example? You see, you have no answer to that! What does it matter? Two goats have knocked each other around a bit…And your husband? Is he in Jaffa too?"

"No. He's in Rosh Pinnah, threshing."

"That's the difference! That's the difference! Flags! Slogans! Manifestos! The poet sings of the land of his delight and the farmer threshes it! All speech is empty and meaningless without Yehiel! What use to him is a priest without a congregation? And what's the little one called?"

"Naphtali, named after the land of Naphtali. I call him Tuli."

"Tuli, Tuli, Tuli!" Imber tickled the baby and then stopped abruptly, as if afraid of making a fool of himself. "And my mother called me Herzli…so we're going to meet at the 'Melaveh Malkah', for the end-of-Sabbath singing?"

"I promised!"

"And you're really going with me to Gedera? Promise?"

"I promised!"

"And are you still playing Chopin?"

"No."

"Pity!"

And he walked away quickly, restoring his spirits by inhaling the scent of the flowers in the little beds.

"Dearest one, merciful Father…"

Shimon Rokeah dandled his little son and sang with feeling. The woman who sat beside Fania wouldn't stop talking. The moment she discovered Fania understood English, she latched on to her. From time to time one of the men would open his eyes in astonishment, whereupon Fania returned his look with an air of apparent innocence, as if saying to herself: Speak up! Speak up, ma'am! This is one right they won't be taking from us! Rachel Rokeah popped up in front of them with a plate in each hand, raisins and almonds. Perhaps she meant to use them to cork the mouth of the garrulous guest.

"Four years I've been in this country and it's the first time I've seen salted fish," Fania whispered.

"Only Zerah Barnett could have thought of such a thing," Rachel smiled at the guest. "He imported twenty crates of herring from London!"

"To Jaffa?"

"Yes. Go to the Armenian shop."

Fania and Mrs. Barnett followed Rachel to the window. The lighthouse beacon had already been ignited, competing with the last radiance of the day. The sea was turning black, but the windows of the Franciscan monastery were ablaze with the fire of sunset. From below came the sound of a Bedouin flute.

"I get seasick just looking at those sails," Mrs. Barnett commented. "The last voyage we took, the sea was so rough and the current was so strong, we were swept all the way back to Beirut. Four times we had to go back and forth. Four times!"

"Have you been in Jaffa long?" Fania asked her.

"No. Until now we've lived in Petah Tikva—if you could call it 'living'! I wouldn't put cattle in those huts of ours! But I understand that in Rosh Pinnah things aren't much better, and you were there before us."

"Not me. I came here only four years ago."

"Only! Every year in this country I've aged ten years. I'm not as young as you, and Zerah has already turned fifty. I don't have the strength for new beginnings…He makes money in London, comes to this country and loses it! I asked him for a divorce!"

"Oy! I didn't know!" Rachel Rokeah's eyes opened wide in consternation.

"I'm here, am I not? Even a divorce I'm incapable of getting. Rabbi Salant backed me, but I obtained a divorce about as much as you did. You can rely on Zerah! If he wants to be rid of me, nothing will stand in his way. That isn't what he wants now. I told the rabbi Zerah had gone insane and the rabbi agreed with me. And Zerah was so happy! 'If I'm mad,' he told the rabbi, 'then my divorce has no validity!' You're laughing? I don't find it funny. 'What kind of a rabbi are you?' he attacked Rabbi Salant. 'The rabbi from Shekalov lost his parents, his wife, his sons, his daughters and his sons-in-law to the plague, and he didn't abandon the Land of Israel! "I was like one lying in the heart of the sea and burning in blazing fire!"' he quoted the words of the rabbi from Shekalov. And the two of them—my Zerah and Rabbi Salant—burst into tears! And embraced! They forgot about me!"

Rachel Rokeah and Fania roared with laughter. The men opened their eyes and peered at them with surprise. More guests were coming in through the open door: Imber, Eleazar Rokeah and Doctor Stein. All eyes lit up, as if the triumvirate had brought good news with them. Eleazar circulated among the guests as if he were the bridegroom.

"Are we late? Has the blessing of the food been sold yet?" he asked.

"No, not yet."

"What are we raising funds for today?"

"For your hospital!"

Fania pricked up her ears. Could she sell medicines to this hospital? Eleazar's eyes rested on her for a moment, and she sensed the effort he was making to remember who she was. Since that night in Gai Oni they hadn't met. On account of the "Elijah's Chair" that he gave them she was pelted with stones, and it was also due to him that she felt Yehiel's arms around her for the first time. There was an excess of fervor in his movements, his enthusiastic looks, his voice. How old was he? Thirty? He was dressed in "European" style, the black ribbons of his tie descending from beneath the two tiny triangles of his stiff collar, jammed against his lower jaw. He laughed suddenly and she listened to what he had to say.

"This is what's known as 'making a virtue out of necessity', seeing that poor old Stein here wants to be an agricultural worker. 'Doctor Stein,' Monsieur Hirsch said to him, 'every doctor can be an agricultural worker, but not every agricultural worker can be a doctor.'"

"Another lunatic!" whispered Rachel Leah Barnett, curling her lip in distaste.

"Hirsch wouldn't have made me change my mind, or made my comrades change theirs," said the doctor, "but we suffered another blow: Hirsch told the Biluists that by order of the Alliance Israelite Universelle in Paris, he's going to stop giving us work in Mikveh Israel, starting from the summer of 1884. What could I do?"

"What about the other comrades?"

"I met Hertzenstein here in Jaffa. He's going into the timber business. Some of the others will be working in the Jerusalem branch of his operation, Harkavi and Ozer Dov Lifschitz and Chertok..."

"Are they all Biluists?" asked Fania.

"Yes."

People looked up and stared at the woman who was butting into the men's conversation. She was both strange and a stranger in their midst. Suspicion and malice dogged the footsteps of this youngster, moving unescorted from place to place, earning her livelihood like a man and supporting her little family, and not intimidated by Turk or by Bedouin. She felt her neck and her cheeks reddening with that infernal flush, but she fixed her gaze on Eleazar Rokeah's face, and he narrowed his eyes, exerting his memory in vain. The woman who sat next to her moved further away, increasing the space between them.

"What's all this about, Mr. Eleazar, the immigrants from Europe don't want to work the land?" she asked sweetly. Her voice was too loud, too tremulous, and the silence was heavy. "And in Gai Oni, in our innocence we thought that only we, the people of the old settlement, are incapable of working the land, lazy and incompetent as we are."

His brows unknitted at once and she knew he remembered who she was.

"Didn't you write a letter to the Biluists in Constantinople, telling them that the settlers of Gai Oni, on whose behalf you worked so hard, simply don't want to work?!"

"No! No!"

"You wrote that natives of the Land of Israel aren't suited to agricultural work, and your only hope lies with people from abroad and first and foremost the Bilu movement. And now the Biluists too have proved a disappointment to you!"

"Yehiel is the only one left out of seventeen families!"

"You were the first to defect, Eleazar Rokeah!"

"They threatened my life!"

"And what about Yehiel's life? Insured with Lloyd's of London? No matter, Eleazar Rokeah, Hebrew farmers who are worthy of you will emerge yet!"

"I've lost faith in the Biluists? Where do you get that from? Is this what you're doing in Jaffa? Spreading rumors? I…I…" Eleazar Rokeah waved his arms, his eyes flitting from person to person. "They came to this country to work the land and not to work in Hertzenstein's sawmill! I know, I know, you all think I love fomenting strife and dissension. You don't understand! The fanatics in Jerusalem have even succeeded in breaking Montefiore's spirit, the man they were looking to as their benefactor! We shall have no salvation as long as there are consumers of charity in our midst. Only the furrow will bring us salvation!"

"Bravo!" Fania clapped her hands. "Yehiel has been clinging to the land through four years of drought! Where were you, Mr. Eleazar, those four years?"

People began to speak all at once, affronted by this young woman's "impertinence".

"Fania!" Bella Rokeah-Mandelstam tried to silence her, slapping her arm lightly. "Ten years of his life Eleazar Rokeah has given for the dream of settling the land…"

"That's what they want! My life! Until my blood has been shed they won't give me any peace."

"Who's this 'they'?"

"The Halukkah crowd! Leaders of sects! Everyone who wants to keep the hungry and abject, hungry and abject!"

"So much hatred!" sighed Mrs. Barnett, pulling at Fania's sleeve to sit her down again beside her. "My mother always used to say it's hatred that unites the Jewish people. How many are they, these Bilu people, in total?"

"In Gedera there are nine," said Doctor Stein. "And one woman."

"Whose wife?"

"According to the Bilu constitution," Uncle Shura explained, "Bilu members are not allowed to marry."

"Not allowed?" exclaimed Mrs. Barnett. "It's a commandment in the Torah!"

"And the revival of the Land of Israel is also a commandment in the Torah!" the uncle stood up tall and proud. "These saintly people decided to work for the good of others and not to feather their own nests, as long as the community needs their sacrifice."

"Their sacrifice!" Eleazar Rokeah couldn't restrain himself from spitting out the words with scorn. Fania came to the conclusion that there must be something good about these Biluists if Eleazar hated them too. Perhaps it had been a wise move, agreeing to visit Gedera with Imber. When would she next have an opportunity to see the Biluists with her own eyes? She glanced around the room until she caught sight of Imber and realized he was looking at her with an expression of amusement.

"Their sacrifice! Yes, their sacrifice!" the uncle cried emotionally. "For three years they have been wandering round the country like gypsies, drinking water from wells swarming with insects and sleeping ten to a room, and getting verbal abuse for not growing beards like the people of Petah Tikva and Yesod Hamaaleh!"

"David Gutman tells me you were in Yahud," Zerah Barnett turned to Eleazar Rokeah.

"Yes. I was there with Visotzky."

"You brought them money?"

"For them there's always money!" the uncle complained.

"Not so!" Eleazar Rokeah protested. "Unlike the Biluists, the people of Petah Tikva have never been subsidized out of public funds. And these are men with families, and not bachelors! And there are more of them than there are inhabitants of Gedera! Their only sin is that they don't blow shofars. They work the land and they revere God!"

"Has Rosh Pinnah received money?" Fania asked Eleazar.

"No, not Rosh Pinnah!"

"Why not? There, too, they are working the land and revering God!"

"Fania! What's the matter with you?!" Bella Rokeah-Mandelstam couldn't restrain herself any longer and she succeeded in silencing Fania, who suddenly remembered that they were supposed to be celebrating the marriage of Bella and her uncle, and sat down on the bench, blushing and confused. She wouldn't speak to Eleazar Rokeah again, for better or worse. How dare he turn his back on his comrades when he could be helping them? They are the ones giving substance to his dream! No! She would never speak to him again. There was no denying his captivating charm, but there was something else about him, something intimidating. More and more his behavior reminded her of her neighbor, Yakov Bushkila, and secretly she wondered if Eleazar too was addicted to Syrian nargilehs...

"Gentlemen, the blessing!" a certain Mr. Landau announced in a loud voice, thus boosting the price of the food-blessing. The room was filled with quiet mumbling. Fania turned her back on the blessers and stood again by the windows, letting the humming enfold her in an opaque cloud. The house of the Schloss family stood on a hill, by the gate of the city. Down in the bay the sea was rolling, rocking the passing clouds in its lap. It seemed that the sound of the sailboats could be heard even here, as they flapped their white wings. Fania tried to ease the pounding of her heart. She sensed the hostility of the people. Of all the things said, what seared her memory was not the argument with Eleazar, but words casually spoken by the doctor—"Nine Biluists in Gedera, and one woman." As if she isn't a person! Nine human beings and something else. A goat, a mule, a woman...This woman must be stronger than her comrades, since she needs greater powers of body and spirit than those of the men if she is to be capable of living with them in isolation. And who was it who made this remark? An intellectual, a doctor who trained in Leipzig, an idealist! Again and again in recent times, the grievances of her own predicament had reared up before her eyes. It seemed it was only in the marketplace that she and her activities were taken seriously. Her uncle, the standard-bearer of progress, had hinted to her that she would be better off returning to the protection of her husband, and even in this enlightened society all were embarrassed when she opened her mouth to join in the conversation, as if she were a child interrupting the grown-ups. If she could, she would stand on the table and shout her complaints at the top of her voice. But behavior such as this would only reinforce their conviction that a woman's place was at the kitchen sink. What nobility of spirit there was in her Yehiel! Without high-flown slogans, he respected her right to lead her life as she chose. As time passed, and she became better acquainted with the world he sprang from, her appreciation of him deepened all the more.

That which divides between sacred and profane...

Shimon lit the Havdalah lamp. The servant came in carrying a tray with little cups of coffee and cakes faintly scented with rose water. An atmosphere of domesticity prevailed in the abode of Rachel Rokeah. Only I wander in distraction from place to place, thought Fania. My accommodation is temporary and my family disintegrating, my husband has no wife and his children have no mother, a home that is no home and a marriage that is no marriage...

"Shimon admires Yehiel," said Rachel, as if reading her thoughts. "He says if he hadn't become a farmer he could have been a great Torah scholar. He was a prodigy, and the family pinned its hopes on him."

The servant brought nargilehs into the room and Mr. Landau took a silver box from his pocket and offered tobacco to his fellow guests. Fania suddenly remembered something Yehiel had told her, that when in Jaffa he had worked for a few days in Landau's tobacco refinery. She looked curiously at this man, whose life had touched Yehiel's. There was nothing of Yehiel about him.

"How much do you pay for tobacco?" Landau asked Shimon.

"I buy in bulk and pay less that way. Five francs for half an occa. Persian tobacco."

"That's a good one to smoke at the end of Sabbath."

"Why the end of Sabbath?"

"The Persians put belladonna in their tobacco. Don't you feel sleepy after smoking it?"

"Yes…perhaps…"

"Soon you'll all be only smoking cigarettes."

"Will you be distributing them free?"

"No. The excise duty on tobacco is soaring from day to day."

"How is Schmerling? Has the merger between you worked out?"

"Oh yes! He's a feisty Jew, keen on new ideas. We've just set up a branch in Shechem."

"And who's working there? Jews?"

"Jews, definitely! We imported twenty families from Jerusalem. Feibel Kahanof is the factory manager and all the clerical workers are Jews as well."

"You didn't find enough Jews in Shechem, so you had to import Jews from Jerusalem?" asked Eleazar Rokeah indignantly.

"Don't give me a hard time!" Landau replied. "We're providing a livelihood for a hundred Jewish families. Do the Jews from Jerusalem need a slaughterer? A tailor? A miller? They're all on the payroll. Not only that, the land on the hill is suitable for the cultivation of tobacco, and it may be that over time we'll develop that as well. The 'Reji Uthman' company wants to open new branches, and

I've suggested to Schmerling that we farm out the marketing rights for tobacco in Galilee and Samaria. A little rashness does no harm in business..."

Suddenly it seemed to Fania that only Landau was talking. All the other voices turned into an amalgam of noise. Her head began to buzz with ideas, ways of linking up with Landau's Galilean tobacco operation. In her pocket she already had enough cash to go into partnership with him. And why not? What's to stop her? True, the population of Jerusalem is twice the population of Safed, but Safed is closer to Tiberias and Tyre and Sidon and the new settlements... she can combine the marketing of tobacco with the marketing of medicines...she's on her way...

Above the heads of the people her restless eyes met Imber's mischievous smile. The man was reading her thoughts! She had no doubt of that. Is such a thing possible? In one of the meetings of the women's circle in Rosh Pinnah they read in *Havatzelet* about a Jewish doctor of Galician origin, living in Vienna, who was making impetuous and hysterical attempts to prove that spiritual activities are in fact generated by the spirit and not the mind, as was previously thought. Can we study the map of the spirit as we study the anatomy of the body?—asked the writer of the article. And Fania and her friends considered the question at some length. Now, encountering Imber's all-seeing eyes, she remembered that article. Can one man read the thoughts of another? Dive into his heart and not drown? She remembered the blind Bedouin poet she saw in the café near the market, holding his hand to his temple, as if listening to distant voices, and speaking out in a hoarse and ringing tone—until a hefty and able-bodied man fell swooning at his feet. Witnesses ascribed supernatural powers to the poet and said he had discovered the terrible secret of the man who had fainted.

"Well, Fania, whereabouts in Galilee do you reckon the cigarette factory should be built?" Imber asked in a loud voice.

"In Safed."

By now they were both standing beside Landau, affecting a casual tone of conversation.

"Acre has a port."

"Yes, but how many Jews live there? One hundred? A hundred and fifty? From Safed it's a convenient journey to anywhere. To Lebanon. To Transjordan."

"Are you from Safed?" asked Landau.

"No, from Rosh Pinnah."

"The Jews of Safed don't smoke cigarettes."

"And in Shechem they do? And in Jaffa? When the operation gets under way in Safed you'll find buyers among the twelve thousand inhabitants."

"Yawash yawash, Fania!" Imber smiled, "You'll be scaring Mister Landau yet!"

"I'm not that easily scared. I believe in cigarettes. Do you know anyone who's capable of handling this?"

"Yes."

"Who?"

"Me."

Suppressing a sly smile, Landau moved to the corner of the room, Fania and Imber following close behind.

"If you're taking on the tobacco concession in Galilee you'll have to commit yourself to selling a certain quantity. What happens if you don't meet your commitments? Can you give me financial sureties?"

"Yes."

"'Rezi Uthman' imposes penalties on those who fail to achieve their quotas. Until now it hasn't happened because I supervise the buying and selling myself. A Greek from Damascus has offered the company his services in the North, and the choice will be between him and us…"

"I'll consult my husband and give you an answer."

"When?"

"Two weeks from now?"

"Will you send via 'Messager Maritime'?"

"No. Their ships don't serve the north of the country. I'll send my answer via the Austrian postal service."

"Excellent, Madame…"

"Silas. Fania Silas. I'm married to the cousin of Shimon and Eleazar."

I'll consult my husband! The words emerged from her mouth unbidden, as if she needed to assure Mister Landau that she was a proper settler, she had a husband and could therefore be relied on. One way or the other, from the moment her ears heard what her mouth was saying, happiness engulfed her. The light of the candles danced and the room buzzed with emotional whispers. The smells of coffee and roses sweetened the air. Fania felt as if she had finally received something she had been waiting for. Yes, in a few days she would be back in Rosh Pinnah, embracing Yehiel!

"He was a righteous man..."

Sweet sadness of longings hovered over the faces of the singers. No longer was this a bevy of prosperous guests, but a family, people who had travelled a long way together. Together they were angry, together they rejoiced, together they yearned. Fania smiled at Bella and she smiled back at her with warmth. Even Rachel Leah Barnett no longer looked like a troublemaker, just an anxious woman. She had made a poor bargain: her fur-trading husband had turned into a farmer and wanted to work on the land. Fania felt someone was watching her, and turning her head she found it was Eleazar. She traded him look for look and the thought occurred to her that in fact, Yehiel was fulfilling Eleazar's dreams. Eleazar talks and Yehiel does. It seemed, out of that entire idealistic clique, only Yehiel remained, still bearing the burden he had imposed on himself. "A prodigy" he had been called by both Allegra Adis and Rachel Rokeah. It was true, he stood head and shoulders above those around him. When I come home, she thought, I'll invite the neighbors to join us in celebrating the Melaveh Malkah. I'll put wine on the table and we'll sing and sing... If only she hadn't agreed to accompany Imber to Gedera.

Chapter eleven

The horse's back was damp with sweat. Fania decided to stop and let him rest. Although his name was "Storm", there was virtually no wind left in him. What a pity Yehiel and the children would see him for the first time when he was so worn out!

Only a few hours had elapsed between her decision to buy a horse and the moment when she cautiously led him into the yard of her uncle's house.

"You're not a child, Fania!" the uncle exclaimed. "Children do impulsive things like this, deciding they want something and rushing out and buying it! I suppose now you'll be gallivanting around all over the place…"

"But he's cute, isn't he?" she laughed and stroked Storm's chestnut mane. Her own horse, with brown freckles on his pink nostrils. From now on she would no longer be dependent on the charity of wagoners! She hugged and kissed her uncle, demanding: "Go on, say he's cute! Say it!" and she wouldn't let him go until he admitted that yes, the horse was cute, and yes, she did the right thing buying him.

In fact, it was her uncle's wife who was indirectly responsible for the purchase of the horse. She asked Fania to go with her to Señor Azriel Levi's shop, where a consignment of iron cooking stoves, manufactured in Marseilles, had just been delivered. There and then Fania decided that the era of Arab-style ovens was over! She too would buy a stove. Just the one? Why not buy three! The profit she made from resale of the two extra ones would cover the cost of the one she was keeping. "You're a businesswoman, Fania!" Bella Rokeah-Mandelstam laughed, and Fania smiled and thought to herself: you wouldn't be laughing if you didn't have men to support you, dead and living…

When the stoves arrived in the yard, the question arose of how to transport them to Rosh Pinnah. She could have sent them by sea, courtesy of the Austro-Hungarian shipping line or the Italian packet, but their ships sailed directly from Jaffa to Beirut, and from there goods had to be transferred by the cartload…When were they finally going to start building the Sultan's famous railway? Two years had passed since they were told by Oliphant—she heard him say it with her own ears—that the trustees had, thank God, been awarded the licence to build the railway, and the engineer Schumacker and his associates had finished drawing up the provisional plans. It seemed it was just a matter of days, and work would begin. But she knew only too well how things worked in the east. Any scheme, however good it might be, would always be held up by all kinds of obstacles! Another *firman*, another palm to be greased…Depressed as she was by gloomy contemplation of the bureaucratic webs that bound her hands and feet until she felt like some kind of golem cast out into the darkness—she suddenly shook herself free in a spirit of mutiny, the youthful, impertinent and brazen spirit of mutiny that had guided her steps recently, and it was then that the idea of the horse was born. With a horse of her own, she won't be dependent on any ship or railway, she'll be in charge of her own fate. Shashon and Simha, the pair of Jaffa wagoners, negotiated on her behalf with a trader importing horses from the Syrian Desert, and she gladly entrusted them with her last majedas. It was a long time since she had been as happy as she was now, on taking possession of the horse. He gave her a sense of freedom and independence. She saw herself spurring over the hills of Galilee, down into the valleys, stopping beside a spring…If any regrets occurred to her she was quick to dispel them, since now, having obtained the license to market tobacco in Galilee, she would need to travel long distances and a horse of her own was an absolute necessity!

Storm cropped the grass, raising his head from time to time and looking at her with his big moist eyes. Tamara plucked clumps of grass and offered them to him. For a moment she was frightened when he rolled back his upper lip and exposed his big teeth, but when his tongue licked her little hand she laughed. What kind of children am I bringing up? she wondered. What part of my past will be filtered into their bodies and their minds? And what will be left of me when I'm not around anymore? She changed Tuli's nappy and put a dry crust of bread in his hand. His eyes, blue at birth, had in the meantime taken on the darker hue of Yehiel's eyes. For a whole month they had been away from their home, and in all that time he hadn't come to visit them once. His obstinacy and pride were apparently stronger than his feelings for his family.

In the people she met in Gedera there was the same obstinacy, and although the encounter with them depressed her, she couldn't help but be moved on their account. In fact, when she joined Imber she had no idea what to expect. Doctor Stein had been forced to stay behind in Jaffa, and they decided to hire the services of Simha and his wagon. They found themselves trudging along a road that was no road, their feet kicking up the dry dust, wondering if the wagoner knew which way he was supposed to be going. To the west, over the sand-hills, was the rumble of the great sea, and sometimes, when they stopped walking, they felt a faint breeze on their faces.

"You promised to take us to Gedera!" Imber ranted at Simha. "That's right! And that's where I'm taking you!" replied the wagoner, and he started chanting a favorite psalm, unmoved by Imber's wrath. What's his problem? Does he expect him to kill his horse? The horse is tired too…And so they trailed along behind the wagon until they reached the Arab village of Katara. It was obvious from the looks of the peasants that they didn't care for their new neighbors. There was no sign of a new settlement, not a vegetable patch, not a path. At last a small wooden shack came into sight, and two young men who were standing beside it digging a hole with shovels.

"God Almighty!" whispered Imber. "For two years I've been hearing nothing but Bilu this and Bilu that—and here it is!"

The boys stopped working and looked at the strange trio: the Jaffa wagoner with grey beard reaching almost as far as his waist, a man dressed in European style with a wild look in his eyes, and a young ruddy-faced woman in Bedouin garb.

"Is this Gedera?" asked Imber.

"Yes. You are all welcome!"

"Delighted to be here! This is Mrs. Fania Silas from Rosh Pinnah, this scoundrel is Simha the wagon-driver from Jaffa, and I'm Naphtali Hertz Imber from Haifa."

One of the two boys straightened up suddenly, and waving his hands as if conducting an orchestra he recited Imber's poem:

Dig in the hills with all your might,
Dig by day and dig by night
Dig and with a joyful sound
Find precious jewels in the ground
One that will be the cornerstone.
They say we are idle and we are weak,
And now you have your chance to speak!
Let all the world, our neighbors, see
Industrious as the ants are we!

"Is that him?" his friend asked, and held his head in his hands. "Every day he wakes us up with your song, Mr. Imber! This is Horowitz and I'm Leibowitz. If you go to the orchard, you'll hear the comrades singing your 'Hatikva.'"

Fania recognized those eyes, burning with hunger and delusion. These beggars, with their empty pockets and the sky the only roof over their heads—whatever possessed them to plant an orchard of all things? It will be years before it bears any fruit, and what will they do in the meantime? Perhaps the curse of Jaoni has landed on their heads too, and they have no money to buy seeds and agricultural implements. Two men wouldn't have been left here to dig a hole if the situation were otherwise...

"The aperture is too broad," said Fania.

"This is going to be a baking oven."

"I know. And the aperture is too broad."

She helped the boys to mark out the dimensions of the baking chamber and to fix the precise location of the shelf separating the combustible materials from the food.

"We've been getting our bread from Rishon le-Zion. Now we've decided to build our own oven."

"I remember you from 'Mikveh'!" Imber said suddenly to Horowitz. "He was such a diligent worker that Hirsch was forced to reinstate him after he'd dismissed all the Biluists. Isn't that right? That was you, wasn't it?"

"Yes."

"Are you Lithuanian?" Fania asked Leibowitz.

"Yes. And you?"

"From Elizavetgrad."

"In which year did you arrive in the country?" came the inevitable question.

"In 1882. And how long have you been here?"

"Two years."

"I need drinking water for the horse," said Simha, "for me as well. But first of all, you boys can help me unload the cart."

The men carried the sack of flour that Fania and Imber had brought with them into the shack. Once inside the shack, the wind really hit them, whistling between the window and the door. Dried mud covered the floor, and the musty smell of poverty wafted from every corner. The full area of the shack was no more than five square meters, and wooden benches running from wall to wall served as beds for the young men. In the middle of the room stood a round table, and between this and the "beds" only a very narrow passageway was left. So much dejection and desolation! Fania wondered if her home in Rosh Pinnah would look like this to the eyes of a stranger. The water in the jarrah was green and scummy, and although their hosts assured them it had been filtered they were reluctant to drink it.

"What's this? You don't have a well?"

"No."

"Where's this water from?"

"We made a deal with the Arabs of Katara and they were supposed to be selling us water from their well. But we didn't know that they don't draw water in the winter. In the winter they use the water in the wadis and the waterholes and we're forced to do the same. Wissotzky promised us two thousand roubles from the funds collected by 'Lovers of Zion' for the construction of a well, but at the moment we haven't succeeded in getting a permit. We're hoping Avraham Moyal will manage to get us the permit before the summer. We shall have to wait and see..."

"Meanwhile the Arabs of Katara have told us they're not selling us water anymore. They exploit every opportunity to bully us; now they've realized we're even poorer than they are, and the brotherhood of working men is something they've never heard of," Leibowitz smiled a bitter smile.

"Can we go to the orchard?" asked Imber.

"You go!" Horowitz said to his mate. "I'll carry on here. It's our turn to keep watch and cook, and that's why we decided to dig out the oven."

"I'll go by myself."

"You see those two hills there? The smaller one we call Mount Moses, after Sir Moses Montefiore, and the taller one we call Mount Judith, after his wife, Lady Judith. An expert from 'Mikveh' was here, the Hungarian Kazioni, and he surmised that Mount Judith would be suitable for planting. That's where you'll find our young men."

"How many of them?"

"Seven. It's better that way," he hastened to add, "considering that between us we have a total of ten spades, two hoes and one donkey."

Fania and Leibowitz went to Katara with the donkey and bought a big sack of charcoal, and all the way the man was brimming over with excitement, singing Russian songs and liturgical chants and asking a thousand and one questions about Rosh Pinnah and about Jaffa. "For two days now we've been digging that oven, and all the time I've been thinking to myself: wonderful, we're going to have an oven, but what have we got to bake in it? Our last thirty majedas we invested—donkeys that we are—in the donkey we bought in Jaffa! And now we have an oven and charcoal and flour for baking bread. And the young men will return from the orchard as smoke rises from the new oven, and from far away they will savor the smell of fresh bread!"

"Why did you plant an orchard?"

"We had no seeds and we couldn't afford a plow."

"And livestock?"

"The nine of us are the livestock here. And we're prepared to harness ourselves to the plow, if we ever get one!"

"In Rosh Pinnah we used to glean after the Bedouin, like Ruth and Naomi. But we didn't have years of training and preparation behind us, not to mention the 'Lovers of Zion' with branches all over the world. What went wrong?"

"It seems to me it's all gone wrong."

For some time they walked on in silence behind the donkey. Finally Fania asked:

"What will you do when the flour runs out?"

"I don't know!"

"You must have some idea."

"We published a letter in *Hamelitz*, appealing to the 'Lovers of Zion' for support until the first harvest…"

"And you didn't get any reply…"

"Correct."

"How much land do you have?"

"Three thousand dunams."

"And you have no plows or seeds or livestock…I know this story. What are you living on?"

"Pines is sending thirty francs to each one of us. You've seen how we live. And Pines was told in a telegram from Warsaw that 'Lovers of Zion' have set aside nine hundred roubles for us, to buy seeds."

"And what about accommodation? And economics? That orchard won't bear any fruit for three years yet!"

"They're going to send another seven hundred roubles."

"And in the meantime?"

"In the worst case we'll take out a loan using that money as collateral."

"So many times you've announced your willingness to sacrifice yourselves for the sacred objective, and now the Jewish people have apparently decided to put you to the test!" said Fania with a chuckle, but since he didn't smile she asked in a more sober tone: "Why don't they send the money directly to you?"

"It's better this way! Last year they sent us the money, and Ossovitsky wrote—and it was reported in *Hamelitz*—that we were stuffing ourselves with roast chicken and wine, and in the evenings we were singing and dancing and whooping it up. And at the same time he wrote—and this was the most hurtful thing of all—that we had let the wheat in the fields burn! Better that the money goes to Pines…"

"I knew a member of Bilu once, Sasha Zusman."

"Sasha! Really! The painter! What's he doing now?"

"I don't know. He visited us in Rosh Pinnah about six months ago."

"He wasn't a true Biluist. He came to this country before we did and worked with some English priest."

"Tristram."

"That's the one! He painted fruits and insects…I saw some of his pictures. After that he settled in Jerusalem and joined a group dedicated to reviving old handicrafts, like metalwork and blacksmithing. How do you know him?"

"I told you. He was in Rosh Pinnah."

"And you don't know where he is now?"

"No, I don't know."

"His wife and his baby daughter were murdered in a pogrom in 1881."

Fania ran to the side of the road and vomited. Her eyes smarted with tears and her throat was nauseous. She wiped her face and returned to Dov Leibowitz, who stood waiting for her, patting the back of the donkey mechanically.

Zevi Horowitz and Dov Leibowitz waited for their comrades returning from the field like the Shulamite waiting for her lover. Again and again they looked at the smoke rising from the oven, not believing the miracle had really happened. They spread a sheet on the table and told the plantation workers they would be serving up roast goose with red currant gravy. To Fania and Imber they explained that every evening they dined in their imagination on quails and swans, and it was up to the duty cook to "prepare" the meals accordingly.

And to her surprise Fania saw a woman among the workers returning from the field. Darya Sirot was an attractive girl, with jet-black eyes and hair. Imber linked arms with her and she was clearly embarrassed by the excessive affection that he was showing her. It seemed to Fania that Darya's face was familiar to her from somewhere. But at once she dismissed the idea from her mind. How could she possibly know her?

"I've lost a button," said Hazanov, and Darya promised that after the meal she would replace it. Sure enough, when the plates were removed from the table and the group finished the prayer of thanksgiving for the food, Darya piled up a heap of clothes on the bench and set to work with needle and thread, listening in silence to the conversation of her comrades. Fania peered at her again and again, trying to remember who she was, where their paths had crossed. A tremor of fear fluttered in her heart and she didn't know why. She tried to exclude Darya from her thoughts and to listen to the conversation of the men in the room. They were in a mood of feverish enthusiasm, suppressing doubts beneath a barrage of impassioned declarations, and then suddenly falling silent, as if they had used up all the air in their lungs. Perturbed by the silence, they hurriedly started talking again, all at once, and then they laughed and were embarrassed again by their laughter which had broken out for no particular reason…

Fania remembered the first party she ever attended. This was for the birthday of her classmate, Mashinka Wolf. She wore new shoes made for her especially by the "Italian" cobbler. The girls all gathered in one corner of the room, chattering and giggling incessantly. Opposite them stood the boys, congregating around the table and the supplies of lemonade, looking impudently at the girls and setting off fresh gales of laughter. Something in her mind made a connection between that party and this one. A kind of fine and delicate thread, from a spider's web, and if she takes care not to sever it, she can follow it back to the memory that is boring into her brain… When the party ended night was falling, and her sister Lili arrived with her fiancé Kalman Leib to take her home. As they were standing in the vestibule, putting on their coats and hats and gloves, a boy and a girl, both about eighteen years old, emerged from the apartment. They passed by them quickly and went out into the street. Kalman Leib revealed in a frantic whisper that this was Dina Wolf of Narodnaya Volia, the revolutionary movement plotting to overthrow the Tsar. Dina Wolf had gone into hiding about a year before and the authorities had put a price on her head. "What are they thinking of, harboring her in their house when it's full of children? If she's caught, it won't just be her facing the firing squad, anyone associating with her will be in danger!"

"Hush, not in front of the girl!" Lili warned Kalman, and Fania pretended she had heard nothing. Years later, when members of Narodnaya Volia assassinated Alexander II and riots broke out in the city, the house of the Wolf family was the first to be attacked. The rioters set it on fire, along with all its occupants, on April 27, 1881. Some two weeks later, when the fifteen-year-old Fania, more dead than alive and a reluctant survivor, was still in bed in her neighbor's home in Elizavetgrad, she heard one day an agonised whisper urging somebody to remove herself—and at once—from this house and from this city. "You've done your part!" her neighbor added, her voice hoarse and angry, "All this blood will be on you and on your head! Come here and see the girl who's had to take refuge in my house! A drunken Cossack raped her while his cronies were slaughtering her parents…" In the doorway stood none other than Dina Wolf. One of her shoulders was raised in a rather clumsy posture, perhaps because the neighbor was pulling on her arm, and her white face was hunched into her neck like a trapped bird.

It's her! Dina Wolf! Fania looked up and stared fixedly at Darya Sirot. Is it her? Only twice she saw her, and briefly too. Can she trust her memory? And if the slightest hint of a doubt exists, will *she* remember her? Who knows how long she stood there in the doorway and looked at her as she lay in her neighbor's house? All those days had blended together in a dense and frantic haze. And if she really is Dina Wolf, is she liable to reveal her history, tell the truth about Tamara? Oh God, why did she come here? Will the former revolutionary recognize, in the woman dressed like a Bedouin with damascene headdress, the girl she saw four years ago? No! Impossible!

"Who's in the chair tonight?" asked Hazanov.

"I am," said Zuckerman.

Fania listened attentively. It turned out that every evening they chose a chairman for their meetings so that no one person could dominate proceedings. There are nine of them altogether and they're all acting like businessmen, she reflected gloomily.

"What's on the agenda?" asked Izik. "I want to write letters. Can you post some letters for me?" he asked, turning to Fania.

"Certainly!"

"You can write those letters now," said Zuckerman, and everyone laughed.

"Izik is on guard tonight," one of them explained to the guests. "It's in his interests to keep the meeting going, so he spends more time in here and less time out there on patrol. Zuckerman is on guard tomorrow night, and he wants a shorter meeting so he can go to bed early and build up the energy he's going to need. We have disagreements like this every evening..."

"On the agenda," Zuckerman raised his voice, "the demand from 'Lovers of Zion' in Warsaw to know how much money each and every farmer needs."

"Money! Money! Money!"—someone thumped the table. "I used to think only the rich were interested in money, and now I see the poor are even more obsessed with it."

"Have you abandoned the communal principle?" asked Imber.

"Certainly not, as you can see for yourself! We live together, and we share the cooking and the laundry and the sentry duty, as well as the work in the orchard. We've already planted four thousand saplings on Mount Judith, and when we finish the planting we're going to share out the land between the comrades so each one has his own plot."

"And what will you do with the rest of the land?"

"We leased it to our neighbors in Katara. Now they're giving us a hard time and pretending it belongs to them."

"What kind of an account are we going to send Warsaw?" asked Fuchs. "An account of the houses that haven't been built? The seeds that haven't been bought? The well that was never dug? There's a bunch of tradesmen and hucksters sitting over there and treating our idealism with contempt!"

"They're entitled to know what's being done with their money!" someone protested angrily.

"It isn't their money, it's our money! Those clubs in Odessa and Warsaw exist for our benefit! We send an account, and then what happens? They call another meeting and discuss it again and send another letter and write another article! How long? Until we starve to death?"

"We're not starving to death!" Zuckerman objected.

"Really? In the time it's taken them to decide who they're going to send to this country to inspect conditions in the settlements, three babies have died on us. And the solution they came up with? The tea baron Kalonymos Zev Wissotzky, may his light shine brightly!"

"And what's wrong with him?" Zuckerman demanded to know, leaping up from his seat. "I don't like this pointless hatred!"

"It isn't pointless hatred! This is hatred based on facts! I don't believe Wissotzky will do anything at all for us!"

"He will! When he sees with his own eyes the state we're in—he'll act!"

"I still trust him, but Eleazar Rokeah I don't trust."

"What's the connection?" Fania asked.

"Rokeah is Wissotzky's secretary. Wissotzky is old, in his sixties, and he's taken on as his secretary a young man with all the right qualifications—knowing the country, an Arabic-speaker, an avowed lover of Zion. And then what? This Rokeah has decided he's going to be the leader of the Bilu society, and the Bilu society doesn't want leaders. We're not pandering to the vanity of Eleazar Rokeah or anyone else. And now this man, who bears a grudge against us for not agreeing to his demands, is going to be Wissotzky's secretary. My friends, I don't expect *anything* from Wissotzky's visit! Anything!"

"Brothers, Biluists!" Imber leaped up from his seat, cheeks flushed, eyes flashing, and his tie adrift from his collar. "Shimon Bar Yitzhak said, 'Some fight with gleaming swords and some with the points of spears, but we fight in the name of the Lord of all the worlds!' Forget Rokeah and forget Wissotzky! Gedera is the Jewish people's answer to Warsaw and Yalta and Nijni-Novgorod! Nine celestials have broken out from the circle in which sixty thousand members of our race are trapped. I too have read the libelous reports published in the papers: 'Here is the mountain that gave birth to a mouse!' they say. 'Out of an army of five hundred Maccabees, the sole survivors are nine tired and desperate youths, pleading for charity'. You should be silent and let your actions speak for you. See how many commandments have been upheld so far: the commandment of return to the Holy Land, the commandment of settling there, the commandment of ingathering the exiles. Of course you make mistakes! You weren't born with spades in your hands. Only those who do nothing do nothing wrong. Take pride in your mistakes! Take pride in your failures! It's by virtue of such mistakes and failures that seven new settlements have sprung up from the beautiful land these last three years. And Gedera exists and nine youths from Bilu are living there and working ten plots of land. Don't let your spirits weaken, don't worry and don't hurry! My hope for you is that like that enigmatic creature, the orangutan, you will be tied by your navel-strings to this earth all the days of your lives! On this cornerstone shall arise a mighty and royal city!" And he began chanting one of the "Songs of Degrees" from the Book of Psalms.

Simha and the boys joined in. Darya put down the sock she had been mending and gazed out of the window. The sun was setting behind the distant hills. The donkey began braying mournfully, and faraway the dogs of Katara wailed in response. The landscape facing them was desolate, with sparse bushes that looked like mallow sprouting on the yellow hills. Far away a caravan of around a hundred camels was passing, and all eyes watched it in bemusement. "The Bedouin are taking their herds back to Horan," someone commented. For a moment Fania caught Darya's eye and both of them looked away hurriedly. Is it her? Does she recognize me? What will I do if she remembers? How come Fania has heard so little about the girl living alone among these men? She had heard gossip about the Bilu society, allegations that they were nihilists and non-observers of commandments, careless with public money and similar things in that vein, but she knew virtually nothing about this woman and the kind of life she was living here. She must be behaving with extreme caution, giving no one the opportunity to malign her. Is she in love with one of them? Are the boys in love with her?

A few of the boys started preparing themselves for the night's sleep. The overcrowding was such that some of them preferred just to stretch out on the bench. Anyone needing to go out was liable to collide with the bodies of his mates as he threaded himself between the benches and the table.

"Fania is related to Eleazar Rokeah," she heard Imber telling someone.

"How is that?"

"She's married to his cousin."

"And what is he saying? About Gedera, I mean."

"Nothing. He's busy setting up a library and a hospital in Jaffa. I'm helping to run the library, and your friend Mark Stein will be the hospital doctor."

"Mark Stein! He knows how to choose his partners! Eleazar Rokeah, Mark Stein…" Leibowitz spat out the doctor's name in a tone that clearly said: *There's another traitor for you!*

Izik, who had been engrossed for the past hour in writing letters, handed Fania two envelopes which he wanted sent from Jaffa. Then he picked up a rifle, called to the dog and went out of the shack. After a while the sound of his effusive song wafted to their ears:

The waves are churning
As the wheels are turning
All in the heart of the deep blue sea…

"You can imagine you hear the surf," said Imber, his head tilted as he listened to the song of the sentry. "Come on Simha, we'll sleep on the cart." The poet and the wagoner went outside, and Fania turned to Darya:

"Where are you sleeping?"

"In the donkey's shed."

Fania followed Darya and lay down on a pile of straw. The shed was nothing but a roof and a pair of panels like wings, fixed to the wall of the main shack. It was a moonlit night and stars sparkled in the sky. The donkey breathed steadily and exhaled a warm vapor.

"Where are you from?" Darya asked softly. Fania didn't answer, pretending to be asleep. The sentry walked back and forth and poured out his heart in song:

I thought one day I would be a lady
In the hand of the Lord a glorious crown
And now my love is far away
And all my skin is turning brown...

Crazy! thought Fania to herself. They are crazy and so am I! All of us! Utterly insane! She'll be leaving in the morning. She doesn't want anything more to do with these deluded dreamers. She's already got a lunatic of her own, back at home. You can tell that they're hungry in body and in spirit. With what fervor Izik sat down to write his letters! As if he's afraid he's been forgotten and erased from memory. All the same—it's obvious they're not going to leave. They'll cling to the thorns, eat mallows, drink the infested water, live and die with the land. She's met communal workers before in Jaffa, the people with lofty slogans, but these were molded from a different fabric... And she? What does she think she's doing, roaming from place to place like a gypsy? Yehiel shared his home and his bread with her, and she abandoned him! The person most precious to her in the world! Again and again the song of the sentry was heard, repeating the only verse he apparently knew, *I thought one day I would be a lady*...Darya mumbled something in her sleep and the donkey answered her with a snort. He's lonely too, poor thing. How lonely these people are! she reflected, her compassion kindled. Then she suddenly felt ashamed of herself, shame blended with a powerful desire to return to Yehiel and bear the yoke with him. The humility in him boosted his standing in her eyes even more. At least in this group people can keep one another's spirits up, while Yehiel is carrying the burden by himself, deserted even by his wife…She found herself struggling for breath and she was afraid of waking Darya. If only daylight would come! She got up quietly and went outside the hut.

"Who's there?"

"It's me, Fania."

"Has something happened?"

"No, no. Can I walk around with you for a bit?"

"Of course!"

For some time they walked without speaking. The night was cold and Fania wrapped her arms around her body.

"That's Yavneh," Izik pointed to a hill wrapped in the blue light of night. Then he pointed to another hill. "We're going to build our houses over there. Where we are now, the peasants of Katara can see right into our mouths, but from there we'll look out over the sea and the Judean hills and Yavneh…"

"In Jaoni too we started off living cheek by jowl with the peasants. The first pioneers thought that close association would breed brotherly love."

"Yes! You mean like Cain and Abel?"

"Where are you from, Izik?"

"From Cherson."

"Have you worked in Mikveh Israel as well?"

"Where haven't I worked? I went as far as Alexandria in the quest for work. You think we're crazy, don't you?"

"No crazier than me. Everyone who comes to this country is a little bit crazy, don't you think?"

"Perhaps."

Suddenly she tripped over a pile of something and fell to the ground. Her feet and hands fumbled among stones and planks and Izik grabbed her dress and began pulling, trying to get her back on her feet. Floundering between the heap beneath her and the man above her she somehow succeeded in standing up again, swaying drunkenly. Suddenly she heard a kind of faint moan from Izik and he hugged her body tightly. She almost fainted from shock. She started pushing him away, panting and groaning softly, trying not to make a sound. He was shorter than her and his big head was rammed into her neck. "Please! Stop that!" she pleaded in a whisper, hitting out with her fists at his stomach and legs. At last he detached himself from her, breathing hard. For a moment she stood still, taking deep breaths to ease the palpitations of her heart. Then she started cautiously extricating herself from the pile. Izik cleared his throat once or twice as if meaning to say something, and then he sighed.

"These are our houses," he pointed to the heap of tiles and kicked it. "The validity of the building permit has expired…and by the time we get another the wood will have rotted and the tiles will be cracked and we'll be like the proverbial broken vessel."

"The public doesn't like you."

"The public? Who's the public? You?"

"Me too."

"Eleazar Rokeah?"

"Him too.

"He hates us because we chose Pines as patron of the Bilu society," Izik snorted angrily. "We don't need administrators. All that bureaucracy is a sick curse."

"They claim you don't keep the commandments."

"Is that all? Hirsch expelled us from Mikveh Israel because we're lazy and impertinent and we hate the Arabs. He wanted us out of the country and was even prepared to pay our passage to America. Two thousand francs he set aside for that! Levontin opposed us because he supported Hirsch, and so did Erlanger, who said we weren't 'practical'. This is a chorus singing with one voice. Digur—I almost forgot him—he too said we were taking the subsidy and not working. The old men of Rishon le-Zion don't want us because we don't keep the commandments, and on the other hand they say there's no point helping bachelors when there are families needing support. David Gutman said they should take the land away from us and distribute it among the existing settlements. Ludwig Zamenhof wrote that we are petty-minded glory-seekers and sowers of discord, destroying ourselves with slander and intrigue, and the only difference between us and the charity Jews is that they study Torah and we write letters. Wissotzky says he doesn't want to support us because we're not students! Who else? Who have I forgotten?"

Fania burst into laughter.

"Thank-you, Fania,"

"For what?"

"For laughing. Come on, I have to heat some water. The comrades will be getting up for work soon."

When she turned to go into the hut he touched her arm.

"I can cope with the hungry body," he whispered, "but in me it's the spirit that's hungry. Look over there, Jerusalem." He pointed to the hills in the east, encircled by a thread of gold.

When she looked back at him she found him peering at Darya, evidently fast asleep in the depths of the straw heap. When he had gone she bent down to pick up her shawl.

"You didn't waste much time," Darya whispered. "Don't look at me like that, I won't tell Imber. I'm not a gossip."

"What are you talking about?" asked Fania. But she realized Darya had seen her in Izik's arms. Is she in love with Izik? Is that why she's here? And what about him? What does she mean when she says she won't tell? Does she think…I'm Imber's woman? Oh my God!

"I saw the two of you."

"You didn't see anything! I slipped, and he helped me up."

"I said, I won't tell Imber," Darya whispered stubbornly, emphasizing every word. She looked at Fania, her brows knitted into an expression of contempt.

"I have a husband!" Fania's voice was high and shrill, and she knew how ridiculous she must be sounding. "Imber is my friend! A wonderful man! But I have a husband. And a home, and children. And I'm going back to Rosh Pinnah today…"

Shame and anger blinded her. Because Darya didn't say any more, she turned away from her and left the hut. She tried to remember her first encounter with these people. How did they look at her? What did they say? The smiles, the friendliness—were these just a mask, covering up what they really felt? Was this what they thought of her? Imber's mistress? God help us! How eager she had been to come here! The kindness and the warmth she had shown them, helping them cook pitas in their new oven! The care and compassion with which she listened to their conversation last night! And all the time they thought she had come here for illicit pleasure! She remembered the passage in *Anna Karenina* describing the journey of Vronsky and Anna to a small town in Italy and their meeting with Golinichev. Here, too, people were saying in their hearts: see how eager and affectionate is this young woman who has left her husband and children for the sake of an adulterous liaison with this charming lover—with Imber! How can she prove to them they're mistaken. What's she going to say? Everything suddenly looks so ugly! This shack! The isolation! The poverty! Is this what they think of her?

Fania peered again and again into Tuli's face, as the baby lay on the back of the cart between the bundles and the stoves. The cart lurched over stones and potholes, and Fania kept a firm grip on the reins. Tuli's black eyes were slanted like Yehiel's, and his face clear and bright. His red, moist mouth was broad, and when he laughed or cried, a little dimple opened in his chin. She longed to pick him up, but was afraid he would burst into tears when she had to put him down again. Tamara ran back and forth, plucking a flower, chasing a butterfly, throwing a stone, chattering. Again and again her beauty reminded her of the man who was her father. She was grateful to Yehiel for the simple way he accepted Tamara into the bosom of his family. He never spoke again about the circumstances of her birth. Sometimes she wondered if he remembered all of this. If only I could have been his first wife, she thought, as he is my first husband! But were it not for that black day in Elizavetgrad she would never have come here at all. The Land of Israel would have remained a vague concept popping up in her father's prayers. Sometimes weeks passed without her remembering the calamity that befell her, and sometimes the memories came bubbling up like incandescent lava from the depths of her heart, bolstering her impression that her "healthy" life was a delusion. This was a "conditional" life, an "in-between" life, lived as if waiting for the plague to reawaken. She wondered about the people who didn't sense the torn flesh beneath her skin. Were they the same as she? Pretending to be healthy rustics, and inside—utter confusion! Hence this yearning of hers to "give" to Yehiel, she thought suddenly. She wants to compensate him! But no, that isn't it! She always loved giving presents, even as a child. They were a family of avowed present-givers, her parents and her sisters too. Rustling wrapping paper and parcels tied with string and ribbons were a part of their lives—not to mention the satisfaction of surprising and delighting the recipient of the present. Now she's returning to Rosh Pinnah with hands full. True, there isn't much money left in her pocket, but she's bringing with her a horse and a cart and cooking stoves and a license to sell "Razi" tobacco in Galilee, in addition to the "Park Davis" pharmaceutical franchise and two vine saplings obtained in Gedera. These she will plant as soon as the rains have come. And she'll ask Yehiel to build a bower in the yard. The vine will climb over it and in the summer they can sit in the shade of the booth, just stretch out a hand to pick a cluster of grapes—and eat their fill!

Fania felt she loved Galilee, loved the green sward of the foothills, the banks of flowers and the chirp of the birds—so refreshing after the aridity and heat of the coastal plain. The closer she came to Rosh Pinnah the more excited she became. If only she could learn to conceal her emotions—she's behaving like a bride on her way to meet her groom!

From a distance she saw a few houses standing half-built. Near Ayn Abu Halil she met Yosef Friedman, one of the Romanians, and with him a youth she didn't recognize and Leibel Sifris. Leibel was a close friend of Yehiel, who had known him since childhood. A native of Safed, he wore a tunic and a belt, and his hair was a shock of curly ringlets in the Safedi fashion. All through the week Leibel worked in Rosh Pinnah for paltry wages, assiduously observing the midnight prayers, and spending the Sabbath with his family in Safed.

"Look here, lad, this is Fania Silas, your landlady," said Yosef Friedman.

"My landlady?" she repeated blankly.

"No!" Friedman laughed, "You're his landlady! He's staying in your house."

"I…that is…Yehiel…"

Fania reassured the flustered youth, wondering where she was going to accommodate him. In the shed? In the kitchen? How she wished she could be alone with Yehiel, just he and she together.

"The Baron sent him and his comrades to get some experience in agricultural work with us here in Rosh Pinnah. In the fullness of time they will, God willing, take the place of those bureaucrats who are determined to ruin us."

The boy fixed Fania with a curious look.

"I bring you greetings from the wife of your landlord in Jaffa, Hannah Becker. She heard I was on my way to Rosh Pinnah…"

"Oh! Thank-you!" Roses bloomed suddenly in her cheeks when she remembered the good woman. Four years had passed since the day they arrived in Jaffa, and many guests had stayed since then in that hostelry, and still she remembered her. And she had just spent months in Jaffa and hadn't visited Mima Becker even once!

Her eyes scoured the summit of the hill, looking for "her" four walnut trees, up there on Hirbet el Yahud. She couldn't wait to go there and sit under the trees with a book in her hand and the wind on her face…

"What's new?" she asked.

"Rabbi David Shub has opened a school for the children here. Did you hear about it?"

"No!"

"He's teaching them in Hebrew. And it's not just the Torah either, but there's history and geography and botany too. There aren't any textbooks, so he took some of the books that used to be in your house. You don't mind, Fania?"

"No, no, not at all! And what else is there? More building, I see!"

"Look!" Leibel picked up a fruit resembling a large lemon from Friedman's cart and flourished it. "Our citrons are being exported to Australia!"

"Mr. Frank, our commissioner in Beirut, found us a buyer in Australia. I'm sending five hundred citrons."

"And what else?" she asked eagerly.

"We're planting a new variety of fruit. Not a lemon and not an orange but resembling both of them."

"And what else?"

"Riva is ill."

"Oy!"

"Nothing new there…I didn't want to tell you but it seems I have."

The whole settlement was revealed before her eyes: the new houses that had been built on the hillside were bigger than those of the original inhabitants, whitewashed and gleaming in the sunlight. The cypress tree sealed the row of diminutive grey houses, dwarfing her house which stood close by. Yehiel appeared at the gate of the yard, with his long strides, Moshe and Bella hovering beside him. Bella flung herself into Fania's lap, hugging her thighs with her thin arms, and then left her at once to climb up on the cart and look at Tuli. Both she and Moshe were barefoot, like all the other children of Rosh Pinnah, Jewish or Arab, and their patched clothes were torn.

"Come on, Moshe, lead the horse into the yard," Fania said to the boy who had stopped beside her, smiling and hesitant. His narrow, black eyes lit up with happiness when he took the reins from her hand. His cool fingers touched hers, and she bent down and gave him a resounding kiss on the cheek before he had time to take evasive action. How handsome was Yehiel! The wings of his short coat flapped with every step that he took, and the hint of a familiar, crooked smile flickered over his lips. When he held out his hand to her, he said "Fania," and she pressed her cheek to his hand. For a moment he hesitated, and then he remembered they were standing outside and withdrew his hand from her cheek.

"Tuli!" Fania pointed to the baby still lying in the cart, and Yehiel gazed at his son, a kind of twitch in his chin betraying his emotions. Fania knew exactly what he was feeling, the seething, surging wave that cannot be contained, that veils the eyesight to the point of blindness. If only she could stand her forever, she and Yehiel and the baby. If they could stop this moment that is theirs, with the happiness enfolding them! Yehiel lifted Tuli out of the box, and the baby wriggled suddenly and opened his mouth to cry, but changed his mind when he felt the big warm hand on the nape of his neck and let his head rest on his father's chin.

"Saida Fania!" Maryam Alhijah greeted her with a laugh, appearing suddenly with a pitcher of water balanced on her head.

In the Alhijah family's little garden there were now beds of shallots and radishes almost identical to those in the Silas family's garden…Yehiel had been sharing seeds with the neighbors…

"Moshe and Bella are staying at their house," said Yehiel, and Fania stared at him in astonishment.

"We have guests at home."

"Who?"

"Rivka, and her husband, and their baby."

Rivka! Again! So, was that why he came out to meet her, not wanting *her* as a witness to the homecoming? All at once the old hatred was rekindled in her heart. This woman is sitting in my house while I'm rushing round from place to place and never relaxing for a moment—who knows how long she's been here? Fania was so enraged she was afraid to go inside, in case her voice or her eyes betray her.

"And two boys."

"I've met one of them. Why are they in our house?"

"The 'Lovers of Zion' sent them, to learn about agriculture."

"Yes, but why in our house?"

"A party of six came to Rosh Pinnah. Only two of them are staying with us. We had the space, or we did until Rivka arrived here with her entourage."

"And Lulik?"

"Yesterday, when the guests arrived, he ran away. But he came back in the night."

"How long has Rivka been here?"

"Since yesterday."

Now she noticed the phoenix that Sasha painted on the outer door. The clouds of fire were flaking and the wings had split.

Fania sensed that Yehiel was delaying her deliberately. She looked at him quizzically.

"Riva..."

"What?"

"She's dying."

"I heard something about that..."

"We'll go and visit them afterwards."

"Yes..."

"It's because of her that Rivka's staying with us."

Rivka was sitting indoors with a big baby in her lap, bigger than would be expected considering her dimensions. A gleaming silk headscarf covered her hair, and it was studded with little beads that sparkled in the sunlight filtering in through the window. Her husband surprised Fania. A fleshy man with a florid and puffy face and bandy legs like two thick poles, and an air of stubborn confidence, he was standing by the window haloed in the light, which seemed to be showing him a degree of deference.

"Fania, this is Ishmael Nisan Amzaleg, Rivka's husband."

"You didn't tell me how beautiful she is! If she was my wife, Yehiel, I wouldn't let her out of my sight, in case she got kidnapped by a sheikh!"

Fania was embarrassed and turned her attention to the baby in Rivka's lap. She loved most children, but this baby was so like his father it was hard to smile at him.

"Are you related to Haim Amzaleg, sir, the British consul in Jaffa?" she asked.

"No! His origins are in Gibraltar and my family hails from Morocco."

"How is Bella?" asked Rivka. "My aunt Bella Rokeah is married to Fania's uncle," she reminded her husband.

Rivka hadn't yet digested the fact that Fania, this homeless Muscovite, had married her favorite relative—when along came the girl's uncle and married her aunt!

"I wouldn't live in Jaffa if I was paid to!" announced Ishmael Nisan Amzaleg. "The streets are full of sewage!"

"And Shimon Rokeah has married a Muscovite too," Rivka continued, warming to her theme.

"I met Eleazar," Fania told Yehiel. "He's back in the country as secretary to some Russian grandee, Wissotzky, who's on a mission for the 'Lovers of Zion', inspecting conditions in the settlements."

"Yes, I know."

"Has he been here yet?"

"No. He was tired and he stayed in Haifa. He sent Pines instead."

"What's Eleazar up to?" asked Rivka.

"He and Shimon have set up a society called 'Sons of Zion' with the object of giving aid to the poor, and a separate society called 'Israel Aid' specifically helping the needy of Jaffa. And he's founded a library and a hospital for the immigrant community."

Yehiel spread his hands as if saying: there's a real hero for you! Fania curled her lip. The memory of their last meeting was bound up with the image of Imber and with their joint excursion to Gedera, and she felt her cheeks flushing. The insult thrown at her by Darya Sirot still rankled, and she prayed earnestly that none of these things would ever come to Yehiel's ears.

"I've got a license to trade in tobacco," she announced. "Do you think I can export tobacco to Lebanon?" she asked Ishmael.

"I don't know, I'm not in the tobacco trade. You want me to check?"

"Yes, please."

"A tobacco license!" Ishmael laughed and slapped Yehiel's knee. "She'll be the ruin of you!" he roared suddenly. "*Kirche, Kuche, Kinder!* the Germans say. Church, kitchen, children—that's where a woman belongs! Tobacco indeed!"

"I sell medicines too, Mister Amzaleg."

"Ishmael bought a book of papers to roll cigarettes and there was a German poem printed on it," Rivka tried to steer the conversation toward another topic.

"Hertzenstein from Jaffa printed Imber's *Watch on the Jordan* on tobacco papers," said Fania.

"In Hebrew?!" Ishmael was fuming again, and Fania felt she

could now excuse Rivka for *anything*, having seen the braying donkey she had to put up with. "I'd never buy tobacco papers with a Hebrew poem printed on them! Burning Hebrew letters? God preserve us! Did you hear, this year we've started exporting olive oil to Pollonia and Romania. The 'Messager Maritime' line has opened a new route linking the Mediterranean with the Black Sea. On the barrels I wrote 'Kosher' in Hebrew letters. They don't burn barrels!"

"Are the newlyweds still living in Bella's apartment?" asked Rivka.

"Yes, though recently they've started talking about moving to a new neighborhood..."

"What's wrong with where they live now?"

"It's still only being discussed. Shimon Rokeah wants to build a new quarter in Jaffa, for Jews exclusively, like the new quarters being built in Jerusalem. He and Eleazar are talking about it..."

"If Eleazar's talking about it, it's definitely going to happen!" Rivka smiled.

"Anyway, they have their first two tenants. Bella has agreed to the project because she's loyal to anything that has the name Rokeah written on it, and my uncle is going along with it because he thinks it's a revolutionary idea. Would you like to live in a quarter like that?" she asked Yehiel.

"You've been home one hour," Yehiel grimaced, "and already you're talking new quarters! If I'd known you were coming I'd have built a triumphal arch in your honor!"

"Why? What have I said?"

"You've only just arrived—are you already wandering off again?"

"I'm not wandering off anywhere! I just asked a question!"

"Don't ask! Since when have you asked questions? You want to live in a new quarter?—I'm not stopping you!"

Fania went out to the other room, her throat constricted and her eyes filling with tears. She said to herself again and again: Don't cry! Just don't cry! From the next room she heard Rivka's voice:

"I'd definitely move to a new quarter."

"What's wrong with Beirut?" Ishmael's voice was raised again.

"Nothing wrong with it, nothing at all! But my relations live in Jaffa."

"And mine live in Beirut!"

Yehiel appeared in the doorway and said to Fania: "Come on, let's go and see Riva."

Riva's eyes were big and bright. The lids seemed to have receded from them. Her skin was white and smooth as ivory, and only two little red dots showed on her face, as if a painter had touched it with the tip of his brush. She smiled at Fania, with a look that was both apologetic and offended. Fania sat down beside the bed, and touched the back of the cool, puffy hand. It was clear that Riva had to struggle to turn her head, and the place where her head had been resting until now was marked by a deep indentation in the pillow. Issar asked Yehiel to sit beside Fania, so Riva could see them both without straining her neck.

"The children?" she asked, her voice reduced to a croak and her whole body tensed with the effort of articulating the two words.

"They're here. They came back with me. I'll bring them to see you tomorrow."

Riva smiled and closed her eyes. Fania and Yehiel sat together on the only chair in the room which stood beside the bed. Issar sat on a small couch covered with an old tapestry. He had been sleeping here since his wife fell ill. He was very tired, rubbing his eyes from time to time.

"Go to the other room and rest for a while," Fania whispered to him.

"Go on, go!" she urged when she saw him hesitate. It was clear that Issar was relieved to have someone telling him what to do. He rose and went to the other room. A soft moaning emerged from Riva's mouth. There was something majestic and awesome in those ivory features which drew Fania's fascinated gaze.

"Doctor Blidin is giving her morphine," Yehiel whispered. They were sitting in congenial discomfort on the one chair, listening to Riva's breathing. So, finally they had been left alone. Fania tried to remember all the things she wanted to say to him and couldn't remember a single one of them. Part of his body rested on hers, and Fania sensed the warmth and softness of her breast and belly, cushioning him. Her body said to his body: "I'm not angry. You were right." She wound her arm around his waist, as if to keep him from falling from the chair. If only this moment could last, she thought, taking care not to move. From her sleepy, inert body erupted a volcanic surge of passion for this beloved body clasped gently in her arms. She turned and kissed the smooth patch of skin between collar and nape, the only place where his skin was exposed. A tremor passed through Yehiel's body, and he stood up and drew her after him to Issar's little couch. They leaned their backs against the cool wall and stretched their legs out in front, watching Riva. The room was small and low-ceilinged, almost identical to the rooms in their house.

"Why didn't you come to me in Jaffa?" she asked.

"Why did you leave?"

"I waited for you."

"Are you staying now?"

"I love you, Yehiel."

"And is that why you go off by yourself so often?"

"Yes."

"Don't leave me."

"I'm not leaving."

"You promise?"

"Yes."

From the tips of her toes to the curls on her head happiness bubbled in her, an irresistible force. Yehiel peered at her playfully as if saying, what am I going to do with so much happiness?

"Yehiel?"

In the doorway a lean youth appeared with a rifle slung over his shoulder. He recoiled at the sight of the man and the woman sitting so close together on the couch.

"Sorry…I was looking for the spade…"

"I left it under the planks. This is my wife, Yehoshua. Fania, this is Yehoshua Ben Aryeh. He came here three months ago from Romania."

"Yes…well then…I'm going on guard."

Flushed with embarrassment, the boy left the way he came. Fania and Yehiel grinned. Yehiel kissed her lips lightly, like the peck of a beak. Then he stood up as if he remembered where they were sitting. Fania was a little disappointed that he hadn't returned her declaration of love.

"What are you doing with his spade?"

"It's my spade, actually. Poor fellow, when he arrived he was shocked by the behavior of our new administrator, Monsieur Oshri, and he wrote a letter of complaint to Erlanger. He didn't know the way they do things—you scratch my back…etc. Erlanger sent a copy of his complaint to Oshri, and since then the boy has been mucking out stables all day and standing guard at night. As if all that wasn't enough, when he arrived in the country he told Erlanger he was going to build his own house, with his own hands. He just needed the materials. 'Go on then!' the people here responded. 'You've said it, now get on with it!' They knew he hadn't the faintest idea how to build a house. And so now, not only is he mucking out stables by day and guarding at night in exchange for a few paltry bishliks, he's supposed to be building himself a house, too…The boy was desperate and he decided to leave the place. And then we decided to help him. Each one of us contributes a day or two of work to get the house started."

"I see that the Moineshti contingent have added yards and gardens to their houses, in European style."

"That's right."

She would have liked to ask him, what about us?—but she knew that if they had any prospect of changing their accommodation, he would definitely have told her. For a moment a shadow deepened on his face, and then he peered at her.

"What is it?" she asked.

"You're different from all other women."

"All women are different from all other women. Why say it now?"

"Any other woman would have asked, 'what about our house, Yehiel?'"

"You didn't promise to build me a new house."

"There you are! That's how you're different! Wouldn't you like to have a new house?"

"Of course I would!"

"Oshri will never authorize a house for me. And I'll never ask him for it. The hand that offers expects to be kissed. I hate that way of doing things!"

"We'll build ourselves a house! With our own money!"

Yehiel looked down at his hands. On his bowed head she found grey hairs that she hadn't seen before.

"Was someone here?" asked Issar, appearing in the doorway and rubbing his eyes again and again. He apologized for intruding on their time. In his place, she wouldn't have treated them with such deference.

When Fania and Yehiel returned to their house, they found there the two boys who had come in from work and even found the time to wash before sitting down at the table. Rivka had spread a cloth on the table and set out the bread Fania brought from Jaffa, as well as olives, figs, hard-boiled eggs and cheese. She's treating my house as if she owned the place, Fania thought.

"The cheese is from my parents' house in Ein Zeitim," said Rivka. "And the figs we brought from Beirut. Nothing compares with Beirut figs!"

Is she still in love with Yehiel? And her husband, doesn't he notice what's going on? What does she hope to achieve with all this posturing? Is she cherishing, somewhere deep down, a hope that one day I'll go away and never come back and she can move in and take my place?

"Gershon! Michel! You haven't met your landlady!" Since Fania and Yehiel had sat together on the one chair beside Riva's bed, it was if their hearts were opening up. His eyes followed her and everything about her gladdened him. They sat down side by side, while Bella and Moshe put Tamara between them, leaning over her like a pair of brooding birds. The two children scratched from to time at the insect-bites on their faces and arms. Bella's eyes were still showing symptoms of trachoma.

"You shouldn't bring young men into a house where there's a

lady like this!" Ishmael wagged his thick finger in Yehiel's face. He laughed uproariously, and Fania was afraid that the bread and the cheese and the olives he had stuffed into his mouth were about to be regurgitated.

"Where are you from?" she asked the boys.

"Baron Rothschild sent them to you as a present," cried Ishmael, chewing as he talked and scraping up the last morsels of food from his plate.

"You want coffee, Ishmael?" asked Rivka.

He mumbled something slurred and unintelligible, ignoring his wife's diversionary tactic. Fania didn't look at Rivka. Involuntarily, she thought of those thick fingers groping her body.

"They are the proof that one merchant can succeed where a hundred busybodies fail!" His menacing finger, coated in fragments of cheese, was now turned towards the youths. "At the conference in Katowitz they talked and talked and talked and nothing came of it! Until a fur trader from Berlin took a hand—what was his name, Rivka?"

"Zimel."

"Zimel! Until he went to Baron Rothschild and persuaded him! If it weren't for this Zimel you wouldn't be sitting here today! A merchant calculates his moves, he doesn't jump in and go ahead. He waited for the right moment, and on the twenty-fifth anniversary of the foundation of the Alliance Israelite Universelle he went to Rothschild with greetings in the name of 'Lovers of Zion,' and it was only then, when the bread was well and truly buttered, that he presented the bill! That's the kind of language Rothschild understands!"

"Rothschild sent you?" Fania asked one of the youths.

"Yes. The 'Lovers of Zion' chose six young men to learn about agriculture in the settlements and Rothschild paid our passage. The idea is to turn us into instructors for the future."

"Someone was asking about you and I can't remember who," said Ishmael to Fania, peering inquisitively at his wife.

"When?" asked Rivka.

"In Beirut, someone...I'm trying to remember. Who do you know in Beirut?"

"I don't know anyone there!"

"You know me!" he laughed and thumped the table. Tamara was frightened but the two older children, accustomed to the noisy antics of their "uncle", suppressed their mirth. "Come and see us in the summer," Ishmael said to her, as if they were alone together. "When everything's burning down here, up there it's as cool as the Tyrol. Isn't that right, Rivka?"

"That's right."

"You can travel by the Messager Maritime packet. It leaves Jaffa every other day and the voyage to Beirut takes exactly twelve hours. A house like ours you've never seen in your life, I promise you!"

Fania rose from her seat and turned to Yehiel and the youths:

"Help me bring the stoves inside. In Jaffa there was a delivery of cooking stoves from Marseilles and I bought one for me and two for resale. You see, Ishmael, here in Rosh Pinnah we have some things you definitely don't have in Beirut!"

When the stoves were brought into the kitchen, all stood and feasted their eyes on the wonders of technology.

"Would you like to have a stove like that, Rivka?" Ishmael asked.

"Yes, I would."

And so, without further ado, the sale of the first stove was concluded. Meanwhile Yehiel stayed out in the yard, fetching fodder and drinking water for Storm. On returning to the kitchen he said to Fania: "The horse and the cart, whose are they?"

"Ours."

She was alarmed to see the change that came over Yehiel. His face clouded with anger that he couldn't hide. If only there weren't all these people here! The place suddenly became very overcrowded. Yehiel's abrupt breathing sounded like a growl.

"We have a horse, Fania," he whispered in a choking voice. "Our king and saviour, Elijah Shaid, appeared in Rosh Pinnah and gave us horses. And stables. And factors who hand out fodder every evening to those who bow down low enough, as well as Jews like Aryeh and Segel who clean their stables for them."

"But...if that is so, then it must be a really good thing to have a horse of our own and not be dependent on the Baron's charity," she mumbled nervously.

"I want to plow and sow...not run a stable!" he shouted suddenly. His outburst scared everyone and Tamara started to cry. "I didn't leave Safed for this!"

"But, Yehiel," Fania pleaded. "I bought the horse with money I earned myself, from sheer hard work! I didn't get it as a present from anyone! And it didn't cost a lot anyway, just six imperials, that was all. And it's a good horse. Jaffa to Rosh Pinnah in five days. He can help out on the farm as well..."

"These luxuries are a disaster!" cried Yehiel. "They've turned all of us into charity cases! People have stopped working. Why work? The Baron will bail us out. Treat the Baron's henchman with respect—you get a horse. Polish his shoes—you get a house..."

"The Baron also paid off all of Rosh Pinnah's debts," Ishmael's voice boomed out suddenly, "fourteen thousand francs!"

"Those leeches from Alsace will suck our blood until there's nothing left of the settlements!"

"Yehiel!" If only she knew how to calm him down. She sensed it wasn't on her account that he was angry, but she had never seen him so agitated.

"What's the source of Oshri's power? The farmers and their lust for leisure! What kind of people are we? The 'Halukkah' is aptly named. It means division—and it has divided the people into two camps: beggars on one side and corrupt moneylenders on the other! And what have we here in Rosh Pinnah? A new version of the Halukkah! Rivka!" he cried suddenly, his eyes blazing, "You remember! You remember how the peasants used to be in Jaoni! No harvest?—they became tenants on their own land, paying the 'kism' to the landowners and eating what was left. When there was nothing left, they moved to Horan until after the rains..."

"You sent Rokeah and Pines all over the world to appeal for help!" a furious Ishmael suddenly cut in. "Who didn't you appeal to? I read Rabbi Israel Teller's articles in *Hamaggid*, the articles in *Yizrael* and *Hashahar* and *Havatzelet*...from all of them the plea arose:

Money! Money! Money! Money for Jaoni! Money for the settlement of the Land of Israel! Well, you got what you asked for, and there's a price to be paid! You think I didn't contribute? I contributed all right! Why are you being so hard on Fania? What has she done to upset you?"

Exploiting his role as her saviour, Ishmael put his arm around Fania's shoulders, and she hurriedly pulled herself free from his grip. His touch made her skin smart.

"There is money," Yehiel answered him angrily. "It's for buying land, not fancy carriages for ladies! Five francs a dunam costs today! Tomorrow it will cost ten, and the day after—out of our reach!"

Yehiel went outside, slamming the door behind him. Fania started clearing the plates from the table. Something was extinguished in her heart. Her grievance felt deep and sore. Yehiel shouted at her in the presence of all these people, in Rivka's hearing! Yehiel, always so sparing in speech, Yehiel who never raises his voice—and on the first day of her return. The best way to escape from the crowd thronging her house is to go to bed. Five days she has been on the road, and she can't yet digest everything that has befallen her from the moment she set foot on the threshold of her home. She lay down on the mattress, between Tuli and Tamara, and the rhythmic breathing of the children drove her to sleep.

Chapter twelve

When she woke in the morning Fania realized that she had slept on the mattress set aside by Yehiel for Ishmael and Rivka and their baby. As she had taken the only mattress in the house, all the others were forced to sleep on mats. This turned out well in the end, as it meant the Amzalegs left them the next morning and moved to Ein Zeitim. They only returned for Riva's funeral.

"The Land of Israel was bought with suffering…" said Rabbi Motel in his eulogy for Riva Frumkin, daughter of Shlomo Zalman. Michel and Gershon threw clods of earth on the freshly dug grave. Ishmael linked arms with Issar, who was staring straight ahead of him with his tired eyes. He was wearing a European suit and a stiff hat, and Fania wondered if these were left over from his wedding day.

Three days had passed since Riva went to a better world, and they had been unable to bury her. Her wasted body was not allowed to rest even after the spirit had left it. The court in Safed ruled against burials in Rosh Pinnah, while Issar refused to bury her in Safed. The presiding judge had the temerity to declare, in Issar's hearing, that he didn't expect Rosh Pinnah to survive much longer. The place would be wilderness again, and abandoned Jewish graves would be unprotected.

"I don't understand them!" cried Fania indignantly.

"What's so hard to understand?" said Ishmael. "The old men of Safed want the people of Rosh Pinnah to become dependent on their charity."

After Riva had lain unburied on her bed for two days, Rabbi Motel Katz called to see Issar and told him that everywhere in the Land of Israel was sacred ground; a site for the grave had been allocated and the funeral would take place the next day at noon.

A cold wind blew and grasped the tunics of the men and set the women's headscarves flapping. Fania stared at the dark dust piling up on the isolated little grave. The sound of prayer came to her ears as if from far away. Riva's body was tiny, like the body of a child...She had been like a second mother to her, when she needed a mother. Fania wondered now how she had looked when she arrived here four years before. Were her wounds visible to the eye? Yehiel took her into his house without asking questions, as if he was picking up a stray cat. Did she look like a stray cat? Did Riva guess what had happened to her?

The easterly wind howled like a banshee. Issar bent down suddenly and covered his face with his hands.

Fania looked up at the sky. If the rain fell, it would leak through the crack in the roof of the factory she was leasing in Safed. The building, formerly an apartment house, had been constructed with thick walls of solid masonry, and although it looked robust, wind whistled through the crack in the roof. The landlord explained that like all the buildings of Safed, this one too had shallow foundations, and that was why the fissure opened up; sealing it would be a simple job. So far she hadn't found the time to attend to it, and now she was afraid of the rain soaking the bales of tobacco stored there. How would she keep the building warm in winter? In Rosh Pinnah there was a brass stove—the Mangal—in every home, fueled with wooden faggots, but if she were to bring a stove like that into the factory, the tobacco was liable to catch fire, Heaven forbid! The days were growing shorter, and she bought a storm lantern for the workers so they could carry on until four in the afternoon. Like the other business premises in Safed, shops and bathhouses, they closed and locked the shutters half an hour after sunset. The dark streets of the town sent the local people scurrying to their homes. What do they have to look for in the streets? Thieves? Lepers? Mad dogs? Ever since she opened the factory she had lived in a state of constant fear. The livelihood of four workers' families depended on her! She didn't fear for herself, she knew she could endure anything. But what would happen if for example the workers forgot to extinguish the paraffin lamp? Yehiel suggested she should pay half a majeda to a handyman who lived near the factory in return for turning off the lamp every evening. Fania was nervous about employing the handyman, as he seemed to have lost most of his fingers, but she did as Yehiel advised. A few days later Rabbi Motel told her she had done a sacred duty, as the man would have otherwise died of hunger.

"What happened to his hand?" she asked.

"Yehiel didn't tell you?"

"No."

"The Rabbi sent the handyman to Beirut, to fetch from there the Halukkah funds sent from Amsterdam. An Arab attacked him in Kasmia and tried to steal the money. The handyman held on to the purse with all his strength, but the Arab cut off his fingers and got away with the purse."

"Oy!"

"In the end they caught the thief and punished him appropriately."

"Meaning what?"

"They cut off his fingers. Why didn't Yehiel tell you? Sparing you, I suppose. Now he's afraid, the handyman that is, that electricity will put him out of a job."

"What's that?"

"In the French legation in Jerusalem they've installed electric lighting. It doesn't run on oil, wood or coal."

"So how does it work?"

"It's a current flowing through metallic cables; it gives heat and light, without any need for combustion."

Fania decided that if her business succeeded she too would install electric light in her factory, copying the French legation. For the handyman she would find alternative employment. But at the moment the business wasn't operating at a profit. Her expenses were higher than she had expected: the cost of the lease, commission to Mr. Landau and his associates, payment for raw materials from Nablus and Jaffa, salaries for the four workers. She used to wake up in the night drenched in sweat, paralytic with anxiety. Why did she need this business? She remembered with a feeling of awe the days when she gleaned ears of corn with the peasants of Jaoni to slake her hunger. She was proud of those days. She glanced at Yehiel. He was standing behind Rabbi David Shub and his brother-in-law Rabbi Motel Katz, beside Rivka's parents. They still saw him as their son-in-law; after all, the blood of Rachel, their daughter, flowed in the veins of his children. Now he stood hunched, hands folded on his stomach, as if he was in pain. His face was lined and his narrow eyes sunk deep in their sockets. God! If only my business could succeed! Fania prayed in her heart. How much she wanted to lighten the burden placed on his shoulders. The hard years had engraved their marks on his body and soul. He had been the first of the pioneers of Jaoni, and the last to benefit from the transformations that had taken place there. She asked herself how long he could carry on bearing this yoke, and was alarmed by the thought. Yehiel seemed to sense her scrutiny because he raised his head and looked at her, his eyes intent and his expression softening. He needs me! she said to herself, weighing the shift in the balance of power between them. She drew strength and energy from the difficulties stacked in her way, while he was being ground into dust. It wasn't hunger that bowed him, or hard work, but the humiliation of dependence on the bureaucrats. He hated them and hated the system that promoted them. A new instruction had just been issued by Monsieur Yitzhak Oshri. Every day, the farmer was required to stand before his door, ready and prepared to set off on any mission dreamed up by the great panjandrum. Yehiel declared that he had no intention of being one of Oshri's lackeys. The other farmers were angry with Yehiel for not enduring with them the burden of the decree, but their protests were silenced when Oshri stopped paying Yehiel the monthly subsidy of ten francs and the allowance for fodder for the horse. Suddenly the farmers seemed to be distancing themselves from Yehiel, as if they couldn't forgive him for being more stubborn than they, as if they feared he might infect them with a suspicion of mutiny. And Yehiel, instead of being upset—rejoiced!

"He can't evict me," he explained to Fania. "We're occupying Oliphant's land, not the Baron's."

He was digging holes in the ground to make the foundations for a bower. After the rain, they planted the vines she brought from Gedera at two corners of the house, and now Yehiel was putting up supports for the vines with the thick branches that Moshe and Bella had gathered for this purpose. Two years would pass before the vines needed these supports, but perhaps this was his way of saying he believed in this land.

But the land wasn't supporting them. If it weren't for the onions and radishes in their vegetable patch, and if it weren't for Fania's enterprises, they would all be going hungry.

Every day, when she returned from Safed in the afternoon and saw the farmers lining up at the door of the barley store, each with a basket in his hand, she blessed Yehiel in her heart. Oshri had found himself a fine way of humiliating the farmers! Instead of doling out the fodder once a month, he set up a storehouse and put one of his minions in charge of it, to distribute the barley on a daily basis. Ishmael claimed this was a good way of falsifying the accounts and earning illicit profits, while Yehiel lamented the loss of the barley that the mice were eating.

Yehoshua, Riva's first-born son, said "Kaddish". When the people looked up from the solitary grave, the first to be dug in the soil of Rosh Pinnah, they were confronted by a sight that made them gasp. Fire was raging in the fields, flames soaring to the sky. For a moment people looked on in horror and then broke into a run and headed for the fields, young and old, women and children, running here and there as if possessed. At the graveside only a few remained, and Issar stared at the fields with a look of blank incomprehension.

"Your saintly mother is ascending to Heaven in a fiery chariot," he told his son.

The Arabs of Jaoni suddenly appeared, shrieking like ravens, and people came running past carrying hoes and buckets. Fania stayed with Issar and his son in a kind of covenant of grief. From far away came the anguished cries of the owners of the fields, bewailing a whole year's work going up in smoke before their eyes. The sky turned purple from the volume of the sparks thrown up in the air, and the stench of burning filled the void. Suddenly Lulik appeared before them, running and shouting, "Jews! Fire!" Fania left the group of mourners around Issar and ran toward her brother. "Lulik!" she shouted, trying to stop him. But his legs were lighter than hers, and like an arrow loosed from the bow he sped towards the fire, his maniacal cries mingling with the shouts of the farmers tackling the blaze. From a distance she saw him rushing into the heart of the flames and disappearing from sight, engulfed. When at last she reached the edge of the scorched ground she was grabbed by Yehiel who held her back, clutching her in a grip of iron. She struggled with him until her throat was choked by tears and moans and until she saw her brother Lulik again, laid out before her as charred as an ember. His mouth was pink in his blackened face and she didn't dare touch him. For a moment he opened his eyes and it seemed to her he recognized her, then he twitched and lay still.

Fania sat out the "seven days of mourning" in Issar's house. The bereavement of the two families became the bereavement of the whole community. A full year of work had been obliterated in an hour, and no one knew how the fire had started. All of Rosh Pinnah was crammed into the little room, like a herd of frightened goats. People raised all kinds of weird conjectures, returning again and again to the moment when the fire was first seen, as if by reliving this moment they could decipher the cause of the disaster. People prayed for the safe passage of the souls of Riva and of Lulik, and at the same time they prayed for themselves too, asking for the strength to withstand all the woes that were assailing them.

What will happen now? they asked again and again. What will happen now? All their hopes had been pinned on the crops that were destroyed in the field. In the new cemetery they dug another grave, and all the people of Rosh Pinnah, great and humble alike, came to pay Lulik their last respects.

Fania reflected indignantly about her brother, about his short and embittered life, extinguished like a stray spark. He was the thread binding her to her parents. Perhaps that was why she clung to him so, hoping for a miracle. She realized now that she had been clinging to him, and not he to her. Did he have any idea where he was? Did he know who she was? With his death another of the links tying her to her past was severed. Would she ever understand why things happen? Are they part of some greater order? Of some process driven by logic? Sometimes she was aware of Moshe's bemused looks, as if he was waiting for an explanation from her. I only wish I could explain, she thought, and if only someone would explain it to me. Now Lulik was a kind of secret pact between her and Moshe, a vague and confused pact, like a momentary flash, a transient lesson that she tried in vain to grasp.

She heard and didn't hear the murmur of the people who filled the room from morning till night. When Yehiel came in, all fell silent, as if afraid he might hear what they were saying. There was a high barrier of suspicion between them and him. They couldn't forgive him for taking himself out of the circle of the needy, for going hungry and not holding out his hand. All had moved long since into spacious houses built with the Baron's money, they all received the monthly allowance, their daughters wore pretty dresses, their wives had redeemed their jewelery from the pawnbroker…Fania knew it was pointless passing judgment on these ill-fated people, but their treatment of Yehiel enraged her. Seven years he had clung to the land, pouring his heart's blood into it, and at the very least he deserved friendship.

In the afternoon, Fania and Issar were left alone. Tuli slept in his cradle and Tamara on the small couch. Soon people would be returning from the fields to recite "Mincha". They were both silent, worn out by grief and by the mourners streaming in and out from dawn to dusk. Wrapped up in themselves, they listened to their hearts.

Suddenly a little black bird came in through the window. It flew around the room, perched for a moment on the candlestick and circled the walls, chirping merrily. Fania held her breath. A strange thought flashed into her head: it's Lulik! When the bird had disappeared, leaving the same way as it arrived, and its chirping was swallowed by the wind, Issar stood up and lit the lamp. He looked at Fania and an enigmatic smile hovered over his face. His smile scared her. Was he thinking what she was thinking? It wasn't by chance that he got up just then and lit the memorial lamp. The atmosphere in the room became strange and intimidating. Suddenly she felt an overwhelming urge to do something! Anything! To toss aside the shawl of bereavement that was covering her shoulders! For four days now she hadn't visited her factory in Safed. Who knows what's happening there? Did they wrap up the bales of tobacco? Have new deliveries arrived yet? Any sign of customers? Can she be sure no packages have been stolen? She simply can't afford to replace them…

The morning after the "seven days" Fania went up to Safed, and sure enough, as she expected, another consignment of tobacco had arrived from Jaffa. From the previous consignment, a total of three packs had been sold so far. Since the day she went into the tobacco business she had made a point of observing smokers, to see if they were inhaling the smoke of cigarettes manufactured by "Razi". The world was divided then between those who smoked "Razi" and those who didn't smoke "Razi". She soon discovered that the Arabs preferred to smoke the tobacco grown by Druze. She was almost tempted to smoke herself, but was afraid of being pelted with stones. The money she received from Ishmael for the stove had long since been spent. She was forced to borrow money from Rabbi Elya, head of the Vilna community in Safed, just so she could pay her employees' wages. At the end of the second month she dismissed three workers, and the one she retained was Bezalel Ben Moreno, the boy who rescued her when the people of Safed were throwing stones at her. At night he slept in the factory, an arrangement which suited them both: he had a roof over his head and she had a reliable watchman. She went on paying the half majeda to the handyman with the shorn fingers, even though she didn't need his services anymore. As time passed and still no customers were found, she began to fear the tobacco would rot. Day by day her debt to Rabbi Elya mounted. And she didn't dare tell Yehiel that not only were they not trading at a profit, but they were also sinking deeper and deeper into the mud. In the end she loaded eight packs of tobacco on Storm's back and sent Bezalel to Beirut with a letter addressed to Mr Ishmael Nisan Amzaleg. In her letter, Fania asked Ishmael to find a sub-contractor who could sell her tobacco in Lebanon. After two weeks of waiting, Bezalel returned safely and handed her three "purses" of money. Ishmael wrote to her in reply that he'd been unable to find her a sub-contractor because all the big companies had their own agents. Even "Razi" was represented in Lebanon by Herr Franck. He also asked her not to send him any more consignments of tobacco. What she had already sent was stowed in his warehouses and he didn't know if he would ever manage to shift it. He advised her to get out of the tobacco business without delay. With his customary sensitivity he implied that he was sending the money as an act of charity. Perhaps he had heard from Bezalel Ben Moreno about her plight; she would need to interrogate the youth. The thought of being beholden henceforward to Ishmael soured her mood. As soon as she moved into profit she would repay the money to the last farthing! Most of the money she received from Ishmael went straight to Mr. Landau to pay for the tobacco stocks she already had. She also took Ishmael's advice and wrote to Landau that she wanted to give up the company franchise because "Razi" tobacco just wasn't selling in Galilee. When Landau's reply arrived, she was stunned. She had forgotten that according to the contract she signed she was committed to paying a penalty in the event of failing to sell the tobacco. Now Landau was demanding the payment of the penalty. As if all this wasn't enough, tobacco rotting in the warehouses and all her investments going up in smoke—she still had to pay off the "Razi" company! Fania was furious with herself. She'd leaped at the chance of being a "Razi" agent without first checking out the state of the market. When will she finally grow up? She's past twenty now, and her blunders are harming not only her but her family too. How happy she was when it seemed to her that with her acumen she had succeeded in hooking Mr. Landau, and now she was coming to realize that she was the one who swallowed the bait he cast for her. Would an experienced businessman like Landau have awarded a license to anyone without first finding out who that person was? No! She was naive and Landau had exploited her naivete! He hadn't lost a brass farthing in her business; the risk was hers entirely!

Fania was beside herself with worry. She ran to the field to share with Yehiel the calamity that had befallen her, but in the field there was no sign of him. Two farmers stood in what was left of the scorched crop, winnowing busily. Straw and chaff flew in the air and their movements matched the swinging of the shovel. Beside the farmers stood her "lodgers", Gershon and Michel, gathering up the grain and filling sacks with it. When she asked them where Yehiel was, they looked at her in surprise: "Yehiel's in Yesod Hamaaleh, isn't he?"

"What? Since when?"

The boys were confused and fell silent. If Yehiel hadn't seen fit to tell his wife what he was doing, who were they to do it for him?

"Where are the other farmers?"

They shrugged, embarrassed.

"We're just hired hands," said Michel.

"And bachelors!" Gershon stressed.

"I don't understand!"

Bit by bit the full story emerged. A few days after the end of the "seven days" vigil, it was Issar's turn to do the bidding of His Excellency Monsieur Oshri. But instead of presenting himself before the factor's door, Issar went out to the field as he did every day. Oshri punished him for this by cutting his allowance in half, but Issar said, "He can starve me to death, but I serve only God and work only on the land. I was here before Monsieur Oshri and I shall be here after he has gone. Lucky is the man who isn't dependent on Oshri..."

Other farmers took encouragement from Issar's defiance. Suddenly they were ashamed of their readiness to sell their freedom and their pride for a mess of potage. The Baron's factor shouted "Mutiny!"

and cut their wages. He stopped paying some of the farmers the monthly subsidy, and they were forced to sell their clothes to feed their children. Rabbi Moshe David Shub, head of the community, sent a letter of complaint to Mr. Shaid, but since an order had come from the Baron to establish "discipline" in his settlements, Shaid replied by telegram asking Shub to persuade the farmers to submit to the factor. Meanwhile Oshri bribed two of the residents with favors, and they testified that the idle hooligans of Rosh Pinnah had slandered them. Oshri himself alleged that farmers had assaulted him. Vormesser, manager of the settlements, demanded that the farmers apologize to Oshri. So long as they didn't apologize, they would receive no wages. The farmers heard this and dispersed, looking for work in foreign fields.

"How come I don't know about this?" Fania was appalled.

"I don't understand..." Gershon mumbled.

"I'm so ashamed! Busy with my own troubles...and what now?"

"I heard a rumor..."

"What?"

"Secret discussions in the settlement..."

"I won't tell!"

"They say that Moshe David and his brother-in-law Motel Katz met in Safed with Yehiel Michal Pines and he advised them to apologize and promised he'd have Oshri removed and replaced with another administrator."

"And if he isn't removed?"

"He will be!"

Now she remembered things she had heard in Safed. The grocer who said to her in his unique blend of Yiddish and Arabic, "In the meantime, until the threshing, how are you going to manage?" And Rabbi Elya, the money-lender, who gave her a warning, the full significance of which escaped her: "The interest rate is low, Madame Silas, but this is temporary. When you people get the *shtitza* back, we shall raise it." It turned out that she had benefited indirectly from the troubles of Rosh Pinnah! How did she fail to notice what was going on under her nose?!

"They know about this in Safed?"

"Everyone knows about it!"

"Who is Yehiel working for?"

The boys shrugged. Perhaps they really didn't know and perhaps they didn't want to tell her what Yehiel himself hadn't told her. She looked at the two farmers, sifting their grains in a winnowing shovel. Their lips were sealed tight in bitter obstinacy. She couldn't be angry with them.

"And they?" she asked the boys, pointing to the farmers.

"Those two confessed their 'sin' and were forgiven."

Miserable traitors! In a foul mood Fania turned toward her house. She dragged her feet and her heart was heavy. How many torments had Yehiel suffered while she saw nothing! How is it possible? How did she come to this, not knowing what was happening to him? And what does he think of her? Is he comfortable with her not knowing? Or is he offended?

Toward evening Yehiel came home, paralysed with fatigue. Fania heated some water in a bowl, and while he washed his sweaty limbs, she prepared his meal. When he finished eating she asked,

"Since when have you been working in Yesod Hamaaleh?"

"Since a week ago."

"Why didn't you tell me?"

"You didn't ask."

"I didn't ask! How could I ask if I didn't know?" Despite her determination to stay calm, she burst out angrily: "All of Rosh Pinnah knows where my husband's working, everyone but me! I went looking for you in the field!"

"I didn't want to worry you."

"What will people think of us?"

"I don't care what people think of us."

"And you don't care what I think about you?"

"What do you think, Fania?"

"I think it's stupid and ugly that a whole settlement—children and old people too—is starving itself because of the arrogance of a heartless factor!"

"What do you suggest?"

"Apologize to him."

"Never!"

"You don't understand, Yehiel! What do you think? He's tearing out his hair and shedding tears over your revolt? No! He's celebrating his victory! He can't be acting any other way! This is the Baron's principle!"

"I have principles too!"

"But at what price!"

"The dream is great. People are small. Salvation won't be achieved by people whose honor has been besmirched."

"Oshri is stronger than you."

"The dream is stronger than him. Oshris will come and go… and we're staying. We stayed in Jaoni after it had been deserted, and we stayed after the drought set in. Why should we have anything to do with that corrupt slave-master? We don't live by his command!"

"Oh yes we do! That's precisely it!"

"Why does he intimidate you, Fania? What are you afraid of? Whatever he says, we have forty families here instead of the four that were here four years ago, and twelve hundred and fifty dunams…"

"So then, I'm right! The achievements are more important than the stupidity and malice of Monsieur Oshri! He can't drive you out of your homes and away from your fields! What do you look like, Yehiel! You could have at least told me…"

"You didn't tell me that the tobacco isn't selling."

"How do you know that?"—she was astounded.

"From the Adis family. Ishmael told Rivka you sent him tobacco to sell and she wrote about this to her parents. So, you confided in Ishmael but not in me."

"That's why I was out looking for you in the field. To tell you… oh Yehiel! Landau is demanding payment of a penalty for the tobacco I haven't been able to sell! I was stupid enough to commit myself to paying that kind of penalty…"

"Sell the tobacco. Pay him off."

"There are no buyers!"

"There will be."

"No, there won't! I've tried everything!" Fania collapsed suddenly like a little girl on Yehiel's chest. When she had calmed down a little she heard his rapid, abrupt breathing. She looked at him in alarm. His eyes were closed and beads of sweat covered his forehead.

"Yehiel! You're sick!"

"No, no…just tired…"

"What are you doing in Yesod Hamaaleh?"

"Working for Fishel Salomon. We're preparing the land for sowing."

"And how much is he paying you?"

"A franc a day."

"From dawn till sunset. That's a fine deal Fishel Salomon has gotten out of you! If you're working for next to nothing you could get the same here in Rosh Pinnah! That's a peasant's wage!"

"And am I better than a peasant? But I'd work for him if it was even for nothing. It's a pity you haven't seen him in action—he works in a state of spiritual elation! The priests and Levites who carried the Ark of the Covenant to the Temple couldn't have felt more holy exhilaration!"

Fania sensed a note of indignation in Yehiel's voice.

"The farmers there need loans to buy mules and plows and to pay government taxes. They want to put their land in the Baron's name as a guarantee for the loans they've already taken out and for the extra loans they're applying for. Fishel is refusing to sign. 'I don't want loans,' he says, 'I work the land and I bring forth food from the earth!' But he doesn't want to cut himself off from the community so he's prepared to mortgage all the rest of his property—everything but his land."

"The arguments in Rosh Pinnah weren't enough for you, so now you're getting yourself involved in disputes in Yesod Hamaaleh too…what are they planning to grow there?"

"Flowers. The Baron sent some French agronomist there and he said the place was suitable for manufacturing perfumes."

"In Jaffa I met Baron Ustinov's gardener and he actually asked me about Yesod Hamaaleh!"

"I've met him too. Nessim Bakhor Alhadif. He was working with the agronomist."

Yehiel rose from his seat, flexing his limbs cautiously as if his muscles ached.

"Fishel swears that if he ever gets to plant a tree on his land he'll go to Jerusalem and give thanks to God by the Wall...maybe I'll join him...I need to sleep now, Fania."

"When are you getting up?"

"After the second watch. Don't worry." He looked for the expression on her face.

"I am worried!"

"Let go of the factory."

"That's what I have to do."

Easily said! And who's going to buy the moldering tobacco? And where will she find the money to pay Landau off if she doesn't sell the tobacco? Fania lay on her bed, thoughts buzzing in her head like bees in a hive. She reckoned she heard a kind of gurgling sound from Yehiel's chest. She listened intently, holding her breath, but moments later he relaxed and was breathing steadily again. In her heart she swore that never, ever, would she have anything more to do with trade! She would stay at home and cook and sew and raise the children, be a dutiful wife and an exemplary mother. Exactly as Ishmael had advised her in his crude style: church, children, kitchen. Even though Rivka didn't quite appear the epitome of happiness...

When she woke in the morning a new idea flashed into her mind. The remaining stove she would sell to the staff of the secretariat. The money made from the sale would more or less clear her debts to "Razi". Such a simple and logical idea—how come she never thought of it before?

The secretariat was housed in an imposing building, perched on the hillside with all the grandeur of a French chateau. The residents of Rosh Pinnah didn't like passing through those gates. The big house was surrounded by gardens and flower beds and there was even a fountain, its waters cascading at the base of the broad veranda, which overlooked the valley to the east. Several times in the course of the year the place turned into a miniature Versailles, thronged with people and parties, when civil service mandarins were visiting Rosh Pinnah.

They tended to arrive in opulent style in their carriages, complete with baggage-train and outriders, and the people of Rosh Pinnah, like the inhabitants of the other settlements, were at pains to placate and impress their distinguished guests.

The door was opened by Muhammad, Shaid's favorite footman. Fania hesitated. Mr. Shaid was evidently in residence. The footman looked her over with a watery, all-knowing stare that made her shudder. For a moment she felt an impulse to run away, but she quickly regained control of herself. To her question, whether the lady of the house was at home, the footman replied, "Wait a moment" and disappeared. Fania walked into the entrance hall. If Shaid was in the settlement, she had better not be seen coming in here. She would never be able to salvage her good name.

A big mirror in a gilt frame was hanging on the wall of the lobby. It seemed years had passed since she last saw herself from head to toe, and she liked what she saw. She was still slim and statuesque, despite having borne two children. Her smooth skin glowed with sunburn and her eyes flashed in the velveteen mask of her face. She turned away abruptly, as if caught red-handed in the commission of a crime. Through the half-open door she saw a big salon with carpets and padded chairs upholstered in yellow silk. They could have financed all the colonists with the money they were wasting on their palaces, their stables and their servants! she thought angrily.

From the interior of the house voices were heard, as well as the clatter of plates and pans. Should she go to the kitchen first and speak to the cook, before approaching the lady of the house?

From inside the "small salon", Mr. Elijah Shaid suddenly appeared and invited her to enter. Fania hesitated. To be fair, the man had saved Rosh Pinnah from ruin, but his reputation as a womanizer was known to all.

"I have business with the lady of the house," she said.

"She'll be here in a moment." A cautious smile hovered over his lips as he motioned her to sit. Fania pretended she hadn't taken the hint and fixed her gaze on the big window. Lace curtains covered it, and she tried to visualize the landscape beyond.

"Women's business?"

"Yes. I want to sell her something."

"For the house?"

"A cooking stove."

"I'm the one who approves purchases. Tell me more."

"I bought a new stove in Jaffa, from Señor Levi. Manufactured in Marseilles. I can vouch for its quality as I've been using a similar one myself, and I wondered…"

"Who is your husband?"

"Yehiel Silas."

"He's not one of the Moineshti contingent?"

"No."

"Where's he from then?"

"From Safed. One of the colonists who settled here in 1878."

"Who's supporting him?"

"He's supporting himself."

"A proud farmer, eh? That's good!"

Fania opened her mouth to protest, but thought better of it for fear of aggravating him. That wasn't her purpose in coming here.

Shaid went to the big window and parted the lace curtains, then beckoned her to approach him.

As he said nothing, she joined him by the window and looked out. Dry leaves fluttered on the floor of the veranda with its red awnings, the black iron fence was already rusting, on the terraced flowerbeds in the garden rose bushes had been planted. A herd of black goats was meandering down into the ravine. To the north-east, according to her estimate, was the snow-capped summit of Hermon, and in the valley, eastward, sparkled Lake Huleh. There, beside that silver bowl, Yehiel was working now. She reminded herself of Yehiel's words: "Oshris will come and go, and we're staying." Shaid's right arm was wrapped around her shoulders, while with his left hand he pointed to the vista unfolding at the foot of the hill.

"All this land, the land of Rosh Pinnah, the Baron has bought. No point in your protesting, someone is supporting you after all. You're lucky that this someone asks for nothing from you in return, except that you work! His colleagues deride him over this, he's told me that himself! After all, why should the farmers work when they can live on the Baron's charity?"

Fania wondered whether to hold her head high and walk out with dignity and empty pockets, or swallow her resentment and walk out—perhaps—substantially richer than before.

"Would you like tea?"

"No, thank-you, I only came about the stove…"

Shaid pursed his lips as if he were sucking a candy and tightened his grip on her shoulders. His face looked like the waxed skin of a white snake.

"Please, Mr. Shaid!" she objected, extricating herself from his hold. "If you want to buy the stove…"

"How much are you selling it for?"

Fania named a sum that would cover her debt to "Razi". Without saying a word, Shaid took out his purse and counted out six imperials into her open hand.

"Don't you want see it first? Or ask your cook to inspect it?"

"You have an honest face."

Excited by the coins in her hand, she laughed suddenly. "I'll send the stove round this afternoon."

"Well, a laugh at last! You're very pretty! I've wanted to meet you for a long time. The peasant woman who plays Chopin, that's you, isn't it?"

"Oh! Imber and his big mouth! I haven't played for ages!"

Shaid took her hand in his and led her to the "great salon", a room characterized by pieces of furniture with curved legs, latticework closets and artfully constructed pillars. This furniture must have come from Beirut, or possibly Alsace. In the corner stood a grand piano.

"Play!" he commanded her with a smile.

"My head still remembers perhaps, but my fingers, Mister Shaid, forgot all this long ago…" she apologized, but even as she spoke a shudder passed through her body and desire suddenly burst out in her like a drop of water shattering in the sunlight. Involuntarily she was drawn toward the piano. When she lifted the lid, wood struck on wood and the sound reverberated around the room. Fania touched the keys, feeling their white smoothness with the tips of her fingers. Her body shook when the first note rang out and then a gentle chord filled the void. Shaid was forgotten as she tried to play, slowly to start with, the *Barcarolle*. The room was awash with mellow brown-golden sounds, like the color of the heavy lace curtains.

"God!" whispered Shaid when she finished. "What are you doing in this god-forsaken spot? Wasting your youth, your beauty, your talent…"

Fania grinned awkwardly.

"Poor Tchaikovsky, not living long enough to hear you play…"

"Is he dead?" she was astounded.

"Oh yes! Didn't you know? A few years ago, cholera."

"Oy!" Fania remembered her teacher, who admired Tchaikovsky to distraction. She would never know if she was herself Nadezhda von Meck, his mysterious patroness, or just a friend of the patroness. When she was first taken to her, the woman in black with the big teeth and the dark freckles looked like a real witch. But how beautiful she seemed to her just a short while later! Her playing enthralled the little girl. Her devotion to music and the intimate tone in which she spoke of her favourite composers turned the "black witch" into a queen. Queen of music.

"Would you like to teach music in the school?" Shaid asked.

"I couldn't do that…" Fania stared at him in amazement, flexing the joints of her fingers.

"In the school we're short of a music teacher. No! Don't answer now, there's no hurry. While we're waiting for the school to get up and running, you could be training for the job. The Conservatoire in Paris is one of the best in the world."

"Paris!"

"And in the process you can enjoy your Tchaikovsky, hear *Eugene Onegin* at the opera and see the 'Sleeping Beauty' at the new ballet."

"I have four children, Mister Shaid."

"All yours? How old are you?"

"Twenty…two of them are my children by birth, but they are all mine."

"And I have sixty children, young lady. The children of Rosh Pinnah. And by the end of the century there could be more than a hundred here. I know I am reputed to be a predatory wolf, but as you will see for yourself the truth is that I know people, and I'm capable of judging their worth. You have no idea, my sweetheart, who you are and what you are…Come here."

Fania went and stood beside him at the window. He screwed up his eyes, gazing at her intently.

"I studied medicine in Paris…" he mumbled distractedly. "Allow me?"

He was peering into her eyes, lifting her curls away from her nape. His fingers glided over her neck, and then he put his ear to her heart. When she recoiled in fright, he put his arms round her and hugged her. Disgusted, she tried to push him away, but struggling only fanned his combative streak. All fired up, he pressed her to his body with surprising force, muttering French endearments into her cleavage. Her senses misted over and the cries from long ago reverberated in her head. She felt the fear swelling in her and forced herself not to cry out. Don't yell, don't scream, keep your lips sealed and get out of here quickly and quietly, she told herself, trying to pry from her skin the fingers that were sticking to her like leeches. When she finally succeeded in releasing herself from his grip she ran to the door, only to find it locked! Fania turned to Shaid in horror.

"Come here my little wild cat…come on…" He held out his hands to her, exposing his yellow teeth in the provocative smile of a wrestler in the ring.

"Open the door!"

"Please…don't be afraid…you're so beautiful…"

Fania pulled out the revolver that was concealed in her dress and took aim at Shaid, shaking from head to foot.

"Open the door!"

At the sight of the revolver Shaid burst into laughter and held his head in his hands. She had to fight the impulse to shoot him in the head, and instead she shot through the lock on the door and fled from the room. The sound of the shot was still reverberating in her head when she reached the yard. She hid the revolver in her clothing and slowed her steps. Steady, steady, she said to her pounding heart, if I'm seen running from here all the malicious tongues in Rosh Pinnah will be wagging. She strained her ears to hear, in case anyone was following, and returned to her home at a measured pace, praying in her heart she would arrive safely and not faint on the way.

"Fania!"

Fania stopped, taken by surprise, and for a moment stared blindly at the young woman who had called her name. Then the mist cleared and she fell into the arms of Helen Leah.

"What's the matter with you?"

"What? What do you mean?"

"You looked at me without recognizing me! Fania! You didn't see me!"

"No…it's nothing…"

"Something's happened! Yehiel?"

"No…no…"

And all at once the dam was breached and she started to weep. The tears flowed like a cataract from her eyes. Unbidden, their legs led them to the hill and there, sitting on a rock in the shade of the big walnut trees, she told Helen Leah the whole story: about the standing corn that was burnt and about Riva Frumkin who died of fever and Lulik, roasted alive in the field, about the tobacco business that failed, about the hungry farmers and Yehiel, having to work in Yesod Hamaaleh, and finally about Shaid. When she came to describing the shot she fired, Helen Leah threw her head back and howled with laughter. Tears of mirth streamed down her cheeks, and in the end Fania couldn't help but join in.

"You didn't have to go to him, Fania."

"I didn't go to him! I didn't know he was there!"

"He's 'helping' us too," Helen Leah smiled mischievously. "Thanks to the daughter of Mendel Schindler—you remember her?—he's helping now with the building of our synagogue. And Franiya Deutsch he sent to Paris to study in a seminary and now he's betrothed her to one of the farmers."

"He offered me the chance to study in Paris!"

The two young women howled with laughter again.

"You have the money with you?"

Fania took the six imperials from her pocket.

"I'm going to burn these!"

"Don't you dare! Business is business! You sold him a stove and got a fair price for it. Promise me you're not going to burn the money, Fania! Promise!"

"This is tainted money!"

"The man's going to demand his stove. He's paid for it after all. And if you have no money, how are you going to pay Landau?"

"Oy!"

"So what are you going to do?"

"I can't destroy the money!"

"Well said! Congratulations!" Helen Leah turned to scrutinize her friend, laughter and curiosity in her eyes.

"What am I going to say to Yehiel?"

"Will you tell him about the…encounter with Shaid?"

"No!"

"You're growing up at last! He's got enough problems without all of this."

"And what are you doing here, Helen Leah?"

"And it's nice to see you too, Fania! You've finally noticed me!" Helen Leah started laughing again. Her black eyes disappeared between their lids and with her hands she had to wipe away the tears of laughter all over again. Fania was so happy to have a friend like this! If she weren't so shy, she'd be hugging and kissing her!

"I want to move my parents to Zamarin."

"And will they agree to that?"

"I'll persuade them! I don't want them to go on living here! My father is healthy, thank God, but he's fifty-three years old. Today he had to go to Safed and plead with Matityahu Hason to give him fodder on credit. 'It doesn't matter if I starve but the donkey has to eat!'

he said. Monsieur Oshri was with us in Zamarin before he came here, and I know who he is and what he is. An arrogant upstart! Someone told us that he stopped paying the subsidy to the farmers of Rosh Pinnah. How long has that been going on?"

"Nearly three months."

"Where we live, my father can work, and that's all he wants to do: to work! And even if he doesn't work in the fields there are other jobs he can do. We already have a house, thank God…"

"My congratulations to you, Helen Leah!"

"Thank-you, thank-you. The men go out in the morning to the fields, and leave just the German builders in the settlement. I'll be glad to have my parents living with me! When are you coming to visit me, Fania?"

"As soon as I can! I want to visit you very much. Did you know? I bought a horse and a cart. My own!"

"*Our* own."

Fania looked at her friend quizzically, who smiled warmly and explained, "A wife doesn't say 'my', Fania. She says 'our'. *We* bought, *we* built, *we* wanted, *we* thought, *we* felt…"

"We understand."

Helen Leah told Fania what was happening in Zamarin, which had been called Zichron Yakov since passing under the patronage of the Baron. Helen Leah was one of the few wives who lived in Zichron Yakov with their husbands. Most of the women and children lodged in Haifa, in the Odessa Hostel, whereas the men tended to work three weeks and then spend a week with their families. Since the Turkish government was refusing to give them building permits and this was a cold winter, they were residing in the Arab huts that they found on their land.

"It's because of a goat that I have a house now," laughed Helen Leah.

"Eh?"

"Some Arab shepherds turned up suddenly and insisted on sleeping with us in the huts. They'd paid three hundred francs in tenancy charges for the right to pasture their flocks on Zamarin land in the winter. They claimed that accommodation in the huts was included in the deal. Our Galician friends had no choice, and in the end they refunded the money to the shepherds, on condition that they leave the place. But until that was sorted out they slept with us in the huts. These were little mud huts, with just one entrance, and the overcrowding was terrible. One of the shepherds even brought his goat inside our hut, and that was the last straw. I told David I wasn't sleeping with a goat! I took my blanket and lay down outside, under the sky. David insisted I go back, and I refused. That night it rained and in the morning I was feverish and coughing. David went to Vormesser, our factor, and threatened that if no houses were built in Zichron Yakov we were going to leave the place. That's something even the Baron's factors don't want. What would they do without us? So, thanks to the Arab shepherd and his goat, I have a house today!"

The laughter of Helen Leah had such a pleasant sound, and her words were spoken with such wisdom and charm, that Fania forgot all about Shaid and his antics.

Chapter thirteen

On the narrow road leading up to the hill, a small figure appeared. Concern clouded Fania's face when she recognized Moshe. He was supposed to be at school. The headmaster, Rabbi Moshe David Shub, wouldn't have let him out of school without a good reason. There was fear in his eyes and he was short of breath, speaking with difficulty.

"Leibel the postman came back from Yesod and he says you've got to go there and get Dad."

"Where's Leibel?"

"On the way to Safed."

"What else did he say?"

"That's all. Shaul Mizrahi asked him to tell you."

"What's the matter with your Dad, Moishele?" asked Helen Leah. "Didn't Leibel tell you?"

"Fever."

Fania set off quickly down the road, Helen Leah and Moshe following close behind.

"I'll stay with the children, Fania, don't worry!" she heard her friend's voice behind her. Fania nodded. A cold mist enveloped her, as if she had fallen into a well, as if Yehiel had betrayed her, as if he had abandoned her at the roadside. And he's the strong one! The brave one! If anything happens to him…Her thoughts went that far and no further.

If anything happens to him…again and again the words drummed in her head as the little cart jolted on the hill road, down towards Yesod Hamaaleh. She took care not to overstretch Storm, not wanting the horse to slip, Heaven forbid, and injure himself. She needed him now more than ever! She remembered Yehiel's disturbed sleep, his stooped back, his tired face. She should have realized he was sick. God, if anything happens to him…It wasn't often that she stopped to reflect on the form that their shared life had taken, and now, immersed in her worries, she saw their life as it really was. Absolute freedom he had given her. She was free to pursue her business activities, travel the roads, stay away from home. He respected her right to lead a life separate from his. Not one of the women she knew, not even Helen Leah, was allowed to behave as she did. Yehiel never said anything to imply that this freedom was a gift from him, or that her actions were unacceptable. She was part of the new society he aspired to create; did he see this as another sacrifice he had to make? Unbidden, the thought occurred to her that she hadn't been a trustworthy partner to him in his back-breaking toil, his life of penury and disappointment. A "child-prodigy", his long-standing acquaintances called him. If he wanted he could have chosen a different, an easier life, he could have created a future in which every passing day was another brick added to the structure. And she, instead of helping, had been flitting around from place to place like a mindless sparrow…

Rain began falling. And the further she descended into the valley, the stronger it became. Through the veil of the rain the lake appeared. The cart-tracks were filled with water, forming deep puddles that impeded Storm's progress.

On the way into Yesod Hamaaleh she met Rabbi Fishel Saloman as he was leading his oxen back from the field. The evening plowing was his responsibility, and he was lifting his feet in a goose-step motion, trying to avoid the sticky mud that was building up on his shabby boots. She didn't dare ask him how Yehiel was faring.

"Get up on the cart, Rabbi Fishel."

"Then who will lead the oxen, Mrs. Silas?"

He isn't saying anything about Yehiel, she thought. Is that a good or a bad sign? Rabbi Fishel himself has come down with malaria before, so the disease holds no fears for him. He believes that God in Heaven will help him and salvation will surely come. Has he not prayed assiduously? Has he not observed all the commandments meticulously? If only she too had a faith like his.

"Where is my husband, Rabbi Fishel?"

"In the house."

Then Yehiel is definitely sick! There was only one "house" in Yesod Hamaaleh and she remembered it well from her previous visit. The house accommodated the children and the women as well as the invalids. The other families—five families from Mezhirich, the Mizrahi brothers, Rabbi Fishel and his laborer, Israel Ashkenazi—all of them lived in the tents that Ashkenazi erected—no doubt inspired by the verse *How pleasant are your tents, O Jacob, and your habitations, O Israel.*

Yehiel lay on a mattress close to the wall and thrown down beside him was a Bedouin blanket. In the dingy room the cold was bone-chilling. Water dripped from the ceiling into buckets, and the hollow monotonous sound added to the gloom. Rags were piled up in the corners of the room—bedding for the women and the children. Sweat poured from Yehiel's body as if he had been working in the fields on a blazing summer day. The mattress was drenched with water and stained with the dark residue left behind by other invalids. Fania poured Yehiel a drink of water and tried to force some of the quinine she had brought with her into his mouth. His lips refused to open, and she stared at him anxiously, wondering what to do. She couldn't take him back to Rosh Pinnah in this rain, but leaving him here wasn't an option either. Here he would never be cured! And where was a doctor to be found? Oh, why didn't she think of this in Rosh Pinnah?

The rain drove people inside, into the house. From time to time the door would open, and together with the wind and the rain and the mud one or other of the workers from Safed or the Arab hirelings would enter, those who had no tent of their own amid the "habitations of Israel". Fania shuddered in the cold and looked up gratefully at the woman who offered her a cup of hot tea.

"The end of all flesh is at hand!" the woman whispered as if passing on a secret. "My dear Yitzhak died of malaria two weeks ago," she added. A tremor passed through Fania's body. We have to get out of here! she thought.

Rabbi Fishel came into the house, stopped in the doorway and removed his muddy shoes. The cold had turned his toes red and his feet were puffy from the damp. She hurriedly averted her gaze from his feet. He hummed one of the psalmist's chants to himself, and then placed his shoes close to the cooking-stove, walking through the cold room barefoot.

A youth with a black beard, blazing eyes and a kind of flat cap squashed on his head, came to Yehiel and wiped his body with a damp cloth, dabbing gently at his skin to cool it. A moment later he brought two quilts and laid them beside the mattress. "When he shakes," he explained to Fania in a bizarre form of speech, differing from the style of the "Poles", also of the Sephardis. The young widow, who was still sitting close by her and watching her actions, said: "Kurdish. Yehudah Barazani. He came on foot over the dark mountains and here his grave will be."

"Come, Sarah!" cried Fishel to the widow, to move her away from the flustered Fania. More and more people came into the room. It seemed there was no space left for even one, and here came another bedraggled couple, another family...The rain drove into the house even the occupants of the "habitations of Israel", and a chill wind rushed in whenever the door was opened. Sometimes Yehiel recognized her and a kind of apologetic smile flickered on his lips. His hair and beard were damp with sweat. His shoulders reared up from within a body that had grown leaner still in recent months, and his eyes were sunk in his grey face. If it weren't for all the people around her she'd have lain down beside him, to protect him with her body from the dreaded disease. Her heart reproached her for the months she had spent in Jaffa while the one she loved most of all was wearing himself out with backbreaking work, in dire hunger, in despair…she should have been beside him, to help in any way she could…

The men prayed the afternoon and evening prayers while the women cooked on the ancient iron stove. The olive-husks that served as fuel filled the room with a pungent smell. I have to get Yehiel out of here somehow! she thought. She herself felt faint from the vile air and the overcrowding in the room.

"Since we are all here, sitting as brothers together," Rabbi Fishel raised his voice, "I have asked Daniel Barukh to tell you of the proposal from the 'Lovers of Zion'. So speak, Daniel, and may your words enlighten us!"

This Daniel Barukh was shy and he spoke in a whisper, eyes fixed on the dripping window. The people fell silent and sat up on their mats, listening attentively. Involuntarily, Fania strained her hearing too.

"This isn't my idea," said Daniel Barukh, sounding apologetic. "There's no need to go over our problems again, they are well known! But in brief: first and foremost the land in Yesod needs to be registered in the name of the farmers, yes? All the bureaucrats in Tabu, without exception, are demanding bakshish. Secondly, we need building permits too, yes? And here, bakshish isn't enough. We need to find out how things work, know how to get the permits, who to turn to and how to turn to him. Wissotzky has asked Avraham Moyil, the money-changer from Jaffa, to take on this mission. So he will be the man mediating between 'Lovers of Zion' and the settlement. We are instructed to respect his judgment."

"Well? Get to the point!" people began pressing the speaker. Daniel Barukh again fixed his gaze on the water streaming down the window pane and then continued in the same apologetic whisper,

"Moyil suggests that the farmers of Lake Huleh be transferred to Petah Tikva…"

The people in the cold, steaming room, held their breath. Even the women at the cooking stove stopped working. Someone, man or woman, laughed briefly and fell silent.

"Near Petah Tikva there's good land and it's possible to live there and produce food from the earth…"

"And what happens here?" someone asked.

"The Biluists will be coming here from Gedera. Most of them are bachelors. The land in Gedera can be sold to one of the Jewish companies looking for land to buy up, and the money made from this will be the saving of Yesod Hamaaleh."

"Jewish business!" someone started laughing hysterically. The laughter was cut short by an angry shout: "We're preparing this land for the benefit of the Bilu crowd? What are they, better than us, those reprobates from Kharkov? Over my dead body! As long as I'm alive they won't take my land from me!"

Suddenly all were shouting at once. Angry cries reverberated in the void of the crowded room, and Fania, turning to see if the noise was disturbing Yehiel, saw that he had pulled one of the quilts over him, up to the eyes. He was shaking despite the thick layer covering him.

"Jews!" Rabbi Fishel's voice rose above the other voices, "Why all the shouting? They can't remove us by force. This land still belongs to the Abu brothers, not the 'Lovers of Zion'."

"It isn't as simple as that, Rabbi Fishel," said Daniel Barukh. "It's true that the land doesn't belong to 'Lovers of Zion', but it isn't ours either. I don't want to depress you all, but our creditors are demanding repayment of the money we borrowed from them. Don't we need money to buy food as well? Money to buy seeds? And who's going to help us, if not 'Lovers of Zion'? I'm afraid that if we don't agree to their demands they won't offer us their help in the future. I've sent telegrams to Eleazar Rokeah and asked him to come here at once and see with his own eyes how we are working and living. It's good to see for oneself…"

"Why Eleazar Rokeah?"

"Wissotzky sees the land through Rokeah's eyes. It was Wissotzky who entrusted Moyil with the job of managing the settlement interests of 'Lovers of Zion', and he who appointed Rokeah secretary of the 'Lovers of Zion' committee. They say he has connections with the authorities too, and he's a friend of the *Kiamkam*."

"They say…" Fania grumbled to herself. No doubt it's Rokeah himself who's been spreading these rumors. A spark of interest was ignited in Yehiel's eyes. Apparently he picked up the reference to his friend and beloved mentor.

"You can inform the head of the committee, His Royal Highness Avraham Moyil, and Eleazar Rokeah, his secretary and Wissotzky's champion, may his light shine, that we are not leaving Lake Huleh!" someone shouted. "The land here has been irrigated with our blood!" All at once the crowded little room was filled with a cacophony of indignant voices.

"Jews! Jews!" cried Rabbi Fishel, a conciliatory smile on his face and his hands making soothing gestures, "These are the tribulations of the Messiah! Tribulations of the Mess-i-ah! Tribulations of the Mess-i-ah!" he chanted at the top of his voice, gradually drowning out the other voices and succeeding somehow in calming the people down.

"We should not insult Mr. Moyil, nor Rokeah, nor Wissotzky," Rabbi Fishel declared with finality. "Their intentions are good. Their objective is the same as ours, to sanctify the dust of the land."

"And they will hold the purse-strings!" someone shouted scornfully.

"Of course! And we need them."

"We're not pleading with them!"

"Pleading? Perish the thought! The story is told of a certain rabbi who went with a deputation of the worthies of his city to collect money for an important matter. When they arrived at the great man's house, one of his associates said to him: 'Please, let's not go in there. Everyone knows the great man is miserly and coarse of spirit and he is liable, Heaven forbid, to treat you with disrespect.' The rabbi answered him: 'Man is the most noble of creatures, and yet, when he wants to milk the cow he has to kneel down before her! Eh?" Rabbi Fishel looked round at his friends, his eyes blazing with the fire of holy passion. "When the Children of Israel were encamped in the Sinai Desert, the Holy One Blessed be He said to them: 'I have borne you on the wings of eagles and brought you to me, and now if you will heed my voice and keep my covenant you shall be a treasure to me above all nations, *for all the earth is mine!*' And how does Rashi interpret this?" Rabbi Fishel closed his eyes, put his hand to his temple and listened to the voices breaking out from his head.

Then he opened his eyes and fixed all those surrounding him with an impassioned gaze: "'If now you accept this duty upon yourselves, it will be pleasant for you from here onward, *since all beginnings are difficult.*' Now accept this duty upon yourselves," he repeated, waving a finger in the air, "since all beginnings are difficult! The tribulations of the Messiah…the tribulations of the Messiah…" he began to chant and the Hassidim from Mezhirich joined in the chorus.

"The end of all flesh!" the widow whispered in Fania's ear, and she jumped up from her seat and shouted at her: "That's enough! Leave me alone!" The people in the room turned to look at them in surprise, and someone hurriedly led the widow away from Fania, admonishing her gently.

Yehudah Barazani returned to Yehiel and rubbed the quilt covering him with his hard, bronzed hands.

Some of the people were arguing over the points raised by Daniel Barukh, their eyes flashing with anger and fear. They gathered together in small groups until the candles began to flicker, and one by one they went away to prepare their sleeping places for the night. Instead of the argumentative voices, it was the sound of the storm raging outside that was heard now. Fania wondered what was happening in her house at this time. Rosh Pinnah was situated at a higher level than Yesod Hamaaleh and thus exposed to stronger winds. Was Helen Leah sleeping in their house, with the children? Had the children woken up in fear, scared by the thunder and the howling wind? Was Tuli alarmed, seeing the strange woman? After all he hardly knew her…

After the third watch she woke to the sound of the men praying. Yehiel was shivering with cold all night. In the viscous, spidery darkness she lay beside him, keeping the quilt wrapped tightly round his body. From time to time he would be gripped by a spasm, and she woke from her fitful sleep and rubbed the quilt, as Barazani had done. In the morning the rain stopped, but water was still dripping through the leaking roof. I must get Yehiel out of here! Fania thought again and again. This overcrowded room would only make his condition worse. At home she could care for him. So many things to be done before the start of Sabbath! She would go to Safed and fetch Doctor Rosen, even if she had to drag him from Safed to Rosh Pinnah by his beard! He tended to charge his patients half a majeda per visit, and who could tell how much he'd charge for a journey to Rosh Pinnah? Luckily, she still had in her pocket the money Shaid gave her. When in Safed she could also visit Rico La Pulvera and buy malaria remedies from her. Who knows? Perhaps that woman, with her herbal concoctions, the "kurvas di campo", could succeed where a doctor might fail. Such things had happened before…And she could cook nourishing soup from cows' feet, also a proven treatment for malaria, and get lemons from Yosef Friedman's garden…God! So much to do, and Friday already!

Fania wrapped Yehiel in the blanket she brought with her from Rosh Pinnah. Shaul and Shmuel Mizrahi, Yehiel's friends, helped her load him on the cart. Rabbi Fishel, shod once again in the shoes that were still soaked through, was also there to see them off and wish them well.

He didn't try to persuade me to stay, she thought. Is he afraid Yehiel might infect the other settlers? Or is he afraid Yehiel won't recover in Yesod Hamaaleh? A shudder gripped her, and it seemed she could still hear Sarah the widow whispering "the end of all flesh". From time to time she glanced behind her. Yehiel lay there like a wet sack, staring at her; every time she turned she met his gaze. The quinine she forced into his mouth had done its job and the shaking of his body had stopped, but his face was black and a kind of white crust covered his lips. Once she thought she heard him sigh and she reined in the horse.

"Do you want to rest?" she asked.

"Do you?"

"You're the invalid!"

"My poor girl…"

"I'm all right!"—and already she was covering his face and hands with kisses as if apologizing for her own health. She had spent a night of fitful sleep, but still she felt the blood coursing fiercely through her veins. Oh, she was alarmingly healthy! She enjoyed taking deep breaths of the cold air, enjoyed walking on the muddy ground, and looking out over the rain-washed hills, and scanning the grey sky with its windows of blue…

"You fill me with happiness, Fania. Just like the moment I saw you for the first time, in Mima Becker's hostel. Even more than then. You're beautiful, wild and magnificent. Don't ever change!"

"Oh, Yehiel, I love you so much!"

Her face was wet with tears and her heart seethed with joy and remorse, worry and relief. She wiped her eyes and nose on her sleeve, and laughed when she saw her tears had dripped on his neck. Yehiel moved under the blanket, and she was startled for a moment but laughed again when she saw him taking deep breaths. Her young and passionate body longed to embrace his body, and inwardly she prayed he would recover soon, and then she could compensate him for all the months she had been away from him. A smile hovered over Yehiel's lips.

"Once you told me that if you had the choice, you wouldn't have married me!" she said.

"On the contrary, I said that if *you* had the choice, *you* wouldn't have married *me*…"

"Why didn't you tell me?" she cried, impassioned. "Why did you let me leave you? Why didn't you tell me I'd gotten it wrong, I didn't understand…"

"I had no right to stop you going. When I met you in Jaffa you were so lost and scared, like an injured bird caught in a trap…and I was the hunter…I exploited the fact that you'd lost control of your destiny. And I knew what I was doing…I wanted you so much."

"I'll never leave you! Not ever!"

Sweat broke out again from Yehiel's body and he stirred and twitched uncomfortably until he pushed the blanket away from him. Fania took up the reins again. Her face she raised to the wind to feel its cold draft, and she knew it would be blowing on him too like this and cooling his overheated body. She was wondering about Yehiel, reflecting on the way that even now, when they had just told one another of their love and were feeling so close, so very close together—still there was something he was keeping to himself, like this disease. What kind of a love is it that doesn't let her suffer the same pangs he's tormented by? So many things she has to say to Yehiel, she needs to talk and talk and talk. She remembered her conversation with Helen Leah. How good is friendship! How good is the simple chatter between lovers!

On the ridge she made out the black tents of the Haratim, who were working alongside the peasants of Jaoni. Her heart was filled with a new happiness, the happiness of homecoming. The night in Yesod Hamaaleh had strengthened still further her sense of belonging to Rosh Pinnah. As if she needed to go into exile for her heart to know where her homeland was. Now, as the landscape became familiar, she stopped looking at it. So much work awaited her at home. She had to approach Rabbi Moshe David Shub and ask him to accept Tamara in his school, although she was only five years old, and she must write to her sisters too. Two months had passed since Lili's letter arrived and she hadn't yet had time to reply to it. And the stone on Lulik's grave—what was she going to write on it? She must borrow hurricane lanterns from Issar, in case she gets held up in Safed after dark…

Suddenly, appearing before her as if he'd sprung out from under the ground, was Rabbi Haim Yonah Segel, the slaughterer. A horse-feed bag was hung around his neck and he was waving his arms to stop the cart. He was a shocking sight. His head was bare, he had lost most of his teeth and on his forehead was a deep welt that looked like a whiplash. Some moments passed before he managed to say anything coherent.

He told Fania that Turkish soldiers had arrived in the settlement, demanding payment of the "worko" tax. It seemed that Yitzhak Oshri had found a new way to harass the farmers. When he realized they would rather starve than apologize to him, he "suggested" to the *Kaimkam* in Safed that his soldiers should be sent on a tax-collecting expedition. In vain the farmers protested that according to their contract with Mister Shaid, the secretariat should be paying this tax. The soldiers didn't believe them. It was the factor himself who hinted to them that the farmers had money. They started assaulting and humiliating the farmers, until they and their families took to their heels and fled. They were up in the hills now, hiding among the rocks.

"The children!" Fania cried.

"There's no one left in the settlement."

"Did you see them? See where they went?"

"The houses are all empty. The soldiers broke into the houses... they ate the bread that was baking in the ovens and gobbled up all the other food that the women were preparing for the Sabbath."

"You saw the children? Helen Leah! Did she take Tuli?"

"I didn't run away," wailed Rabbi Haim Yonah, "I'm not a farmer! I'm not liable to pay this tax and I have no quarrel with Mr. Oshri. But those ravenous beasts were angry that there wasn't more stuff to loot and they took it out on me. They put this food-bag round my neck and took me round from house to house demanding oats for their horses. They didn't believe me when I told them the farmers don't keep oats in their houses and it's all locked away in the central granary..."

"And you were in our house too?"

"I was."

"And who was there? Try to remember, Rabbi Haim!"

"No one was there. I told you. The settlement is deserted." The slaughterer's voice broke and he burst into tears. "And as for *him*! *He* was standing in the doorway of the secretariat building with a big smile on his face! He was smiling...You can't go to Rosh Pinnah now. The soldiers are still on the rampage there."

"I must go there."

"They'll beat you up. They're looking for someone to bear the brunt of their anger."

"Where did the people run away to?"

"They went towards the Hirbet. Thank God, at the last moment my Leah decided to join them and took the children with her."

"Get up on the cart, Rabbi Haim. We'll go up there. And take off that nose-bag!"

"What's up with you?" he asked Yehiel, suddenly noticing him for the first time.

"Fe-e-e-v-e-e-er," Yehiel's teeth chattered.

Fania ascended the hill by a circuitous route, not wanting to be seen by the soldiers down there in the village. Yehiel was again covered by the blanket, and he was quiet as well. He didn't ask Rabbi Haim Yonah any questions, he kept his eyes fixed on her all the time, and his silence alarmed her. I have to get the doctor to him, and quickly! she thought to herself. But how? How? She'll take Yehiel to "Hirbet" and go to Safed herself to call Doctor Rosen. The walnut trees came into view, and she was soon to find that her favorite hideaway had become the hideaway for the whole settlement. She was agitated and flustered by worry, fearing at one moment for the children and the next for Yehiel. Sometimes she walked beside the horse and sometimes in front, urging him on with blandishments and caresses, with gentle slaps on his flanks. Now and then Storm turned to look at her with a big and tolerant eye. What would she do without him? The two daughters of Haim Yonah suddenly came running to meet him with cries of "Tata! Tatiano!" and after them others appeared. Moshe and Tamara popped up from a crevice, and then she caught sight of Bella, sitting on a rock with Tuli in her lap.

"Don't come too close to Daddy!" Fania warned the children.

"I told you Mummy would fetch Daddy!" Moshe called out to Bella, with relief in his voice. Fania stroked his head. She knew he was embarrassed by her kisses, but how sweet it sounded, being called "Mummy"! Moshe was a Silas through and through: speaking little and economical with displays of affection. While she, a full-blooded Russian, loved hugging and kissing her nearest and dearest…Helen Leah was the next to appear, her pale face showing both relief and concern, closely followed by Rabbi Moshe David and his brother-in-law Rabbi Motel.

"Fania! For Heaven's sake!" cried Rabbi Moshe David Shub with feeling, but his face fell when he caught sight of Yehiel. "What's the matter with him?"

"Fever."

"Oy! We need the horse. A matter of life and death. We were just about to set out for Safed on foot, my brother-in-law and I, to persuade the governor to pull his troops out of the settlement…and the Sabbath will soon be upon us! You heard what happened?"

"I'm going to Safed too, to the Doctor. I have to fetch him."

"F-F-Fania…" stammered Yehiel with lips blue from the cold, and her name sounding strange in his mouth, like breathing into a snowdrift. "Give Shub the horse!"

"Yehiel, you need the doctor!"

"Shub will call the doctor."

Shub and Katz will sort out the business of the settlement with the governor first and only then approach Doctor Rosen. And in the meantime precious time is passing…what is she to do? Yehiel looks so strange…He was never a great talker, but this silence…and what if because of the Sabbath the doctor refuses to come out? Suddenly she felt helpless with fatigue. She was having difficulty breathing with all the commotion erupting in her chest. Yehiel closed his eyes and opened them slowly, as if moving his eyelids was an effort for him.

"We'll go to Doctor Rosen first," Rabbi Moshe David promised her. "We'll tell him a life is at stake, and he can come out here on his own horse."

"Storm is going to need feeding and watering. He's tired too."

"Thank-you, Fania."

The men spread a woolen blanket on the ground and laid Yehiel on it. Rabbi Alter Schwartz took off his cloak and covered Yehiel with it, and then bent down to retrieve the provisions that had been wrapped in the cloak: pitas, olives and freshly-laid eggs. What would I take with me if I was forced to flee so suddenly? Fania wondered. She took off her headscarf and laid it down as a pillow for Yehiel. The green tassels peeped out from under his nape, and a weak smile rose to his lips when he felt the touch of her hair on his cheek. When she straightened up, Rabbi Moshe David and Rabbi Motel were already seated on the cart. The clatter of the wheels knocking against fallen stones swamped her with a kind of intoxication. Everything happened as if in a strange dream.

The children, although sharing the worries that were eating at the hearts of the grown-ups, took advantage of their unexpected holiday. The little girls, usually at work alongside their mothers, were playing now, jumping and running, the tinkling of their glass bracelets accompanying their movements. The parents didn't stop them, as if they were thinking: Let the children enjoy themselves while they can. Fania found herself a round stone and sat on it, not taking her eyes off Yehiel. She heard and didn't hear what was going on around her. Some distance from his head she saw little pine-mushrooms and wondered how she could pick them when her kerchief was serving as Yehiel's pillow...Hayaleh, daughter of Rabbi Alter Schwartz, seemed to read her thoughts, and asked her:

"Would you like to borrow my *sarafa*?" and already she was taking the thin snood from her head and shaking out her curls. She was speaking in the vernacular specific to the Jews of Hazbia, which she must have heard in her parents' house. Alter was a friend of Yehiel's, one of the seventeen original pioneers of Jaoni, and now he sat some distance away and prayed. Perhaps it was he who sent his daughter, thinking this was no time for Fania to go bare-headed, or was it the girl's own generous gesture? From time to time Yehiel's gaze would focus on Fania's face, and she preferred to sit with head exposed rather than cover it with a borrowed snood. She smiled at Hayaleh and shook her head. She was almost a young woman. Soon they would pack her skirts with cushions, pinch her cheek and introduce her to her bridegroom. She too would be harnessed to the wheel of drudgery that was grinding women into dust. How strange it is to see these women now, sitting here with nothing to do, hands folded in their laps. From dawn until night they are at work, a day for laundry and a day for baking and a day for cleaning...and now suddenly it's a picnic, a trek into the bosom of Nature...

Is Rabbi Alter's cloak enough to keep Yehiel warm? She could do now with the quilt from Yesod Hamaaleh and Barazani's strong hands. Was that only yesterday? Fania took the decision not to look towards Safed, because Rabbi Moshe David and Rabbi Motel had only just set out. But her eyes were drawn of their own accord in the direction from which the doctor would come. And suddenly she was scared. What if they don't tell the doctor exactly where they are? And supposing he gets lost in the hills and doesn't find them. Yehiel's dry lips had turned blue in the meantime, and the bristles on his cheeks darkened and lengthened. Now and then he opened his eyes, and when his gaze fell on her there was something velveteen softening the expression on his face. It seemed he was sinking deeper and deeper.

Helen Leah stood beside her with Tuli in her arms. Fania wondered at herself, not wanting to take the baby from her friend's hands. Helen Leah told her how this morning she had been spreading a slice of bread with olive oil and went out to the garden to pick shallots for extra flavor, and that was when the Turkish soldiers suddenly appeared in the settlement, and she ran away with all the others and it was only when she reached the top of the hill that she realized she still had the slice of bread in her hand…

Fania looked at her friend. How strange things are. Is she supposed to be interested in a silly story about bread and shallots? Her eyes scanned the ridge and at once returned to Yehiel. Time crept so slowly. She didn't want to think about time, but however hard she tried, everything turned to time and time alone. Yehiel had stopped shaking and stopped sweating, and she found his repose more frightening than the convulsions that had racked his body all night. From time to time she brushed the flies from his face and shook off the ants and beetles that were running over his clothes. Birds dived from the sky and the children yelled. Moshe sat some distance away from them, hands tucked into the sleeves of his shirt, and hunched up like a snail. Someone had put a sheepskin coat over the boy's shoulders. Two months before a Turkish soldier had turned up in their yard, taken out a tent that he had hidden under his coat and sold it to Fania for two loaves of bread. From the fabric of the tent she sewed shirts for the children, and so that they could still be worn in years to come, she lengthened the sleeves, and in cold weather Moshe hid his hands in them. If only he would come and sit beside her. So strong—the impulse to hug the thin shoulders and press him to her body! Such a short time they have spent together. He's her son and she has no idea what he's thinking, what he's feeling…and soon he'll be putting on *tefillin*, getting betrothed and leaving home! Lately he's been playing truant from the "Talmud Torah" school and hiding in the Alhija house. When she found out about this she made him promise not to do it again, and also promised to transfer him to Rabbi Moshe David's school. She well remembered the stories Yehiel told her about the "Kuttaf" school where he was a pupil, about the slaps and the pinches and the thrashings and the verbal abuse that he endured at the hands of the so-called "Sage". Betrothal at the age of fourteen was a real lifesaver, he said. Did he love Rachel? She never dared ask him which of the two of them he loved more.

Issar came and sat beside her, and Hayaleh Schwartz was holding Tuli now and rocking him, while Helen Leah wiped her tears away. What is this? Why is she weeping? They think Yehiel's going to die! What nonsense! Who doesn't get a touch of fever these days? And Yehiel's even stopped shaking and sweating.

"Seated in the shelter of the Most High", said Yehiel suddenly in a loud and clear voice, his familiar voice. Fania was overwhelmed by joy and the wild blood burst into her head. She laid her hand on his forehead and he opened his eyes and said "Fania", then closed them again. His eyeballs moved under the lids with a delicate movement, like the fluttering wings of a butterfly.

What is this? What's he up to? A kind of anger filled her. How selfish is this torment, that is his alone! How selfish is this silence! How much time has elapsed since they came here? The sun is setting behind the hills to the west. It seems years have passed since they set out from Yesod Hamaaleh. When did she last see Rabbi Moshe David and Rabbi Motel?

Between the hills a mounted figure appeared. Fania looked at the figure, trying to remember who she was waiting for. The doctor! Relief is at hand. She leapt up from the seat and ran toward the rider.

"Doctor Rosen!" she yelled, as if only now she was becoming aware of the risk she was taking. From behind she heard the shouts of people warning her to be careful and avoid the horse's hooves, and through a mist she saw a tarboosh above her and the horse rearing up on his hind legs and the mud on his hooves...When the doctor moved towards Yehiel the mother of Rabbi Moshe David stepped forward and blocked his path.

"Where are Moishe and Motel?" she demanded to know. People tried to move her aside but she stood her ground, as if planted in the earth. Fania understood the way this woman was thinking and the heart-stopping fear she must be feeling. Whenever she encountered her, she looked at her with reverence and compassion, remembering what was said of her when she arrived in Rosh Pinnah. The old woman had gone down to the harbor of Beirut holding the hand of her three-year-old grandson and supporting her daughter-in-law. The wife of Rabbi Motel carried in her arms the body of her dead daughter, pretending she was still alive. The baby was four days old when her father went to the Land of Israel to buy land in Jaoni. The immigrants from Romania were afraid that the Turkish government would impound the ship and put all those aboard in quarantine if news of the baby's death leaked out. The mother and the grandmother were instructed to hide their sorrow and act as if the baby was still alive. And this they did. Now Fania stared at her as if dazzled by a blinding light.

"They're already in Rosh Pinnah, Mrs. Yankowitz. Both Rabbi Motel and Rabbi Moshe David," said the doctor. "You can all go back to the settlement. They succeeded in collecting the money they needed in Safed and they've paid the tax."

But nobody moved. All stood their ground, waiting in silence to hear the doctor's diagnosis. They had gathered some distance away and only Fania sank down again on her stone. In the morning she had chosen this stone at random, and since then it had been hers, no one else would even think of sitting there. After examining Yehiel, Doctor Rosen took a small phial from his case, sprayed liquid on his hands and rubbed them together. Then he sat down beside her on the ground. What a nice man, she thought.

"I'm sorry, Mrs. Silas…"

What is he saying? What's he got to be sorry for? He took the trouble to come out here despite the impending Sabbath. His eyebrows were close together and she looked at the little bridge of hair linking them. She wanted to ask him about Storm. How had he coped with the rigors of the journey? Had they given him water and fodder? Where is he now…Someone cried out suddenly, and the voice went up and down the hills and joined people together. Did the cry come from her? The misty face of the doctor receded further and further from her, and she wanted to stop him so she could finally hear his conclusion. But she couldn't say a word. Inside her head something exploded and a new wound spread in her and filled her whole body.

Chapter fourteen

Fania walked along the wadi of Jaoni, on the way from Safed to Rosh Pinnah. Her legs were heavy and she stared into the yellow, viscous fog that had enfolded her since the death of Yehiel. Today she sold Storm, and with the five pounds that she received for him she paid her debt to the grocer. Until the next threshing season, she could breathe easily again.

Her uncle Shura and his wife Bella visited her on their way to Beirut, and urged her to register for the new housing development now under construction to the northeast of Jaffa, on land formerly owned by Aharon Schloss. It seemed Shimon Rokeah was realizing his dream of building a Jewish quarter modeled on the new quarters in Jerusalem. The parlor in the Rokeah house seemed so far away, far away in place, far away in time.

"It's more than a year since Yehiel, peace be with him, passed away," said Uncle Shura. "What's keeping you here? The poverty? The loneliness! You have no livelihood, your children are ragged and hungry, and as for you—God preserve us! In Jaffa you could revive your pharmaceutical business. Señor Azriel Levi is even prepared to rent the license from you for a monthly fee..."

She didn't know how to answer. Again a kind of fog covered her eyes, as if the world outside was behind a closed door. Since Yehiel died she had worked with blunted senses, coming and going without feeling and without thought. At night she would go to bed and stare at the ceiling until blessed sleep descended on her. Her uncle was right, of course, but four children were dependent on her, and how could she embark now on new adventures? In Rosh Pinnah there was work for her, and not just work but the kind of work she liked, arduous labour that exhausted her strength and dowsed her senses. Since Yitzhak Oshri was removed from his post, Rosh Pinnah had been buzzing with activity. The area of the settlement had increased, extending now over thirty thousand dunams, and planting was in full swing. On the ground that she herself had helped to clear five years before, each settler was now planting five thousand vines. Having no land of her own, she worked as a hired hand in Issar's orchard, cultivating the Malaga vines, imported from Spain specifically for use in the production of raisins. Some of the vines in the settlement came from as far away as India, on the initiative of the Baron's French agronomist. Issar's son, Yehoshua, had also planted an orchard and being unable to help his father, he was glad to know that she was working for Issar alongside the share-croppers. For the moment her remuneration was tiny; until the sale of the first crop all that Issar had in his pocket was the ten francs he received from the Baron's fund, and this was shared between them. The money was barely enough to buy flour and charcoal, and she was glad she didn't need to feed the horse anymore. Although she was sorry to let Storm go, she consoled herself with the thought that now he would be adequately fed.

She went out to the orchard at dawn, after Issar had come back from the synagogue, and returned home in the afternoon, when the children finished their lessons in the school. They understood each other without words, the old widower and the young widow. Talking was hard for them and the company of other people was irksome. Sometimes she looked up and saw Issar's face awash with tears and she would silently join in his weeping. The shared grief was no consolation, but at least they didn't need to apologize or explain away their tears. Only in work did the pair of them find relief. The residents of the settlement understood their feelings and didn't harass them with charitable gestures. On the small shoulders of Moshe and Bella lay the responsibility of milking Issar's cow and feeding the donkey before going to school. The goats and sheep he received from the Baron he handed over to his son, who took them to pasture with his own flocks. On Sabbath Eves Fania would wash the children and scrub her hair, and when they were all in clean clothes they would go for "Kiddush" at the house of Helen Leah's parents. Her own house wasn't a home, it was a place for eating and sleeping. Besides a roof over their heads she couldn't give her neglected children anything—least of all warmth or happiness, because her heart was as still as the grave. She would sit as if only her body was there while they sang the "*Yedid Nefesh*" or "*Tzur Mishelo*", watching the slight movement of the light spread by the smart new lamp, and the flicker of the candles dying in their sockets. The children learned to love the Romanian food served in the Moses household, the *mamliga*, the maize cake which they divided up with a cutting wire, and the spicy soup, the *chorba*. Fania didn't cook a great deal, except at festival times when she tended to bake *hammim* and brew jam, to give the children something of a festive feeling. If it weren't for them, she would lie down at night in the same clothes she had worked in, and go out to work in the same clothes she had slept in, but they were growing up around her, fresh and luxuriant, like green shoots emerging from the stump of a felled tree.

Yehoshua Frumkin, Issar's son, told her one day that someone was interested in buying her house. When she didn't answer he plucked up the courage to add:

"You could move in with my father, and I'd be happy to see that! I have a home of my own and a family of my own, and my father, as you know, refuses to live with us. And I worry about him! He's not young anymore. You wouldn't need to pay any rent, just help him out with the cooking and the cleaning and the laundry. The children will bring a breath of fresh air into the house. Even if they disturb him that would be better than the isolation he's imposed on himself. Working and sleeping, working and sleeping, how long can he carry on like that? How long?"

"And if he should die?"

"My father?!" Yehoshua was shocked, as if such a thing was inconceivable.

"Where will I go with four children?"

"I wouldn't ask you to vacate the house until you'd found a new place to live. And I'm prepared to guarantee that before witnesses."

"Who wants to buy my house?"

"I don't know. Someone from Beirut."

So you see, I'm not leaving Rosh Pinnah! she told Yehiel in one of their imaginary conversations. Look at me, I'm an agricultural worker! A fruit-grower! Carrying on where you left off. Issar needs me. And the children need a man, a head of the family. Issar will be like a grandfather to us…

After Passover, Moshe announced he didn't want to go to school anymore. He was ten and a half years old and he wanted to work, like his friend Isa Alhija who was going out to the fields every day with his father.

"Your father was a prodigy!" said Fania.

"I don't want to go on learning."

"What do you want, Moshe?"

"To be a farmer. Dad was a farmer, too."

"After he'd gone to school!"

"The peasant children work and learn as well."

"You're working now. At five in the morning you're up helping on the farm. That's enough! You're Moshe Silas, and you come from a long line of scholars. You have obligations."

"To work!"

"To study!"

And perhaps it's better this way? The boy will grow up to be a farmer, like one of the peasants. Isn't that what Yehiel was aiming for? To create a people like other peoples, a nation of agricultural workers. And if she dies the boy will have an occupation. If she dies…these things happen. Yehiel too was healthy and strong and young. She had to guarantee the future of these children. She felt the lack of a wise and experienced person to be consulted for advice. Suddenly she was expected to decide somebody's destiny, his future, the course of his life and perhaps the lives of his children too! She wasn't capable of thinking that far ahead…

"For the time being you stay on at school!" she declared, deferring the final decision from day to day, from week to week. Again and again Moshe played truant from school and joined Isa and Samir Alhija. Once he was seen in Majuez and once someone said he had met him by the well. Fania decided to remove him from the influence of his friends, and took him to Safed, enrolling him in the Talmud Torah school run by the Sage Merkado Ayil Kosho, Merkado the Lame as he was known. From morning till night the children sat on filthy mats, and Fania wondered if this was really doing the boy any good, as his aunt Leah claimed.

Since Yehiel died, the two women had grown closer together. Fania's tragedy spoke to the heart of the bony and bad-tempered woman in a language she understood: she knew all about sighing, shedding tears and cursing. Moshe lasted a week in Sage Merkado's school, and on Friday he returned to Rosh Pinnah and announced he wasn't going back to that prison. The soles of his feet bore the signs of lashing with the "flakka", and these convinced Fania that he had a point. She looked at the thin little face, the triangle of freckles on the temple, "the luck of the Silases", the stubbornness flashing in the eyes, Yehiel's eyes, and didn't know what to do. Since she was incapable of deciding, Moshe started going to the orchard with her and Issar, and working beside her really did seem to make him happy. It was as if she and Issar had agreed to hide their distress from the boy. Issar used to hum monotonously from the Passover liturgy, as if his mumbling could dispel the devils from his heart. One day Moshe asked her if he didn't know any other songs, and she found herself singing the song about the mariner who made sails from his girlfriend's underwear. All that day, Issar and Fania and Moshe were singing "Yo ho ho and a flag on the mast!" Little by little Moshe's cheeks gained a little color, and although Fania knew it was her duty to send him to school, her heart wouldn't let her deliver him again into the hands of that limping child-beater.

One day as they were working in the orchard, they saw a figure approaching. Rabbi Moshe David Shub, the headmaster of the local school, in person. He came to offer Moshe a compromise.

At that time a silk-weaving enterprise was starting up in Rosh Pinnah. Every farmer planted a thousand mulberry trees on his land and two experts had been brought in from France to teach the local lads the art of weaving. Thirty boys were already working in the plant, under the supervision of the experts, and more were expected to arrive soon from Hazbiya; they would lodge during the week in Rosh Pinnah and go back to their families for the Sabbath. The youngsters were learning a respectable trade and also bringing a few coppers into their homes. "There can be no doubt, the silk industry is the industry of the future," said Rabbi Moshe David, "and it will guarantee the future of Rosh Pinnah for generations to come." Rumor had it that more experts were being brought in from Beirut, and once the trees had matured and were producing enough leaves to feed the worms on an industrial scale, the weaving-shed would be enlarged and steam-powered looms installed, for the manufacture of garments. Rabbi Moshe David had suggested to the manager that he take Moshe on to work in the afternoons, on the strict condition that he spent the morning hours in the school. "We're not Bedouin," he said to Moshe, "we're Jews. And Jews study the Torah." He went on to say that when he reached Bar Mitzvah age he could finish his studies, and by then he would have a trade which was sure to stand him in good stead. Rabbi Moshe David hesitated for a moment and then added with a smile: "You can bring Isa along with you, if you like."

The "compromise" suggested by Rabbi Moshe David Shub was acceptable to all, and the only dissenting voice was Bella's. She insisted on working alongside her brother and threatened to run away and join the Bedouin of the Zangariya tribe if her demands weren't met. The threat raised a smile to Fania's lips, but she was afraid the girl might do something rash and put herself in danger. She went to the weaving-shed herself and cajoled one of the instructors to accept Bella into the workforce. She had to promise not to budge from Moshe's side while he, as the older brother, promised to look after his sister. So Bella was taken on at nine years old to work in the silk industry, the only girl among thirty boys.

After classes in the school the two of them would run home, slake their hunger and set out at once for the weaving-shed. They worked there for four hours, until nightfall. On Sabbaths Fania let them sleep until midday. They looked so small and helpless in their sleep! When all the family were dressed in clean clothes, they sat under the awning of vines in the garden for the Sabbath meal, and after the meal they set out for a long walk. Usually the same route—up the gully of the wadi as far as the walnut trees. The one who enjoyed these walks most of all was Tuli. All through the week he was in the care of Fatima, their neighbor, and now he was getting to spend time with his family. Of all her children, only Tuli was the fruit of her love, but she felt no need to give him more attention than the others. They were all bound up in her consciousness with a sense of irremediable loss. Sometimes, when she sat in the shade of the trees watching them at play, she would compare her pampered childhood with their deprived childhood. Or perhaps they, having known no other life, didn't feel deprived! Did she really enjoy playing with glass marbles more than they enjoyed playing with animal bones? And the rag-doll that she made certainly gave Tamara more pleasure than all the dolls she had possessed as a child had ever given her. What is happiness? Can it be measured? Is she imprinting her grief on her children? Which part of the complex tapestry of her life will be woven into the fabric of their lives and passed further on, to their children, from generation to generation?

Fania quickened her pace. She promised Fatima she would be back by noon today, but her business at the factory had taken longer than she expected. The lease had long since expired, but the landlord had let her store the tobacco there for as long as he didn't need the building. Now he had found a new tenant, and the remaining tobacco had to be cleared out. She set for Safed at dawn and having walked the full distance, she arrived in the town flushed and panting, with parched throat. There Bezalel Ben Moreno was already waiting for her, her partner these last two years in the failing tobacco business. He invited her to his house and his young wife, Zipora, gave her cold water to drink as well as a little cup of freshly ground coffee flavored with homemade jam. Zipora was all of fourteen years old and had been betrothed for two years before her marriage to Bezalel. "I was so small," she told Fania with a laugh, "when they sat me on the big chair to announce the betrothal! And on the day of my wedding my mother made me wear four skirts so Bezalel wouldn't notice how thin I was!" Fania was glad to see curls of Zipora's black hair protruding from under the headscarf and to know that marriage hadn't turned her into a puritan. What kind of old woman am I! she thought to herself, letting the child-bride fuss around her and play the role of the dutiful wife.

"What work are you doing these days, Bezalel?"

"You know Yakov Abu Hai, the French consul? I'm his *kavass*!"

They both smiled. She tried to imagine him running in front of Señor Yakov, wearing the "formalia", that embroidered waistcoat, and carrying a silver baton. Both of them had travelled a long way since the day she was pelted with stones in Eleazar Rokeah's house.

In the factory a dismal sight awaited them. The remnants of the tobacco had been shovelled into a sack, exuding a vile smell. Bezalel had set aside a few strands that were still usable. He handed her the ten francs which was all he had left.

"No!" she protested. "This is a payment for your work!"

"Perish the thought! The money's yours. Your profit!"

"But I haven't paid you anything!"

"I'm not taking a cent from you! All your money was lost when the tobacco business crashed."

"Without you I wouldn't have sold a single leaf!"

"You have young children, Mrs. Silas."

"I'm selling my house in Rosh Pinnah. I don't need charity."

"Nor do I."

Finally they came to an agreement: the money went to Fania and what was left of the tobacco was Bezalel's, to be disposed of as he saw fit. She left him one franc to cover administration costs, compensation for the loss of his "livelihood". She and Bezalel put away the surplus tobacco leaves and cleaned up the building. This was work Fania was only too glad to do! A full stop to the tobacco business! Good-bye Mr. Landau! Good-bye "Razi"! How Yehiel hated the tobacco trade! Now that there was a little money in her pocket she could buy wheat and oil and charcoal, and in Issar's backyard she would plant vegetables. Would Issar be pleased to see shallots and radishes growing in Riva's kitchen garden? Or would the sight break his heart?

Last week Yehoshua Frumkin brought her four Turkish pounds sent by the broker handling the sale of the house. This was an advance payment on the total asking price of twenty pounds. The buyer promised to pay another four pounds next month and the remainder he would hand over when in occupation of the house. Money! Money! Money! It isn't the rich who think about money all the time, but the poor! Who said that? Well, in her parents' house they didn't talk about money, but there, poverty wasn't a constant presence, like a boulder weighing down on the chest. Of all the fears that afflicted her, the one constantly uppermost in her mind was the fear that there would be no food to feed the children. When she received the advance payment, she borrowed Issar's donkey and went to Safed to buy lentils and rice, oats and olives. She stowed these away in the storeroom in the cellar of the house. Now, with spring on the way and money in her pocket, now was the time for stocking up on supplies. When the rains came the roads would be impassable and the hillside tracks hazardous. In the past she used to go out on these shopping trips with Yehiel and return laden with baskets in the driving rain or with the sun beating down, and this memory too pricked her heart with its sweetness. It seemed Yehiel was continuing to accompany her, every step of the way. At night she still heard his breathing. Sometimes it seemed to her he was watching her and she turned around quickly. It seemed the shape of his body was still imprinted on the mattress, and she became used to lying precisely there, in the hollow of that indentation. Sometimes she looked at the door expectantly: He's coming in! He's alive! It was all a mistake, a bad dream! Sell the house? Expel Yehiel from his dream? After all, this house and this land were the goal of his life. Again it fell to her to fulfill the dreams of another. Did she ever have dreams of her own? And perhaps everyone's like this? Fulfilling the dreams of others? No! Leaving the house means ripping Yehiel out of her life! "I haven't decided yet," she told Yehoshua Frumkin, and already she was thinking of flour and pulses and blue ribbons for Bella's and Tamara's hair.

The buyer didn't haggle over the price, and Fania feared he might think he was getting one of the Romanian houses, the ones built with timber specially imported from Romania. Hers was one of the Jaoni houses, a stone-built cottage situated close to the peasant quarter. What would she do if he claimed he had been duped and demanded his money back? Not many Jews liked living close to the peasantry. For the moment she wasn't required to leave the house, but as time passed her agitation grew. What has she done?! This house isn't her property! It's Yehiel's house! And the children—what will become of them? And if she should die, Heaven forbid? Will they be homeless? In her imagination she saw them joining the ranks of the poverty-stricken, hanging around the soup-kitchens, begging for scraps or for worthless coins distributed from the dirty handkerchief which constituted the "social fund"...

The sun was high in the sky. The children were sure to have returned home by now, and Bella would have collected Tuli from Fatima's house. Soon they would need to go to the weaving-shed. Since Bella had been given the job "as a favor" she was always afraid of arriving late and perhaps not coping with competition from the boys. These were children of her own age, but they worked from dawn until nightfall, seventeen to nineteen hours every day for a measly half a bishlik. How heavy was the burden laid on the little girl's shoulders! At her age Fania was still playing with dolls and playing the piano and reciting the fables of Karilov while reclining on a hammock slung between the white poplars in the garden. Aunts and uncles pinched her cheek and cried out in wonderment "How lovely she is!" and her mother would grimace and spit to ward off the evil eye and exclaim: "Much good may it do her!" Her mother was right, more so than all the others. Who could have known, there among the poplars, how her fortunes would be overturned? The Land of Israel? What was that? An old fairy tale! A dream! Did I have dreams too? She tried to remember. She'd been drifting in a haze from place to place, trailing along behind events, skimming the surface and never stopping to reach out for the spiritual essence of things.

The fringes of the wadi were covered with a thin layer of violet flowers and she thought: How dare they bloom? The houses of Rosh

Pinnah appeared on the slope and Fania quickened her pace, catching herself from time to time on the mildewed branches of the raspberry bushes growing on the banks of the wadi. She remembered the days when she had to "sense" the direction she was going in. Now a clearly marked path crossed the hilly ground. My feet carved out that path, she thought, and felt a twinge of pride. She paced along the edge of the crater, lifting the hem of her dress. Whenever she travelled she tended to wear Bedouin garb. From a distance she looked like one of the shepherds, and the bandits of Galilee didn't bother her. Anyway, scrambling over rocks was more comfortable with trousers worn under the skirt.

Bella stood by the door of the house, looking out into the street. She was supposed to be at the silk factory at this time and Fania realized something had happened. Her legs went on walking, moved by the pulsating force that had animated them up to now, but her eyes darkened suddenly, as if a cloud in the sky was hovering directly above her, its wings covering her with their shade. She had to fight the impulse that attacked her, to take to her heels and run. Erect and determined, her face betraying no sign of her panic, she took one step and another toward the bad news.

"Moshe is sick!" said Bella, and burst into tears.

In the little, low-ceilinged room, too many people were crowded. Fatima was kneeling, leaning against the wall with one of her children in her lap. Issar Frumkin sat upright in "Elijah's Chair", his eyes closed, as if listening to distant voices. Tamara was holding Tuli in her little arms, and now, when he saw his mother standing in the doorway, his head lolled backwards again and again. Tamara rocked him, taking a firmer grip on him, and it seemed any moment the two of them would fall down together on their tender heads. Fania plucked Tuli from Tamara's arms and ordered Bella to take the children out to the yard and keep an eye on them there. She thanked Issar and Fatima for their concern, but it wasn't until she had assured them again and again that she didn't need them anymore, they finally left and the room was still. Now there were no more excuses and she turned, her heart pounding, to Moshe.

Moshe lay on the bed, his skin on fire, sweat pouring from his head and his closed eyes sunk deep in their sockets like two purple lakes.

"He's been shaking all morning," said Bella, who had returned to the room.

"We'll make him some sweet tea and give him quinine and he'll soon feel better."

"Is it fe-e-e-ver?" asked Bella in a quavering voice.

Fania wetted a cloth and wiped Moshe's feverish body the way Barazani had done for Yehiel when they were in Yesod Hamaaleh. She gave Bella all kinds of tasks to try keeping her out of the room, but the girl completed the tasks in no time at all and came back, peering from the door as if afraid to enter. Fania's heart reproached her for going to Safed, for selfish reasons of her own. This poor little girl—no wonder she's frightened.

"He'll get better, Bella, don't worry. He'll be better in the morning."

If only I could believe what I'm saying, she thought to herself. He was suddenly so tiny. Greyish freckles sprouted on his burning skin like a kind of fungal growth, his red hair blazed and the light eyelashes cast a shadow, like a secret, on the groove between the incandescent lids. Even in his sleep he was solemn, Yehiel's son. Poor little old man. There was no frivolity in him, no youthful mischief. He fulfilled his obligations with sullen rectitude and it seemed he was the same in sleep and in sickness. Fania wiped his face and neck, resisting the impulse to bend down and kiss the soft cheeks.

From time to time Moshe opened his eyes slowly, and she smiled at him. How long had she been sitting beside him? An hour? Two hours? All at once it was dark and she rose from her seat to light the lamp. It seemed his breathing was easier, but still she didn't dare leave him.

"Here!" Bella handed her a slice of bread spread with olive oil.

"Thank-you, Bella."

"I've fed Tuli and Tamara."

"Good."

Fania had difficulty speaking. Her heart fluttered between her ribs and her breathing was constricted as if stones were blocking her throat. Bella hesitated for a moment, then left the room. I should be encouraging her, she thought, but what can I say to her…It seemed the time of crisis had passed, but she didn't dare believe what her eyes were seeing. Yehiel too looked as if he was on the way to recovery and death snatched him away, literally from her hands. By the flickering light of the lamp it seemed Moshe's face had turned darker still, and her heart melted with compassion for the little boy who lost his mother and then his father, leaving her his only defender and savior. How small he was suddenly! "My son," she whispered to herself, and perhaps it wasn't too late to get him used to calling her "Mummy". After all, she was his mother, his only mother! The red hair on his head was more like hers than like the hair of the Silases or the Adises! According to her feelings he was her son, her child, flesh of her flesh, just like Tuli or Tamara. When he recovers…

The convulsions stopped and the choking and the eruptions of sweat eased as well. Moshe was sleeping peacefully now. For a moment her eyes closed and she woke with a start. No! She must not sleep.

The rustling sounds from the next room were stilled. Fania got up to see what the youngsters were doing. The three children lay on the mat. Tamara and Tuli were asleep while Bella turned frightened eyes to her.

"You should go to bed, sweetie."

"Moshe's going to die!"

"Don't even think that! I'm looking after him!"

"Daddy died."

"Moshe's going to get better. He's sleeping peacefully now, and you should do the same."

"You looked after Daddy and he died."

"Get up! Come and take a look at him."

Bella stopped by the door and glanced at the bed, afraid of going any closer. Moshe was breathing steadily and his face was smooth and relaxed. The faint rasp that accompanied his breathing was the only sign that he was unwell.

"I'm staying awake," said Fania, kneeling beside the anxious child. "I'll sit with him till morning and then you can take over. You need to get some sleep now so you can take care of him tomorrow."

Bella nodded solemnly and went back to her mat.

Fania looked for something to occupy her so she wouldn't fall asleep. Months had passed since Sonia's letter arrived. She had put off replying from day to day and from week to week. A letter to her sisters was always something like a balance sheet: what's there, what isn't there. Yehiel isn't around anymore, the factory has gone out of business, the house is up for sale, the boy is sick…Why is she staying on here? No father, no Lulik, no Yehiel. A few frail, frayed threads were all that remained, tying her to this place. The logical course of action would be to get up and leave! Except that at some time during the harsh and cruel years of living here, there had been crystallized in her—a sensation rather than a conscious thought—the awareness that this was her only and her final home. She despised those Jews who wander from place to place, in a quest for new ideas, elusive fortunes, old fears. Yehiel said to her once: "We must do the best that we can, that is all there is." And to this flimsy hope she held firm: to stop wandering, to set up a home and cling to it, for better or worse, to the best of her ability. No, she wouldn't even try to explain these things to Sonia. She herself wasn't entirely clear about them, and simpler things than these she had difficulty explaining. Inwardly she promised God that if He spared the life of Moshe, she would stand on her own feet and manage her home as before. Again she would devote herself to the pharmaceutical business, and not let it slip through her fingers. And perhaps she would consider her uncle's advice and hand over the Park Davis franchise to Señor Azriel Levi in exchange for a monthly payment. What would her sister have to say about this? In her last letter, sent from the State of Louisiana, her sister revealed that she too had been embroiled in the tobacco industry. Sonia wrote that she had come to this state because others from their hometown of Elizavetgrad had settled there, but now she was thinking of moving to another location.

Our Jews devote more strength and energy to arguments than to working on the land—Sonia wrote—*I'm fed up with discussions on the issue of whether Jews are capable of being agricultural workers or not and I'm fed up with people debating the relative merits of Robert Owen and Tolstoy as role-models! Yosef wants to sell our land and move to the State of Oregon. The pioneers of the "Eternal People" group have established a settlement there, New Odessa they call it. I'm not enthusiastic. I'm tired of pioneering, especially as this settlement is based on the sharing principle. Incidentally, Yosef tells me that your Rosh Pinnah was the first commune in the Land of Israel. Is that right? Fanichka! You never tell me anything! Does a commune mean sharing everything? You must write and tell me about this. In New Odessa the group subsists by supplying wooden sleepers for the local railway. They say the climate there is nice. But I've also heard that they believe in vegetarianism and sexual freedom, and that's not what I'm looking for. In the first place, I'd scratch out Yosef's eyes if he dared to share his bed with other women (and I have neither the energy nor the inclination to reciprocate!), and secondly: I've come to the conclusion that I'm set in my ways. Jacky chatters away in English like an American born and bred, but as for us, living in a group that's predominantly Jewish, the natural thing is to keep on speaking Russian and Yiddish and preferring spicy cabbage soup and herrings to apple cakes and maple syrup. And as for you, my Fanichka, are you still playing the piano? I hope so! If your life had followed a normal course you would be a famous pianist today…*

If! If only…

Fania sank into thought and suddenly froze in her seat. It seemed to her she heard the sound of movement in the yard outside. But no, it must have been a cat, or a rat, and she was startled, that was all! And supposing there was someone there! She was sitting by the lamp and her silhouette would be clearly visible through the window. What was the time? Midnight? Two in the morning, three? Again she heard the rustling sound and then the creak of the door of the shed. The rusty hinges played their familiar tune. She peered at Moshe. It seemed he had sunk into a deep sleep. With a pounding heart she took the revolver from the drawer and went quietly outside. Should she cry out? Her neighbors would come running to her aid. But what if it was just a cat after all? She hid in the shadow of the cypress, and from where she stood she threw a stone at the door of the shed. And then another. For a moment nothing happened, and then the door opened and a gigantic figure stood in the door-frame.

"Who's there?"

"Halt! Who are you?"

"Fania?"

"Sasha?!"

"Where are you?" Sasha moved out of the shed.

"I'm over here…you startled me! What are you doing in the shed?" Her legs began to shake and she leaned against the trunk of the tree.

"I didn't want to alarm you."

"I nearly fainted!"

A bat suddenly flew from the top of the tree and Fania emerged from her hiding place. The faint light of the stars touched the big figure but didn't illuminate it. Fania turned toward the house, postponing the questions for later. When they reached the door of the house, Sasha stopped and stroked the panel with his hand.

"Is the phoenix still there?"

"The colors have faded a bit. But he's still there."

In the house, by the light of the lamp, they studied each other. She remembered he was tall and broad-shouldered, but not on this scale—he was a giant! How could her memory be so faulty? Perhaps it was because she was pregnant when they met and her attention was focused on the baby inside her.

"Any chance of you putting the gun down, Fania?" he asked finally.

"Where have you come from?"

"From Beirut. I know it all," he went on to say. "I met Ishmael Nisan Amzaleg and his wife. You…you're still dressed? I mean," he added hastily when he saw her surprised expression, "haven't you gone to bed yet?"

"Moshe is sick." She pointed to the bed, speaking in a whisper.

"What's the matter?" He was whispering too.

"Fever. It's eased off a bit now."

Sasha moved closer to the child and laid a hand on his forehead. Moshe stirred, mumbled something and was silent again.

"Has a doctor been called?"

"No," Fania shrugged. "What's the point? He'd tell me to give him quinine and I've already done that. They say the water supply is polluted. But we all drink from the same well. What are you doing here?"

"I'm here for the silk-factory."

"You're the expert from Beirut?"

"That's me!" Sasha smiled, seeing the surprise on her face. Then he turned serious and said: "I want to be a farmer."

"Here?" A scornful kind of laugh emerged from her mouth. Or a whimper.

"Why not? I heard that Ossovitzky has bought ten thousand padans and he's dividing it up between the farmers."

"Yes. They're planting orchards...mulberry trees...what did you do in Beirut?"

"I worked in a silk-factory."

"Moshe and Bella are working in the silk-factory in the afternoons. Poor little mites. I'll be glad, knowing you're there too. I'll feel more secure. They say there's a future in it, silk."

"How old are they?"

"Moshe's ten and a half, Bella's nine."

For a moment a cloud passed over Sasha's face. But he made no comment and Fania was grateful for this. If he'd delivered a moral homily she would have thrown him out of the house.

"Can I see *my* baby? How old is he?"

"Tuli? Nearly two."

Fania lifted the lamp and Sasha looked at the three children sleeping on mats. The room was cold and wind whistled through the cracks in the windows, sealed up with straw. This was their lullaby. Still, soon it would be summertime and the windows could be opened. Tuli and Tamara were covered by Yehiel's old overcoat, and Bella was curled up in the woollen blanket. For a moment she felt sorry for herself. When they returned to the other room, she rounded on Sasha:

"You ran away!"

"Your hair is turning white, Fania!"

"I'm a hundred years old!"

"You're beautiful! Even more than I remembered. Of course, I met you when you were pregnant. Do you know what they call you?"

"What does who call me?"

"The Queen of the Land of Naphtali!"

"Oh, Imber!" Fania shrugged dismissively.

"He wrote a poem about you."

A flush reddened her cheeks, that old flush of embarrassment which used to be her constant companion, less so since Yehiel's passing. She remembered the slander laid against her by the gossips in Gedera, and was livid with resentment.

"Is the baby named after him?"

"No! After the Land of Naphtali!"

"What are you so angry about?"

Again she shrugged her shoulders.

"In Beirut I met a Turk who leased a room to Imber. You know how he made a living in Constantinople?"

"As a pedlar."

"And in Yiddish too!"

"He met the Oliphants in Constantinople."

"He was in love with the wife."

"Yes, that's what I thought. How do you know?"

"It wasn't a secret. It certainly wasn't a secret after he published his funeral dirge."

"What funeral dirge? Is Lady Alice dead?" Fania queried, aghast. "When?"

"Last year. It's a long poem and I only remember a few stanzas. It's heady stuff—all about hearts and tombs and darkness and plumbing the depths of despair…Can I stay here, Fania?"

"What will the neighbors say?"

"Fania! That isn't like you!"

"Oh, but it is!" she replied angrily. "Yes it is! I'm responsible for all these children. You've seen them. I'm a biological miracle! A woman of twenty-one with a son who's ten and a half years old."

"I'll stay in the shed."

"You've heard that Lulik is dead?"

"Yes."

"All right then." Suddenly she gave in and her anger evaporated at once. "Anyway, I have to leave the house in a few days."

"Where are you going?"

"To Issar Frumkin's house. Riva is dead too. Did you know?"

"Yes."

"We'll make a fine couple, Issar and I."

"Are you going to marry him?!" he asked in amazement, and Fania burst into laughter and covered her mouth with her hand.

"No! Idiot! Of course not! But I'm selling the house and we're moving in with him. If you don't find work in the silk-factory you can work in his orchard. Pay is meager, but a job is a job!"

"You're working in his orchard?"

"Yes. Today I cleared out my factory in Safed. Every day something comes to an end. Like in Imber's poem—hearts and tombs and darkness, wasn't it? You've heard about the tobacco too?" she asked when he didn't respond.

"Yes."

"Who told you? Ishmael?"

"I met your uncle and aunt at Amzaleg's house in Beirut. They came to visit Bella's sons who are studying at the university there."

"My uncle!" she snorted angrily.

"What about him?"

"His heart's full of love for all humanity!"

"And what's wrong with that?" he smiled.

"Wrong! When Yehiel died he came to the funeral and then went back to Jaffa right away. As if I wouldn't accept his help!" She added hurriedly with emphasis: "What I mean is, with all his grand ideas about saving humanity he can't see the people right under his nose."

"I'm under your nose."

"Difficult to miss you!" she smiled.

A quiver passed over Sasha's face.

"Would you like to stay here? In this house?"

"I can't!" Suddenly she turned her back on him and walked to the window, looking out into the pitch darkness, at a little star flickering in the heights. "Poor Yehiel! I can't sleep at night, all the time I'm seeing him, watching and waiting. Waiting! Perhaps young Miss Fania Mandelstam will finally be good enough to make up her mind whether she wants to stay in the house of her late husband and her children…He never demanded, never preached, never cajoled. It was what I wanted that counted. And now, when he is no longer here, now she is firmly resolved to stay! I pray that God will spare me until my children are grown and on their feet. Then…"

Her voice quivered. She had never spoken with anyone of these things. Who was there to tell? She took a deep breath, shook her bronze locks, and turned back to the room.

"I bought the house, Fania. I'm the man from Beirut."

For some time they were silent. The words he said filtered very slowly into her brain, as had often happened recently. As if there was some blockage there, as if the very sound of the words was fading away. Sasha leaned forward and for a moment she thought he was going to take her hand in his. Then he glanced at Moshe and sighed. It seemed the silence in the room was set to last a while longer. And then Sasha said:

"I was married. Sonia Brill was a midwife, a poet and the tallest Jewess in Kharkov. And we had two little girls. Nina was two years old, Leah was seven months…We spent the Seder night in Poltava, with my in-laws. I went back to Kharkov and they stayed behind for a while…if only I had stayed…"

"If only!" Fania exclaimed and nodded her head, as if having accounts of her own to settle with that "If only".

"I couldn't go on living there. I felt that every step I took I was wading through Jewish blood. One of our people, from Kharkov, went with the delegation that confronted General Drentalan after the pogroms in Elizavetgrad. Do you know what he said: 'The Jews should go to Jerusalem'!"

"I'm from Elizavetgrad."

"I decided that was what I would do. I would go to Jerusalem. I wanted to forget but I can't, not ever."

"We're stronger than we think, Sasha. It seems we can't take any more and then something else happens. And we endure that too. Is that a sign of strength or of weakness?"

"I don't know."

"God tests us again and again."

"I decided I would never raise another family. I would be the headstone on their grave. So I thought. How many years have passed since then? Six? And I'm ready to pick up the pieces, glue them together and start from the beginning."

"That's what we Jews do, we start from the beginning. Again and again and again. On our bodies we bear the scars as if they are our shame. Hiding the terrible secret from our children, why? Obliterating it from memory, why? Why?"

"Because it's impossible to live with it, Fania."

"We should have cried out till the skies cracked open, even if it meant dying in the process. We need to yell, Sasha, yell! Remind the world of its shame. Remind it that *we* are the crucified Christ. Why are we ashamed?"

"Perhaps it's because we're human…meaning…we're ashamed of the acts of humanity…Fania?"

"Yes?"

"Silk…there's a future in it. Today there are thirty looms in the factory. I spoke to the manager in Beirut and he's planning to double that number. I'm a professional and my livelihood is assured. What I mean is…I need you, Fania! Will you let me help you?"

Fania stared at him, bemused. Then she thought that if he embraced her, the top of her head would just reach his collarbone. And then her eyes filled with tears.

About the Author

Author photo by Lihi Lapid

Shulamit Lapid

Shulamit Lapid was born in Tel Aviv in 1934. She majored in Middle Eastern studies and English literature at the Hebrew University of Jerusalem. A former chairperson of the Hebrew Writers' Association, Lapid is the author of six novels, five collections of short stories, six suspense novels, three plays, a book of poetry and six books for children and youth. She has received the Prime Minister's Prize for Literature (1987), the International Theater Institute Award (1988), the German Krimipreis (1996) and the Newman Prize.

The fonts used in this book are from the Garamond family